CREAM
AND
PUNISH
MENT

ALSO BY SUSANNAH NIX

Starstruck Series

Star Bright

Fallen Star

Rising Star

Lucky Star

Chemistry Lessons Series

Remedial Rocket Science

Intermediate Thermodynamics

Advanced Physical Chemistry

Applied Electromagnetism

Experimental Marine Biology

Elementary Romantic Calculus

King Family Series

My Cone and Only

Cream and Punishment

Pint of Contention

Penny Reid's Smartypants Romance

Mad About Ewe

CREAM

AND

PUNISH MENT

SUSANNAH NIX

Haver Street Press

CREAM AND PUNISHMENT. Copyright © 2022 by Susannah Nix

FIRST EDITION: January 2022

ISBN: 978-1-950087-12-9

Haver Street Press | 448 W. 19th St., Suite 407 | Houston, TX 77008

Edited by Julia Ganis, www.juliaedits.com

Ebook & Print Cover Design by Cover Ever After

For all the kids who got lost in books to escape the world.

TANNER

"You're a big dumb ugly poo-poo head!"

I peered through the eyeholes of my costume at the angry urchin who'd flung this insult at me. He appeared to be about six or seven, and his round cheeks were as red as pomegranates as he worked himself into a temper tantrum worthy of Veruca Salt.

Glancing around, I attempted to identify the parental figure he belonged to. Unfortunately, none of the nearby adults seemed inclined to claim him. Not that I could blame them. If he was my kid, I'd probably pretend not to know him too.

"I want ice creeeeeeaaaaaaaaaam!" he screamed at the top of his lungs as he stamped his feet on the pavement. "Give me some ice cream RIGHT NOW!"

Grudgingly, I was forced to respect his commitment to his goals, although I dearly wished he'd find someone else to focus his impressively loud displeasure at.

People were staring now, and I scanned the vicinity for an amusement park employee to come to my aid and escort this miniature ball of rage to the security office. Or anywhere, really, that was far away from me. I'd have done it myself, but I wasn't allowed to speak while in costume in front of the public. It was one of a long list of rules you were expected to follow when assuming the role of Sheriff Scoopy, the official mascot of the King's Creamery ice cream company.

I felt like I'd stepped into a television sitcom. This was the part at the beginning of the episode where you'd hear a record scratch sound as the image freeze-framed on me in my absurd predicament with a voiceover of me saying, "Yup, that's me. You're probably wondering how I got into this situation..." At which point the episode would jump to a flashback explaining how a grown man with a college education had ended up dressed as a giant ice cream cone while being verbally assaulted by a child.

A week ago, I'd had a management job at the King's Creamery corporate headquarters. I'd worn dress shirts and slacks to work every day instead of a puffy ice cream cone costume with a comically large cowboy hat and clown-sized boots. I'd had a desk, for god's sake, and a computer.

I missed my desk.

As much as I'd hated that sales management job—and I'd hated it a *lot*—I hadn't appreciated how lucky I was to have it until I'd been demoted into my current one. My last job might have felt like purgatory, but this one was literal hell.

Which was the lesson my dad had intended to instill when he'd demoted me to my current position. Yes, I worked for my father. Actually, until today I'd worked for my half-brother Nate, who was the vice president of sales at the ice cream company our great-granddad had founded. Nate reported directly to our father, who was the company's current CEO and chairman of the board.

Over the last ten years, I'd worked my way up in the family business from an entry-level merchandiser position, restocking our ice cream in grocery store freezer cases, to regional account manager for the southwest division. Unfortunately, the higher I rose and the more responsibility I was given, the more obvious it became that I was not cut out for sales.

To put it plainly, I was not a good schmoozer. I did not enjoy chewing the fat or shooting the breeze or any other such thing. All of which made me uniquely bad at my job. So bad that my division's sales numbers had been on a steady decline since I stepped into the position. My father and brother had repeatedly expressed their dissatisfaction with my performance, but the final nail in my coffin had been the latest batch of quarterly sales numbers. After my brother had finished tearing me a new asshole in front of the entire corporate sales staff, my father had called me into his office and informed me he was transferring me to another part of the company.

Silly me, I'd actually been relieved. Little had I known what punishment my father had devised to teach me a lesson. He'd assigned me to the theme park, where I was now being paid minimum wage to gambol through the crowds of guests in ninety-degree heat wearing ten pounds of synthetic padding.

So that was my record-scratch moment. Pretty dull, as abject professional failures went. It wasn't particularly television worthy, even if my present circumstances might be entertaining the growing crowd of onlookers.

As the angry child at my feet unleashed a fresh string of insults featuring an impressive variety of euphemisms for excrement, I was relieved to see one of the nearby amusement park patrons look up from her phone with a world-weary expression that could only belong to this brat's progenitor.

She made her reluctant way toward us, halting a full ten paces distant as she put her hands on her hips and shouted, "Sagacious Braeden Tingle, you stop that right now!"

Sagacious? Why on god's green earth would anyone do that to a defenseless child? It was the most unfortunate name I'd ever heard, and in my brief tenure at the park I'd already encountered a Katniss, a Parsleigh, and a kid named Senator. If he hadn't spent the last several minutes screaming insults at me, I would have felt sorry for the poor kid who'd been condemned to go through life with the name Sagacious Tingle.

"NO!" Sagacious screamed at the woman, who appeared more bored than alarmed by his appalling behavior. "I want ICE CREAM!"

"I told you, you've had enough ice cream for one day."

This unsatisfactory answer caused the child-sized hooligan to convulse with a fresh surge of rage. "No no no no NO! Ice creeeeeeaaaaaaaaaam!"

I wasn't going to say it—or anything, because I wasn't allowed to talk—but this was what you got for naming a baby Sagacious.

"Come on now." His mother let out a long-suffering sigh. "Cut it out and apologize to Sheriff Scoopy."

"I HATE Sheriff Scoopy!" Sagacious rounded on me, red-faced and snotty, his beady eyes burning with such furious intensity it made me recoil. If I believed in the devil, I would surely think this child was his kin. "I hate you I hate you I hate you! You SUCK!"

Then the little shit reared back and headbutted me square in the dick.

Motherfuuuu—

I bit down on my lip to keep from cursing out loud as white-hot pain radiated up through my stomach. Breaking Sheriff Scoopy's code of silence to cuss out a child in the middle of the family-owned amusement park would probably get me not just fired but disowned.

You'd think the padded ice cream suit would have absorbed the blow, but no. This fucking thing wasn't even good for that much.

"Sagacious!" the mother snapped, but I heard a note of laughter in her voice. Apparently she found it amusing when her evil offspring assaulted beloved children's characters in the genitals.

Adding insult to injury, as the stars in my vision cleared, I glimpsed a familiar head of blonde hair heading my way.

Lucy.

Of fucking course. Because why not? The universe was clearly conspiring with my dad to punish me, so now was the perfect moment for my ex-girlfriend to show up.

Unfortunately for me, she worked in the marketing department of my family's company, which was probably why she happened to be wandering the park with an expensive camera in her hand.

Perfect. Let's absolutely memorialize my lowest moment in high-definition pixel data.

Six months ago, I'd told Lucy Dillard I loved her, and she'd responded by dumping me like a used condom. My declaration of love had been so repugnant she hadn't even put her shoes on before fleeing my house. The way the blood had drained from her face, you'd have thought I'd said I wanted to eat her liver with some fava beans and a nice chianti.

Her hasty exit from my bedroom and my life had taken me completely by surprise. When I'd decided to share my deep and abiding feelings for her, I definitely hadn't expected her to break up with me on the spot and leave me naked in my bed, wondering what the hell had happened. I'd genuinely believed we'd connected on a deep level and that she'd been giving me clear signals she felt the same way.

So when she'd fled in panic at the prospect of getting serious, like it had never occurred to her as a possibility, I felt like I'd been gaslit. It had called into question everything I'd felt and believed—not just about our relationship, but about everything else. If I'd misjudged Lucy's feelings for me so badly, what else was I completely wrong about? Could I even trust my own instincts anymore?

I'd been struggling to put it behind me ever since. Even though we'd only dated for five weeks, six days, and twenty-two hours, I'd meant it when I said I loved her. I'd loved her almost from the moment we first met, in fact.

Maybe that sounded strange. Love at first sight was all well and good in stories, but in real life most people didn't seem to believe in it. I hadn't believed in it either until I'd started talking to Lucy that night at the Rusty Spoke and fallen under her spell. Something in her spoke to something in me, and just like that, I knew I loved her.

Only I guess it was another way for the universe to stick its thumb in my eye, because Lucy hadn't gotten the love-at-first-sight memo. It was just me hanging out there on Love Island by myself with an arrow through my heart.

And now, the object of my unrequited affection was here to witness not only my precipitous decline in professional circumstances but also my humiliating physical defeat at the hands of a child. Truly, this was a stunning new low in the shit-heap of my life.

My only saving grace was this fucking costume. Lucy wouldn't have any way of knowing it was me inside this thing. Unless someone had told her. But I guessed they hadn't, or she wouldn't be headed straight for me right now—probably hoping to capture some heartwarming shots of Sheriff Scoopy interacting with his adoring public.

Speaking of which, Sagacious's violent attack on my nutsack seemed to have exhausted his reserves of anger. He'd ceased screaming and was giving me a slack-mouthed, bleary-eyed stare that disconcertingly reminded me of a zombie.

Right as Lucy drew near and lifted the camera to her eye, I

heard my new little friend utter the most terrifying words a child could say: "I don't feel so good."

With my reflexes dulled by the pain still throbbing through my nethers, and my oversized cowboy boots inhibiting my movement, I only managed to stagger a half step back before Sagacious projectile vomited what appeared to be at least five gallons of chocolate ice cream all over me.

A second ago, when I'd thought Lucy was witnessing my lowest moment?

Yeah, no.

This moment right here was the actual low point.

———

TWENTY MINUTES LATER, I stood in the employee locker room with my eyes closed and my head propped against my locker, unable to get the stench of puke out of my nose. I was hoping if I stayed here long enough with my forehead pressed against this cold steel surface, I'd fuse with its matte gray nothingness and disappear altogether.

After Sagacious had spewed chocolate-flavored vomit all over me, he'd promptly burst into tears. My ex-girlfriend had leaped to his mother's assistance, sparing a sympathetic look at me as she escorted mother and hellspawn to the park's first aid center. So Lucy definitely hadn't realized it was me in the Sheriff Scoopy suit, or she would have been laughing her ass off instead of feeling sorry for me. *Thank god for small favors.*

I'd limped back to the employee locker room alone, and after struggling my way out of the vomit-covered costume, handed it over to a thoroughly disgusted laundry attendant.

Now I wasn't sure what to do with myself. Technically, I had another three hours left of my shift. But without a costume to wear, I couldn't perform my job.

My *job*.

Christ.

What a joke my life had become. This job was a joke, my career was a joke, and I was the biggest fucking joke of all.

Kudos to my dad. His plan to humiliate me had been an unmitigated success. He and Nate would probably piss themselves laughing when they heard about this.

For the time being, I decided I might as well stand here with my head against this locker until someone told me to do something else. My supervisor would probably show up eventually and give me a new assignment. She might send me to scoop ice cream at one of the park's many refreshment stands or reassign me to custodial services so I could spend the rest of my shift cleaning toilets.

Maybe she'd even fire me. I doubted it, however. A park guest services supervisor wasn't going to fire the CEO's son. Not without my father's say-so, and he'd never approve it. He liked having all of us chips off the old block under his command. He wanted us beholden to him for our careers, our livelihoods, and our self-respect. That way he could keep us under his thumb by threatening to take it all away if we didn't play our assigned roles to his satisfaction.

At this point you might be asking why I didn't quit if I hated it here so much. Couldn't I go out and find my own job? Why not start from scratch and embark on a new career I didn't hate so much?

Good questions, all of them, and ones I'd asked myself many a time.

It was that whole starting from scratch thing that tripped me up. I wasn't great at taking risks or dealing with uncertainty. The thought of leaving the security of the family business to make my own way in the world terrified the living shit out of me. Maybe ten years ago, when I'd been younger and the world had seemed full of possibility, I might have managed it. Before I'd gotten settled in here and grown accustomed to earning a comfortable paycheck.

The entirety of my professional experience was in sales—the one line of work I knew for a fact I hated. And I'd only ever worked for my dad's company. Who would want to hire someone like me? I wasn't even qualified to work at Whataburger. Did I really want to start over at my age? A thirty-two-year-old competing with fresh-faced college grads for entry-level jobs making pennies an hour?

I didn't love working for my dad, but I didn't hate it *that* much. Once he judged I'd completed my punishment, he'd find me something better to do. I just had to eat some crow first to show I was a team player. Maybe I'd actually like whatever new job he assigned me to after this. Even if I didn't, it'd still be better than anything I'd be able to find on my own. Besides, if I stuck with it and managed to please my dad, I'd be rewarded with a stake in the company eventually. My financial future would be set. If I left, I doubted I'd ever see a dime of the family money.

It might be different if I had a burning aspiration to do something else. I'd have a reason to take the risk and go it on my own. But I had no idea what I wanted to do, much less what I'd be any good at. So here I remained. Because why not? At least it paid well. Or it had, until my recent demotion.

"You trying to mind-meld with that locker or what?"

I turned at the sound of my sister Josie's voice. Technically my half-sister. Whatever.

My dad had been married three times, and my immediate family was so complicated it practically required an infographic to explain it. Josie was one of four kids from my dad's first marriage, along with Nate, my former boss. After our dad divorced their mom, he married my mother and had me and my younger brother Wyatt. My mom also had a son from a previous relationship, my half-brother Ryan. After my mom died of breast cancer when I was twelve, my dad married again and had two more kids. As if that wasn't enough, in addition to all my half-siblings, I also had an adopted older brother named Manny.

Like I said, it really helped to have an infographic.

Manny, Nate, and Josie all held executive leadership positions in the family business as well as shares in the company. Manny was the executive vice president of plant operations, Nate was executive VP of sales, and Josie was executive VP of marketing. I was supposed to be following in their footsteps and working my way up to...something. Probably Dad had thought I'd take over as VP of sales after Nate eventually moved up to COO.

Instead, I'd ended up here. Knocked down to a job usually filled by a high school student.

As VP of marketing, Josie was responsible for the company's branding, which included the Sheriff Scoopy mascot. That was likely why she was here right now. No doubt a report had gone up the chain of command about the scene in the park today. Anything to do with the company's image or a potential public relations problem, Josie took extremely seriously.

Her tall, willowy frame was immaculately attired, her brown hair sleekly styled, and her gaze steady and razor-sharp as she stood in the doorway of the locker room. Josie always looked perfectly put together, because Josie always *was* perfectly put together, no matter what kind of crisis was happening around her.

"I never broke character while I was in costume," I told her. "I never said a word to that kid."

"I know." Her mouth pulled into a smirk. "I saw the video."

Oh god.

Of course there was video. We had security cameras all over

the damn park. Nate had probably emailed it to the entire sales organization by now.

I sank down on the bench and dropped my head into my hands. "Awesome. Fantastic."

"Are you okay?" Josie's voice softened in sympathy. "It looked like that little brat got you right in the junk. Hopefully the padded costume gave you some protection."

"Not enough," I mumbled.

Josie sat down on the bench beside me. "Tanner, what are you doing here? Why are you working in the theme park?"

I turned my head to peer at her. "They didn't tell you?"

"No, the first I heard about it was when I saw the report about the incident today."

I knew it. I knew Josie had gotten an alert about it.

Pushing myself upright, I gripped the edge of the bench. One of my fingers encountered a calcified wad of old gum stuck to the underside, and I wiped my hand on my thighs. "I've been reassigned."

She stared at me blankly. "Reassigned?"

"Fired, I guess, would be more accurate."

"Nate fired you?"

"I think it was probably a joint decision that he and Dad came to together." Nate had been the one to break the news, but he'd done it in Dad's office with the two of them presenting a unified front.

"That sucks," she said. "Let me guess—working in the park was Dad's idea?"

"Until he figures out what to do with me."

"So he's punishing you."

"Yep."

Her shoulder bumped against mine. "Hey, at least you don't have to work for Nate anymore." She offered me a smile, and I exhaled a wry laugh. "Look, I love the guy, but if I had to take orders from my big brother, I'd strangle him with my bare hands within an hour."

Josie was probably the smartest one of us, because she'd gone out and blazed her own professional trail before agreeing to work for the family business. She'd built her résumé at advertising agencies in Dallas and New York before moving back to Crowder a couple of years ago to bring all the advertising for the creamery in-house. In addition to scoring what I assumed must have been an outrageous compensation package to lure her back, it gave her leverage the rest of us didn't have. Josie could always go somewhere else and get another job as good as or better than this one if she didn't like the way Dad treated her.

I stared down at my hands. "Sorry I didn't get out of the way of the vomit. I can't seem to do anything right these days."

She laughed. "Do you know how many times that suit has been vomited on?"

I absolutely did not want to know, although I could imagine. "Gross."

"How do you feel about marketing?" I glanced at her and she shrugged. "Weren't you an English major? I assume you can string words together well enough to write copy. Want to come work for me?"

"What about Dad?" I doubted he'd allow Josie to throw me a lifeline until I'd been humiliated to his satisfaction.

"I'll handle Dad." Josie arched a wry eyebrow as she glanced around the locker room. "Unless you'd rather stay here and play Sheriff Scoopy?"

"I'll write whatever copy you want. I can do it." I didn't know anything about marketing, but I was willing to learn if it meant I never had to put that costume on again.

"Good. I happen to have an open job I need to fill." She patted my knee and got to her feet. "Come to my office Monday morning at nine."

"Thank you," I said, gratitude forming a lump in my throat. "Seriously. I owe you big time."

"Go home and take a shower. You smell like puke."

There was just one teeny tiny little problem that didn't occur to me until a full ten minutes later, when I was in my car driving home.

Lucy worked in marketing.

My ex and I were about to become coworkers.

Could you report someone to human resources for singing the baby shark song at work?

My coworker Arwen was currently humming it out loud in the cubicle next to mine, and if that didn't qualify as a hate crime, it ought to.

Arwen sang under her breath all the time in the office. It seemed to be an unconscious habit. The few times I'd pointed it out she'd seemed surprised she was doing it. She'd promised to cut it out, only she hadn't.

Usually I could deal with her incessant humming by tuning it out. I'd gotten to be quite good at tuning things out. It was one of my useless superpowers, along with peeling an apple in one continuous ribbon and waking up five minutes before my alarm went off. But right now it was eight thirty on a Monday morning, I was short on sleep *and* coffee, and the baby shark song was definitely the most insidious earworm of all time.

I glanced at my work BFF in the cubicle on the other side of me. Linh's head was propped on her hand so her wavy black hair masked her face from my view. As if she could feel my attention on her, she turned toward me, pushing her red glasses up her nose as we exchanged a look of mutual exasperation. That was one of Linh's superpowers—always knowing when I was telepathically trying to communicate with her.

I clicked over to the company's internal communications app and typed a direct message to her.

Is there a baby shark song exception to murder? Because there should be.

It could be worse, she replied.

How???

She could be singing "It's a Small World."

RUDE, LINH. REALLY HATEFUL.

I heard her snort at her desk and directed my most maleficent glare at her—which, admittedly, was not all that scary. A Disney villain I was not. My small stature, yellow-blonde hair, and freckled face undermined my fearsomeness.

I heard Linh's fingers tapping on her keyboard and waited for her message to come through.

You're her supervisor. Say something to her.

Not technically, I typed back.

Arwen was a graphic designer in the in-house marketing department at King's Creamery, where I was a content strategist in charge of the company's website, blog, social media accounts, and email newsletter. While yes, I'd effectively been performing the role of content manager since our former supervisor, Jill, left three months ago, I hadn't officially been promoted into the position. Allegedly it was coming, but we were under a company-wide promotion and salary freeze until at least the end of the year. In the meantime, I was expected to do my former boss's job *and* my job for the same money—and without any actual supervisory authority.

I wasn't comfortable sitting Arwen down and giving her a

stern talking-to about the singing. I'd already mentioned it several times, as nicely as I could, but that was as much as I felt empowered to do.

You could ask Byron to talk to her, Linh suggested.

I didn't like that idea either. Arwen wasn't doing it on purpose to be a jerk. I didn't want to complain about her to our creative director, Byron, for something so trivial. Also, I was pretty sure it would make me look petty and ineffective in Byron's eyes, potentially hurting my chances of ever getting that promotion I deserved. Basically, I was stuck in a worst of both worlds situation.

YOU could ask Byron to talk to her, I typed back.

Linh was a web developer, so technically she was part of the IT chain of command, and Byron was only her dotted-line boss. It didn't matter if he thought Linh was petty, because he needed her to keep our website running.

That's gonna be a pass from me, she replied. *You know how I feel about lizard boy.*

We called Byron lizard boy because he spent so much time playing golf that his face and forearms were tanned and leathery, and his skin pulled taut like a pair of lizard-skin boots.

Anyway, I have headphones, Linh added.

When I looked up, she stuck her tongue out at me and pulled on her cherry red Beats just as Arwen started another cycle of the baby shark song.

Did you know there were nine different verses to the baby shark song? I hadn't until this morning, but now I'd be reciting them all in my head every day until I died.

Grabbing my favorite *So Many Books, So Little Time* coffee mug off my desk, I headed to the break room for a fresh infusion of caffeine to dull my baby shark headache. On my way there, I happened to glance toward the elevator, and my heart seized up when I recognized the person stepping out.

Tanner.

I nearly pulled a muscle whipping around the corner in my haste to avoid my ex. Fortunately, he hadn't been looking my way, so hopefully he hadn't seen me.

What the heck was Tanner doing on the fifth floor? He worked in sales, two floors up. I almost never ran into him, which was good, because running into him was mega awkward.

We'd broken up six months ago, and every time we'd encountered each other since, Tanner's spiteful glare had communicated exactly how much he hated me. Which was a lot. I was the one who'd ended it, so I couldn't blame him for nursing some resentment. But honestly, we'd only dated for a few weeks. It wasn't like we were even that serious.

Only apparently it had been serious to Tanner—serious enough for him to drop the L-word on me.

That was why I'd had to end it. He'd gotten way too invested way too fast. It was too much pressure. I'd just been trying to have a good time, casually dating a nice guy. I hadn't been looking to get serious—with him or anyone else.

It wasn't as though I hadn't liked him. He was smart and funny and hot in that Clark Kent kind of way that was totally my catnip. I would have been perfectly happy to keep things the way they were: seeing each other once or twice a week, having some fantastic sex, and going back to our separate lives in between.

We'd had a good thing going until he went and got serious on me. Why couldn't we have kept it casual? I didn't have room for another commitment in my life right now. Thanks to my family, I already had more obligations than I wanted.

Once Tanner said the L-word, there was no turning back. We couldn't just hang out and have a good time anymore. Since I had no intention of falling in love with him, I'd had no choice but to bail.

I'd done it in the kindest way I could, under the circumstances. I'd told him straight out that I didn't feel the same way, and therefore I didn't think we should see each other anymore.

Ever kicked a puppy square in the face before? Just reared back and let the fuzzy little guy have it right in his adorable puppy nose? I hoped not, because that would be unforgivably cruel. But that was how it felt to break up with Tanner. The hurt look in his eyes still haunted me sometimes when I was trying to fall asleep at night.

Nevertheless, I firmly believed I'd done the right thing. I could have taken the easy way out and pretended everything was cool for a while, then ghosted him at the first opportunity. A cowardly yet effective breakup technique, and one I'd been on the receiving end of enough times to know exactly how much it sucked. But no. I hadn't done that to Tanner. Instead I'd been honest with him, because I thought he deserved that much. Because I respected him.

Although it probably hadn't felt like respect from his perspective. He'd looked at me like I'd run over his cat, which was unfair because I'd never hurt a cat. I loved cats, and Tanner's cat Radagast was very sweet, even if he was a million years old and occasionally slightly incontinent.

Obviously, Tanner had been surprised by my response to his declaration. You don't tell someone you love them unless you think there's a good chance of them saying it back. Whatever future he'd been imagining for the two of us—marriage, babies, a white picket fence—I'd blown it to smithereens and thrown it back in his face.

In his defense, he'd accepted it without a fight. You never knew with men, how they were going to take rejection. But Tanner hadn't yelled or acted out. He hadn't tried to wheedle or coerce me into changing my mind. He hadn't argued at all, once

I'd explained how I felt—or didn't feel. He'd let me go and hadn't voluntarily spoken to me since.

It was just that every time we ran into each other, it was painfully obvious he'd rather be anywhere on earth other than in my presence. Unfortunately, Crowder was a small town, so we couldn't avoid crossing paths occasionally. Especially since my brother Matt was in a band with Tanner's brother Wyatt. So if I ever wanted to go hear my brother's band play, there was a good chance Tanner would be there.

Oh, and also Tanner worked at the same company as me, which bumped up the odds of running into each other even more. Only Tanner didn't just work for King's Creamery like I did. His family *owned* it.

So anyway, that was the saga of me and Tanner. I'd smashed his heart into itty-bitty pieces and now he hated me. What I didn't know was why he'd just gotten off the elevator on the fifth floor.

Trying to play it cool, I peeked around a fiddle-leaf fig to see where he'd gone. Into his sister's office, apparently. I could see the vague shape of him through the patterned glass, sitting in one of the chairs across from her desk. They were probably just visiting. Family stuff or whatever. No big deal.

I completed my journey to the kitchen and refilled my cup with the aggressively mediocre complimentary coffee provided by the company. On my way back to my desk, I flicked a surreptitious glance at the VP's office to satisfy myself that Tanner was still in there. He was. Coast clear.

Arwen was still mumbling the baby shark song to herself when I sat back down at the cubicle beside her, but I barely noticed it anymore. I was too distracted by the fact that Tanner was on my floor. I kept craning my neck, trying to see the elevators so I'd know when he left and I could relax.

"What are you doing?" Linh asked, frowning at me.

"Nothing," I said as I typed out a new direct message to her. *Tanner's here.*

Where??? she replied immediately.

In Josie's office.

Her response came a few seconds later: *Be cool, Soda Pop.*

My head jerked up at the sound of voices approaching, and my stomach clenched in alarm as Josie led Tanner into the creative director's office. Byron didn't have privacy glass, so I was treated to an unobstructed view of the three of them talking. Byron had gotten to his feet, and Josie was introducing Tanner to him.

"Who's that in Byron's office with the VP?" Arwen asked, swiveling her chair to look at them.

I didn't answer her. I was too busy trying not to have a panic attack over the fact that my ex was in my boss's office.

"That's Tanner King," Linh answered when I didn't. "One of Josie's younger brothers."

"He's cute," Arwen said, and I cut a look over at her. "What?" She blinked at me innocently. "He is."

I probably forgot to mention that Arwen was as beautiful as her fictional namesake. Her parents really nailed it when they named her. Tall, graceful, shiny dark hair, bee-stung lips, big boobs. Your basic nightmare if you were the kind of woman who assumed other women were your competition in a zero-sum game to secure the best mate.

Which I was not, and therefore I had no business behaving jealously. Tanner *was* cute, and Arwen had every right to notice. I'd relinquished my rights to him, so I wasn't entitled to act territorial.

"He works in sales," I told her, attempting to make up for my sharp look. "I don't know why he's here."

As the three of us watched, Josie bid the two men goodbye and exited Byron's office, leaving Tanner there. Her gaze skimmed right past us as she headed back to her own office. I'd only spoken to Josie a handful of times, and I wasn't sure if she knew about my history with Tanner. It was a source of persistent, low-grade anxiety that I might have hurt my chances of advancement in the company by having the nerve to break up with one of the almighty King sons.

Byron and Tanner were sitting down now, Byron at his desk and Tanner with his back to us. Byron seemed to be talking an awful lot, and I wished, not for the first time, that one of my superpowers was reading lips. When it became clear they weren't doing anything worth watching, Arwen got bored and turned back to her computer. Linh gave me a sympathetic look before doing the same.

I tried to follow suit and concentrate on the feature I was writing for this week's newsletter. A key component of the King's Creamery branding was our social consciousness. We weren't just a family-owned business with deep roots in rural America, we were also a company with a conscience. Every month, our content marketing platforms highlighted a different environmental or human rights issue. So in addition to the usual product promotions and silly "What Ice Cream Flavor Are You?" quizzes, I had to write a series of weekly features about the issue of the month.

This month we were focusing on the school-to-prison pipeline, and I had to have the second weekly feature finished by the end of the day so I could send it to the public relations director for approval. Unsurprisingly, they were finicky about what we could and couldn't say when discussing potentially contentious political issues.

My focus had already been crap today, but Tanner's unexpected proximity posed an unbearable distraction. If I raised my eyes from my monitor even a little, he was right there, directly in my eyeline. I couldn't see his face, but I could see the back of his head and his neatly trimmed golden brown hair. The way his head tilted slightly to the right when he was talking and slightly to the left when he was listening. The white dress shirt that pulled tight across his broad shoulders. The way his right arm was cocked to the side and casually draped over the armrest while his left remained hidden, presumably resting in his lap.

Yikes. I really needed to stop creeping on him like a creepy creeper.

Dragging my gaze downward again, I forced myself to keep my eyes glued to my screen. Unfortunately, my mind refused to get on the bandwagon. The harder I stared at the words I'd been writing, the more they seemed to mock me by blurring into abstract shapes detached from any meaning. There was a word for when that happened. Wordnesia. When a task your brain usually performed on autopilot—like reading or writing—hit a mental speed bump, and the conscious part of your brain realized it didn't know what it was supposed to be doing.

The back of Tanner King's head was one big honking mental speed bump that my brain refused to drive over.

Fifteen minutes later, I'd finally managed to write one pathetic sentence about school suspension rates and incarceration when movement in Byron's office derailed my attention yet again. He and Tanner were on their feet now, moving toward the door. I lowered my head as they emerged, pretending to concentrate on my screen while I tracked them in my peripheral vision.

Whatever their mystery meeting had been about, it was over now, thank god. Byron would walk Tanner out, and he'd be gone gone gone so I could get back to my regularly scheduled day without the back of his head derailing my productivity.

Only Byron didn't lead Tanner toward the elevators. He appeared to be leading him straight to me.

Please no. Please don't bring him over here.

But that was exactly what he was doing. Byron was looking

right at me, and I wished one of my superpowers was invisibility so I could fade into the bland gray office furnishings and disappear completely.

As Arwen and Linh turned in their chairs to track Byron's approach with Tanner, I summoned my *This is Fine* face. I had a first-rate *This is Fine* face. So good, it might even be considered a superpower. It was infinitely useful for any occasion when you needed people to think you had everything under control and were definitely not panicking inside. Like, for instance, the sudden appearance of your boss at your desk with your bitter ex in tow.

Tanner stood partially behind Byron, looking tense as his gaze flitted around the office. I had the impression he was lurking behind Byron on purpose, as though I might suddenly attack or turn him to stone if he accidentally made eye contact with me.

"Good news," Byron said cheerfully. "Content marketing is finally getting the extra pair of hands you've been needing since Jill left."

My eyes went wide, and I amped up my *This is Fine* face a few notches, affecting an expression of pleasant surprise rather than growing dread.

He can't mean Tanner. Tanner works in sales. He has a job already—a much better job than this. He doesn't even have marketing experience. Also, he'd never in a million years agree to work with me.

"Everyone, this is Tanner King." Byron stepped to the side, leaving Tanner exposed to our scrutiny. "That's right, he's one of *those* Kings," Byron added with an obsequious wink I knew Tanner must be hating. "And he's going to be joining you on the content marketing team starting today."

My stomach plummeted through the bottom of my chair and landed on the floor at my feet with a splat. Nevertheless, my

This is Fine face stayed firmly in place, proving once again to be my most useful superpower.

Tanner's *This is Fine* face was not great, and it was especially terrible when it came to me. At the moment, his face looked every bit as consternated as I felt. Was consternated a word? I couldn't remember anymore. It sounded made up. There went my wordnesia again.

Anyway, Tanner looked unhappy, which I didn't understand. I didn't understand any of this. What was he doing here, why would he agree to this, and why did he look so unhappy about something he'd surely had a say in and known was happening?

Unlike me, who'd been completely ambushed by this unpleasant development.

Byron made the introductions. "This is Arwen Nussbaum, who does all the graphic design for the team, and Linh Tran, our web developer." Tanner mustered a shy smile for both of them, almost looking friendly for a second—until Byron got to me. "And this is Lucy Dillard, our content marketing strategist."

For the first time, Tanner's eyes met mine, and I felt it like a physical blow. It took all my effort not to flinch away from his steely blue gaze, which was at once so cold and so beautiful. My *This is Fine* face cracked, my pleasant expression slipping as competing feelings of discomfort, guilt, and apprehension lodged in the back of my throat.

"We've met," Tanner said, his voice flat but still deep and familiar, stirring memories of former warmth that made his current hostility sting even more.

Byron glanced between us, his expression curious, obviously hoping one of us would volunteer more details. I waited for Tanner to say something else, to explain to everyone that we'd briefly dated and now my existence was abhorrent to him. But as the silence between us thickened, it became clear he'd said all he planned to say.

I was uncomfortably conscious of everyone's eyes on me, but particularly Byron's. He expected me to be gracious and welcoming to the VP's brother and make a good impression for the sake of the team.

So I summoned all my *This is Fine* energy and produced a smile. In response, Tanner's mouth pulled into a flat line, as if his brain had issued an order to smile back, but his face had refused to comply.

"My brother and Tanner's brother are in a band together," I said, knowing it would be enough of the truth to satisfy Byron's curiosity. If Tanner didn't want his new coworkers knowing about our relationship, I was more than happy to keep it between us. In fact, that would be my preference.

"Well great. That'll make things easier." Byron smiled wider, oblivious to the tension in the air. Maybe it wasn't that noticeable, even though it felt like an emergency alert shrieking inside my brain. "Lucy, I'd like you to train Tanner on producing the newsletter so you can hand it off to him."

"He's taking over the newsletter?" I said, desperately cranking my *This is Fine* face up a few more degrees. The newsletter constituted half my job. Granted, I was currently doing the work of two people, but the newsletter was my thing. It was what I'd first been hired to do. And now it was being taken away from me.

"That's right," Byron said, flashing his over-whitened teeth. "He'll be writing all the features once you've got him up to speed, which will give you more time to focus on the website and social media."

"Okay." I smoothed down the front of my shirt as I nodded. "Sure."

"Great!" Byron turned his perky smile on Tanner. "You can take the empty desk directly across from Lucy. Make yourself at home." He let out a chuckle. "Look who I'm talking to—you know this place better than any of us. But if you need anything at all, Lucy will take care of you. Right?"

"You bet." I gave Byron a thumbs-up, doing the best *This is Fine* face of my life as Tanner stared at me like I was a bug he wanted to squash under his shoe.

3

TANNER

This was so much worse than I ever could have imagined. Possibly even worse than being head-butted in the dick and puked on. It was at least a close second.

There had to be at least fifty people working in the creamery's marketing department. My sister could have assigned me to work with any one of them. But who did I end up working with? Sitting directly across from? Being *trained* by?

Lucy goddamn Dillard.

Of course.

Apparently I still had some penance to pay for whatever I'd done to piss off the universe.

I couldn't blame Josie. She didn't know Lucy and I had dated. If she had, she almost definitely wouldn't have put us together like this. Maybe I should have told her, but I wanted this job, and I wanted it without the extra scrutiny and pitying looks I'd get if she knew about my history with Lucy. I'd figured I could handle seeing Lucy around the office. I could learn to smile and be cordial, as if I didn't still have a scab where my heart had cracked in two.

It had never occurred to me that we'd be working side by side. By the time I'd realized, I was already in the creative director's office, hearing about the role he'd generously created for me. I hadn't wanted him to know Lucy and I had dated, because I didn't want to lose this opportunity.

When Byron had first mentioned her name, for a second I'd felt like I couldn't breathe. Fortunately, my autonomic nervous system had taken over, and I'd managed to keep my expression neutral while the reality of the situation sank in. Lucy wouldn't just be some random peer whose desk I'd walk by occasionally. She was my new team lead. My *mentor*.

Then my new boss had walked me out to the bullpen and introduced me to my new coworkers. I'd barely noticed the other two as I greeted them, because Lucy had arrested all my focus the way she always did. Even now, when I wished I could ignore her, when I'd been trying for months not to *feel* anything, she still managed to be the center of my universe whenever I was around her.

I hated how calm she seemed about this. How agreeably she'd smiled when Byron had introduced us. Like it was nothing to her, not even the slightest bit uncomfortable. I suppose it *was* nothing to her, because *I'd* meant nothing to her. Seeing me again was a minor inconvenience.

God, how I envied that. The freedom of not having feelings.

I glanced at my watch, but it was only ten thirty. I'd never known time to pass so slowly. For the last hour, Lucy had been sitting with her chair right up next to mine as she walked me through the team's workflow and processes—the file structure they used for storing documents on the shared drive, the company style guide I was supposed to follow, the department-specific channels in our corporate communications app. The whole time, I'd been able to smell her perfume, faint but unmistakable. It was the same perfume she'd worn when we were together, and it brought on a wave of powerful sense memories. There ought to be a law about that. After you broke up with someone, you should be required to switch to a different perfume to avoid giving them unnerving flashbacks to more intimate and loving times.

As if that wasn't bad enough, whenever I leaned forward for a closer look at the computer screen, a wayward strand of her hair would tickle my face. I wanted to move it away, but then I'd be touching her hair, and that wasn't something I was allowed to do anymore.

I was only barely holding it together. You know that thing you do at the dentist or during an uncomfortable medical procedure where you disassociate yourself from the unpleasant thing happening to you? That was how I'd been getting through this orientation session.

"The content channel is just the four of us and Byron. We're our own little bubble, separate from the rest of the art department and copywriters." Lucy reached for my mouse, and I flinched when her arm brushed against mine.

My attempt at emotional detachment didn't work so well when she touched me and that small, innocent point of contact jolted through me like an electric cattle prod.

"Sorry," she muttered without looking at me. "You can probably familiarize yourself with the other channels on your own, but this one right here is the one you really want to pay attention to, because it's where the important updates about upcoming promotions and product changes get posted."

"Got it," I said, praying for this godforsaken tutorial to end.

Seeming to sense my discomfort at last, she pushed her chair back to give me more space, and I let out a controlled breath. Lucy's gaze lifted to mine, and I finally saw something in her expression that resembled an actual emotion. A whole constellation of them, in fact, warring with each other as they flashed across her face. Uncertainty. Embarrassment. Concern. Maybe even a little guilt, although she composed herself again before I could be sure about that one.

Still, that one fleeting glimpse acted like a splash of cool, soothing water on all the overheated parts of my brain. I wasn't the only one struggling here. This wasn't easy for her either. She was simply a lot better at hiding her discomfort than I was.

She lowered her eyes and smoothed the front of her blouse. It was brown and gauzy, covered with tiny pink flowers, and her fingernails were painted almost the exact same shade of pink.

"Do you think..." she began, her voice lower and softer than before. Her fingers twisted in her lap as her eyes lifted again, and I saw more of that same uncertainty. "Could we talk for a minute? In private?"

I swallowed hard and nodded.

She got to her feet and inclined her head for me to follow. We went into a nearby conference room, and she closed the door behind us. I didn't know what to do with my hands while I waited for her to say whatever she'd brought me in here to say. I tried crossing my arms, but that felt too hostile. Letting them hang at my sides was too awkward, so I shoved my hands into my pockets.

Lucy turned to face me, still grasping the door handle. She was eight inches shorter than me, so she had to tip her head back to meet my eyes. "I don't understand why you're here. You're a regional account manager. You work in sales."

"Not anymore. I've been reassigned."

"Why?"

I understood why she wanted an explanation, but I didn't want to tell her. My gaze dropped to the floor while I considered and discarded various lies. There wasn't a good way to explain a demotion this big, and I'd only look more pathetic for lying about it.

"It was decided that I'd be more useful in another job," I said as diplomatically as I could.

Lucy blinked her soft brown lashes at me as she parsed the truth behind my careful phrasing, too smart not to understand the implication. Her expression shifted into something most people would probably describe as kindness. But all I saw was pity, and it made me feel about as worthless as that wad of gum stuck to the underside of the locker room bench.

"I'm sorry," she said. "That sucks."

I shrugged one shoulder. "I never liked sales anyway."

"I remember." Those two little words, spoken so gently, pierced my chest like a poisoned Nazgûl blade. "Did you ask to come work in marketing?"

"With you? No." As soon as the words left my mouth, I realized how harsh they sounded. How bitter. How much of an asshole I must seem to her.

And here she was, trying to be kind.

She winced like I'd poked a bruise, and another flash of guilt crossed her face.

"I mean..." I flailed to express myself better, remembering when I used to be a nicer person than this. "I never would have asked to work in your department, because I wouldn't want to make you uncomfortable."

Her chin dipped in acknowledgement—or maybe gratitude. "And yet, here you are." An attempt at lightness, but one that sounded forced.

"My dad had me reassigned to the theme park. But Josie offered to find me something else and"—I grimaced, rubbing a hand over the back of my neck—"I wasn't in a position to turn her down."

Lucy nodded slowly. "Can I ask, does Josie know about us? About our history?"

"No. She has no idea we were ever..." I couldn't decide which word would be the least painful way to describe what we'd been, so I settled on: "Acquainted."

Another small wince cracked her expression before she recovered enough to give me a dubious look. "So it was pure chance that you ended up on my team?"

"I swear. I had no idea what she had planned for me until she took me into Byron's office this morning." I needed Lucy to believe me. I might be a bitter asshole, but I didn't want her to think I'd arranged this on purpose to get close to her or get back at her or anything else she might be suspecting. "I was as surprised and dismayed as I imagine you were."

Her hands smoothed her shirt again. A nervous habit, I realized. One I hadn't noticed when we'd been dating. Maybe because she hadn't had reason to be nervous around me before. The thought that she did now made me sad.

A determined muscle clenched in her jaw. "So we both agree this situation is less than ideal. But I suppose it can't be helped. We're stuck with each other."

"It can be helped. If you're too uncomfortable working with me, I'll tell Josie I can't take the job."

It would probably destroy any respect my sister might have for me and burn one of my last lifelines at the company, but I wasn't willing to make Lucy's life a living hell in order to make mine a little better. She shouldn't have to pay the price for the mess I'd made of my career. This job actually meant something to her. I remembered the way she used to talk about it. She'd gone to college for marketing. This was her dream career. I wouldn't be the one to ruin it for her. I wasn't *that* much of a bitter asshole.

Lucy shook her head. "I don't want Josie to know—"

"I don't have to tell her. I can make up a reason that doesn't involve you."

"No." Lucy's lips pressed together, pink and glossy, and I

couldn't help remembering how it had felt to kiss her. "I can't let you do that. I don't think you'd be here if you felt like you had a choice."

"Everyone always has a choice."

"Still." Her voice was softer. "You need this job, don't you?"

"Maybe," I admitted.

She nodded. "I need this job too. Which means we'll both have to make the best of it and try to get along. Do you think you can do that?"

"Yes."

"Then I need you to make more of an effort to be pleasant. I can't have you glaring at me all day long like you hate me."

"I don't hate you." That seemed like an important point to clarify. My feelings for her were tangled and painful, but hate didn't play any part in them. "I'm sorry if I was glaring."

"You were. You have been. Every time we see each other."

"I'm sorry. I didn't realize I'd been doing that." I ducked my head, embarrassed that my feelings had been so apparent. The last thing I wanted was Lucy knowing how much she'd hurt me or thinking I still hadn't gotten over her. I *hadn't* gotten over her, but that was beside the point. "I'll do better."

"We could come up with a code word, if that would help. Something I could say to let you know you're glaring at me so you'll stop."

"If you want."

"How about jinkies?"

"Jinkies?"

"It's what Velma says on *Scooby-Doo*."

"I know what it's from." Why did Lucy have to be so fucking cute? She was honestly standing there quoting Velma, who'd only been my first fictional crush. It was the cruelest part about all of this—I couldn't even properly dislike Lucy because we were so goddamn perfect for each other.

Except for the small matter of her wanting nothing to do with me, obviously. Minor obstacle, that one.

"It's a word I wouldn't normally use in a sentence, but I can say it around the office without arousing too much suspicion. Unless you have a better idea?"

"No, it's fine." It was a good idea. Because Lucy was really smart and really good with people, and just generally better at navigating things than I was.

"Okay. So if you hear me say jinkies, you'll know to fix your face and try to be less of a jerk."

I didn't like that she thought I was a jerk. That wasn't the kind of ex I wanted to be. "I'll make an effort to be civil from now on. Nice, even."

"I'd like that. I'll be nice too." She gave me a tentative smile. "From here on out, we'll be two coworkers on friendly terms."

It was a great plan, except for one thing. Something I hadn't fully realized until now, standing here having an actual conversation with Lucy for the first time since she'd broken up with me.

I was still just as in love with her as ever.

4

LUCY

Tanner wasn't glaring at me anymore. That was something.

I'd only had to say "jinkies" once this whole week —which was good, because Linh had looked at me like I'd had a mental break when I whisper-yelled it at my desk out of nowhere on Tuesday. I'd had to make up a lie about accidentally biting the inside of my cheek, and I'd felt so bad about lying that I'd bitten my cheek so it wouldn't be a lie. On the plus side, Tanner had looked appropriately chastened when I'd said our code word and had quit frowning at me across the low divider between our cubicles.

As far as I could tell, he'd been telling the truth about not realizing he was doing it. The guy simply had a resting surly face around me, which was lovely. But at least he seemed to be making a genuine effort to cut it out.

He'd pretty much stopped looking at me entirely, in fact. An improvement over active hostility, granted, but I found it disconcerting. Our little island of cubicles was set up like a four-leaf clover so we all faced the center. It was supposed to encourage collaboration, but Tanner was at the workstation diagonally across from me, which put us directly in each other's eyelines. In order to avoid flashing his *I Hate Lucy* face, he kept his eyes down completely unless he was talking to Linh or Arwen.

Which, by the way, he did a lot. He seemed to be getting on like gangbusters with the two of them. Tanner could be shy, but he was also very nice—to most people. Those of us who'd broken his heart excepted. So it hadn't taken him long to warm up to the members of the team who weren't me.

Especially Arwen.

Not that I was jealous. I definitely was not. I also wasn't bitter that he was being all friendly with everyone else while treating me like I had the plague. You know why? Because I was not a bitter person. I was a nice person. Even nicer than Tanner.

So it was totally fine that he'd been asking Linh and Arwen how they were doing every morning while ignoring me. I wasn't the least bit bothered that he never made eye contact with me or addressed me unless he was forced to—and even then he either stared at his shoes or at a spot on the wall past my shoulder. Totally no big! My feelings weren't even hurt yesterday when he'd announced he was going to the good coffee cart downstairs and offered to bring Linh and Arwen something back. *Pfft*. I could get my own coffee, thanks for not asking.

So what if this morning he'd brought kolaches from Leshikar's Bakery—which were totally my favorite—and even though he'd said they were for everyone, I didn't feel like that included me. I'd only had to sit there smelling that heavenly, fresh-baked dough while everyone else crammed their faces with delicious pastries. Whatever!

It definitely wasn't why I was in a bad mood right now. That had more to do with Byron and the team meeting I was currently sitting in.

We had one of these meetings every Friday to review the content strategy for the upcoming week. In general, our team was left mostly to ourselves. Byron had his hands full supervising the art department and copywriters who produced all the rest of the company's national advertising and marketing materials, and our little content marketing team ran like a well-oiled machine that didn't require much of his attention. Largely due to me, thank you very much. Since Jill had left, I'd kept things chugging along smoothly, creating all our content schedules, getting creative assets and approvals from other departments, making sure our messaging was pushed out to our social channels on time, tracking engagement data, and adjusting our content strategy accordingly.

Usually, these Friday meetings were quick and perfunctory. Byron would stare at his phone, only half listening, while I went over the plan for next week. Then he'd rubber-stamp everything I'd proposed and we'd adjourn. Easy-peasy lemon squeezy.

Today's meeting? Not so much.

It was the end of Tanner's first week, and therefore his first time taking part in the team meeting with Byron. I blamed Tanner's presence for Byron acting so weird today. For starters, Byron hadn't looked at his phone once since he'd sat down. For another, he kept interrupting me to ask questions about next week's schedule. He *never* had questions about the schedule. He barely cared about the schedule, except to make sure there was one in case he got asked about it. Now he suddenly cared about everything. In the last thirty minutes, he'd questioned my ice cream trivia, quibbled with every suggestion in our summer activity ice cream pairing feature, and currently he was grilling me about the recipe for S'more Than a Feeling ice cream sandwiches. Which, yes, I had made up myself, and they were freaking delicious.

"Plain graham crackers though?" Byron rubbed his chin like he was contemplating quantum mechanics instead of ice cream desserts. "Can't we come up with something a little more interesting?"

"Graham crackers are an essential ingredient in s'mores," I pointed out.

"What do you think, Tanner?"

Tanner's head jerked up. "Umm...I like graham crackers fine."

"Sure. They're fine. That's what I mean. Who wants 'fine'?" Byron snapped his fingers. "What if we used cookies instead of graham crackers?"

This perfunctory meeting that typically lasted only ten minutes had somehow turned into a protracted brainstorming session. Byron had to be doing this for Tanner's benefit, because he didn't want his boss's brother to know he usually phoned in the content marketing meetings. But if this was the way Byron was going to be from now on? I was going to lose my effing mind.

"The problem with that is we'd have to include a recipe for the cookies," I started to explain.

"What kind of cookies would go with s'mores?" Arwen asked.

"Chocolate chip?" Byron suggested. "Everyone likes chocolate chip, and they go with everything." He looked at Tanner. "How do you feel about chocolate chip?"

"I like them," Tanner said with a shrug.

"It's better to keep the recipes simple," I told Byron, making sure my *This is Fine* face didn't slip. "Expecting people to bake homemade cookies might make the recipe too complicated."

"Snickerdoodle?" Byron frowned and shook his head. "No, definitely not."

"What about peanut butter cookies?" Tanner said, starting to show some interest.

I tried again to get my point across. "The thing is, we get

much higher engagement when we keep the recipes super simple. Our newsletter subscribers have consistently shown they prefer treats they can throw together in five minutes. And also, I've already taken photos of the s'mores ice cream sandwiches I made with graham crackers. If we change the recipe, I'll have to do the whole photo shoot over."

"Does peanut butter and marshmallow go together?" Byron asked Tanner.

Had I died? Was it my ghost sitting here in this meeting and that was why no one was listening to me? I pinched my arm to make sure—and also to keep myself from shouting at everyone to shut up with all this cookie cross-talk.

"Peanut butter and marshmallows is totally a thing." Arwen was getting into it now too. "What's it called again when people put them together in a sandwich? My grandmother made me one once."

"Fluffernutters," Tanner said.

"Right!" Arwen beamed at him. "That's it."

Tanner beamed back at her. "I've never had one. Are they good?"

"I can't remember," Arwen said. "We should go out and get the ingredients at lunch so we can make them."

My *This is Fine* face didn't waver. I was *This is Fine*-ing like a champ.

"As much as I'd love to watch you eat that truly disgusting-sounding sandwich," Linh cut in, "Lucy's right. If the recipe requires people to bake homemade cookies, I can guarantee our click rate will be fifty percent lower."

God bless Linh. I would have kissed her on the mouth if it wouldn't get me in trouble with human resources.

"We learned that lesson from the great brownie sundae debacle last year," I added before Byron could derail the conversation again. "It's tempting to come up with the most delicious and ambitious recipes, but it's important to remember that thirty percent of our subscribers are under eighteen. A significant number of those are under twelve. They're not looking for *America's Test Kitchen*."

"Sounds like maybe we should stick with the graham crackers," Tanner said without looking at me. It was impressive how he'd managed to go through this whole meeting without once letting his eyes turn in my direction.

"Yeah, okay," Byron said. "Tanner's probably right."

My molars ground together hard enough to emit a supersonic whine. *I* was the one who was right. *Me*. It was *my* recipe and *my* opinion that had prevailed.

"What else?" Byron asked, looking around the table.

"That's everything," I said. *Thank god.*

"That's it?" he repeated as if there should be more.

"Yes," I told him. "We've covered the whole schedule." Finally. It only took us forty-five minutes longer than usual.

Byron looked disappointed. "How's it been going getting Tanner settled in?" Before I could answer, he turned to address Tanner. "What does Lucy have you working on?"

Tanner kept his eyes fixed on Byron, still pretending I wasn't in the room. "I've been adapting the copy for the upcoming newsletter into tweets and Instagram captions."

"Tweets?" Byron looked disappointed again. "Surely we can come up with something better than that." He looked at me. "Did you know Tanner has an English degree?"

I fixed my *This is Fine* face back in place. "I am aware of that, yes."

In fact, it was one of the first things I'd ever learned about Tanner. The night we first met, at one of my brother's shows, we'd spent hours talking about our favorite books. I could guarantee I knew a lot more about Tanner's interest in literature and writing than Byron did. For example, I knew Tanner had written his senior thesis on E.M. Forster and Virginia Woolf, that he'd reread *The Lord of the Rings* every year since he was twelve, and that his favorite author was Ursula K. Le Guin.

All of which was great, but it didn't mean he could jump right into this job with no experience. Tanner was smart and an excellent writer, so I had no doubt he'd catch on quickly, but the fact remained that he knew nothing about marketing or writing copy for social media. When he'd sent me the tweets he'd written yesterday, I'd covered his draft in so much markup it had looked like one of Cy Twombly's abstract expressionist paintings.

"I'll bet we can come up with something a little more interesting for him to work on," Byron continued before I could state my case. "Let's put him to work on next month's SJW stuff."

I had to forcibly unclench my jaw before I cracked one of my molars. Byron's habit of referring to the important issues facing our country as "all that SJW stuff" had always irritated me. The fact that he'd just undermined me in front of the whole team? Also not great. But I was downright incensed by Byron's implication that the work I'd given Tanner was somehow beneath him. It was the same work I'd been doing for my entire tenure at this company. Why wasn't it beneath *me*? Why did Tanner need something more interesting to do after all of five days on the job? Why was it fine for *me* to do the less interesting work but not him?

The answer was obvious, of course. Because Tanner's last name was King.

My *This is Fine* face kicked into double-overdrive to hide all the fuming I was doing on the inside. "If that's what you want," I told Byron serenely.

Writing those issues features was one of my favorite parts of this job, not to mention one of the most challenging to navigate. Walking the delicate tightrope between the company's progressive branding and our goal of building customer loyalty required a level of finesse it had taken me years to master.

But fine. Byron wanted Tanner to write it? I'd let Tanner write it.

And then I'd rewrite everything he'd written.

"Good. I think we're done here." Pushing his chair back, Byron directed his attention to Tanner again. "Do you have plans for lunch today? Let me take you out to celebrate the end of your first week on the team."

Arwen followed them out of the conference room while I silently gathered all my notes and pens.

"Byron never invited me out to lunch," Linh said as she watched the two men walk across the bullpen together before parting. "I mean, thank god, because he's the last person in this department I'd want to go to lunch with. But still." Her eyes slid to me. "He ever invite you out to lunch?"

"No," I said. "He never did."

"I think Byron has a crush on your boy Tanner."

"He has his lips firmly planted on Tanner's butt cheeks, that's for sure." I glanced through the glass and saw Arwen chatting with Tanner, probably making new fluffernutter plans.

Byron's not the only one around here with a crush on Tanner.

A lump tried to lodge itself in my throat, but I flipped open my water bottle and washed it away. I had much bigger problems than any totally inappropriate feelings of jealousy I might have about my ex.

I knew exactly what was happening. I could see the oncoming train speeding toward me.

That promotion I'd been promised? The one I'd worked my ass off to earn?

Byron was going to give it to Tanner.

5

LUCY

I was not, in general, a moody person. A positive attitude and an even temperament had done more to see me through life's challenges than sulking and complaining ever had. Not that I didn't occasionally suffer feelings of melancholy or aggravation—I just didn't believe in inflicting my foul moods on the people around me.

Still, today's meeting with Byron and my unsettling takeaway from it had put me in a grouchy frame of mind that followed me all the way home that night. When I let myself into the kitchen, only to be confronted by the same collection of dirty dishes I'd walked past that morning on my way to work, it was all I could do not to stamp my feet in frustration.

I was not the only occupant of this house, nor was I the only one physically capable of doing dishes. Yet I was the only one who ever seemed to do them with any regularity, despite the fact that I *was* the only person in this house who worked a full-time job. I did *most* of the chores, in fact, including the majority of the cooking, cleaning, and shopping.

Gritting my teeth, I stalked out of the kitchen and found my younger brother asleep on the couch. Without bothering to be quiet about it, I slammed my purse down on the pine coffee table and began gathering up the dirty dishes and trash that had accumulated since I'd picked up last night.

"Hey, Luce," Matt mumbled around a loud yawn. "What time is it?"

"It's almost six o'clock."

"Oh, cool." He pushed himself upright and rubbed his unshaven face.

My little brother—who was a year shy of thirty—shared my blonde hair, but where mine was thin and mostly straight, his was thick and wavy. It had been months since his last haircut, so his shaggy, nap-tousled mop stuck up in random spots on his head.

"Did you work today?" I asked, trying to keep the crabbiness out of my voice.

If he'd put in some hours, I could partially excuse the mess he'd left for someone else to clean up. Matt worked as a food delivery driver with one of those services where you signed into an app to be matched up with orders to pick up and deliver. The pay was crap, but Matt liked the flexibility of setting his own hours, allegedly so he could work around his band's gigs and practices, although I strongly suspected it was more so he could sleep late and play Xbox. Between the low pay and his disinclination to work more than twenty hours a week, he was barely earning enough money to cover his bar tabs, much less contribute to the household expenses.

"Nah." He ran a hand through his fluffy hair, which made it stick up more. "I was too hungover."

I should have guessed as much from the detritus I'd picked up, which included several cans of Monster Energy, an empty orange juice carton, a half-eaten bag of Flaming Hot Cheetos, and a bowl that seemed to contain the milk-bloated remains of Crunch Berries cereal.

"Gimme those," he said, leaning forward to grab the Cheetos out of my hand. "You don't have to clean up. I was gonna get to it."

"Were you?" I muttered under my breath.

"Lucy? Is that you?" our mother called from the back of the house.

"Yes, Mama," I called back.

"Did you wake your brother? You should have let him sleep."

"It's fine." Matt crammed a handful of Cheetos into his mouth. "I needed to get up anyway."

Our mother appeared from the back of the house and went straight to Matt without so much as a glance at me.

I was pleased to see she was wearing makeup and a nice dress. Hopefully that meant she'd gone to work today. She never left the house without putting on her face, which included bright red lipstick, false lashes, lots of contouring, and so much foundation you could scrape it off with a fingernail.

She pressed her hand to Matt's forehead as if he'd had the flu instead of too many shots of Jim Beam—or whatever it was he'd been overserved last night. "Are you feeling better, honey?"

"I'm fine, Mom. I told you it wasn't anything." He swatted her away gently and hauled himself to his feet. Offering me a contrite look, he took the stacked dishes and trash out of my hands. "I'll take those."

Our mother beamed a smile at him as he carried them into the kitchen. "Aren't you a sweetheart, cleaning up for your sister?"

"He's not doing it for me," I said, fighting to keep the petulance out of my voice. "It's his mess."

My mother waved her freshly manicured hand airily. She didn't believe men should have to clean up after themselves. That was how she'd been raised, how she'd treated our father when he still lived here, and how she'd raised Matt, to my perpetual irritation. Unfortunately, she didn't seem to think she should have to do much of the cleaning either, which meant the majority of it fell to me now that my younger sister Becca was off living in San Francisco.

"How was work?" I asked my mother.

She worked as an independent hairstylist and beauty consultant, which meant she paid calls on her clients in their homes to do their hair and makeup. Sometimes she got booked for wedding parties or other special events, but most of her clientele were elderly folks who were unable to leave their homes without assistance. There weren't all that many house-bound seniors in Crowder who could afford to pay for her services, so most months she didn't bring in enough money to cover the mortgage and other household bills.

She'd earn a lot more money if she worked in a salon, but that required committing to a regular schedule of full-time hours, which my mother resisted as much as my brother did. She'd been let go from two different salons for excessive absences and failure to bring in enough clients. At this point I was just grateful she was earning any money at all.

"Oh, you know. Fine." She smoothed a lock of hair that was the color of red velvet cake. I had no idea what my mother's natural hair color was—probably gray these days—because she'd been dyeing it bright red my entire life.

"Did you go to Spring Oaks?"

"Yes, but only four ladies wanted their hair set today. I was out of there by two o'clock."

One of the local nursing homes allowed her to come in on Fridays to style any of their residents who were interested in hiring her services. She offered them a steeply discounted rate, but was usually able to see five to ten clients in one day, which made it her most profitable—and busiest—day of the week.

When she rallied herself to go, anyway. Some weeks she decided she didn't feel up to it.

"I don't suppose you went to the grocery store?" I asked hopefully. I'd left the grocery list on the counter for her this morning, and she'd promised she'd try to squeeze in a trip to the HEB.

"Oh no, I didn't have time. You'll have to go tomorrow."

Of course I will.

"Is that a new manicure?" I asked her.

"Yes, what do you think?" She showed off her perfect nails, oblivious to the contradiction in what she'd just said. In her world, a manicure always took precedence over something as mundane as grocery shopping. "The color's called Sunset Soirée. Isn't it divine?"

"Very nice." It was never any use arguing with my mother. Even the mildest criticism could send her into a blue funk that sometimes left her incapable of getting out of bed for days, much less leaving the house to go to work.

When my father had announced he was leaving her for his administrative assistant, my mother took to her bed for six full weeks. I'd been twelve at the time, and I'd kept the house running by myself, making sure Matt and Becca got to school every day and scraping together meals for us from what I could find in the pantry. After we'd eaten our way through most of the chest freezer and I'd exhausted my piggy bank and the contents of my mother's wallet, I'd finally broken down and called my Uncle Curtis to tell him what was going on, and he and his wife Janet had driven down from Fort Worth to "handle the situation."

Things hadn't ever been quite that bad since, but my mother still reacted to heartbreak and disappointment by falling into a state of low spirits and refusing to leave her room. Even something as small as expressing my displeasure over the fact that she'd chosen to get a manicure rather than do the grocery shopping could easily set off one of her moods, so I kept my irritation to myself. Better to say nothing than risk upsetting her.

"Is everything all right?" my mother asked, focusing on me for the first time since I'd come home.

"Yes." I increased the wattage on my *This is Fine* face. "Just a long day at work is all. But thank you for asking."

I didn't like to tell my mother when I was having problems at work. I didn't like to tell my mother about any of my problems. She always responded in one of two ways. Either she'd minimize and dismiss my problems as "not worth worrying about" or she'd overreact by getting so upset on my behalf that I ended up trying to comfort her. Neither of which was helpful when I was feeling down or overwhelmed.

"Poor Lucy." She took my chin in one hand as she smoothed my hair back from my face with the other. "They work you too hard at that place, baby girl."

I smiled, enjoying the attention from her. "It's not so bad, Mama. I like my job."

"Are you sure you're feeling all right? You're looking wan— much more so than usual. Maybe you've got the same tummy bug as your brother."

"I don't think so."

"Don't frown like that. It will give you wrinkles." My mother studied my face, tilting it toward the dim overhead light. One of the bulbs had burned out and the fixture was desperately in need of dusting. I mentally added both to my weekend to-do list. "Maybe it's that lipstick you're wearing. I've told you before that shade of pink washes you out."

I pulled out of my mother's grasp and plumped the pillows on the couch where my brother had been sleeping. There was a smear of bright orange Cheeto dust on one of them, and another on the couch cushion next to it. Vacuuming the upholstery went onto the chore list as well.

The state of the house was a persistent source of stress and embarrassment for me. After my father left, my mother gave up maintaining domestic appearances, and the house had been slowly but determinedly sliding into dilapidation ever since. Nearly twenty years of neglect had left it so cluttered there was no such thing as a flat surface anymore. I tried my best to contend with the accumulating mess, but almost nothing ever got cleaned or put away unless I did it myself. I couldn't keep up with everything that needed doing, and I couldn't get my mother and brother to contribute enough to make a difference.

Believe me, I'd tried. For years I'd begged, pleaded, and harangued them about it, until finally I'd given up because all the nagging took too much of my energy. I couldn't even get them to stop undoing my efforts. As soon as I managed to get something in the house clean, one of them would stroll through and mess it up again. Last weekend I'd spent two hours making the kitchen spotless, and as soon as I'd finished my mother had come in to whip up a batch of her special homemade facials and left it looking like the aftermath of a food fight.

"I wish you'd let me color your hair." My mother tapped a red fingernail against her lips as she contemplated the problem of my unsatisfying appearance. "A warm brown shade would do wonders to brighten up your face."

I turned my back on her and headed into the kitchen. "My hair is the same color as Matt's."

My mother drifted after me. "Yes, but Matt is a Summer and you're a Spring. His complexion is so much richer and deeper than yours."

My richer- and deeper-complexioned brother had his head stuck in the fridge. "Is there anything to eat for dinner?" The dirty dishes he'd brought in had been abandoned on the counter with all the others, which was apparently his idea of cleaning up.

"No one went to the store today," I said as I began unloading the clean dishes from the dishwasher. "So probably not."

He closed the fridge. "That's okay. I'm not that hungry anyway."

"Don't you have a show tonight?" my mother asked. "You need to keep your energy up. We can send Lucy out to the store real quick."

"I'll grab something later. Don't fret, Mom." He leaned down to kiss her cheek on his way out of the kitchen. "I'm going to take a shower."

I had no regrets about making my brother fend for himself, but my mother was another matter. If I didn't make something for dinner, she was liable not to eat anything at all. "There's probably some soup in the pantry," I said. "I could heat it up for us."

She waved her hand at my suggestion. "Oh no, don't worry about me. I've got a dinner date tonight."

"With who?" I asked as I sorted silverware into the drawer.

"No one you know. I met him at the Chevron on the state highway. His name's Tony."

I tried not to wince. "You're going on a date with a man you met at a gas station?"

"We got to chatting as we filled up our tanks. He's an auto transport driver. He delivers cars all around the state."

"So he's a trucker?"

"No, he doesn't drive a big rig or anything. It's a concierge service. He has a trailer he tows behind his F-250. He was delivering a Porsche to somebody in Austin this afternoon, and we're meeting up for dinner on his way back to Houston tonight."

"Fingers crossed he's not a serial killer."

"Honestly, Lucy. A serial killer? You have such an overactive imagination."

That might be true, but I didn't think my concerns about my mother's date for tonight were entirely without basis.

She petted her flawless hair in the reflection on the oven door. "Goodness, I look a fright. I need to go touch myself up before I meet Tony." She turned to look at me. "Are you singing with your brother's band tonight?"

I shook my head as I loaded dirty mugs and glasses into the dishwasher. "Nope. Not tonight. They're just doing their usual show at the Rusty Spoke."

Matt had begged me to lend my choir skills to singing backup vocals for his band, but I'd told him I was only willing to do it on special occasions. Even though I liked singing, I didn't particularly enjoy doing it in front of an audience, and I didn't have time to show up for every random gig. I'd only agreed because I wanted to support Matt's efforts with the band, which were finally earning him a little money now that they were taking it more seriously. If me singing at a couple of shows could give them a leg up, I was willing to make the sacrifice.

"You should do something to treat yourself tonight," my mother said. "Like a nice bath bomb or a facial. You can use my bathtub if you like."

"Maybe I will." It wasn't the worst idea. After this week, I could use a little self-care. My chore list could wait until tomorrow.

"While you're in there, would you be a dear and work your magic to unclog my sink? It's been draining a little slow."

"It's not magic. I showed you how to do it yourself." I'd also warned her not to brush her hair over the sink or wash the strays down the drain or it would keep clogging.

"Oh honey, I can't risk ruining my manicure on a dirty job

like that. You're so good at it, it'll only take you a minute." Blowing me a kiss, she wandered off to get ready for her date.

After I'd finished cleaning up the kitchen and started the dishwasher, I retreated to my own bedroom for some privacy and quiet time. Technically, I shared my room with my little sister Becca, but since she'd left for college five years ago, I'd had it mostly to myself. It was my oasis of serenity and tidiness, the one part of the house I could control, and I kept it immaculate. No clutter or mess would ever be found in here, nor anything left sitting out that wasn't meant to be there.

After turning on my air purifier and lighting one of my candles to mask the scent of weed drifting in from my brother's room next door, I changed into my favorite Captain Marvel pajamas, grabbed a selection of graphic novels from my bookcase, and sank down in the nest of throw pillows arranged on my snowy white duvet.

I longed for the day I'd finally be able to move into my own apartment, but sometimes it felt like I'd never get there. My mother depended on me, not just for help around the house and emotional support, but also to help pay her expenses. She'd blown through her divorce settlement by the time I'd graduated from high school. By the time I finished college, she'd been fired from three different jobs, racked up a truly terrifying amount of credit card debt, and fallen behind on her mortgage payments. I'd dragged her to a credit counselor who put her on a debt repayment plan, and as soon as I landed my first full-time job I'd started contributing to the household expenses.

But now I was stuck. I couldn't afford to help with her bills and get my own place. Not yet, anyway. I'd been saving every cent I could spare, but I was still a long way away from making my dream a reality.

As I settled back on the bed, the sound of my brother's Xbox bled through the paper-thin wall between our rooms. I hunkered down deeper in my pillows, trying to ignore the litany of machine gun fire and explosions.

"Lucy!" my mother shouted from the bedroom on the other side of me. "Do you know what I did with my keys?"

"No," I shouted back through the wall. "I wasn't home the last time you used them."

"Please, honey, will you just come help me?"

This was why I needed that promotion. Aside from the fact that I deserved it, I needed the salary bump—desperately—if I was ever going to get out of this house.

One day.

One day I'd come home to a quiet, empty home that was just as spotless as I'd left it. My very own Fortress of Solitude where everyone would leave me alone.

6

TANNER

"You need to bang her out of your system," my younger brother pronounced with his trademark delicacy.

I'd asked Wyatt to meet me at Dooley's Bar after work on Friday, at the end of my first week in my new job. We were sharing a much-needed pitcher of beer while I vented to him about my romantic-slash-professional predicament.

This situation with Lucy was obviously untenable. I couldn't keep having all these feelings for her. Not only was it awkward and inappropriate now that we were coworkers, it was utterly fucking pathetic given her clearly stated disregard. I needed to bring my emotions to heel.

Unfortunately, short of Lucy revealing herself as a serial killer, animal abuser, or devotee of dark magic—and that one might not necessarily be a dealbreaker—I couldn't imagine myself spontaneously falling out of love with her. Not while I was being confronted on a daily basis with how lovely and funny and smart and essentially perfect she was for me in every respect.

"Does that ever work?" I asked, raising a skeptical eyebrow at

Wyatt. "Wasn't that what you were trying to do for years to get over your feelings for Andie?"

"Yeah, no, it didn't work for me at all," Wyatt agreed, shaking his head. "But hey, it might still be worth a try, right? At least you'll get a good time out of it, even if it doesn't cure you of Lucy fever."

As unappealing as I found Wyatt's suggestion, he might be onto something. If I wanted to stop pining for Lucy, I needed to move on and find someone else—someone with the power to displace her in my affections.

I needed a romantic distraction.

The most obvious candidate to jump out at me was my new coworker, Arwen. She was attractive, friendly, and she'd been named after a character in one of my all-time favorite books, which seemed like it ought to be a sign. Unfortunately, I quickly identified two problems with Arwen as a potential love interest.

The first—and biggest—involved the questionable wisdom of dating a coworker. What I really did not need was to be trapped working on the same team with *two* ex-girlfriends instead of just one. Which, given my lifetime batting average in the dating department, was not an improbable outcome. I also worried it might make Lucy uncomfortable. Most likely she didn't care about me enough to give a damn one way or the other, but I preferred not to take the chance. I'd already made her life amply unpleasant. Not only had I inadvertently been a jerk to her for the last several months, now I was inflicting my unwanted presence on her daily in her place of work. Courting Arwen right in front of her face seemed unconscionably callous.

The second reason Arwen didn't strike me as a promising romantic partner was that, in an attempt to make conversation with her my first day, I'd mentioned I had a cat named Radagast, and Arwen had responded with a blank stare. When I'd explained that Radagast was a character from *The Lord of the Rings* books, she confessed that she'd never read them. Then she'd gone on to tell me that she hadn't even liked the movies because they were, in her words, "too long, too boring, and what was the deal with all those endings?"

Everyone was entitled to their opinions, obviously. I didn't expect the whole rest of the world to love the same things I loved. Nonetheless, it felt like a good indication that Arwen and I were not meant to be soul mates. Which was just as well, on account of the whole coworker thing.

"What I need is to start dating again," I told Wyatt. "I need to meet someone who can make me forget Lucy."

"Yes. There you go." Wyatt smacked his hand on the table-top. "Good plan. Pick yourself up, dust yourself off, and get back out there. Which app are you thinking of?"

"No dating apps." I shook my head firmly. "I'm not doing that again."

I knew it was how a lot of people my age found their sexual and romantic partners, but my past experiences had not been stellar. Online dating might be great for people living in a city big enough to provide a greater degree of anonymity and choice. But in a small town like Crowder? It was fraught with peril.

For one thing, the odds of accidentally swiping right on someone who later turned out to be one of your second cousins were alarmingly high. Yes, it had happened to me, and yes, I was still scarred by the flirty messages we'd exchanged before we realized our mistake.

The problem was that everyone knew everyone in Crowder. You couldn't throw a rock in the eligible dating pool without hitting either someone you'd grown up with or someone who was connected to someone you knew. In addition to the afore-mentioned second cousin, my potential matches had included a girl who'd dumped me in tenth grade, one of my former high school teachers, a coworker's wife who claimed to be in an open relationship, and my father's longtime personal assistant, who I was now burdened to know was "up for anything." Overall, the experience had provided me with too much information I wished I'd never learned about the love lives of people in my circle of acquaintance, and very few viable dating candidates.

"Don't worry, bro. I've got this." The black vinyl booth creaked as Wyatt shifted to dig his phone out of his back pocket.

"What are you doing?" I tugged at the collar of my shirt, wishing I'd gone home and changed instead of coming straight from work. The inside of Dooley's was uncomfortably warm, despite the cavelike darkness inside the bar. Every time the door opened, a shaft of blinding sunlight pierced the gloom as another blast of broiling summer air poured in to nudge the mercury higher. Coming here in wool dress pants had been a miscalculation.

Wyatt didn't look up as he scrolled through his phone. "I'm searching through my contacts for the perfect woman to make you forget all about Lucy." He was wearing a tank top and jeans, and he looked a hell of a lot more comfortable than me, as per usual. Wyatt always appeared effortlessly comfortable everywhere he went. Me, not so much.

People said we looked alike, and I guess technically we did, but that was where the resemblance ended. He was a scruffy, tattooed musician who attracted female attention as easily as breathing, and I was his reticent, buttoned-down, easily ignored alter ego.

Going through life as Wyatt's duller doppelgänger had taught me that there was a lot more to sex appeal than bone structure. Attractiveness was all about attitude and personality, two things Wyatt oozed out of his pores and I sadly lacked.

Shockingly, women weren't as interested in the introverted, bookish brother as they were in the overtly flirtatious one in a rock band.

"You still have women in your contacts?" I asked him. "Andie doesn't mind?"

For the first time in his life, my "love 'em and leave 'em" brother was in a serious, committed relationship with a woman he was utterly besotted with—and it had only taken thirteen years of mutual pining for them to get their shit together and admit how they felt about each other. I'd half expected the natural order to break down when Wyatt took himself off the market, but so far no obvious cracks seemed to have appeared in the space-time continuum.

He threw a sardonic look at me as he reached for his beer. "Does my girlfriend mind that I still speak to fifty percent of the human race even though I'm madly in love with her? No, she doesn't."

"I was referring more to the fact that you're hanging on to the phone numbers of all the women you've slept with."

"Okay, first of all, I don't even *have* numbers for most of the women I've slept with. And secondly, I haven't slept with every woman in my contacts. Some of these women are customers and others are simply friends."

I eyed him over my own beer. "But a nonzero number are friends and/or customers you've had sex with, right?"

"True," he conceded with a shrug. "But Andie trusts me completely, just like I trust her."

This new, love-bitten version of Wyatt was taking some getting used to. Not that I wasn't pleased about the changes in him. Since he and Andie had gotten together, he'd been happier than I'd ever seen him. I just wasn't used to hearing him speak so earnestly about his feelings. I was supposed to be the sensitive, monogamous romantic of the two of us.

"Ideally, I'd prefer someone you haven't had sex with," I told him. "Although I know it's a tall order."

Wyatt rolled his eyes at me as he continued to scroll through his phone.

I took a sip of my beer. "I don't suppose you're coming to Dad's birthday dinner next week?"

He snorted. "Hell no."

My brother wasn't currently speaking to our dad. Wyatt's rebellious nature had frequently clashed with our father's controlling tendencies over the years, but this was different. This time they'd fallen out over one of Dad's business ventures—a real estate startup that had employed some underhanded practices that had nearly caused Wyatt's girlfriend to lose her house. As far as I knew, Wyatt hadn't spoken to Dad in several months. I didn't blame him for nursing a grudge, but I missed having him as an extra buffer at family functions.

"Are you ever going to forgive him?" I asked.

"Maybe when he asks for my forgiveness."

"So no." Barnyard hogs would take to the skies before Dad ever apologized for anything.

Wyatt shrugged. "We've got a gig in Austin that night anyway."

"Oh yeah? That's great."

Wyatt's band had been getting more traction in the local music scene lately. Thanks to Wyatt's songwriting, they'd gained a loyal following here in Crowder and generated enough buzz to start booking some shows out of town. The other three members of the band were friends of Wyatt's from high school —including Lucy's brother Matt. It was at one of their shows where I'd first met her, in fact.

Wyatt shrugged. "It's just a weeknight gig at a dive bar on the Drag, but everyone's gotta start somewhere."

"Is Lucy going with you?" One of the songs Wyatt had

written was a duet, and Matt had recruited Lucy to perform it with them at a few of their local shows. The first time I'd ever heard her sing was up onstage with my brother after we'd broken up, and it had just about knocked me flat.

Wyatt arched an eyebrow. "Why? You gonna come to Austin to see us play if she is?"

"No, I was just wondering how she was going to balance all your gigs with her full-time job." It seemed like a lot, performing a weeknight gig seventy miles away, then showing up for work at eight o'clock the next morning. Obviously I hadn't talked to her about it lately, but when we'd been dating she'd never mentioned any dreams of being a professional singer. Lucy didn't particularly strike me as the type to sacrifice a steady job to run off and join a rock band.

"She's not. We can't pay her enough to make it worth her while, and it's not really her thing, anyway. She's only been doing it as a favor. She's singing with us at the folk festival though. I assume you're coming to that?"

"Yeah, of course. I wouldn't miss it."

The Crowder Folk Festival was a local annual music event that our late grandfather, Earnest King, had started in the sixties to capitalize on the growing music scene in Austin and bring more people into the country-western dance hall he owned here in town. These days our uncle Randy ran both the dance hall and the festival, but this was the first year he'd agreed to let Wyatt's band play.

Wyatt lifted his phone to his ear, and I leaned forward, frowning.

"Who are you calling?" I asked, afraid he was rushing me into something I wasn't sold on doing yet.

He raised a finger in the universal sign for *hold your horses* as he spoke into the phone. "Hey, babe. I need your opinion on something."

I relaxed when I realized he'd only called his girlfriend and not a prospective love interest he was about to foist on me.

"Tanner needs to get laid," he told Andie. "Any ideas who we should set him up with?"

I rubbed my forehead as the level gauge on my self-esteem reservoir dropped another few notches.

"What about Megan?" Wyatt asked Andie. "Oh shit, really? Well, never mind." He looked up at me and shook his head. "Megan's seeing some tattoo artist up in Austin," he explained as though I knew who the hell Megan was.

"Maybe we should forget the whole thing." I was having second thoughts about asking my womanizing brother for dating advice—even if he was a reformed womanizer. "I don't know how I feel about going on a blind date with a total stranger."

"No weaseling out," Wyatt told me. "Did you hear that?" he said into the phone. He took a sip of beer as he listened to Andie's response. "Yeah, okay, that's a good idea." He spun the phone away from his mouth as he addressed me again. "What if we did a double date? Then you'd have us there as buffers. Keep it like a casual, friends hanging out sort of thing so there's less pressure?"

"Yeah, all right," I allowed. "That might not be so bad."

In the past, Wyatt had always made the worst kind of wingman, because he'd instantly monopolized the interest of every woman in a five-mile radius, thereby rendering me invisible. But now that he'd hung up his player's hat, I might have a fighting chance. Especially with Andie there to reinforce the fact that Wyatt was spoken for.

"Okay, don't kill me"—Wyatt ducked his head as he spoke into the phone once more—"but what do you think about Brianna?" He winced and held the speaker away from his ear as Andie's voice grew loud enough to travel across the table to me, although I couldn't make out what she was saying. "Yeah, I know, but Tanner needs an easy win to boost his confidence and —I mean—that's Brianna, right?"

"I'm not a charity case," I muttered. "Jesus."

Wyatt ignored me. "Of course this is about Lucy. Hey, did you know they were working together now? Why didn't you tell me?"

I held my hand out and waggled my fingers. "Give me the phone."

Andie was friends with Lucy, and if Lucy had been talking to her about me, I wanted to know what she'd said.

"Hang on, Tanner wants to talk to you." Wyatt passed his phone over to me.

"Hi, Andie," I said, pressing it to my ear.

"Hey," she answered. "Why do you need to get laid? Is this Wyatt's brilliant idea or yours?"

"Did you talk to Lucy about me?" I asked, ignoring her question. "Did she tell you I was working on her team now?"

Across the table, Wyatt rolled his eyes as he topped up our glasses from the pitcher.

"Yesssss." Andie sounded hesitant. No doubt because she knew I was about to press her for info.

"What did she say about me?"

"Tanner, come on."

"Andie, please just tell me." I'd known Andie since she was a kid, and I was pretty confident I could wheedle the information out of her if I tried hard enough.

"Look, she didn't say much, okay? She doesn't really talk about you around me, because you're Wyatt's brother."

"But she said something."

"Just that you were on her team now and she was having to train you."

"And? She must have told you how she felt about it, or else why would she bring it up?"

"Look, she's my friend. I'm not going to betray her confidence—just like I wouldn't betray yours. Unless you want me telling her everything you've ever said about her?"

"You are annoyingly scrupulous."

Wyatt gave me a commiserating nod over his beer. "I know, right?"

"You're not still acting weird around her, are you?" Andie's voice had gone stern.

I rubbed the sweat off the back of my neck. "Did she tell you I was being weird?"

"No, that's my own personal observation. Whenever you see her, you get all withdrawn and sulky, and it makes her feel like shit. You can't do that to her at work."

"I know," I said. "I'm trying to cut it out."

"Good. See that you do. Now, why do you need to get laid?"

I sighed. "Because I'm still hung up on Lucy."

"I already knew that," Andie said.

"Working together every day isn't making the situation any better. It's making it worse. At this rate I'm never going to get over her unless I take drastic action."

"And you think sex is the answer? That sounds more like Wyatt than you."

"I think I need to do something to help me move on. For both my sake and Lucy's."

"So are you looking to date? Or are you just trying to screw her out of your system? Because I gotta be honest—I don't think the latter's going to work for you."

"Yeah, that's not really my style."

Wyatt shook his head like I was a lost cause. Which was rich, coming from the guy who'd professed his deep and abiding love for his girlfriend up onstage in the middle of a children's concert while dressed as Sheriff Scoopy. I wasn't exactly clear on why he'd needed to wear the Sheriff Scoopy costume, but I gathered it had something to do with humiliating himself to prove the extent of his devotion to her.

Neat, huh? The same job my dad had sentenced me to was the most demeaning thing Wyatt had been able to think up for his grand romantic gesture. That was probably where our dad had gotten the idea, in fact. *Thanks for that, bro.*

"Okay, cool," Andie said. "Give me back to Wyatt."

I passed Wyatt back his phone.

"So?" he said to Andie. "What do you think?"

While the two of them debated which poor, unsuspecting woman to pawn me off on, I leaned back in the booth and sipped my beer. It was interesting that Lucy had mentioned our new work situation to Andie. Maybe she was more fazed by it than she'd let on.

I knew it couldn't be because she still had feelings for me. It had taken me a while, but I'd finally accepted that Lucy hadn't ever felt anything real for me. Only one of us had been playing for keeps, and it wasn't her.

If she was bothered enough about me working on her team to tell Andie, it meant my presence was a nuisance to her. While it might be tempting to take petty satisfaction in the thought of making her life unpleasant after she'd broken my heart, that wasn't who I wanted to be. My mother—god rest her soul—hadn't raised me to be the kind of man who made a woman's life miserable because she didn't love me the way I wanted her to. However I might feel about her, Lucy didn't owe me her affection. But I did owe her the courtesy of not making her life unpleasant on purpose.

"Yep," Wyatt said into the phone. "That works. Let me know what she says. Love you." He hung up and tossed the phone onto the table before reaching for his beer. "Andie's calling her friend Kaylee to see if we can set something up for tomorrow night."

"Is she cute?" I asked warily.

"No, she's got a hunchback and a third nostril." He rolled his eyes. "Come on. I told you, I got this."

Somehow, I didn't find that particularly reassuring.

7

LUCY

Today was the Monday-est of all Mondays that had ever Monday-ed. First, I'd woken up at four a.m. with my period and a killer case of cramps. After I'd finally fallen back asleep, I wound up snoozing through my alarm so I didn't have time to make coffee or breakfast.

When I got to the office—hangry, under-caffeinated, and still feeling crampy—I'd discovered Tanner had brought kolaches from Leshikar's Bakery again, damn him. But no matter how hungry I was or how delicious Leshikar's kolaches were, I refused to eat his suck-up kolaches. Especially after Byron exclaimed over them as if Tanner was the first person in the entire history of the office to bring in breakfast for the team.

Never mind that I'd brought in homemade cinnamon rolls two weeks ago. Homemade! Not that it mattered. I could bring in fresh baked goods every day of the week, and I still wouldn't be getting that promotion. Not with Tanner here.

As if all that wasn't bad enough, while I was sitting at my desk, resentfully gnawing on the stale granola bar I'd found in the bottom of my purse, I was forced to listen to Tanner and Arwen flirting three feet away from me. He'd stopped at her desk to compliment the graphic on her screen, and now she was giving him some kind of Photoshop tutorial. Which Tanner was of course completely enthralled by. No living soul had ever been more fascinated by layer masks than Tanner was by Arwen's explanation. They were getting along like two flies in a jam jar.

It shouldn't bother me, but it did. And the fact that it bothered me bothered me even more. The sound of their friendly banter rubbed against my brain like cracker crumbs in my bedsheets. My teeth ground together every time I heard Arwen's tinkling laugh or Tanner's warm chuckle. I tried not to look at them, but it was impossible to tune them out and concentrate on the copy I was supposed to be writing.

Without my permission, my gaze jumped to Arwen's desk. Tanner was standing next to her with his hand resting on the back of her chair. I couldn't help noticing how her dark hair brushed against his bare forearm where he'd rolled his sleeve up. As I watched them, Tanner leaned in closer to point at something on the screen, and Arwen giggled as she pushed his hand away.

They really were disgustingly cute together. I could already picture their save the date cards, which Arwen would of course design herself. Their wedding colors would be lilac and turquoise—her favorites—the ceremony held at First United where Tanner's family attended church, and the reception would be a black-tie dinner and dancing affair at the Crowder Country Club. After a honeymoon in Europe, they'd have five adorable children and buy a beautiful old house in the historic district that they'd lovingly renovate themselves like Jimmy Stewart and Donna Reed in *It's a Wonderful Life*.

Wow. What was wrong with me?

Get. A. Grip.

Exhaling in irritation, I swiveled my chair so I couldn't see them anymore without twisting my whole body. I needed to quit fixating on Tanner and focus on my own work. Sitting here resenting him wasn't going to improve the reality of my situation. Nothing was likely to improve the reality of my situation, other than some sort of divine intervention that took Tanner out of the running for my promotion. Like if he were suddenly struck dead by a stray piece of space junk falling from the sky. But since I didn't believe in divine intervention—and I didn't actually want Tanner to die by space junk or any other means—there was no point in fixating on it.

Then, for the icing on the shit cake that was this day, as I sat there grumpily contemplating the copy on my screen, I felt an uncomfortable twinge between my legs that I immediately recognized. My stupid menstrual cup was trying to slip out of place. Again.

I swear to god, this day.

What was it about this dang menstrual cup? Some days it fit perfectly snug and other days, no matter how hard I tried, it refused to stay in place. Of course today had to be one of the latter days. On top of everything else, what could be more perfect than wrestling with my menstrual cup in a public restroom? *Love it.* Totally my favorite thing to do at the office.

Squeezing my pelvic floor for dear life, I stood up and penguin-walked down the hall to the bathroom. Relieved to find it empty, I slipped into a stall and set about fixing my wayward menstrual cup.

Unfortunately, the cruel whim of fate hadn't finished playing with me today. As I hovered over the toilet to perform the complex feat of contortion required to extract the silicone cup wedged in my vagina, the sudden release of suction caused the slippery thing to launch itself out of my fumbling fingers. I watched in horrified slo-mo as it flew into the air, tumbling end over end and sending period blood flying everywhere.

Every. Freaking. Where.

Tears of panic and frustration sprang to my eyes as I surveyed the damage. The inside of the stall looked like one of those gruesome television crime scenes that sent the rookie beat cop running to retch into the nearest garbage can and required a blood spatter expert to determine exactly how many people had been disemboweled.

Cursing my own stupidity under my breath, I grabbed a handful of toilet paper and attempted to wipe up as much of the blood as I could. Five minutes later, I emerged from the stall with a wad of toilet paper stuffed in my underwear and my bloodstained hands clutching the accursed menstrual cup I'd rescued from the unsanitary bathroom floor.

One look in the mirror brought on a fresh slew of frustrated tears. My light pink blouse was streaked with blood. Not, like, a few small spatters either. Huge splotches of bright red splashed across my chest like the ghost of Jackson Pollock had mistaken me for a canvas. There was no washing this stain out in the sink and hoping no one would notice. Even worse, I'd foolishly left my phone at my desk so I couldn't text Linh for emergency assistance.

I was screwed.

Biting back tears, I scrubbed my hands and menstrual cup with antibacterial soap vigorously enough to make Lady Macbeth proud. There was nothing to be done about my shirt, so I went back in the stall and reinserted my menstrual cup, shoving that infernal device so far up my cooch I'd probably need my OB to extract it for me. My attempt to clean up the evidence of my bloody crime had left the stall looking like a toddler had been through on a finger-painting rampage, but there was only so much you could do to remediate a biohazard with cheap toilet paper. Every surface would need to be disinfected before it was safe for public use, which entailed a trip to the break room down the hall to get the spray cleaner from under the sink.

Cautiously, I poked my head out the bathroom door and peered down the hall. The coast appeared to be clear. But I'd need to be quick, both so I wasn't seen and in order to get back before some poor unsuspecting soul tried to use the bathroom and stumbled on the horror show I'd left behind. The way my luck was going today, it would probably be Josie King herself, and I'd never be able to look my VP in the eye again.

I slipped into the hall and fast-walked to the break room, pausing to peek around the corner and ascertain it was empty before proceeding inside. For once, fortune was on my side. I scampered over to the sink and grabbed the disinfectant and a roll of paper towels.

Unfortunately, that was where my oh-so-brief bout of serendipity ran out. Silly of me to think I'd catch a break. As I turned around with my cleaning implements in my hands, I heard the unmistakable sound of footsteps approaching.

Worse, they sounded like the heavy tread of male footsteps. Heading right for the break room—and me, with my blood-soaked shirt.

Panic and embarrassment burned in my throat. There was nowhere for me to hide in here. Frozen in place, I hugged the paper towels and disinfectant to my chest, attempting to cover the stains on my shirt.

As the maraschino cherry on top of the crappy ice cream sundae that was my morning, freaking *Tanner* walked into the break room. Of course. Who else could it possibly be but him?

He came to a dead stop at the sight of me and blinked. Neither of us spoke as we stared at one another, equally disconcerted to find ourselves in the same room, but for vastly different reasons. His eyes dropped to the cleaning supplies in my arms before returning to my face.

A frown creased his brow. "Are you okay?"

"Yep." I nodded, blinking rapidly as my cheeks burned hotter. "Just doing a little cleaning."

"You look like you've been crying."

"Allergies." Forcing my legs into motion, I attempted to dodge around him on my way to the door. "If you'll excuse me —" In my agitated state, I lost my grip on the disinfectant and lunged to retrieve it before it could hit the floor.

"Is that *blood*?"

"No." I spun around, presenting my back to him.

"Then what is it?"

"Paint?" It wasn't the most convincing lie I'd ever told. In retrospect, I probably should have worked out my cover story *before* I'd ventured out of the bathroom.

Tanner loomed in front of me, making me jump. Tears of embarrassment burned my eyes and clogged my throat.

"That's not paint." His eyes lifted from my shirt to my face, and his frown grew deeper. "Are you hurt? Did you cut yourself?" He started to come closer, and I threw a hand up to ward him off.

"It's not that kind of blood!"

"What does that mean? What kind of blood is it?"

I shook my head, squeezing my eyes shut. "Would you believe I murdered someone, and you've caught me in the act of cleaning up the evidence?"

"No, I wouldn't." Tanner's voice was softer than I'd gotten used to hearing it recently, and it made my throat burn even more. "Tell me what happened."

"It's...you know." Opening my eyes, I gestured at my uterus, not wanting to say the words out loud.

He stared at me blankly, still not getting it.

"It's period blood, okay?" I held my hands up, letting him see the full extent of the damage.

"Oh!" He relaxed. "Okay. Whew. For a second there I thought you'd severed an artery."

"No, I just spilled my menstrual cup all over the bathroom stall and myself, and now I have to go decontaminate the ladies' room because it's covered in my uterine lining!"

Tanner rolled his lips between his teeth, trying not to laugh. I couldn't fault him for it. The situation was probably hilarious when you weren't the one standing around your workplace drenched in menstrual blood.

"Go on," I said. "It's okay. You can laugh. Enjoy my humiliation. I don't blame you." I tried to laugh at myself like a good sport but it came out sounding hollow and creepy, like one of those demented dolls that came to life and murdered people.

Tanner's expression gentled. Instead of laughing at me, he took the roll of paper towels, tore off a piece, and offered it to me. "What can I do to help?"

I accepted the paper towel and wiped my eyes, taken off guard by his kindness. "Nothing. It's fine. Thank you for the offer, but I don't need any help."

He scrutinized me, then set the paper towel roll on a nearby table and untucked his dress shirt.

"What are you doing?" I asked in alarm.

"Giving you my shirt." He proceeded to unbutton it, exposing the white V-neck undershirt underneath.

I shuffled backward, mortified. "Oh, no. Please don't."

"Would you rather walk around the office looking like an axe murderer?"

"It might earn me some respect." His mouth quirked at one corner, and I couldn't help smiling a little in response. "I'll figure something out. I couldn't possibly—"

"Just put it on." He shrugged off his shirt and held it out.

"But you can't walk around the office in your undershirt all day."

"My brother Nate always keeps spare shirts in his office. I can borrow one from him." He gave the navy blue shirt an impatient jiggle.

Reluctantly, I turned around and let Tanner guide it over my arms. It had a subtle geometric pattern and hung down to my knees. If I'd had a belt to cinch it at the waist, it would have made a passable shirtdress.

He took the disinfectant bottle from me so I could button the shirt to cover up the evidence of my bloody accident. While I was doing that he grabbed the paper towel roll and headed out of the break room with my cleaning supplies.

"Wait!" I hurried after him, clutching his shirt closed over my chest.

He stopped in front of the ladies' room and knocked on the door.

"What are you doing?" I asked, alarmed anew.

"The bathroom still needs cleaning, and you're the only one of us wearing a nice shirt." He tipped his head at the door. "Check to make sure it's empty. I don't want to surprise anyone."

"I can clean up my own mess," I told him as I pushed open the door and peeked inside.

"All clear?" When I nodded he bustled in past me. "Which stall?" He guessed correctly on the first try, pushing inside and peering down at the blood-smeared site of my disgrace. "Oh yeah, found it."

"*Tanner.*" My whisper-yell was sharp enough to make him turn around. "I can't let you do this."

He stared at me blankly. "Why?"

"Because it's embarrassing and...and *gross.*"

"It's just period blood. It's not like I've never seen it before."

This was true, although it was something I'd rather forget about. Back when we'd been dating, I'd started my period on an overnight sleepover at his house. You would think a grown woman on birth control pills would have a better handle on her menstrual cycle, but clearly not. I'd woken in the morning and been appalled when I discovered the bloodstain I'd left on his sheets, but Tanner had simply put them in the washer like it was no big deal and asked if I needed him to go to the store for me.

Talk about ideal boyfriend material. It was really too bad I hadn't been in the market for one.

"Besides," he added, his expression flat, as if he'd had the same memory and found it as painful as I did, "I don't want you getting bleach stains on my shirt." Before I could argue further, he went into the stall and closed the door behind him.

I bit my lip as I listened to the sound of the spray bottle pump, at a loss for what to do. Short of parkouring my way over the stall and dropping down on Tanner's shoulders like Spider-Woman to wrestle the cleaning supplies away from him, I didn't seem to have any choice but to accept his gentlemanly assistance.

On the one hand, having my resentful ex clean up my biological hazmat spill compounded my humiliation a thousandfold. But from a practical perspective, out of everyone in this building, Tanner was the only one who'd voluntarily exchanged bodily fluids with me already. When you looked at it like that, perhaps it wasn't such a big deal. He might resent having to do me any favors, but he was the person least likely to be revolted by this particular favor.

One of the things I'd admired about Tanner when we were dating was his strong sense of decency and the fact that he never let self-interest prevent him from doing the right thing. He was the sort of man who picked up other people's litter on the sidewalk and stopped to help strangers in need even when it was inconvenient. Today I happened to be the stranger in need, and Tanner was simply doing for me what he'd do for anyone else.

He really was a profoundly good person. In so many ways

he'd been perfect for me. It was tragic bad luck that we'd met when we were both looking for such different things. Tanner was obviously in the market for commitment, while all I'd wanted was a little company and a temporary distraction from the pressures of my own life. That was as much as I could handle right now. I wasn't giving up what little freedom I had to take on the additional responsibility of a boyfriend. Just the thought of it made me physically recoil.

But maybe, if we'd met at another time in my life, I might have been able to love him. In a few years, when I had my own place and I'd dug myself out from under the constant, crushing burden of responsibility I felt toward my family, maybe then I'd be ready for a serious relationship. Tanner and I might have been happy together if we'd met in that imaginary future instead of now, when I was barely holding my shit together.

My eyes started to prickle again as I stood there uselessly, waiting for him to finish cleaning up my mess. I reached for a paper towel and blew my nose again, blaming my overactive mucus membranes on the aerosolized bleach in the air.

Tanner emerged from the stall a few minutes later. "That's done," he said as he chucked the dirty paper towels in the trash. "Fit for public use once more."

"Thank you. I don't even know what to say."

"Don't worry about it," he replied gruffly as he washed his hands.

I handed him a clean paper towel to dry off with. "You've done your civic duty for the month. You can go now."

He hesitated, looking me up and down. "What are you going to do? Wear my shirt over yours for the rest of the day?"

I shook my head. "I'll run home and change real quick. I just need to get my purse and phone from my desk." Of course, that would require me to walk into the bullpen while wearing Tanner's shirt. Which everyone would know was Tanner's shirt because they'd all seen him wearing it not ten minutes ago. Which would definitely raise questions and eyebrows.

"Maybe I should get them for you," he proposed, having the same thought.

"How are you going to explain what happened to your shirt?" His plain white undershirt was bound to attract its own share of notice.

He shrugged. "I can say I spilled something on it."

"Yeah, but if Linh or Arwen see you digging through my drawers and taking my purse, they're going to get suspicious."

"What do you want to do?"

I bit my lip. "Tell Linh what happened. She can get my purse and phone and meet me in here."

"All right. Sit tight." He turned to leave.

"Thank you," I called after him. "Not many men would be so kind."

He paused in the doorway without looking back at me. "That says more about them than me."

8

TANNER

As per usual, when I parked in front of my father's house, a knot of dread twisted itself around my stomach. I didn't enjoy returning to the house I'd grown up in, and it was only my sense of family duty that kept bringing me back.

Tonight's duty was my father's birthday. My stepmother had planned a family dinner at the homestead in honor of the occasion. I hadn't spoken to my father since he'd condemned me to work at the amusement park, and I wasn't looking forward to seeing him tonight. But it couldn't be avoided. I was expected to pay my respects, and pay my respects I would.

As I stepped inside the spacious ranch-style house, the familiar smell stirred up a host of unpleasant emotions: loneliness, apprehension, grief. The few fond memories I had of my childhood here were overshadowed by all the things I'd sooner forget. My parents' frequent arguing, the weight of my father's disapproval, my mother's illness and subsequent death.

The sounds of splashing water and laughter pulled me out of my melancholy ruminations, and I followed them through the house until I found the rest of the family gathered on the large covered patio next to the swimming pool. My half-brother Ryan and half-sister Riley were in the water playing with our adopted brother Manny's three-year-old daughter. Everyone else either stood or lounged under the big fans that stirred the hot air enough to keep most of the mosquitos away.

I spotted my dad presiding over the grill with Nate at his elbow. Of course he was with Nate. The two of them were always plotting together, always talking about work, neither of them capable of leaving the job behind for one measly evening to relax and have a good time.

They were the two people here I least wanted to face. My instinct was to turn the other way and avoid them both, but I knew I couldn't escape an interaction with them altogether. Better to get it over with early and out of the way. Rip the filial bandage off and hopefully be done with it.

Squaring my shoulders, I dutifully headed over to greet my father. "Happy birthday, Dad."

"Tanner, good to see you." My father accepted my perfunctory embrace before turning his attention back to the grill. In deference to the summer heat, he'd forgone his usual cowboy boots and jeans for Bermuda shorts and Birkenstocks. With his long gray hair and beard, my dad looked a lot like his musical hero, Willie Nelson, although he wore his thinning hair pulled back in a ponytail rather than in Willie's hallmark braids.

I nodded a greeting at my brother Nate, who was attired in his version of casual, a polo shirt, twill slacks, and loafers. Ever since he'd come back from college and started working full-time at the creamery, Nate had been dressing like a Wall Street banker. I got the sense he wanted to set himself apart from the hippie redneck aesthetic our dad had always favored, although in almost every other respect Nate had doggedly tried to emulate our father.

Nate returned my nod with a taut smile, appearing annoyed by the interruption to whatever more important conversation they'd been having.

"I hear you got your sister to rescue you from the theme park," my father commented as he sipped a bottle of Shiner.

"She offered. I didn't get her to do anything."

"Right. That would require you to be proactive."

I tried to ignore the dig and turned to Nate. "Thanks for loaning me a shirt the other day. I'll return it to you as soon as I get it back from the dry cleaner."

I'd had to swallow my pride in order to show my face at Nate's office, begging for the loan of a spare shirt after Lucy's accident. I'd expected scorn or at least a gibe at my expense when I'd told him a lie about spilling yogurt on myself, but he'd simply gestured at his coat rack and told me to take whatever I wanted.

"It's no problem," Nate said, looking faintly embarrassed.

"How do you like marketing?" my father asked in the same tone you might ask someone how they liked cleaning out septic tanks. "I hear Josie's got you writing tweets now." Disdain dripped off every word.

"Among other things," I answered tightly. "And I like it fine."

My father grunted. "Well good. Maybe it'll turn out to be more your speed. Not everyone's cut out for the high pressure of sales."

"We can't all be Nate," I muttered.

"Go get yourself a drink," my father said without looking at me. "You know where they are."

Recognizing a dismissal when I heard one, I wandered off to get the aforementioned drink from the big wooden chest at the other end of the patio, grateful the interaction had been brief and relatively painless. Dad must be in a good mood tonight.

As I was digging through the cooler, I was joined by Manny,

wearing his infant son strapped to his chest in a baby carrier. "Hand me a beer, will you? I can't bend over in this thing."

I pried the caps off two bottles of Shiner Bock. Handing one to Manny, I leaned in for a better look at Jorge, who offered me a gummy smile. "How's my nephew? Is he walking yet? Reading and writing? Doing long division?"

"None of the above. He has discovered his toes though, so he's pretty much ready to start applying to colleges."

"Daddy! Daddy! Daddy!" Isabella yelled from the pool. "Look at me! I'm a flying fish!"

We both turned to watch as Ryan launched Manny's daughter out of the water and into the air, catching her again as she squealed with delight.

"Did you see how high I went?" she shouted.

"I sure did," Manny called back, raising his beer in tribute. "Good job, mija."

"Again!" she ordered her uncle Ryan with the imperiousness of an English monarch. "I want to go higher!"

"So," Manny said, returning his attention to me, "Sheriff Scoopy, huh?"

I rolled my eyes. "You heard about that?"

"Everybody heard about that. Saw the video too. That kid really nailed you." He grinned. "Twice."

Manny was seven years older than me, and I was used to his good-natured ribbing. His dad, Manuel Sr., had been my dad's best friend and COO at the creamery until he and his wife died in a boating accident. Manny's grandparents had been too frail to take full-time custody of a ten-year-old, so Manny had come to live with us. I'd only been three at the time, so he'd been a part of my family for almost as long as I could remember.

"Not exactly my finest moment," I said with a grimace.

"I hear you're working for Josie now."

"Yeah, she took pity on me." My gaze drifted across the patio to where Josie was standing with her boyfriend Carter, watching Ryan and Riley play with Isabella in the pool.

"She's smart to snap you up," Manny said. "I bet you'll be good at marketing."

"I can't be as bad at it as I was at sales, right?"

Manny frowned at me as Jorge waved his arms around like a windmill. "You can't force a square peg into a round hole. I'm impressed you stuck it out as long as you did."

I touched a finger to Jorge's pudgy little hand, and he clenched it in an iron-fisted grip. "Sure. That's the word for it. Impressive."

"You never know. Maybe marketing will turn out to be your calling. How do you like it so far?"

"It's not bad." I shrugged, not wanting to unpack the whole Lucy situation. "Where's Adriana?" I asked, looking around for Manny's wife as a way of changing the subject.

"She's either in the kitchen with Heather or she snuck off to take a nap. My money's on the latter." He sighed like he wished he could join her.

I bent down to address the baby directly. "Are you not letting your parents sleep through the night yet?"

Manny snorted. "Not reliably. On a good night we're lucky to get five hours before Isabella wakes us up demanding breakfast. But the good nights are few and far between." He looked at me hopefully. "Don't suppose you want to take one of the kids off our hands for a few years? We'd be willing to give you a good deal on a long-term lease."

I laughed, shaking my head as I waved Jorge's fist around on my finger. "Does that mean you're quitting at two?"

"Oh, I don't know." Manny's smile turned soft as he gazed down at his son. "Ask us again when this one gets too rambunctious to cuddle."

Sometimes I envied Manny so much it hurt. He had everything I'd always wanted: a wife and kids he adored, a job he was good at and seemed to enjoy, a decent relationship with my father. He even got along well with Nate. Manny got along with everyone. He was easygoing, friendly, and universally liked.

Meanwhile, my foray into the dating pool on Saturday had been an unqualified failure. Andie's friend Kaylee had been pretty and personable, but the two of us couldn't have had less in common—or less interest in getting to know each other better. She'd spent half the evening talking about her passion for hockey—and the other half questioning Wyatt about his music career. The lack of chemistry between us had been so obvious, Andie had actually apologized to me at the end of the night.

Manny set his beer down and plucked Jorge out of his carrier. "Here, take him, will you? I've got to take a piss."

I settled the baby into the crook of my arm, and Manny leaned in to kiss his son's forehead before heading off to the bathroom. Jorge's eyes went wide with alarm at his father's disappearance, and I abandoned my beer to offer him my index finger to hold on to again. Grasping it with both hands, he shoved it in his mouth and gummed it like a toothless puppy.

Make that a puppy with at least one tooth, I revised, wincing as I felt the bite of a tiny fang.

Jorge still largely resembled Jabba the Hutt, but his features were beginning to become slightly more defined. While Jorge happily gnawed on my finger, I peered at his small lump of a nose, attempting to decide if it looked more likely to develop a slight upturn like Adriana's or lengthen like Manny's. Honestly, how did people decide who babies resembled at this age, when they still looked like they'd been molded out of Silly Putty? Was everyone just lying when they claimed an infant had his mother's eyes or his father's nose?

"Hey," Nate said, appearing beside me.

Startling slightly, I looked up from my nephew and tried to cover my unease. "Do you think he looks more like Manny or Adriana?" I asked, presenting Jorge for inspection.

Nate's eyes flicked down to the baby and quickly away. "I don't know. All babies look like Winston Churchill."

He wasn't a big baby guy, Nate. Shocking, since he was otherwise so warm and cuddly.

Jorge started to fuss in response to Nate's glowering indifference, and I shifted the baby onto my shoulder, bouncing him so he'd settle down again.

"Listen, can we, uh..." Nate jerked his head toward the house like he wanted me to go inside with him.

The knot in my stomach tightened as I nodded my assent, wondering what was up. Nothing good, that was for certain.

I didn't dislike Nate, necessarily, but we'd never been close. He and Josie and their older twin brothers, Chance and Brady, had all lived with their mother when I was growing up, so I mostly only saw them at holidays and other special occasions. I'd gotten to know Nate better over the last five or so years that I'd been working for him, but more as a boss than a brother. He wasn't one of those easygoing bosses you could pal around with. He hadn't cut me any slack because we were related, which meant the majority of our relationship had revolved around him giving me orders and criticizing my performance.

As Jorge gnawed on my shoulder, I followed Nate into the empty den and watched him stride to Dad's liquor cabinet, where he opened one of the cut crystal decanters to give it a suspicious sniff. "You want some?" he asked, having decided the unidentified brown liquor was up to snuff.

When I shook my head at his offer, he poured himself a drink, gulping down a mouthful and grimacing before finally letting his intense gaze settle on me. "I just wanted to say that I'm sorry for the way things went down."

I blinked in confusion and shifted Jorge to my other shoulder. "What things exactly? You mean when you fired me?"

"Yeah." Nate seemed nervous, which made me nervous. It wasn't often that he exhibited anything less than perfect confidence and command. The last time I'd seen him this out of sorts was when Manny had cajoled him into holding newborn Jorge at the hospital. "I tried to talk Dad out of it, if it means anything."

"You did?"

"He's been on me to cut you loose for a while, but I convinced him we should give you more time."

"Thanks?" The way Nate had been on my case lately, I'd assumed he was the one gunning for me. I'd never even considered that he might have been in my corner.

"Yeah, well." His lips pressed together in a thin line. "Then he got a look at the latest quarterly sales numbers." Nate tipped back another mouthful of what smelled like bourbon, and his brow furrowed. "He told me to make an example of you. He wanted to send a message that there wouldn't be any tolerance for poor performance."

"Right." I was the sacrificial lamb. After everyone saw Nate was willing to fire his own brother, they'd know he wouldn't hesitate to fire them too. I didn't doubt my public humiliation had lit a fire under the rest of the sales organization.

Nate's knuckles whitened around his whiskey tumbler. "I want you to know, that's not the way I would have handled it, if it had been up to me. Ripping into you like that in front of everyone, that wasn't my choice."

"I appreciate that," I told him, recognizing how much of a concession it was for Nate to admit he disagreed with Dad's orders. He'd always been a loyal lieutenant who did everything exactly the way Dad wanted. His faithful service had secured his position as heir apparent who'd one day succeed the old man as CEO. Assuming Dad ever retired. I could easily picture him hanging on like Queen Elizabeth, still running the company in his late nineties with poor seventy-year-old Nate still waiting for his turn.

Nate dropped his gaze to the surface of his whiskey. "I voiced my objections, but I was overridden. With everything going on, Dad wasn't in a lenient mood."

"What's been going on?" Jorge gurgled on my shoulder, and I felt something warm and wet soak through my shirt. "Hand me a towel, will you?"

Nate passed me a bar towel and made an expression of distaste as I wiped the spit-up off the baby's face and my shoulder. "Where's Manny?"

"He said he was going to take a leak, but I think he might have snuck off to take a nap." Once I had Jorge cleaned up, I draped the towel over my damp shoulder and laid him over it.

"This is just between us, okay?" Nate cast a wary glance around to make sure we were still alone.

"Sure."

"Revenues have been trending steadily down for the last year, and our spending has continued to go up despite the salary freeze. There's going to be more belt-tightening coming. We may be looking at layoffs if we can't turn things around."

"Jesus." We hadn't had layoffs since the nineties. It had been a matter of company pride that we'd weathered the last few economic recessions without letting any of our people go.

I'd been so focused on my own district's sinking sales numbers, I hadn't noticed they were part of a larger pattern. Maybe I should have been relieved that I wasn't the only one who'd been falling short, but all I felt was guilt that my failure had contributed to the crisis.

Nate set his empty glass down and leaned against the counter, gazing across the room at the patio doors. "They're even talking about closing the old ice cream shop downtown."

"Who knows about this?"

"Right now, just me, Dad, Terry, and Bruce." Terry was the COO, our dad's second-in-command, and Bruce was the company's chief financial officer.

"What about Manny and Josie?" I asked.

Nate shook his head. "Not yet. Although I imagine he'll have to tell them before too much longer."

"Why'd Dad tell you and not them?"

A muscle clenched in Nate's jaw. "Honestly? I think he did it to scare me, hoping I'd be able to bring up our sales numbers if I was motivated enough."

"Can you?"

"I don't know." He shook his head with a grimace. "I'm trying."

"There you are, mijo!" Adriana said behind me, and Jorge arched his spine, waving his arms at the sight of his mother. She came over and took him from me, greeting both of us with a kiss on the cheek. "Where'd my husband get off to?"

"He said he was going to the bathroom." When I looked around, I saw that Nate had already slipped back outside without a word.

"That stinker. He's probably taking a nap." Adriana lifted Jorge into the air and blew a raspberry on his stomach. "Daddy's a stinker, isn't he? Yes, he is!"

"Hey! I heard that!" Manny emerged from the back of the house and came over to kiss his wife and son.

Adriana licked her fingers and ran them through her

husband's disheveled hair. "If you're going to sneak off for a nap, at least have the decency to hide your crime by fixing your hair."

"Ugh, stop it!" Manny dodged out of reach and batted her hand away. "You know I hate it when you spit in my hair. And I was only resting my eyes for five minutes."

Adriana's smile was unrepentant. "Heather says the food's about ready, so you should probably go pry our daughter out of the pool and wrestle some dry clothes onto her."

"On it," Manny said, doing an about-face and heading for the patio.

"Good luck!" Adriana called after him. She shook her head with a sigh. "He'll be lucky to get a clean pair of underwear on her."

I smiled. "Isabella still a nudist, is she?"

"I keep waiting for her to grow out of it, but so far no such luck." Adriana regarded me as she bounced Jorge on her hip. "How are you doing? I hear you've had a rough time of it at work lately."

"Manny told you, did he?"

She shrugged. "Manny tells me everything. You doing okay? Working for Josie's not so bad, right?"

"Nah, it's fine."

I was saved from further questions about my professional setback by the sound of my dad's wife, Heather, ringing the antique dinner bell on the patio. "Come and get 'em!" she shouted.

"Come on." Adriana tugged on my sleeve. "There's a buffet set up in the kitchen. We can be the first in line."

I followed her to the spacious faux-Spanish kitchen and fixed up two plates for us while she jiggled Jorge and directed me how to dress her burger. When we were both well-supplied with food, we went out to the patio and claimed one of the round tables by the pool. Josie and her boyfriend Carter joined us a few minutes later. I let the others carry the conversation while I ate in silence and listened. He and Josie had been dating for nearly a year, but she'd only brought him to a couple of family gatherings, so I didn't know him that well.

Eventually, Adriana left to feed Jorge, and Carter wandered off to play washers with Cody, leaving me and Josie on our own.

She eyed me as she stole a tortilla chip off my plate. "How do you like content marketing so far?"

I pushed my plate toward her and leaned back in my chair. "It's good. I think I'm getting the hang of it." The last draft I'd sent to Lucy had come back with only a few changes instead of the eye-crossing sea of markup my previous attempts had received. "I'm grateful for the opportunity."

Josie waved away my thanks. "You're the one doing me a favor. That team's been down a head for a while, and I haven't been able to bring anyone new onboard because of the hiring freeze. Transferring you under me allowed me to finally get Lucy the extra help she needed."

Lucy didn't seem like she needed much help to me, but what did I know? I was just there to do what I was told.

Josie helped herself to another one of my chips. "Byron's been giving me glowing reports of you."

"That's nice of him." I wasn't sure what he was basing his reports on. Other than one lunch where he'd spent the whole meal talking about his golf vacations, and one team meeting during which I'd barely said a word, we hadn't interacted at all.

Unless he had Lucy giving him regular updates on me— which would mean it was Lucy who'd been giving the glowing reports of me.

"Nice isn't the word I'd use to describe Byron." Josie made a face as she reached for her beer. "He's a professional ass-kisser. Probably sucking up because you're my brother. No offense," she added with another hand wave. "I'm sure you're doing great."

So much for Lucy giving me glowing reports.

"Tell me the truth," Josie said, leaning back in her chair and giving me an appraising look. "Do you really like your new job? I'm asking as your sister, not your boss."

"I really like it." I told her honestly. The work itself was far more suited to me than my sales jobs ever had been. If it wasn't for the pay cut and the awkwardness of working with my ex, it'd be pretty much perfect. I probably should have considered going into marketing from the beginning instead of letting my dad push me into sales.

"Good." Josie nodded and took a swig of her beer.

"What would you have done if I'd said no?"

"I don't know. Probably try to find you another position. You're my little brother. I don't want you to be miserable." Josie leaned forward and ruffled my hair.

In the five years I'd worked for him, Nate had never once ruffled my hair—nor at any other point in my entire life, for that matter. Nate was not a hair ruffler. I wasn't sure I'd seen him display any outward sign of affection toward anyone, in fact. Had he ever even had a girlfriend? Or a boyfriend, for that matter? I didn't know him well enough to know the answer. He'd certainly never brought a date to any family functions.

I reached up to smooth my hair back into place. "I'm not miserable."

My sister frowned as she contemplated me. "But you're not happy."

I shrugged. "Who is? Other than Manny and Adriana."

Josie gazed across the patio to where Manny was engaged in a battle of wills with Isabella over how much of her dinner she needed to eat before she could have dessert. Her high-pitched whines were growing louder by the second, a sure sign she was headed for total nuclear meltdown. "I'm sure they have their share of problems like the rest of us. People's lives are never as perfect as they seem from the outside."

"What about you? Your life seems pretty perfect from the outside. Are you happy?"

"Sure." She inclined her head. "As happy as anyone, I guess." The way her lips tightened made me think she wasn't all that happy either.

I didn't know Josie much better than I knew Nate. She'd only been back in Crowder for a couple of years, and we didn't exactly hang out regularly. She might be friendlier and easier to talk to than Nate, but she never seemed to reveal very much about herself.

"Is it serious with you and Carter?" I asked her. She'd brought him to Dad's birthday, so I assumed yes.

She shrugged. "He moved in with me. I guess that makes us serious."

"You did?" I couldn't believe I didn't even know. "When?"

"A few months ago. His lease was up, and he'd been spending so much time at my place that it seemed like the logical next step." She shrugged again. "We're adopting a dog together. That's pretty serious."

"It is," I agreed. "Good practice for having kids."

"Yeah, right." Her mouth flattened and she shook her head, signaling an end to the subject. "Tell me about Lucy."

I nearly choked on my beer. "What about her?"

"Has she been doing a good job training you? What do you think of her as a team lead?"

I relaxed when I realized she only wanted my professional impression. Conscious of the fact that whatever I said could affect Lucy's career, I considered my words carefully. "She's conscientious and knowledgeable. She has high standards, but she's taught me a lot in a short time. And from what I've seen, she keeps everything running pretty much singlehandedly."

Josie nodded as if this was what she'd expected to hear. "Does she seem happy in her job to you?"

That wasn't a question I felt comfortable answering. As grateful as I was to Josie for the job, I wasn't going to act as her mole in the department and report on my coworkers behind their backs. "You're awfully concerned about people's happiness."

"I don't want to lose her." Josie leaned down to swat a mosquito off her ankle. "She's due for a promotion, but with the salary freeze, I haven't been able to give it to her. I'm afraid she'll leave if she doesn't get it soon, and I'll be absolutely fucked."

I swallowed, remembering what Nate had said about increased cost-cutting measures and possible layoffs. "There's nothing you can do to get around it?"

Josie shook her head. "I've tried, believe me. I even went to Dad and asked him to make an exception, but he said it would look like favoritism."

"Could you give her my salary if I quit?" The words popped out of me before I could consider the wisdom of them.

My sister looked at me in surprise. Most likely wondering why I'd offer to give up my job for someone I'd allegedly just met the week before last. It was a valid question. An even better one was why I'd offer to give up my job for an ex-girlfriend who'd dumped me.

"Do you want to quit?" Josie asked carefully.

"No. I told you, I like this job. I just thought…she's more valuable to you than I am, so if you can rebudget my salary to retain her, that would be better for the department and the company, wouldn't it?"

Josie gave me a funny look. "You're valuable too. I'm sure you've got a lot to contribute."

"Sure, but why keep me around if it means losing Lucy? She deserves to stay more than I do."

"You both deserve to stay, and I'm going to do everything I can to keep you *and* Lucy. But even if I fired you, they wouldn't let me give Lucy a raise. Not with things the way they are right now."

I cut a look at her. "What do you mean? The way what things are right now?"

She sat up and glanced around, scooting her chair closer to mine before speaking in a low voice. "This doesn't go beyond the two of us, but there are more cost-cutting measures coming. You might have noticed that revenues are down, but the fact is the company has been hemorrhaging money. If we can't turn things around, every department is looking at major budget cuts and probably layoffs. But Dad hasn't told anyone else how bad it is, so don't say anything to anyone."

I stared across the patio at the back of my Dad's head. What the hell was he up to? Had he told Manny the same thing as Nate and Josie? To what end? Was he playing them against each other somehow? What was the point of making them each think they were in on some kind of secret? To make them think he favored them? Was this some kind of power play? Or was he just trying to shore up their loyalty to him? As ever, my father's intents and purposes were a mystery to me.

Before I could tell Josie what Nate had said, we were interrupted by Heather's appearance with Dad's birthday cake. Josie dragged me out of my seat as everyone gathered around the man of honor to serenade him with the birthday song.

As I watched Dad blow out his birthday candles, I wondered what it would be like to have a normal father. The kind who encouraged and supported his children selflessly instead of using them to further his own perverse agenda. Our dad had always treated us like pawns in his personal chess game, pushing us around the board into whatever positions he considered most strategic for his own ends. If you were a good soldier like Nate or Manny, you might be rewarded with praise and the illusion of influence, but Dad never stopped playing his little games.

"Okay, so we've got the company history quiz, the National Ice Cream Day trivia, and the zodiac sun, moon, and rising flavors meme. We just need one more and we'll be set."

Tanner and I were working together on ideas for upcoming newsletters. Byron had suggested it. Insisted, in fact, during the weekly team meeting this morning. He'd expressed concern that Tanner didn't have enough to do and wanted to make sure I wasn't underutilizing him. Wasn't that nice of him?

So here Tanner and I sat. Working together. The two of us. Alone in the small conference room where our brainstorming sesh wouldn't disturb anyone in our open-plan office. Just like normal coworkers. No one would ever suspect from looking through the glass at us that we were anything other than regular coworkers.

"What about a list of unusual topping ideas?" he suggested.

"We did that a few months ago."

Although I hated to admit it, doing this with Tanner was easier than doing it alone. Jill and I used to brainstorm like this together, but since she'd left I'd had to come up with all the features on my own. It was nice having someone to bounce ideas around with again, even when I knew that someone was only pretending not to begrudge every second he was forced to spend in my company.

Plus, Tanner was getting pretty good at this job. It had taken him some time to get the hang of the kind of writing we had to do for the different platforms, but he was a quick study and an insanely talented writer.

I wasn't too proud to admit he was a better writer than me. It was one of the things that had tripped him up most at first. His writing was a little too good for the kind of content we were supposed to be churning out. I'd had to make him dumb everything down. Content marketing was about driving home a simple, straightforward message, which required less subtlety of craft and more in-your-face shouting sometimes.

"What about something with flavor pairings?" I said. "That always gets loads of clicks."

"Like the movie and ice cream pairings you did last month?"

"Exactly. We've also done pizza and ice cream pairings, cookie and ice cream pairings, and summer activity and ice cream pairings."

"Hmmm." Frowning, he rubbed his hand over his jaw, which was showing a hint of late-day stubble.

Not that I was paying attention to his stubble. Or his jaw. Or his hand, for that matter. Definitely not looking at any of those things.

We'd both been doing a better job of acting normal around each other, and I didn't intend to ruin our streak by ogling him like a weirdo. Ever since he'd helped me out after my accident on Monday, he'd seemed a lot less tense around me. He'd even been making occasional eye contact, as if it no longer caused him actual, physical pain to look at me, which was a huge step forward.

And all it had taken was for him to witness one of the most embarrassing moments of my life. *Yay.*

Whatever. If that was what it took to level the playing field between us, I could live with that. I was just happy we finally seemed to be moving past the past. Not that we were destined to be besties anytime soon. We still didn't talk about anything other than work. But when we did talk about work, it wasn't nearly as strained.

"What about beer and ice cream pairings?" he suggested. "Can we do beer?"

"They've let us do alcoholic recipes in the past, so it should be fine. That's a great idea."

He actually smiled at the compliment, and my chest grew hot and painfully tight. Good god, I'd forgotten what a breath-taking sight that smile of his was.

He wasn't a big smiler in general. His smiles had always been a rare and splendid treat he only bestowed on singular occasions. When we'd been dating, I'd always felt proud of myself whenever I'd managed to coax a smile out of him. Since we'd stopped dating, he hadn't smiled at me once.

Until now.

Belatedly, he seemed to remember who he was smiling at, and it faded as quickly as it had appeared. His gaze dropped to his notepad, and I silently blew out an unsteady breath.

"Are you volunteering to write that one?" I asked, struggling to keep my voice steady. "You're much more of a beer person than me." As soon as I said it, I felt uneasy for bringing up something I only knew about him because of our past relationship.

If it bothered him, he didn't show it. "Sure." One of his shoulders lifted in a small shrug. "Is there anything I need to know, or do I just make up whatever I want?"

"You can pretty much wing it. I don't know if there's beer nerd wisdom about what flavor profiles go with what kinds of beer, but you can read up on it if you want. Or do your own taste test even."

A faint flicker of a smile reappeared as he scribbled on his notepad. "Does that mean I get to expense beer?"

"As a matter of fact, it does. Assuming you can get Byron to approve it, which I'm sure *you* won't have any trouble with."

Tanner looked up at me and frowned. "I don't like him very much."

"Oh?" I made sure to keep my expression neutral. No matter what Tanner said, I wasn't going to be caught badmouthing the boss to his teacher's pet.

"He keeps trying to suck up to me. I guess hoping I'll put in a good word for him with my family." Tanner's lips took on a bitter twist. "Joke's on him if he thinks I actually have any pull around here." When I didn't say anything, he went back to writing on his notepad. "Josie doesn't like him either," he added without looking up.

My eyes widened, but I refrained from responding. It was the best news I'd heard in a long time, but it wouldn't be appropriate to get up on the conference table and celebrate with a dance of jubilation.

"I probably shouldn't have told you that." Tanner was still writing on his notepad and still not looking at me.

"I won't say anything to anyone."

His head bobbed. "I know."

My stomach and heart both lurched at the same time. I hadn't ever expected him to trust me again, or realized how much it would matter to know he did.

"She likes *you* though," he added, still writing.

"She does?" My voice came out sounding squeaky. *Way to play it cool.*

Tanner looked up at me. "She thinks you're a valuable part of the team."

"When did she say that? Were you...talking about me?" The prospect made me queasy. It was terrifying to imagine what might have prompted the conversation and what else might have been said.

He shrugged and looked down at his notepad again—what the hell was he writing on there anyway? "She was asking me how I liked working here so far, and she asked what I thought of you."

"Oh god." I swallowed. "What did you say?" I was almost too afraid to ask, although it was hard to picture Tanner throwing me under the bus. The man who'd loaned me his shirt and cleaned my period blood off the ladies' room floor wasn't the kind of guy to throw anyone under a bus. He might be the only person I'd ever met who actually took the dictum to "love your enemies" seriously.

He glanced up at me, his expression guileless and possibly the slightest bit offended. "All good things, of course."

Of course he had. Because he was a good person. One of the best I knew. He was pre-super-soldier serum Steve Rogers minus the scrappy impulse to get into fights.

"She still doesn't know about us, if that's what you're worried about." He looked down at his notepad again, frowning slightly as his pen scratched on the page. "I told her you were a great team lead and you'd taught me a lot. And she said she'd hate to lose you."

"Thank you. I appreciate that." I wondered what Josie's comment might mean for my promotion. If Josie didn't like Byron but she did like me, would she stick up for me despite Byron's obvious bias in favor of Tanner? Or would she still give Tanner preferential treatment because he was her brother?

"I thought you should know, in case..." He stopped and pressed his lips together.

"In case what?"

"In case you were wondering." I was almost certain that wasn't what he'd originally been about to say. While I was pondering that, he looked up, his expression thoughtful. "Do you ever get that thing where you stare at a word too long and it starts to look wrong? Like it's spelled wrong, but you can't remember how it's supposed to be spelled, and it looks like a random combination of letters you've never seen before instead of a real word? Or is that just me?"

I smiled. "Wordnesia."

"Is that a real thing or did you make that up?"

"It's a real thing. I get it all the time."

"Wordnesia. I like that." He smiled back at me, and for a second we were smiling at each other across the conference table like two nerds who shared a love of words and actually enjoyed each other's company.

This time I was the one who looked down to hide the color I felt rushing to my cheeks. I wasn't used to having Tanner's focus on me anymore. It was unsettling, but in a good way. Which was bad. I shouldn't be enjoying his attention or his smiles so much. We were coworkers now. Nothing more.

He cleared his throat. "Wyatt says you're singing with Shiny Heathens at the folk festival next week."

Okay, so apparently we were doing the friendly small talk thing? This was a big new step for us. Also, Tanner seemed to be having a lot of conversations about me with various members of his family, and I didn't know how to feel about that.

"I am, yes." I stared intently at my notebook, waiting for him to say something else. Eventually the silence stretched out long enough that I felt the need to fill it myself. "Are you planning to go to the festival?" I asked, merely to be polite. I was not invested in his answer one way or the other. I did not care one bit whether Tanner came to hear me sing with his brother.

Look at us, having a normal conversation. Being all friendly and casual.

"I promised Wyatt I would."

"That's nice." So Tanner would be there to hear me sing. Fine. No biggie. I wasn't the least bit nervous and/or excited about that. These flips my stomach was doing were for a completely unrelated reason, probably to do with the frozen burrito I'd eaten for lunch.

"I've heard you sing at a couple of their shows before."

I lifted my head, unable to mask my surprise. "You have?"

I'd wondered, obviously, if Tanner had been to any of the shows I'd performed at. But I hadn't known. I hadn't seen him, because I always hightailed it out of there as soon as we were done without sticking around to talk to anyone. Largely because I'd been so afraid of running into him and seeing that pained expression he always used to get around me.

But he didn't get that expression anymore when he saw me. And he certainly didn't have it now.

"You've got an amazing voice," he said. "I had no idea you could sing like that."

My stomach swooped, and I dropped my eyes to my notebook again to hide how big my smile was. "Thank you."

"You never mentioned you were a singer. Before, I mean. When we were..." He paused, and I held my breath, waiting for him to finish the sentence. "Together."

Something about the word and the way he said it made my insides feel all warm and heavy—in a pleasant way, not a burrito wreaking havoc kind of way. It felt important that we could talk like this now, acknowledging our former closeness without too much discomfort.

I kept my eyes on my notebook as I traced over the letters in my list. "My mom made me take voice lessons when I was growing up. She wanted me to enter beauty pageants, but it didn't work out."

"Why not? You're definitely beautiful enough."

My head jerked up again. *Did he really just say I was beautiful?*

Tanner winced. "Sorry. I shouldn't have said that." He looked like he wanted to curl up on the floor and play dead.

"It's okay." I was gripping my pen so hard it was in danger of breaking. "It's a nice thing to say. Thank you."

"You're welcome," he mumbled to his notepad. "It was just an objective observation."

There. See? Not a compliment. It didn't mean he still felt something for me. Which was right and good. I didn't want him to feel anything. Neither of us were feeling anything at all.

"Anyway," I said, getting back to his question so I didn't have to think about the confusing feelings I was definitely not having. "I hated the attention. Doing pageants was my mother's thing— she used to be a beauty queen—but it wasn't for me. I'd freeze up as soon as I got out onstage and realized everyone was looking at me. "

"You seemed to do okay onstage with Shiny Heathens."

"It's better when it's not just me. I did choir in high school, and that was okay too. When I'm singing with Shiny Heathens, I don't feel like I'm the center of attention—especially not with Wyatt there to pull all the focus." Tanner let out a low laugh, and I felt pleased with myself for diffusing the awkwardness that had cropped up. "I still don't like performing much. I only agreed to do it a few times as a special favor to Matt. He had to badger me into it."

"No one would know from watching you." Tanner was writing on his notepad again as he spoke. "You certainly had me fooled."

"I threw up before the first show I did with them." I leaned across the table, trying to get a look at his paper. "What do you keep writing over there?"

He turned the notepad around and pushed it toward me. There were some notes at the top about the features he'd volunteered to write, and below that he'd listed different kinds of beer with the names of King's ice cream flavors jotted down next to them, all of it in Tanner's neat, graceful handwriting. But in addition to that he'd doodled all around the edges of the page. Beautiful ink sketches of random objects and abstract shapes that intertwined with each other in a way that reminded me of Wyatt's tattoo sleeves.

I pulled it closer, bending my head for a better look. Different kinds of flowers grew out of leaf-covered vines and curlicues. Intermixed with them I made out a few planets, a sun with a face in it, a bee, a butterfly, a weeping willow tree, and a question mark filled in with stripes.

"Wow," I said. "This is really cool. I didn't know you could draw."

He pulled the notepad back toward him with a shrug. "It's just something I do to help me focus in meetings. I used to do it as a writing exercise. Doodling is supposed to help trigger free-thinking and creativity."

I knew he liked to write in his free time and had been working on a book for several years. When we were dating, he'd let me read some of it. It was an epic fantasy set in an alternate reality version of our world with magic and monsters. I'd thought it was wonderful and told him so, but he'd only let me read the first few chapters.

"Have you been doing any writing?"

A crease appeared between his brows. "No. With work and everything, it's been hard to motivate myself."

I suspected some of the "everything" that had kept him from writing was my fault, and I felt a stab of guilt. "Maybe now you'll be able to pick it up again. It's not as if this job is particularly stressful."

"Maybe."

Even when we were dating, he'd been oddly shy about his writing. I assumed from his noncommittal tone that it wasn't something he wanted to talk about with me, so I dropped the subject.

I reached for my phone to check the time and saw I had a new text from my friend Jess. "Shit," I said when I read it, then winced and covered my mouth. "Shoot, I mean. Sorry."

"I'm shocked and stunned by your use of a cuss word," Tanner deadpanned. "I've never in my life heard a woman say 'shit' before."

I'd forgotten how dry his sense of humor could be. And how appealing I found it. His subtle humor had been one of my top five favorite things about him, along with his thoughtfulness, his smile, his hands, and the way he—

Well. That wasn't something I had any business thinking about at work. Or ever, anymore.

He inclined his head at my phone. "What's wrong?"

"Oh, it's nothing. It's just my friend who lets me use her kitchen to take pictures of the recipes for the newsletter. It turns out her in-laws are coming to town for an unplanned visit, so I can't use her kitchen tomorrow like I'd planned. I'll have to find someplace else nice enough to take food pictures."

"You can't do it at your house?"

I barked out a laugh. "No. Definitely not. It has to be somewhere modern and photogenic with lots of natural light." I'd never invited Tanner to my home when we were dating, so he had no idea what our kitchen looked like. I'd been too embarrassed to let him see the state of our house, but more importantly I'd wanted to keep him and my mother apart at all costs.

"My kitchen has a lot of windows," he said. "Would it work?"

I stared at him. "Umm...yes?" He lived alone in a house he'd bought a couple of years ago, a snug three-bedroom with granite countertops, modern fixtures, and a neutral color scheme, which he kept uncluttered and immaculately clean. God, how I'd loved spending time there. "Are you...offering to let me use your kitchen?" I couldn't quite believe he'd willingly volunteer for that.

"Maybe. What's involved?"

"I'd bring my camera and all the ingredients to make the next three recipes for the newsletter. Then I'd just have to assemble each one and take photos of the finished product. They're simple recipes, so it should only take a couple of hours."

"Sure, if it'll help. I don't mind." He frowned slightly. "It's up to you though. If you don't want to—" His phone started vibrating on the table, the harsh sound jarring in the quiet of the conference room. "Sorry." His frown deepened as he looked at the screen. "I need to take this."

While he answered his phone, I tried to figure out how I felt about being invited to his house. Tanner seemed surprisingly unperturbed by the prospect of spending time with me alone in the place where we'd spent most of our intimate moments together.

If he wasn't fussed about it, why should I be?

Why wasn't he more fussed about it though? Shouldn't he be? Two weeks ago he was still glowering at me, and now he was casually inviting me to his house? For work, obviously. But still. Being polite to each other around the office was one thing, but hanging out after hours in his private residence was a whole other level of getting along.

Had he really gotten over his discomfort around me so quickly? Just flipped a switch and moved on? Or had something changed to help him move on all of a sudden?

Like he'd met someone else, maybe.

He and Arwen had gotten quite chummy over the last two weeks. For all I knew they were dating already. Had his newfound interest in her finally extinguished his hostility toward me?

I should be happy about that, if it was true. Hadn't I wanted him to move on? So why did thinking about it make me feel so bad?

The tone of Tanner's voice dragged me out of my ruminations. I'd been trying not to eavesdrop, but he was speaking in a serious, deeper-than-usual voice with an edge to it that had me paying attention out of concern.

"No, I understand," he said to the person on the other end of the phone. "Sure. I can manage that. Twice a day, you said? How long do I have to give them to him?" He propped his elbow on the table and rubbed his forehead. "Okay. Can I pick up the pills tonight?"

A minute later he disconnected the call and set the phone down again. "Sorry about that. I've been waiting for a call from the vet."

"Is Radagast okay?"

Tanner nodded, still frowning. "He's been losing weight, so I took him in for tests. Apparently his thyroid isn't functioning, but the vet's putting him on medication that should help." He was trying to sound matter-of-fact about it, but deep worry lines etched his face.

"I'm sorry he's been sick." Tanner's cat was sixteen years old, but aside from some early-stage kidney failure he was surprisingly healthy for his age. Or he had been, the last time I'd seen him. "I hope the medicine helps."

Tanner's eyes met mine. "Thank you." He looked sad, but also resigned, which was even sadder somehow.

The instinct to walk around the table and give him a hug was almost overpowering, but I managed to squelch it. Barely. "You should go," I said instead. "It's Friday afternoon, we've done everything that needed doing, and Byron's been at the golf course since lunch. No one will notice if you leave a little early."

"You think?" He looked torn.

"Definitely. People do it all the time around here. Go home and cuddle your cat."

"Maybe I will." He got to his feet, gathering up his things. "What about the kitchen? Do you want to come over tomorrow and use my place?"

I hesitated, biting my lip. "Are you sure you don't mind?"

His gaze met mine, and he gave a resolute tilt of his chin. "I don't if you don't."

Why not?

"That'd be great, actually. I appreciate it." I did need a place to take those photos, and Tanner's kitchen would be perfect for it. I supposed I could even teach him how to do it himself and let him take over the whole enterprise after this. No doubt that would make Byron happy.

Okay. So I was spending tomorrow at Tanner's house. With Tanner.

Just the two of us.

And his cat.

And the bed where we'd slept together.

Where he'd told me he loved me.

This is Fine.

10

LUCY

I shifted my grocery bags nervously as I stood on Tanner's doorstep. He lived in one of the newer subdivisions a little farther outside town. This one was about ten years old, and the houses in it all looked more or less the same with only minor variations. The front facades all featured accents of Austin Stone with the wood siding and trim painted in beiges and grays and browns to match the natural limestone.

The handles of my bags had tangled when I'd rung the doorbell, and I tried to sort them out while I waited for Tanner to let me in. My wrist was trapped between the handles of two different bags, which were cutting off my circulation.

As claustrophobia threatened, my struggles to free myself grew more desperate. Right as the door opened, I managed to jerk my hand free, but the movement caused the bag cradled against my chest to tilt, sending the stupid package of cookies I'd bought to please Byron hurtling toward the concrete stoop at my feet.

"Shit!" I made a fruitless grab to save them from being shattered to crumbles, but they slipped through my encumbered hands.

Tanner leaned forward and snatched them out of the air, averting cookie catastrophe.

"Thank you," I said with an exhale of relief. "If those had gotten smashed, I'd have to go back to the store."

The corner of his mouth twitched. "I see you're still cussing up a storm."

I blushed as he lifted the precarious grocery bag from my arms and stepped back to hold the front door open for me. He was dressed casually in a faded gray T-shirt and jeans. It was a good look on him. *Too good.* I'd always had a weakness for the sight of him in jeans, and the way that T-shirt clung to his chest and shoulders was entirely too distracting.

I forced my gaze away from him as I stepped through the doorway. I'd promised myself I wouldn't act weird today, but as the familiar smell of Tanner's house enveloped me, my heart stuttered painfully at the memories that washed over me, causing my steps to falter. The last time I'd crossed this threshold, I'd practically been sprinting the opposite direction with my stomach in knots and the sound of Tanner's "I love you" ringing in my ears.

His hand brushed lightly against my back to ease me out of the way of the door he was trying to close, and I sprang forward into the living room. The house was small for a three bedroom, but tidy and uncrowded. A dark gray couch sat against one wall with a flat-screen TV mounted on the wall opposite. The compact coffee table held several neat stacks of books, with even more lining a small bookcase under the television. As I walked through to the kitchen, Radagast eyed me from his favorite armchair in the corner.

"Is there more to bring in?" Tanner asked as he deposited his grocery bag on the small kitchen island. There wasn't a single dirty dish in sight, and the counters were completely empty except for a couple of appliances and a canister of utensils. *Heaven.*

I set my bags next to his and slid the camera bag off my shoulder. "There's a cooler of ice cream and a box of props in the back seat of my car."

While Tanner went out to get the rest of the stuff, I unpacked the camera and peered through the viewfinder, angling it at different spots around the kitchen to find the best lighting and backgrounds for the shots I'd be taking. As I was doing that, something that felt like a small furry bowling ball bashed against my ankle. Radagast let out an imperious meow and bonked his head against my leg again.

Grinning at the brown tabby, I squatted down and ran my fingernails over his back. He was a little skinnier than the last time I'd seen him, but still energetic enough to demand affection. I dropped into a cross-legged sit on the floor and he immediately climbed into my lap, thrusting his head roughly into my hand.

Tanner came back and set down the last load. "Oh, I see how it is. I do all the physical labor while you sit around playing with my cat."

"Do not meddle in the affairs of wizards, for they are subtle and quick to anger." I looked up and caught Tanner smiling at me, his blue eyes bright as sapphires against his brown lashes. Something warm shot through my veins at the sight, and I smiled in response. "I know who the boss is in this house."

Tanner's smile grew wider. "It's true. He is the boss. You're smart to do what he says."

"I suppose I can get up and get to work now though." I started to move the cat off my lap, but Tanner laid a hand on my shoulder as he stooped to pet Radagast.

"No need." He was close enough that I could smell the clean, cottony scent of him, and it triggered an avalanche of confusing feelings before he straightened again. "Just tell me what to do to get us started."

Who was I to argue? So I stayed on the floor, spoiling the cat, while Tanner unpacked the grocery bags and put the ice cream in the freezer.

"Except the Double Double Fudge and Truffle," I told him. "Leave that out to melt for the ice cream bread."

Tanner glanced over his shoulder, eyebrows raised. "Ice cream bread? Never heard of that."

"Well you're about to help me make some. It only takes two ingredients: ice cream and self-rising flour."

"I was wondering what the flour was for." He shut the freezer and picked up the ice cube trays. "What about these?"

"Those are for our first project. Ice cube tray truffles."

He gave them a skeptical look. "Huh."

After a few minutes, I did get off the floor—over Radagast's protests—so we could get to work. The cat twined around our feet for a few minutes trying to command more attention, but eventually wandered off for another nap in his favorite chair.

Despite my misgivings about this extracurricular project, I was pleased to discover that Tanner and I worked exceptionally well together. He was handy in the kitchen, took directions like a champ, and had a sixth sense for anticipating what I needed before I even asked. He always seemed to be right there, ready to hand me the utensil I was about to reach for or the next ingredient he'd already measured out. The rest of the time he'd swoop in behind me cleaning and putting things away as soon as we finished with them.

His tidying was extra useful since his kitchen was small. The smallness of it meant we were often standing close or ducking around and reaching past each other. It put us in a state of constant physical proximity that would have been unthinkable a week ago.

Something had definitely shifted between us. It had started when he'd come to my rescue last Monday, but our brainstorming session yesterday seemed to have unlocked another level of friendship. At least I hoped friendship was what we were heading toward. Because the more time I spent with Tanner, and the more relaxed he became around me, the more I remembered how much I enjoyed his company.

Maybe a little too much. Every time our arms grazed or our fingers touched, it sent a warm, tingly feeling shooting through my limbs and into my stomach. All this closeness was unsettling for an entirely different reason than I'd anticipated. It made me nervous-excited instead of nervous-apprehensive.

"Are we ready for the ice cream balls?" Tanner asked when I'd filled the ice cube tray with a layer of melted chocolate.

I tilted the tray to make sure all the sides of the wells were coated. "I think so. We have to be really quick about this part so the ice cream doesn't melt too much. Are we clear on our assignments?"

He nodded, taking our project as seriously as I was. "Once I take the balls out of the freezer, we drop one into each well with the chocolate, pushing them down slightly to submerge them."

"Then I'll pour the rest of the chocolate over the top and smooth it with the spatula, quick as a bunny."

"And as soon as you're done, I'll put the tray in the freezer to harden."

"That's the plan." When I'd picked this recipe, I hadn't imagined I'd be assembling it with Tanner, and therefore hadn't considered how often it would require us to say words like *balls* and *harden* out loud to each other.

"Are you ready?" He gripped the freezer handle, waiting for my signal.

"Go."

Tanner brought over the cookie sheet of small ice cream

balls I'd scooped out with a melon baller, and we set to work, racing each other to the middle of the tray. The ice cream balls were cold and slippery, and it was impossible not to get the warm chocolate on our fingers. The faster we worked, the messier we got, and pretty soon we were both laughing and covered in chocolate and ice cream.

Once the tray was full, I poured over the remaining chocolate and tried to smooth it out, which was easier said than done with my fingers all sticky. Tanner pointed out spots that needed more smoothing, then got impatient and took the spatula from me. I let him take over, and he quickly discovered it wasn't as easy as it looked.

"Good enough," I said, taking the spatula back. "Put it back in the freezer. Go! Go! Go! Quick, before the ice cream melts any more."

He shoved the tray into the freezer and slammed the door shut before spinning around and holding his hands up in victory like a contestant on a cooking competition show.

I clapped my messy hands, grinning. "Woo hoo! We did it!"

Tanner grinned back at me as he rejoined me at the counter. "We seem to have made a little bit of a mess."

"At least it's a tasty cleanup." I stuck my thumb in my mouth and licked the chocolate off.

He watched me, his eyebrows lifting slightly, and the corner of his mouth hitched in a subtle, almost imperceptible smile. The potency of his gaze, especially when we were standing so close, brought on another rush of nervous excitement.

"Or we can just wash our hands." Lowering my eyes, I stepped around him to get to the sink.

When he joined me at the faucet, I shifted to make room for him, and we shared the stream of water as we rubbed the chocolate off our fingers. The dish soap was on his side, and he squirted some into his hand. Once he'd lathered it up, he held his hands out to share the excess soap with me.

I laid one of my hands in his palm, and he rubbed it gently between his. Goose bumps shivered over my skin as my heart raced in reaction to his caressing touch. I swallowed thickly, hoping he wouldn't notice as he took my other hand and massaged soap over it too. By the time he let go of me so I could finish washing my hands myself, my stomach was fluttering so much I couldn't think straight.

To distract myself, I grabbed the sponge and wiped up the mess we'd made on the counter while Tanner washed out the bowl of melted chocolate. When I was done, I surveyed the kitchen, marveling how much easier this was with two pairs of hands.

Hot, sexy hands, rubbing over mine—

"You missed a spot." Tanner came toward me with a dampened paper towel and stopped right in front of me. He was so much taller than me I had to tip my head back to look at him. His gaze skimmed my face as he lifted the paper towel to gesture at my cheek. "Right there."

I took the paper towel and scrubbed at my cheek. "Did I get it?"

His lips pressed together in amusement as he shook his head. "Here." He took the paper towel back from me.

My throat went dry as he touched my chin with his other hand, gently tilting my head as he wiped the chocolate off my face. I felt my cheeks redden, but I held still for him despite the erratic beating of my heart.

There was a reason I'd listed his hands as one of my top five favorite things about him. They were strong, but also capable of incredible tenderness. I'd loved the feel of his hands on me. I hadn't been able to get enough of it. My stomach swooped as I recalled the way his touch had driven me wild.

When he let go of me, the loss of contact left me feeling unmoored, and I had to grip the counter to steady myself.

"There," he said, ducking his head shyly as he backed away. "Got it."

"Thank you." My skin prickled where his fingers had warmed it a moment ago. I spun around and pressed my palm against my cheek as I set the oven to preheat.

"What's next?" Tanner asked behind me.

"Ice cream bread." I turned toward him again and smiled like everything was normal and fine. Because it was. Perfectly normal and perfectly fine. We were just two coworkers collaborating on a project together. Easy-peasy. No big deal. "How's our melted ice cream doing?"

He picked up the pint container and pried the lid off. "It's getting close."

I moved to his side and leaned in to peer at the ice cream. "It just needs a little stir to help it along. Here." I grabbed a spoon and stuck it in the melting ice cream, putting my hand over his to hold it steady while I stirred.

This was a completely natural thing to do, and in no way had I done it because I wanted to touch his hand. Definitely I was not taking advantage of the opportunity to caress his long, magnificent fingers while I stirred the ice cream. No, sirree. I also was not spending any longer than necessary stirring said ice cream in order to keep holding on to Tanner's hand. Nor was I enjoying the way he was leaning into me slightly, or the feel of his body pressing against mine.

Nope. Not me.

I'd broken up with Tanner. Freely and of my own accord, I'd made the choice to let him and his wonderful hands go. I was not allowed to start regretting that decision.

It was just...

To be honest, I was having trouble remembering all my

reasons for doing it. They'd seemed like good reasons at the time. I remembered believing with utmost confidence that I'd been doing the best thing for both of us.

But what if I was too hasty?

Looking back on it now, I fully admitted I'd freaked out a little when I'd learned how serious Tanner's feelings for me were. In retrospect, I definitely should have done a better job of communicating my intentions and limitations to him before things had gone so far. But he'd taken me completely off guard with that "I love you." On some level I supposed I must have been aware we'd moved past the initial "just having a good time getting to know each other" stage of the relationship into more serious feelings territory. But I hadn't imagined we were anywhere near "I love you" serious. I'd thought I had more time before I needed to establish realistic expectations. He'd been way ahead of me, taking our relationship to a place I hadn't been ready to go.

But maybe I could have gotten there if I'd given it time. Maybe Tanner would have been willing to be patient with me if I'd asked him to. We could have at least talked about it. We might have found a compromise that allowed us to continue enjoying each other's company. We could have at least *tried*.

Instead I'd panicked and run away like a dummy. I hadn't given him a chance. I hadn't given either of us a chance.

"It looks pretty melted to me," Tanner said, his breath a warm tickle on my hair.

I let go of his hand and backed away. "I think you're right."

"I remain dubious of this whole ice cream bread idea." He hadn't shaved today, and his jaw and throat were nicely stubbly. The urge to reach out and run my fingers over it the way I used to was so strong I almost couldn't resist. If only he'd gotten chocolate on his face so I'd have an excuse to touch him again.

As I stood there staring up at him, the truth of how much I missed him hit me hard in the pit of my stomach.

I missed his sense of humor and his rare smiles. I missed his quiet competence and reassuring presence. His cleverness, his generosity, his handsome face. The smell of his skin, and the way it felt to be tucked inside his arms.

And I wanted...

God help me, I didn't know what I wanted anymore.

11

TANNER

My house smelled like heaven. The scent of the fresh-baked ice cream bread we'd just taken out of the oven was so delicious it was making me dizzy.

Or maybe it was Lucy who was making me dizzy.

Having her here was messing with my head and making me careless. I kept inadvertently falling back into old habits from when we were a couple. Forgetting we weren't like that anymore, and I wasn't supposed to touch her. Like when I'd lathered the soap over her hands. And again when I'd wiped the chocolate off her face. I shouldn't be touching her like she was still mine to touch.

The thing was though, it almost seemed like...

Maybe it was my mind playing tricks on me, but it almost seemed like she was enjoying it? She wasn't flinching away from me anymore when we got too close. And she'd been blushing a lot today, her fair skin turning all sorts of interesting shades of pink.

Sometimes she blushed when she was embarrassed, true. But I happened to know she also blushed a lot when she was aroused. When she was embarrassed, her body language was completely different. She curled in on herself like she was trying to take up less space in the world. It broke my heart every time I saw her do it, but she wasn't doing that today. She was smiling, standing straight, and looking me in the eye. Talking easily to balance my natural reticence the way she used to.

But whenever we touched, or our gazes caught for too long, her freckled cheeks would flare with color, just like they had when I used to touch her in ways that pleased her.

It was all extremely confusing. It made me wonder things, like if my touch still pleased her. Which was a dangerous road to go down.

"Come look at this and tell me what you think," Lucy said, aiming her camera at the ice cream cookie sandwiches she'd assembled in an artful display on my counter.

I moved closer and bent down to peer at the camera's display, which put my face right up next to hers. Close enough that I could smell her perfume, the familiar scent clouding my head even further.

"Do you think the background looks okay?" Lucy's teeth bit down on her plump lower lip, and I felt another wave of dizziness come over me.

I forced myself to look at the camera instead of at Lucy's mouth. "Sure. I think it's fine."

"I usually do flat lays, but I think these will photograph better from the side." She leaned in closer to see the screen, and her hair brushed against my temple.

I straightened and stepped back, putting space between us again as she started taking pictures. "How'd you learn to do this?" I asked as I watched her work.

"I took a photography class in college. It was mostly focused on portrait and candid shots though. I wish we'd done more still life work, because that would be more relevant for this. Mostly I had to teach myself by reading food photography guides on the internet."

Her composition skills were impressive for someone who'd taught herself. She'd arranged the ice cream sandwiches in a stack with one canted next to the pint container, and scattered chocolate chips and mini marshmallows around them on the plate and counter.

She shifted to the side for a different angle and frowned at the camera. "I should probably teach you how to do this so you can take over for me."

"Why?"

"You've got the kitchen for it. You might as well be the one who takes the photos." She shrugged as she snapped more shots. "It'd probably make Byron happy. He seems to want me to hand everything off to you."

"Hasn't your team been understaffed? I thought you'd be relieved to share some of the work."

"I would be, except I'm pretty sure Byron's grooming you to take over Jill's old job."

"He wouldn't do that."

Lucy threw a glance over her shoulder at me. "Wouldn't he?"

"You've got way more experience and seniority than I do."

She went back to snapping photos. "I'm not sure that matters very much. You're the one who's related to the CEO and half the executive leadership."

I remembered what Josie had said about Byron being an ass-kisser—but she'd also said Lucy was overdue for a promotion. The only thing standing in the way was the company's current financial troubles, which I couldn't tell Lucy about. "Listen, don't worry about Byron. My sister isn't going to let him promote me over you."

"You sure about that?"

"I am, yeah. Besides, if he tried it, I'd turn it down."

Lucy straightened and turned around to face me. "Why would you do that?"

"Because I'm not qualified for the job and you are. If anyone deserves a promotion, it's you."

"Yeah, but..." Her brow furrowed even more. "You'd really turn it down? Don't you want to be promoted?"

"Not without earning it. And definitely not at someone else's expense. Contrary to recent events, I do have a little pride."

She cocked her head, her lips twitching as she peered up at me. "That's awfully noble of you."

I rubbed the back of my neck, feeling too warm inside my clothes. "Not really. Hopefully I'll have a financial stake in the business one day. It would be dumb to support a decision that isn't in the company's best interest."

Her eyes narrowed. "That's not the real reason."

Fuck. Had she realized I still had feelings for her? And why was it so goddamn hot in this kitchen?

Her lips curved in a smile. "Quit being so modest and just admit you're a good person."

Lucy had an incredible smile. It had always amazed me how easily she gave it away, as if it cost her nothing to share it with everyone. You might think that would diminish its value, but you'd be wrong. Her openness and generosity only made her and her smile more beautiful in my eyes.

She turned back to the ice cream sandwiches and raised her camera again. "Oh shoot, they're starting to melt. That's the problem with photographing ice cream. You have to work fast before your perfect shot dissolves into a gooey mess."

As she snapped more pictures, I swallowed thickly and tried to get myself under control before I made an ass of myself. It'd be a mistake to go reading anything into our interactions today.

She was a naturally kindhearted and warm person, but that didn't mean anything meaningful had changed between us. She still didn't love me.

"That's probably good enough, right?" Straightening, she leaned against the counter next to me as she peered down at the camera's screen. "Do you think these look okay?"

I leaned over for a better look as she flipped through thumbnails of all the photos she'd taken. The screen was small, and the thumbnails even tinier, so I had to lean in close to see them. Without thinking—I never seemed able to think around her—I rested my hand on her shoulder.

She responded by shifting even closer so her hip pressed against mine as we looked at the photos together. The scent of her perfume filled my head, and her body heat warmed my side where she'd fitted herself against me like she belonged there.

I forced myself to back away. "They all look great to me, but what do I know?"

This whole situation had me discombobulated. And yet I couldn't help enjoying the feeling. I knew it was dangerous. I knew I shouldn't be enjoying Lucy's company so much. I shouldn't be letting myself wonder if maybe she had feelings for me after all. I definitely shouldn't let hope into my heart.

But right now it felt a hell of a lot better than holding on to all that bitterness and hurt.

While Lucy staged the next photo, I put the ice cream sandwiches in the freezer. Once she had everything set up, I fetched the truffles and we pried them out of the ice cube tray and piled them into the bowl she'd chosen for the shot.

"It's missing something," she said, frowning into the camera as she teetered on the stepstool I'd brought out for her to stand on so she'd be high enough to take photographs from above the counter.

I scratched my head as I studied the arrangement. "What if we cut a couple in half so you could see the ice cream inside?"

Lucy beamed at me. "Great idea! You're a genius!"

My heart flipped over and I ducked my head, grateful that for once Lucy was towering over me so she wouldn't be able to see the lovesick expression on my face. As I bisected the frozen truffles, I pretended it was my heart I was carving into, and my feelings for Lucy had been frozen solid so they could be cut away like an unwanted growth.

She instructed me where to place them and declared the new tableau satisfactory. As she leaned from side to side, experimenting with different angles while she snapped her photos, she wobbled precariously on the stool. I was just opening my mouth to warn her to be careful when she lost her balance.

"Shit!" she squeaked as she toppled over.

My hands shot out to grab her hips, steadying her before she took a nosedive onto the floor. "Jesus, Lucy," I muttered, my heart pounding from the scare she'd given me.

"Sorry," she said, looking a little shaken.

"You good?" She nodded, and I cautiously let go of her, ready to seize her again if she started to teeter. "Please don't kill yourself in my house. I can barely afford my homeowner's insurance as it is."

Amusement brought some of the color back into her cheeks. "Is that the only reason you'd be upset? Because of your insurance premiums?" If I didn't know better, I'd almost think she was flirting with me. But that was impossible.

Wasn't it?

"No, of course not," I said. "I also don't want to have to clean up all this mess alone." I felt gratified when it got a laugh out of her. "Did you get all the pictures you need? Can you come down now, please?"

"Not yet. I figured out the angle I want, but the shots got all blurry when I lost my balance." She raised her camera and started to lean over again.

"Hang on," I said raising my hands in alarm. "Maybe I should hold on to you, just in case you start to go over again."

There was a noticeable hesitation before she assented. "That's probably a good idea. I like my job, but it's not worth dying for."

This time I settled my hands on her waist, deeming it a more appropriate anchorage than her hips, which were entirely too close to her backside. Speaking of which, our current position had me face-to-face with her butt. I tried to distract myself by thinking about somber, weighty things like global warming and the rising fascist movements threatening our democratic institutions. But somehow I couldn't seem to summon the proper amount of existential angst with Lucy's lovely round cheeks taking up my entire field of vision.

"Please hurry," I said as she snapped what felt like a trillion photos. "All the blood's rushing out of my arms." And straight to my dick. I needed to get my face away from her ass ASAP.

"All done," she said finally.

Exhaling in relief, I took the camera from her so she could steady herself as she climbed down from the stool. By then the ice cream bread had cooled enough to cut, and I returned the melting truffles to the freezer while Lucy set up the next shot. She placed a thick slice of the chocolate-swirled bread on a saucer, drizzled it with chocolate sauce, and topped it off with a generous dollop of whipped cream. The rest of the loaf sat beside it on a small wooden cutting board with a pink gingham napkin to add a splash of color.

Once again she wanted to photograph it from above, so once again I wound up with my hands on her waist, trying to ignore the fact that I was up close and personal with her rear end. But eventually she declared herself satisfied and handed me the camera. This time when she climbed down she used my shoulder for balance, and my already spinning head blanked out for a second as her slender fingers warmed my skin through my shirt.

"That's it. We're all done." She broke off a celebratory bite of ice cream bread and popped it in her mouth. Her eyes fluttered closed, and she made a noise of pure ecstasy that sank straight into my already tortured manhood.

"Does it taste as good as it smells?" I asked, wishing I had a bucket of cold water to pour over my head.

"Oh my god, yes. Here, try it." She broke off another piece and held it up to my face.

I very nearly opened my mouth and let her feed it to me, but prudence prevailed in time to stop me. Instead, I reached up and took it from her. It was a good decision, because I barely survived the light brush of our fingers. If I'd let her touch my lips, I would have spontaneously combusted.

She watched me as I tasted the ice cream bread. "It's good, right?"

Holy shit. No wonder she'd made a sex noise. I nodded as I swallowed. "One of the best things I've ever eaten."

"Not *the* best? I'm disappointed."

The best thing I'd ever eaten was Lucy, but there was no way in hell I was going to say that out loud.

She broke off two more bites and passed one to me. "We make a good team."

"I always thought so."

Lucy's gaze dropped to my mouth as her cheeks turned an alluring shade of pink, and my body temperature kicked up a few more degrees. You could probably fry an egg on my forehead right now. I turned away and crammed the ice cream bread in my mouth before I embarrassed myself further.

While Lucy packed up the props she'd brought, I went to the freezer to get out the truffles and ice cream sandwiches, pausing to let the icy air cool my face. If only I could freeze these inconvenient feelings I kept having. "What are you going to do with all this food we made?"

"It's yours to keep. Consider it payment for the use of your kitchen."

"Oh no." I set our other creations on the counter next to the ice cream bread and surveyed the extravagant collection of sweet treats. "You're not leaving me to eat all this alone. You have to help so I don't get diabetes."

She checked her phone. "It's almost dinnertime."

"Do you have to be somewhere?" I asked, trying to sound casual.

"No, but we'll spoil our dinner if we eat it now."

"Dessert for dinner. It's totally a thing." I helped myself to one of the truffles and popped it into my mouth. "Live a little."

"Well...maybe just a little." As she bit into a truffle I tried very hard not to be reminded of anything by the way her lips pursed around it as her cheeks hollowed out. "It feels naughty and decadent."

"That's why people like it." If she hadn't been watching me I would have shoved a whole handful of frozen truffles down the front of my pants to cool things off in there. Instead I went and got two plates. "We've been on our feet for hours. Let's have our dessert for dinner in the living room so we can take a load off."

It seemed safer than continuing to orbit each other in the close quarters of my kitchen. Bonus: I'd be able to strategically set my plate of cold ice cream treats in my lap to discourage any embarrassing misconduct down there.

Radagast had staked his claim on the lone chair, giving us no choice but to share the couch. I sat at one end and Lucy took the other, leaving a full person's worth of space between us. Already I was breathing easier.

Once we'd settled, Radagast got up with a big stretch and an even bigger yawn, abandoning his chair to jump up on the couch and pester Lucy for affection.

She lavished him with pets while gently discouraging his attempts to lick her ice cream sandwich. "I think he remembers me," she said when he threw himself onto his back against her leg and exposed his underbelly, begging for tummy rubs.

He'd always had a fondness for women, but Lucy had been his favorite of my girlfriends. Given a choice, I suspected he might have picked her in the breakup over me.

"Of course he does. He missed you."

I missed you too.

Not that it mattered. Exposing my soft underbelly wasn't likely to win me any favors.

"I missed you back," Lucy cooed at my cat, stroking his stomach until he was purring like an outboard motor.

And now I was jealous of a fucking cat. Sullenly, I crammed a giant bite of ice cream sandwich into my mouth, hoping for the sweet relief of brain freeze. Unfortunately, growing up eating the products of the family business every night after dinner had rendered me immune to ice cream headaches. What a useless superpower.

While I was busy eating my feelings, Lucy continued sweet-talking Radagast while daintily nibbling at her plate of ice cream treats. Her preoccupation with the cat allowed me to observe her without being caught staring. She'd dressed casually for our extracurricular activity, in black Converse, jeans, and a pink T-shirt that said *Badass* in cursive letters and now boasted a smudge of chocolate on her right breast. Her face was free of makeup and her hair pulled up in a messy bun, but a few tendrils had slipped loose and one clung to her cheek, perilously close to her mouth. My fingers itched to tuck it behind her ear for her. Instead, I shoved another truffle in my mouth.

"I love his soft little toe beans," she said, rubbing her thumb over Radagast's paw.

I didn't say anything, although I'd spent many an hour admiring his toe beans myself.

Lucy glanced up at me. "Thanks for all your help today and for letting me use your kitchen."

"It's no big deal."

Her gaze sharpened. "It kind of is though."

I crammed a chunk of ice cream bread in my mouth so I wouldn't say anything stupid.

"You know," she continued, "we've never talked about what happened between us."

The last few crumbs of ice cream bread tried to get stuck in my throat, and I coughed. "That's okay. We don't have to." *Please, let's not.* I desperately wanted not to talk about it.

Lucy shook her head. I wasn't getting out of this so easily. "I want you to know how sorry I am about the way things ended. I didn't handle it very gracefully."

Right. She wasn't sorry that she'd ended things between us —only *the way* she'd done it. Good to know. Very helpful. It was exactly the reminder I needed that Lucy didn't love me and never would. Getting my hopes up was a fool's game.

"I never wanted to hurt you." She sounded sorrowful.

"I know that," I mumbled at my lap. She wasn't someone who went around causing pain on purpose. She was the sort of person who rescued moths from the house and carefully released them outside. She'd probably been torturing herself with guilt, afraid she'd damaged my wings when she set me free.

She stopped stroking the cat and reached across the empty

gulf on the couch to touch my hand. "But I'm pretty sure I did anyway."

"It's fine," I forced myself to say. "Really." My wings would heal. Eventually.

The pad of her fingers caressed my knuckles, and by some miracle I managed to keep my hand from trembling. But if she kept at it much longer I was going to flop over on my back and put my head in her lap like the cat had.

"Does that mean you forgive me?"

I offered her a smile even though I was dying a little inside. "There's nothing to forgive."

It wasn't as if she could control her feelings any more than I could control mine. None of us got to pick who we loved. It was just bad luck that I'd fallen for someone who hadn't fallen for me back.

She still didn't look entirely satisfied. And she was still petting my knuckles. My fingers tried to spasm, and I barely managed to suppress it.

"I'd like it if we could be..." I held my breath when she paused. "Friends, I guess?" she finished, and I stopped holding my breath. "Is that too much to ask?"

"I'd like that too," I said like a damn fool.

How would I ever get over her if we were friends? At this rate I'd pine away the rest of my life aching for someone I could never have.

I wasn't entirely sure I cared.

Yes, I loved her and wanted her to be my girlfriend again, but today had reminded me how much I liked her company. I liked spending time with her, no matter what we were doing.

If she was offering me her friendship, why should I turn it down? A little piece of Lucy was better than no Lucy at all.

Right?

She gave my hand a hopeful squeeze. "Really?"

"Sure." Look how easygoing I was. Not a care in the world. Now that I'd committed, I was leaning into the idea. All I had to do was keep pretending I was fine and spending time around Lucy was fine and everything between us was totally fine.

Shouldn't be a problem at all.

12

LUCY

Being your coworker's ex was complicated enough. Being friends with your coworker-slash-ex? Was confusing as heck.

Yes, I realized the whole friends thing had been my idea. It had seemed like a good plan at the time. The mature, healthy thing to do. Wasn't it better to put all that tension behind us and move on to a place where we could coexist amicably? Especially since Tanner and I really did make a good team. We had tons in common, and we got along great when we didn't let feelings get in the way. Maybe we were destined to be friends all along. It was totally possible we had a great future ahead of us as purely platonic best pals.

But the reality of it was proving more difficult than I'd anticipated. Mostly because I hadn't appreciated how hard it was to be friends with someone you were attracted to.

And I was definitely still attracted to Tanner.

Big time.

There was no denying it. The more we were around each other, the more my body reacted to his body in ways I couldn't control.

Every time he looked at me I got inconvenient tingles in my pants. It was becoming a problem, because now that we were friends he was looking at me a lot more often. And talking to me more. And spending time with me when he didn't have to. He'd joined me and Linh for lunch in the break room on Monday. Walked me to my car on Tuesday when we happened to leave at the same time. On Wednesday afternoon, we'd gone downstairs together to get coffee from the good coffee stand.

On the surface, we were totally rocking this whole friends thing. But inside, I was a pants-tingling mess. My hands ached to touch him more or less constantly. My eyes followed him around the office of their own accord. I'd even caught myself leaning toward him once, trying to sniff him in the elevator like an absolute nutbar. I was beginning to think things had been easier back when Tanner was treating me like enemy number one.

On Wednesday, he showed up at work in my favorite shirt, the one he'd worn on our first official date. We were pretty relaxed here in marketing compared to the more conservative sales organization upstairs, and Tanner had settled in enough to trade his wool slacks for chinos and his starched dress shirts for slightly more casual button-downs. And now he'd come to work in the cornflower blue patterned shirt he'd been wearing the first time he kissed me.

Did he remember? Had he been conscious of the significance of that shirt when he put it on this morning? Knowing him as well as I did, I couldn't imagine he'd forget a detail like that. Had he thought about the effect that shirt would have on me? Or had he assumed it would have no effect at all?

It was definitely having an effect. My pants were tingling so much they were in danger of setting off the fire alarm. Especially when Tanner stopped off at my cube to ask me a question. When I spun my chair around, I found myself face-to-face with

The Shirt, looking directly at Tanner's flat stomach. And of course he'd rolled up his sleeves. So unfair. What was it about men's forearms that made them so freaking sexy?

While we talked about the company Instagram account, he leaned back against my desk, his long legs stretched out in front of him and his hands gripping the edge on either side of his thighs. The sight of his hands and forearms and hips and thighs casually arrayed so close to me like that was too tantalizing to be borne, so I fought to keep my eyes on his face. But that was highly problematic territory as well. He was freshly shaved as usual, and the line of his jaw was so strong and perfect. His whole face was flawless—symmetrical and perfectly proportioned around his intelligent, kind eyes. He smelled exquisite too. He always had, and it wasn't cologne but rather some magical combination of hair product, deodorant, laundry soap, and the ineffable essence of Tanner that clung to his skin.

I wasn't even trying to sniff him this time! I could smell him from my chair. It wasn't my fault he'd brought his magnificent man scent to my desk.

It also wasn't my fault that he was so much taller than me that I was in danger of getting a crick in my neck. My eyes naturally drifted downward—first to his shoulders, then his chest, then his forearms, and finally to his hands.

What?

It wasn't my fault! That was just where my eyes naturally fell.

But god, those hands...

"So what do you think?" He'd moved on to describing an idea he had for a series of features in the newsletter. Something something history of ice cream something something. I hadn't been listening that closely because I'd been so distracted by his manly perfection. *Oops.*

"You should propose it at the meeting Friday in front of Byron." What I'd heard of it had sounded like a good idea.

Tanner's ideas were usually good, and he'd been here long enough now that he knew what he was doing.

"You think?" It was freaking adorable that he wanted my approval.

My fingers twitched with the urge to reach out and touch him, to give his lovely bare forearm a reassuring squeeze. I jammed both my hands under my thighs so they wouldn't misbehave. "Yeah, definitely. It's a good idea. Let Byron know it came from you."

"Okay, I will. Thanks." He smiled, and it zipped up my whole spine.

This would all be so much easier if Tanner didn't still give me tingling pants feelings. Also, if my heart could stop beating faster around him, that would be great.

———

AFTER YET ANOTHER long day of trying not to blatantly ogle Tanner, I met up with my brother's band after work for the final rehearsal before the Crowder Folk Festival this weekend. Corey's cousin—Corey played lead guitar—had let them convert the disused barn on his property into a rehearsal space a few years back. They'd fixed it up a lot, adding insulation for the winter, fans for ventilation in the summer, and rugs on the floor and walls to improve the sound quality.

Currently I was chilling on an old vinyl couch that had been draped with woven Mexican blankets to cover the torn uphol-stery. And by chilling I meant sweating. Even after the sun had set and with all the fans going, it was hot inside the barn during the summer months. The guys—Matt, Wyatt, Corey, and Tyler, the bass player—were used to the heat, since most of their gigs were outside. Me? Not so much.

Andie flopped down next to me and twisted the cap off a

bottle of cold water from the cooler. "How's it been going with your new coworker?"

I was glad she'd tagged along with Wyatt tonight. It gave me someone to talk to while the guys argued over the set list for the millionth time. "It's been okay, actually." Aside from all the drooling and ogling. "Better than I expected." *Much* better.

Her eyebrows lifted. "Really?"

I nodded as I sipped my own water. "It was a little awkward at first, but we've been getting along great the last few days. Tanner even let me use his kitchen to take pictures for the newsletter."

She sat up and swiveled toward me on the couch, pulling one of her legs underneath her. "You went to his house?"

"Last Saturday." I shrugged like it was no big deal. "We made some ice cream recipes and took photos of them."

"Together?" Andie said, sounding incredulous. "You and Tanner were alone in his house cooking and working side by side? And that wasn't weird?"

The only part of it that had been weird was how much I'd enjoyed it. And how relaxed Tanner had seemed around me, as if he'd enjoyed himself too. *That* was pretty weird. "It was fine," I told her. "We even talked things out a little and agreed to be friends."

"You and Tanner are friends now?" Andie gave me a long look. "Huh." The way she said *huh* sounded more like *no fucking way*.

"Is that so hard to believe?"

"Not necessarily. Lots of people manage to be friends with their exes."

"Exactly. Why shouldn't we?"

She didn't answer right away. "I guess it depends on the reasons you broke up and how you both feel about each other now."

I picked at the label on my water bottle. "It'll be easier to work together if we're friends."

"Sure." She regarded me for a long moment. "How *do* you feel about him now?"

"I've always liked him," I said, feeling defensive. "That was never the problem."

"What was the problem, then? If you don't mind my asking. Feel free to tell me to mind my own business."

She'd never asked me about my relationship with Tanner before, and I'd never volunteered any details. Andie and I were friendly, but it wasn't like we were besties who told each other everything. I knew she was loyal to Tanner because she was dating his brother, and I hadn't wanted her to feel caught in the middle. Mostly we'd both skirted around the subject. But if she wanted to know, there wasn't any reason not to tell her. I assumed she'd heard Tanner's side of it already.

"We weren't on the same page," I said carefully. "He's a nice guy, but I wanted to keep things casual and he was looking to get serious. I feel bad about it, but he wanted more than I could give him."

"Oh yeah, I've been there." Andie gave me a sympathetic look. "If you don't feel the spark, you don't feel the spark. You can't make yourself have feelings for someone just because they want you to."

"Exactly," I said. "Although, it wasn't as if I didn't have *any* feelings for him."

"But there was no spark, right?"

"There may have been some sparks." A lot of sparks, in fact. Mega sparks. All up and down my whole body every time Tanner had looked at me or touched me. *Especially* when he'd touched me. God, the way he used to touch me...

"So now that you and Tanner are spending all this time

together again, are the sparks still there?" Andie asked, frowning at me.

I didn't know how to answer that. No, actually, I did. I just didn't *want* to answer. Because I was definitely feeling sparks. Lots of them. Every time he stood close to me or we accidentally touched, it felt like it used to. So much so that it was easy to forget things weren't like that between us anymore—and hard to remember why I didn't want them to be.

"You don't have to answer that," Andie said when I didn't reply right away. "Just promise me one thing, okay? Don't jerk him around. If you don't want to be with him, that's fine. But don't get his hopes up and dash them again."

"No, of course," I said. "I wouldn't do that."

"Good. Tanner's a great guy. He deserves better than that."

On that, we were in perfect agreement. Tanner *was* a great guy. And I'd already hurt him once. I couldn't risk doing it again.

———

"WHAT DO you think of this one?" I emerged from Linh's bedroom wearing a gingham dress and stood in front of the couch where Linh and her girlfriend, Alexis, were waiting to pass judgment. I'd brought some potential outfits over to their apartment so they could help me decide what to wear for the folk festival performance tomorrow.

Linh's wrinkled nose communicated her opinion, so I looked to Alexis for confirmation.

"Absolutely not," she said with a shake of her head. "You look like you're about to drop a house on a witch and steal her ruby slippers."

I looked down at myself. "It's not that bad, is it?" They'd shot down every outfit I'd modeled so far, and I was getting discouraged.

"It's definitely not good," Linh said. "I know the whole prairie dress thing is supposedly in right now, but unless you're actively in the market for a sister wife, I'm giving this one a hard no."

"I thought since it's a folk festival I should wear something a little folky."

"But Shiny Heathens is a rock band," Alexis pointed out, brushing her platinum blonde hair off her shoulder.

Linh nodded in agreement. "Do you really want to be dressed like Laura Ingalls when you're up onstage next to Wyatt King and all of his tattoos?"

I let out a grumbly sigh. "Says the woman wearing overalls right now."

Linh laid a hand over her heart, deeply offended. "These are from Anthropologie!"

"The problem is I don't own any cool rocker clothes." My style tended more toward cute pastels and cheerful florals than black nail polish and edgy clothes. I was more of a Taylor Swift than a Billie Eilish—only without the songwriting talent and giant piles of money, obviously.

"Too bad you're not closer to Alexis's size." Linh turned to grin at her girlfriend. "You could loan her your leather pants."

Alexis snorted. "Leather pants in this heat? She'd need to have them surgically separated from her skin by the end of the night." She sipped her wine, studying me like a problem in need of solving. "I do have a leather crop top that might work though."

I was not on Team Crop Top. They were all well and good when you were tall, slim, and athletic like Alexis, but I was not comfortable walking around with my belly and potentially my underboobs exposed to the world.

"What about a romper?" Linh suggested, lounging back on

the couch and resting her feet in Alexis's lap. "They're cool, comfy, and stylish."

Alexis shook her head. "Bad idea. Music festivals mean porta-potties. You do not want to be stripping down to your altogether in one of those horror boxes just to take a pee. Trust me."

"Is that all you brought?" Linh tilted her head and squinted at me. "You're pretty close to my size. I might have something in my closet that would work."

"I've got one more option left to try on first." I went back into the bedroom and stripped out of the vetoed gingham dress. A few minutes later, I reemerged in a red floral maxi dress with a deep V-neck and flutter sleeves.

"Ohhh! Now that, I like," Linh said, pushing her glasses up the bridge of her nose.

"Really?" I asked hopefully.

Alexis got up and circled me, resting one hand on her hip as she looked me up and down. "It's feminine without being too mousy. Weather appropriate. And your tits look spectacular. I think we have a winner."

"Oh thank god." I collapsed on the chair opposite the couch. "I did not want to have to go shopping tomorrow morning."

Alexis handed me the wineglass I'd abandoned earlier, then went to reclaim her spot on the couch. "Are you nervous? Performing at the folk festival is a huge deal."

"A little." I'd never been up in front of an audience that big before. I wasn't entirely sure how I was going to handle it. "Mostly I'm trying not to think about it."

"You'll be great." Linh was my number one cheerleader. I wished I had half as much confidence in myself as she had in me. "And at least you'll know you look awesome."

"Especially your tits," Alexis added, giving me a thumbs-up.

"Y'all are still coming, right?"

"Duh. Of course." Linh raised her eyebrows at me. "Is Tanner coming?"

I sipped my wine, trying to look nonchalant. "He said he was."

She saw right through my ruse. "You two have been acting awfully chummy lately."

"We're friends now. It's a new thing we're trying: being reasonable, well-adjusted adults."

"Is that why the two of you have been having eye sex across your cubicles all day long?" Linh's expression was smug. "Because you're *friends*?"

"We're not having eye sex!" I sputtered, horrified. Was that seriously how it looked? Who else around the office had noticed? Also—wait.

Is Tanner doing it too?

"What exactly would you call it?" Linh asked archly.

"I can't help that his face is right in my eyeline when I'm sitting at my desk," I protested. "What am I supposed to look at?"

"It's not the fact that you're looking at him. It's the *way* you're looking at him."

Alexis swiveled her head back and forth between us, deeply invested in the conversation. "How is she looking at him?"

"Like she's thinking about doing nasty things to him." Linh pointed an accusatory finger at me. "I dare you to deny it."

Busted.

Alexis grinned at my guilty expression. "Still hung up on your ex, are you?"

"Yes," Linh answered for me.

"Hang on," I said. "Tanner wasn't making eye sex looks *back* at me, was he?"

Linh's smug look got smugger as she downed the last of her wine.

"Was he? He wasn't. You're making that up."

"Am I?" Linh shot back, getting up to fetch more wine out of the fridge.

"Don't tease her." Alexis tugged an elastic off her wrist and pulled her hair back in a ponytail. "*Was* he?"

Linh returned with a fresh bottle of rosé. "It sure looked that way to me."

Was it possible? Could Tanner still have feelings for me? Did that mean...

Would he be willing to give me another chance if I wanted one?

Alexis held her glass out for a top-up as she gave me a questioning look. "I thought you were the one who did the breaking up."

"She was," Linh said as she added more wine to my glass too. I detected a note of judgment in her voice. She hadn't fully understood my reasoning for ending things with Tanner, although she'd tried to be supportive of my choice.

"I wanted to keep things casual," I said defensively. "He wanted to get serious."

"And now what do you want?" Alexis asked, putting me on the spot.

I gulped down a big mouthful of wine. "I'm not sure I know anymore."

Linh sat down next to Alexis and fixed me with a penetrating look. "But you're regretting your decision a little, aren't you?"

"Maybe," I admitted.

Alexis shifted so Linh could lean back against her. "What prompted the breakup, exactly?"

I lowered my eyes to my lap. "He told me he loved me."

"And?" she asked, playing with a lock of Linh's hair.

"And I didn't love him back."

"Did he expect you to say it back?"

"People always expect you to say it back. And once it's out there, you can't put the cat back in the bag, so there's all this added pressure. I thought we were having a good time, and he had to ruin everything by falling in love."

Alexis's voice was gentle. "Why do you think falling in love has to ruin everything?"

"Because it always does." Only after I saw both of them looking at me with naked pity in their eyes did I realize how sad and jaded I'd sounded.

But I guess maybe I was sad and jaded. My mother gave up everything for love of my father and became a burden he grew to despise. I was the one who'd been forced to pick up the pieces after he left. And now, because I loved my mother, I was the one who was trapped—thirty-one years old and still living at home so I could financially support her and my brother. I'd lost all of my twenties parenting adults who behaved like children, and at this rate they'd steal the rest of my life from me too.

Why would I want to fall in love and give someone else the power to drag me down even more? I had enough people depending on me already, thank you very much. I didn't need to take on any additional obligations. And I certainly didn't need to open myself up to the kind of heartbreak and disappointment my mother had experienced.

"Love shouldn't feel like a burden," Linh said quietly.

I let out a humorless laugh. "Sure, that's why they call it commitment."

Linh and Alexis exchanged a silent look.

"She's right," Alexis said, fixing her soft brown eyes on me again. "Finding the right person makes everything better, because then you can share each other's burdens. It's not a one-sided arrangement that holds you back. Love should be a partnership that builds you up and frees you to be the person you're meant to be."

I couldn't even imagine what that would feel like. Tying myself down to a person who made me feel free? It sounded impossible.

And yet, I'd spent enough time around Linh and Alexis to know that was exactly what their relationship was like. They were a team who shared everything, supported each other, and faced the challenges life threw at them together.

So obviously it *was* possible.

As I looked at them curled up together on the couch like cats, a hollow ache of longing wrapped itself around my chest. I wanted what they had. I wanted someone I could rely on, instead of always having to be the person everyone else relied on. I wanted someone who didn't mind taking care of me when I needed it. Someone to share my troubles with who wasn't the cause of them. Someone who made me feel stronger rather than more powerless.

"Let me ask you something," Linh said. "When you were with Tanner, did he make your life easier or harder?"

I frowned into my wineglass as I thought about it. "Neither. It was only a casual thing—or it was supposed to be. We just hung out and had fun. We didn't dump our problems on each other." I'd always skirted around the subject of my family with him, explaining my living at home as a way of saving money. I'd never invited him to my house or complained about my current situation.

Neither of us had done much complaining, now that I thought about it. Not that we hadn't talked about ourselves—he'd told me a little about his mother's death, and I'd told him a little about my parents' divorce. But not too much. I hadn't told him the full story—like how my mother had fallen apart afterward—because the full story was too complicated and painful. The full story was still happening to me, still dictating my choices and shaping the course of my life.

"Was it because you didn't want to talk about your problems?" Linh asked in a tone that implied she'd already come to her own conclusion. "Or because Tanner wouldn't have wanted you to?"

"I don't know," I answered with another grumbly sigh.

But I did know, just as well as Linh did. I'd been the one keeping him at a distance. Clearly he'd wanted to know more of me. That was what he'd really been asking for when I got scared and broke things off. That was what "I love you" meant.

"Put it this way," Alexis said. "If you'd needed something, say you were sick or your car broke down, could you have called Tanner for help?"

"I would never have asked him." I didn't like asking anyone for help. If you didn't ask, then you wouldn't be disappointed when they didn't come through. "I can take care of myself," I said with a jut of my chin.

It was something that mattered a lot to me. I didn't ever want to have to lean on other people. I didn't want to become a burden to anyone else.

And yes, I realized there was a contradiction in wanting someone to take care of me but also not wanting to *need* someone to take care of me. I never claimed to be entirely rational. Which, now that I came to think of it, might have something to do with why I'd freaked out over the idea of someone falling in love with me.

"But if you had," Linh persisted. "Is Tanner the kind of person who'd be there for you?"

Yes.

I didn't even have to ponder it. The man who'd come to my rescue when I'd been covered in menstrual blood? There was no question he was the sort of person who could be depended on. And not grudgingly. Tanner hadn't waited to be asked for help. He'd stepped up as soon as he'd seen my predicament, even though it wasn't his problem or his responsibility. Even though he hadn't owed me anything—and in fact he'd had every reason to delight in my misfortune and leave me to sort it out for myself.

It wasn't only that one time either. It was the way he'd volunteered his kitchen for the photo shoot. And how helpful he'd been that day, anticipating everything I needed and providing it before I had to ask.

Now that I thought back on it, he'd always been like that: noticing when I was ready for another drink, offering me his jacket when I got cold, even trading meals with me once when I hadn't liked what I'd ordered. I'd appreciated it at the time, but not as much as I should have. I'd written it off as good manners, but it was more than that. He wasn't just being polite out of habit. He was a genuinely thoughtful and supportive person.

And I'd let him go.

"She knows the answer." Alexis's lips curved as she inclined her head at me. "You can tell by the look on her face."

Linh was giving me a self-satisfied smirk, because she knew about the period blood episode. She knew what Tanner had done for me—and that he'd had every reason not to do it and had done it anyway.

"Yes, fine," I admitted. "He's a great guy. Is that what you want me to say? He's probably perfect for me, and I made a huge mistake by breaking up with him."

"Is that really what you think?" Alexis asked.

I chewed on the inside of my lip. "Maybe."

Linh broke into a broad grin. "I knew it!"

"So what are you going to do about it?" Alexis asked.

I swallowed a mouthful of wine while I thought about it. "I don't know that I should do anything. I already broke his heart once. I'm not sure I deserve a second chance, even if he wanted to give me one."

"Everyone deserves a second chance," Alexis said. "People are allowed to make mistakes."

"And let's not forget the eye sex," Linh said. "I'm telling you, it's not one-sided. That man definitely still has feelings for you. I think he'd take you back if you asked him to."

Was it really that easy? Could I just walk up to Tanner and tell him I wanted to try dating again?

Andie's warning came back to haunt me. *If you don't want to be with him, that's fine. But don't get his hopes up and dash them again.*

But what if I *wanted* to be with Tanner? And he still wanted to be with me?

Was I willing to try again? Would I be able to give him what he wanted next time?

I wasn't sure. The only thing I did know was that I needed to be one hundred percent certain before I did anything.

13

TANNER

I got to the Crowder Folk Festival early on Saturday afternoon to stake out a good spot on the lawn in front of the second stage for the Shiny Heathens set. Not too long after I'd stretched out on the grass, Andie came and found me.

"You're not hanging backstage with the band doing the rock star's girlfriend thing?" I asked as she sank down next to me. Up onstage, the bluegrass band on the schedule before Shiny Heathens was just starting their set.

"I don't want to distract him." She gave a little shrug as she slipped her flip-flops off and crossed her legs in front of her. "He's says I'm not a distraction, but I can tell when he needs to be alone in his own head, you know?"

I didn't know. It never would have occurred to me that alone time was something Wyatt needed. Showed how well I knew my closest brother. Or maybe it was just that he'd been doing a lot of growing recently. He was damned lucky to have a woman like Andie who understood him so well.

"He's pretty nervous, huh?"

Andie tipped her head back toward the sky. "Total fucking

basket case. Barely slept at all last night." She frowned at the clouds gathering overhead. "It's not going to rain, is it?"

"It's not supposed to." I'd checked three different weather apps this morning before leaving the house. "If we're lucky, there'll be enough cloud cover to keep the heat from getting too brutal."

"That'd be nice."

"How was everyone else's mood backstage?" I asked, trying to sound nonchalant.

Andie peered at me over the top of her sunglasses, not the slightest bit fooled. "Just ask me about Lucy. We both know that's what you're dying to find out."

"How was she?"

"A little pale, actually. She's pretty nervous too."

I frowned as I remembered what Lucy had said about performing and not liking to be the center of attention.

"Hey." Andie jabbed me with her elbow. "She'll be fine. She's tough."

"I know."

"How are things between you two, anyway?"

"Confusing," I muttered as I tore apart a blade of grass like it had personally dishonored me.

"Does that mean you're ready for me to find you another blind date?"

I snorted. "No thank you."

She studied me. "Lucy told me you two are friends now. She said you invited her over to your house."

"It was for a work thing. She was in a bind and needed to use my kitchen."

Andie let out a scoffing *pffft*. "Sure. You keep telling yourself that."

I sighed. "What do you want from me, Andie?" I'd been trying to do the right thing and give Lucy what she wanted. For the last week I'd done my best to behave like a friend, but as much as I loved getting to be closer to her, it was exhausting keeping my real feelings hidden all the time.

"I think the more important question is what do you want from Lucy?"

I gave Andie a long look. "We both know what I want from her."

"Still?"

"Still," I admitted despairingly. "I can't help it. I tried to get over her, I really did. But I still love her, and I don't know how to stop."

The sun had disappeared behind a thick bank of gray clouds, and Andie pushed her sunglasses on top of her head as she regarded me narrowly. "You know what? I was going to stay out of it, because it's none of my business and I don't want to take sides. But I can't even with you two anymore. It's too painful to watch you dance around each other like a couple of helpless baby birds."

"What are you talking about?"

"I'm going to break my rule about interfering and tell you something, okay? Lucy wants you back as much as you want her."

A starburst of hope flared to life in my chest. "Did she say that?"

"Not in so many words."

The hope dampened to a sputtering fizzle. "So she didn't say that."

"Just trust me, okay?"

"What did she say, exactly?"

"I'm not going to tell you because that would be breaking a confidence. But my observations belong to me, and it's totally obvious to anyone with eyes how Lucy feels about you. So maybe you two could have an actual, honest conversation about the feelings you both still have for each other and put yourselves and the rest of us out of our misery so I don't have to keep watching this train wreck. I like drama as much as the next person, but at this point I'm over it."

"You should be a therapist. You've got a real sensitive touch with painful subjects."

"I know, right?" She grinned at me as she bumped her shoulder against mine. "So are you going to tell her how you feel, or what?"

The last time I'd told Lucy how I felt it hadn't worked out so well. And it didn't sound like she'd actually said she wanted me back. Did I trust Andie's instincts enough to risk making a fool of myself and potentially ruining the fragile peace we'd built?

"I don't know." I shook my head. "I need to think about it."

Wanting Lucy was one thing, but offering myself up to potentially get my heart broken a second time was something else altogether. I might be feeling the former, but that didn't mean I was prepared to risk the latter.

But I might be.

Truthfully, I didn't fucking know what I wanted anymore.

"Ugh," Andie grumbled, rolling her eyes. "You're so frustrating."

I pushed myself to my feet. "I'm going for a beer." I needed a few minutes alone with my thoughts.

"You're bringing back one for me, right?" Andie called out.

"Of course I am," I called back over my shoulder

"I knew I liked you," she shouted after me.

Unfortunately, I didn't get much time alone with my thoughts because I ran into Arwen on the way to the beer stall. We chatted while we waited in line together, and when I found out she was there on her own, I invited her to come sit with us to watch Lucy sing.

The bluegrass band was finishing up their set by the time I

got back to Andie. While I was gone, she'd been joined by her brother, Josh, and his girlfriend, Mia. Not long after that, Manny showed up with Isabella in tow.

"Do you know if Dad was planning to come?" I asked Manny as Isabella hung off one of my arms, demanding that I swing her.

He saved my beer before I accidentally sloshed it acquiescing to his daughter's request. "He's in the VIP lounge with everyone else. I just came from there."

There was a shaded VIP viewing platform up front next to the stage, complete with comfortable lounge chairs and complimentary concessions. I could have chosen to watch the show from up there, but I preferred it down here on the grass with Andie and the general public. Not having to interact with my dad more than made up for the lack of amenities. Wyatt could have gotten Andie access as his guest, but she hadn't wanted to chance seeing our dad either.

Just before Shiny Heathens was scheduled to take the stage, my brother Ryan showed up in his navy blue EMS uniform. He was working a shift at the festival's first aid tent, but he'd taken a break to come watch Wyatt's show. Isabella flung herself into his arms, and he helped Manny convince her to wear her protective earmuffs so the loud music wouldn't damage her hearing.

When Wyatt came out onstage with the rest of his band, he seemed as comfortable and carefree as ever. To look at him you'd never know he'd been nervous a day in his life. The crowd had filled in a lot since the last act had ended, and most of them got up on their feet when Shiny Heathens started playing.

In contrast with Wyatt, Lucy looked scared as hell when she joined them onstage for the second half of their set. I doubted anyone else could tell, but I knew her well enough to notice the rigid set of her shoulders and the way her smile had frozen in place.

Wyatt must have noticed it too, because he took her by the hand and projected one of his dazzling smiles at her. It worked like a tractor beam to pull Lucy's focus away from the audience that was making her anxious. My whole life I'd envied the ease with which Wyatt captured people's attention, but I'd never been more grateful for it than I was when I saw Lucy relax up on that stage.

Wyatt moved back to his own mic stand as the first notes of the duet started up, but he kept his attention on Lucy. I'd seen them perform this song together twice before, but this time there was a different kind of energy to it. Their eyes stayed locked on one another as Wyatt sang the first verse with a heart-felt passion that caused a hush to fall over the crowd.

I held my breath as Lucy drew herself up straight in anticipation of her cue. As soon as she began to sing, it transformed her completely. Every last trace of tension melted away when her voice rang out strong, clear, and more beautiful than anything I'd ever heard in my life. It socked me right in the chest, nearly bringing tears to my eyes.

An electric ripple moved through the crowd, and I heard Arwen make a noise of surprise beside me. Wyatt could sing, but Lucy's voice was a whole other level. Even Andie, who must have heard them sing this song dozens of times before, was sitting up and leaning forward. I could sense the audience hanging on every note as Lucy and Wyatt sang to each other about finding love, losing it, and getting a second chance to make it last forever.

For the final repeat of the chorus, Wyatt crossed the stage to join Lucy at her mic, their faces only inches apart as they gazed into each other's eyes and belted out the emotional lyrics with an intensity I'd never seen from either of them before.

There was no reason on earth for me to feel jealous. I knew Wyatt's heart belonged wholly to Andie, and he'd be thinking only of her as he sang. He and Lucy were simply putting on a performance. But the emotion they'd created between them was palpable enough to cause an oily stir of resentment in the pit of my stomach.

Not because I had any claim on Lucy, or because I believed I had anything to fear from Wyatt, but because I wanted Lucy to look at me the way she was looking at him. Even if it wasn't real, I wanted it more than I'd ever wanted anything in my life.

The final notes of the song were met by a roar of exuberant applause, and Lucy blinked like she'd just come out of a trance. Wyatt pulled her into a hug, and she clutched him gratefully as he leaned down to speak into her ear.

When they pulled apart she was smiling, her expression easier and less brittle than when she first came out. Wyatt took the mic at center stage again as they moved on to the next song, and Lucy stayed in the background for the rest of the set, sweetening Wyatt's voice with her harmonies. I knew she preferred it that way, but I couldn't take my eyes off her as she stood behind her microphone in her long red dress with her hair catching the stage lights and glowing like a halo.

"You okay?" Andie asked, leaning over to me.

"Fine," I mumbled, far from it.

Any doubts I might have had before were long gone. I knew as surely as I knew my own name that I'd willingly let Lucy break my heart a million times over in exchange for a single chance to have her back.

14

LUCY

I threw up before our set at the folk festival. But only once. Considering the size of the audience out there waiting for us to take the stage, once felt like a win.

My butthead brother teased me about it, but Wyatt was really nice to me. He even came to check on me and shared the thermos of herbal tea with honey that he'd brought for himself. Maybe Wyatt and Tanner weren't all that different after all.

They certainly shared a gift for writing. Wyatt had written all the band's songs himself, although Matt had apparently helped him with some of the music.

If you twisted my arm, I'd have to admit that my brother was a pretty talented musician, thanks to the years of piano lessons our mother had forced on him. She'd had a lot of musical talent as well in her youth, enough that she could have made a career of it herself if she hadn't given it all up when she got married and had kids.

I used to think Matt's band was just another way for him to waste time—something he used as an excuse not to get a full-time job. But recently they'd been taking it more seriously, playing more gigs in bigger venues, and saving up for recording equipment so they could produce their own EP. It was the first time I'd ever seen Matt put real effort into something he cared about.

That was why I'd reluctantly agreed to help when he'd told me they needed a female singer for a duet Wyatt had written. For all my complaining about him, I wanted my brother to be happy and successful doing something he loved. I just wished he'd do it in a way that didn't require him to sponge off me and Mom for the rest of his life.

Playing the Crowder Folk Festival was certainly a decent start. While it couldn't compare to the bigger music events like SXSW or ACL Festival, it drew decent crowds and a slate of seasoned musicians. Held over two weekends and three stages at a ranch outside town, the festival showcased both emerging and established artists, and always attracted talent scouts and record company representatives.

So yeah, I'd puked. But after that I felt a little better. Well enough to keep my cool while I waited in the wings for my cue to join the band for the second half of the set.

As soon as I walked out onstage, however, I started to freeze up at the sight of the crowd spread out over the lawn below us. But Wyatt was right there next to me, and he took my hand, escorting me to my microphone as he introduced me. It was easy to follow his lead and focus on him instead of all the people watching. The fact that he seemed so relaxed and looked so much like Tanner didn't hurt either. I could see Tanner's face when Wyatt smiled at me, which helped me relax even more.

I tried not to think about all the people watching, or about how this show could be the band's big break. And I *really* tried not to think about the fact that if I screwed up today, I could ruin everything for my brother and his friends. Instead, I concentrated on Wyatt and the first song I had to sing with him, which was the duet, an emotional love song he'd written about Andie.

The whole time I was singing my verses, I couldn't help thinking about Tanner and imagining I was singing the words to him instead of to his brother.

At the end of the song, Wyatt gave me a hug, which I was grateful for because it helped distract me from the deafening applause. "You're doing great," he told me. "You've got this."

After that the scariest part was over. I only had to sing backup for the last few songs, which I could pretty much do on autopilot now that I wasn't the center of attention anymore.

As I stood up there singing harmony on another one of Wyatt's love songs, the romantic lyrics brought Tanner to the front of my mind again. I imagined him out there somewhere in the audience I refused to look at. I wondered what he was thinking about and what sort of look he had on his face. Was he smiling? Was he listening to the words I was singing? Was he thinking about me right now the way I was thinking about him?

Before I knew it, our set was over, and we were filing off the stage together as the crowd roared their approval. The guys were justifiably hyped, congratulating each other and basking in their success as we climbed down the stairs behind the outdoor stage.

For a lot of people, performing a show like that would have been the highlight of their life. But for me, it had just reinforced that it wasn't my calling. There was satisfaction in knowing I could do it, but I hadn't enjoyed it, and I'd be fine if I never did anything like that again.

There were a lot of people backstage waiting to talk to the guys and compliment them on the show, including Wyatt's uncle Randy, who took charge of introducing them to people. Some of those people were other musicians playing the festival, and some looked like important music business people.

I hung back, not really a part of the band or their future plans, and watched my brother and his friends enjoy their moment in the spotlight. It was easy to fade into the background with Wyatt around. Matt, Tyler, and Corey were holding their own, but it was Wyatt who shined. His gregarious personality and natural charisma made him the perfect front man.

As I watched him effortlessly charm everyone he talked to, I wondered what it must have been like for Tanner growing up with a sibling like that. Had he felt overshadowed by his popular younger brother? Or had he been grateful to have someone to draw attention away from him? Was Tanner quiet and withdrawn because he'd gotten used to being outshined? Or was it part of his DNA, and he would have turned out like that no matter what?

The next time I had the chance, I resolved to ask him about it. We'd never talked much about his relationship with Wyatt— or any of the rest of his family, for that matter. I hadn't thought anything of it before, because I'd been too busy trying to avoid talking about my own family. But now it struck me as odd.

I'd sensed there was some tension between Tanner and his brother Nate, but it'd been more of a feeling than anything else because he'd never actually talked about it. I'd known Tanner was stressed about his job and didn't love working in sales, but that was as much as he'd ever admitted. The fact that he'd been fired by his own brother meant things must have been much worse than I'd realized.

I felt bad about that. He must have been struggling when we were together, and I'd been mostly oblivious. Too wrapped up in my own problems to stop and wonder what problems he might have been dealing with. Maybe if we'd shared more, we could have helped each other through all of it.

Honestly, I'd been a terrible girlfriend. But in my defense, that had sort of been my whole point in breaking up with him. I only had so much energy to give to other people and things in my life, and there wasn't enough of me left over to keep a boyfriend happy. That was the reason I'd wanted to keep it casual.

But according to Alexis I'd been doing the math wrong. I'd assumed committing myself to yet another person's well-being would mean more work. What I hadn't accounted for was that I'd gain someone looking after my own well-being in return. I'd forgotten that was actually supposed to be part of the deal, because it never had been, in my experience. In theory, the benefits should balance out the costs. Or even outweigh them, resulting in a net gain.

My god, was I seriously treating love like an accounting problem? What had happened to the girl who used to dream about falling in love with a handsome prince who'd sweep her off her feet and spoil her for the rest of her life?

Sadly, I knew what had happened to her. She'd gotten so worn down by life and the responsibilities of adulthood that she'd given up on romance and love and maybe even the idea of happiness altogether. She'd given up so completely that when a handsome prince showed up and tried to sweep her off her feet, she'd told him to take a hike.

What a fool I'd been. This amazingly sweet, sexy, smart, wonderful man had offered himself to me, body and soul, and I'd sent him packing because I couldn't be bothered? I still wasn't positive I deserved a second chance—or that Tanner would be willing to give me one. But I knew now that I needed to find out.

Today had been good for me, because it had reminded me that I was capable of more courage than I'd been displaying of late. Playing it safe wasn't always the answer—there were benefits to stepping out of your comfort zone and taking a risk. I'd just overcome paralyzing stage fright to perform in front of thousands of people. If I was strong enough to do that, I was strong enough to risk rejection in order to tell Tanner how I felt.

If by some miracle I did get another chance with him, this time I'd do everything I could to hold on to him.

"Hey." My brother had come over to the lounge area behind the stage where I was sitting by myself.

I glanced past him at what was left of the people hanging around the band. "Looks like y'all have been making some industry connections."

"Maybe. We'll see if anything comes of it." He shrugged, but his grin belied his attempt to play it cool.

"Did you see the texts from Mom?" Our mother had watched the show from the VIP section and sent us a series of excited texts about the fancy amenities she'd shared with the Crowder glitterati.

"Yeah." Matt dropped onto the outdoor sofa beside me and bumped my knee with his. "You okay?"

"I'm fine." Surprisingly so, all things considered.

He scratched his head, and I resisted the urge to smooth his sweaty hair down. "I know you were nervous about doing this."

"Did the preshow barfing give me away?"

He gave me a small, crooked smile. "I just want to say thanks for doing it, even though I know you didn't want to. You really classed up the act."

Wonder of wonders, had my brother actually expressed gratitude for something I'd done for him? If this was how success went to his head, I wholeheartedly approved.

"You're welcome," I told him. "It wasn't as bad as I thought it would be."

He ducked his head, looking uncharacteristically bashful. "I don't want you to think I don't appreciate you or notice everything you do for me. I'm not always great at showing it, but I'm really fucking grateful you're my sister."

Well, shit...

I blinked, at a complete loss for words. What was I supposed to say to that? My brother and I didn't have sincere conversations or talk about our feelings with each other.

Matt frowned at me. "You're not gonna cry, are you?"

I shook my head. "No. I'm gonna hug you instead."

"Christ." He rolled his eyes, but when I leaned toward him he opened his arms for me.

I couldn't even remember the last time I'd hugged my brother. His birthday, maybe? He stank, but it was a familiar stink, and there was something comforting about it. We should probably try to hug more often. Maybe if we had a few more moments like this, I wouldn't feel as resentful all the time. "Does this mean you're going to help around the house more?"

His rib cage vibrated with laughter. "Probably best not to get your hopes up about that. But I'll try."

"Good." I let go of him and sat up, wiping under my eyes.

"You *were* crying," he said accusingly.

"I was not. It's just your BO is so bad it made my eyes water."

He jabbed me with his elbow. "You're the one who wanted to hug me."

"Consider me suitably punished for the impulse."

"Hey," Corey called out to us. "We're heading over to the beer garden. Y'all coming or what?"

"Yeah, wait up." Matt got to his feet and offered his hand to me. "You ready for a drink?"

"God, yes," I said and let him pull me off the sofa.

The beer garden was just past the giant square of food trucks and stalls, about a ten-minute walk from our stage. As we crossed the festival grounds, the clouds of weed and wood smoke in the air mingled with the odors of stale beer, hot grease, funnel cakes, and meat cooking over butane fires. It was only late afternoon, but a lot of the people around us had been here since the first act took the stage this morning, and they'd had time to put away a lot of beer. Despite that, the atmosphere was laid-back and mostly family friendly.

Now that our performance was over, a wave of exhaustion had settled over me. The adrenaline that had gotten me through it was wearing off, leaving me drained and flagging, and I felt the full weight of what I'd done as thoughts of the audience I'd tried not to look at came rushing back to me.

So when I saw Tanner standing in the beer garden, and he looked right at me and smiled that beautiful, soft smile I'd always loved, what I wanted most in the world was to walk straight into his arms, tuck myself against his chest, and feel surrounded by the security and comfort of him.

I might even have done it. I was already walking faster, my feet automatically taking me straight to him as my mouth curved to meet his smile with one of my own.

Then Arwen appeared beside him to hand him a beer, and he turned his smile toward her. It grew even wider as she leaned in close to lay her hand on his shoulder and speak into his ear.

I'm too late, I realized with a crushing sense of disappointment.

Tanner had moved on after all.

15

TANNER

Andie had arranged to meet up with Wyatt at the beer garden after the show, so the lot of us traipsed over there to wait for him. I didn't know if Lucy would be with him, but I let myself hope. In the past, she hadn't stuck around to hang out with the band after a show, but this was a special occasion. Maybe she'd make an exception this time.

We claimed one of the wooden picnic tables and settled in to wait as distant strains of music drifted over from the three different stages. Ryan had peeled off to go back to the first aid tent, so when Isabella started to get restless I volunteered to take her over to the jungle gym at one end of the fenced-off area to play. After about twenty minutes she got bored and asked for a snack, so I walked her back to the table to let Manny adjudicate her appeals for a funnel cake.

As I was handing her off to her father, I spotted Wyatt heading our way with the rest of his band—including Lucy.

I couldn't control my smile or the way my pulse quickened at the sight of her looking so lovely—but also tired and a little apprehensive. Her gaze tangled with mine, and her face practically broke open with the force of her answering grin.

Just as I was about to raise my hand in greeting, Arwen appeared at my side and handed me a beer. I turned to thank her, and she leaned in to tell me she'd texted Linh, who was at the festival with her girlfriend and was headed over to meet up with us.

When I turned back to Lucy, she wasn't looking at me anymore. Wyatt was giving Andie an exuberant hug, and Lucy had lowered her head, one of her hands plucking at the skirt of that pretty, low-cut dress she wore.

Everyone at our table got up and clustered around the stars of the hour to congratulate them on their triumph. Lucy blushed when Josh complimented her singing, and Wyatt teasingly accused her of stealing the show. Everyone else was hugging her and telling her how great she'd sounded, but when it was finally my turn and I found myself face-to-face with her, I hesitated at the look of...something in her eyes. Embarrassment? Confusion? Disappointment?

Before I could figure it out, it had disappeared, replaced by a false smile. "Hi!" she said, forcing cheer into her voice. "You made it!"

She was fidgeting with her skirt again, her expression strangely brittle, and I hated how small and fragile she looked. So I let my instincts guide me and gathered her in a hug.

At first her body felt as rigid as her smile had looked, and I worried she'd pull away from me. But the next second I felt her sag, not just against me but *into* me, her arms winding around my waist and tightening as she buried her face in my chest.

"Of course I made it," I said, trying hard not to sound absolutely fucking wrecked by how much I'd missed holding her. "I told you I would."

She nodded against my chest, and I felt her let out an uneven breath. "I'm really glad you're here."

While my heart was busy flinging itself against the walls of my rib cage, she pulled out of my arms. Reluctantly, I relinquished the warm comfort of her, digging my fingers into my palms as I breathed in through my nose and out through my mouth.

Lucy cleared her throat, embarrassment peeking through her expression again. "I mean, I'm glad you were able to come see Wyatt's big moment."

"It was a pretty big moment for you too."

"I was just the backup." She ducked her head and waved a dismissive hand, as if she hadn't just done something stupendously impressive.

"You were a lot more than that. You were..." I paused, trying to think of a word better than *amazing*, and she lifted her eyes to mine again. "Transcendent," I decided, although it still didn't quite capture what I'd felt.

Her eyes widened, and I enjoyed watching her freckled cheeks turn pink.

"Lucy! Oh my god!" Arwen threw her arms around Lucy, breathless with excitement. "That! Was! Incredible!"

"Thank you." By the time Arwen released her, Lucy's cheeks had gone from pink to bright red.

"You've been holding out on us." Arwen gave her an affectionate shake. "Who knew we had Lady Gaga working with us all this time?"

Lucy's laugh sounded nervous. "I'm pretty much as far from Lady Gaga as you can get."

Arwen gaped at her in disbelief. "Are you kidding? Your voice? Her voice? They're like totally the same."

"Ummm, I'm not sure—"

"Oh look, here's Linh!" Arwen announced, lifting her arm to wave.

Linh was with a tall woman with shoulder-length platinum hair, and they both attacked Lucy with vigorous hugs. When they were done showering her with praise, Linh introduced her girlfriend, Alexis, to me and Arwen.

Apparently Alexis was friends with Wyatt, because he came running over and caught her in a bone-breaking hug. More greetings and compliments followed, as well as more introductions, since Arwen wanted to be introduced to Wyatt, Matt, and the rest of the band.

A few minutes later, I was seated at one end of our table listening to Arwen, Tyler, and Corey discuss the new head coach of the Texas Longhorns while Lucy chatted with Linh and Alexis way down at the opposite end. Wyatt circled the table with Isabella on his shoulders until Manny bid everyone goodbye and took his exhausted and overstimulated three-year-old home.

Afternoon stretched into evening as the summer sun dipped lower. Multiple parties were sent out to acquire various festival foods, and empty food containers, water bottles, and drink cups piled up in the middle of the table as dusk turned to dark around us.

Lucy wasn't usually much of a drinker, but I couldn't help noticing she was drinking more than usual tonight. I tried not to stare down the table at her, but my gaze kept drifting that way of its own volition. She seemed to be enjoying herself, at least. Whatever had caused the discomfort I'd noticed earlier appeared to have passed.

Eventually, Josh and Mia headed out, followed not long after by Linh and Alexis, who were meeting up with some other friends to check out a band playing on the main stage. Lucy scooted down to talk to Andie, and when Arwen got up to search out a porta-potty, Wyatt slid over next to me.

"What are you doing?" he asked, pinning me with a frown. He'd been drinking at a slow, steady pace for hours and had that overly earnest but slightly unfocused look that drunk people got when they were trying to be serious.

"I'm trying to decide if it's worth getting up to go get a frozen banana."

"No." He shook his head impatiently. "I'm talking about the fact that you're here with this gorgeous woman who's clearly into you, yet every time I look at you, you're staring at your ex."

I darted an uneasy look in Lucy's direction to make sure she hadn't overheard Wyatt. "I'm not here with Arwen. We just ran into each other, that's all."

"But you *could* be with her. You totally didn't need me to set you up when you've got Arwen on deck just waiting for a go sign."

"I'm not attracted to Arwen."

"Why not? Have you seen her? Also, her name is *Arwen*, dude. Why aren't you falling all over yourself to date her?"

I shrugged. "She's nice, but she doesn't do it for me. Also we work together. It's a bad idea."

Wyatt draped a heavy arm around my shoulders, pulling me closer as he lowered his voice. "As bad an idea as getting back with the ex who completely fucked you up?"

"Who says I'm getting back with her?"

"Are you?"

I pulled away from him, tired of being up close and personal with his beer breath. "It's not up to me, is it?"

Andie's chin came to rest on Wyatt's shoulder. "I'm hot and I want to go home," she pouted.

"Yeah, you are." He turned his head to catch her lips as he cupped her face with his hand.

I rolled my eyes as I took a sip of the warm beer I'd been

nursing for the last hour. "There are children present. Don't make me turn the fire extinguisher on you two."

"Come on, let's roll." Andie winked at me as she tugged Wyatt to his feet.

Unlike him, she'd stopped drinking several hours ago, so I figured she was okay to drive him home. While Wyatt was bidding goodbye to everyone, Andie stooped to hug Lucy and the two of them engaged in a whispered conversation. Lucy shook her head at whatever Andie had said to her, which caused Andie to frown and shake her head back.

Curious.

Wyatt and Andie finally took off just as Arwen was coming back, and she waved goodbye to them before sliding in next to me again. Tyler had moved over to the next table to chat up some girl he'd been flirting with, which left just me, Arwen, Lucy, Matt, and Corey. If it hadn't been for Lucy, I would have bailed hours ago. But as long as she was still here I wasn't about to pass up a chance to be near her.

At least she was sitting across from me now, close enough to talk to for the first time in hours. I listened as she and Arwen gave Matt and Corey marketing tips for promoting the band on social media, impressed by how knowledgeable they both were. I never even would have considered half the stuff they were able to suggest off the top of their heads, which showed how much I still had to learn about my new job.

Arwen gamely volunteered her skills to design a new logo and some graphics for the band. When Matt tried to wheedle Lucy into managing their social media accounts for them, I saw her back stiffen, and it set off my protective instincts. Her brother had already pressured her into performing with them despite her dislike of the spotlight, and this felt like taking further advantage of her generous nature. It was one thing to design a few one-time graphics, but managing social media accounts was an ongoing job that would eat up a lot of her free time.

"If you want her to do hours of work for you every week, maybe you should pay her for her professional services," I suggested.

"Yeah, right," Matt said, laughing off the idea, which only annoyed me more.

Lucy's eyes met mine with a mix of surprise and gratitude before she straightened her shoulders and cut a look at her brother. "You're already getting my expert advice for free. If you want more than that, I'll send you my rate card and we can negotiate an hourly engagement." I mentally cheered her on as she smiled thinly at her brother. "I'll even give you a five percent friends and family discount."

"You know we can't afford to pay you." Matt slung his arm around her and gave her shoulder a squeeze. "I just thought you'd want to do it as a favor for your favorite little brother." His voice was easy and coaxing, like someone who was used to getting whatever he wanted.

"Pretty big favor," I muttered under my breath, still feeling salty.

"How about we work out a barter arrangement?" Lucy offered, pushing her brother's arm off her. "For every hour I spend working for you, you spend an hour cleaning up around the house."

Matt snorted like she'd made a joke, and Lucy's posture got even more rigid. I bit down on the reflex to make another comment as my fingers squeezed my beer cup hard enough to make the plastic crackle.

"I'm hungry," Corey said, elbowing Matt. "I'm gonna go get some pizza. You wanna come?"

"Yeah." Matt let go of Lucy and swung his legs over the bench, wavering a little as he got to his feet. "Let's go."

I gave his retreating back a hard stare as I watched him weave drunkenly through the crowd. "Is he always like that?"

"Like what?" Lucy asked.

"Selfish and inconsiderate of your time."

Her jaw clenched, reminding me that was her brother I'd just insulted. "Our mother spoiled him. It's not really his fault."

I was pretty sure some of it was his fault. It wasn't like the guy didn't have free will. But I kept my opinion to myself rather than risk offending her further.

"You really don't have to design a logo for them," Lucy told Arwen. "Don't feel obligated or anything."

"I don't mind." Arwen shrugged. "It'll be fun. It's not like it's that much work, and it'll make a nice addition to my portfolio. Maybe they'll hit it big one day and my logo will be on all their merch."

"All the more reason not to do it for free." Lucy's voice held a note of warning. "At least make them sign a contract agreeing to pay you a license fee for any merch they sell using your designs."

"I guess." Arwen didn't sound entirely convinced. "I wouldn't even know how to write up something like that."

"I can help you," Lucy said, taking a drink of her beer. "We'll go online and find a template you can base it on."

"Did you and Matt drive here together?" I asked her, wondering how she planned to get home. She didn't seem all that drunk, but she'd still been drinking too much to drive, and Matt had definitely been drinking too much to drive.

"We caught the shuttle bus," she said. "I didn't want to get stuck as the designated driver again."

"Me too!" Arwen raised her beer, and Lucy mirrored the gesture before tipping her cup back again.

"I've got my car," I said. "I can give you a ride home whenever you're ready to go. Both of you," I added with a quick glance at Arwen. I couldn't exactly leave her here alone, even if I'd prefer to have Lucy to myself.

Lucy shook her head as she set her beer down. "I don't want to impose."

"It's not an imposition."

"I'll be fine."

"It's really no trouble. I don't mind."

She looked at me for a long moment, her expression unreadable. "I'd rather take the shuttle, but thank you for the offer."

I couldn't decide if she was just being stubborn or if she was pissed at me for calling her brother selfish. Either way, I couldn't force her to accept a ride from me if she didn't want one.

Across the beer garden, I saw Matt and Corey coming back toward our table already, both of them empty-handed. Matt had his arm slung around Corey's shoulders and was leaning on him like he was having trouble walking. At first I thought he was a lot drunker than I'd realized, then I noticed he was walking with a pronounced limp rather than an intoxicated stagger.

Lucy turned to see what I was looking at, and jumped to her feet as they drew near. "What happened?"

"I think I fucked up my foot." Matt's face was pale and creased with pain.

"How?" Lucy asked as Corey lowered him onto the bench.

"You know those big rocks with the festival sign on top where people always take selfies? I climbed up there so Corey could take my picture, and when I jumped down something in my ankle went *crunch*. It really hurts bad, Luce. I think it might be broken."

"Let's get your shoe off." Lucy knelt in front of him, and he sucked in a pained breath when she carefully eased his tennis shoe off.

"Duuuude," Corey said when she'd managed to get Matt's

sock off. His ankle was already turning purple and starting to swell.

"We should take him to the first aid station." I bent down to lend Matt my shoulder and helped him upright as Corey took his other side. "Ryan will know what to do for him."

16

TANNER

The first aid station was a bit of a trek. Tyler was nowhere to be found, so the four of us escorted Matt on his slow hop to the tent that had been set up next to a parked ambulance by the main festival entrance. I was relieved to see Ryan was still on shift, sitting in a folding chair chatting with a few other EMTs. When he saw us coming, he hauled himself to his feet.

"What happened?" he asked, ducking under the awning of the tent as he came out to meet us.

"Matt hurt his ankle," I explained. "It's pretty badly swollen."

"Hey there, Matt," Ryan said, slipping into his genial, reassuring EMT voice. "Think you can make it over to that cot for me?"

Lucy and Arwen trailed behind us as we guided Matt through the tent, and Ryan helped stabilize his ankle as he lifted it onto the cot.

"How'd you hurt your ankle, Matt?"

While Matt repeated the story about jumping off the rock, Ryan rolled his pants leg up and examined him from his knee to his toes.

"Show me exactly where it hurts."

Matt pointed to the outside of his ankle where it was turning purple. "Hurts like a motherfucker."

"I'll bet. Can you wiggle your toes for me? Good. That's great." Ryan took Matt's pulse, wrote it down on a clipboard, and slipped a blood pressure cuff on him as he questioned him about his medical history and recent drug and alcohol consumption.

"You're taking his vitals," Lucy said anxiously beside me. "Does that mean you're worried it's something serious?"

"Not at all." Ryan gave her a gentle smile as he made a note of Matt's blood pressure. "It's just standard procedure. The bosses like us to check all the boxes on the form." He caught my eye and subtly inclined his head toward the tent's entrance.

"Why don't we wait outside so Ryan's got room to work without us standing on top of him?" I suggested, taking his cue. The tent wasn't exactly spacious for someone Ryan's size, and with four extra people hovering around, it was downright cramped.

Arwen and Corey looked relieved to get out of there, but Lucy seemed torn. Reluctantly, she let me guide her outside, where she paced back and forth, craning her neck to see what was happening with Matt inside the tent.

"He's in good hands," I told her. "The best." My fingers twitched with the impulse to offer her physical comfort, but I wasn't convinced she'd welcome it from me right now.

"I know. It's lucky Ryan's here." She was trying her best to seem calm, but I could tell it was costing her. Someone she loved was hurt, and there was nothing she could do to help.

"It's hard to see someone you care about in pain." I knew that feeling far too well. I remembered it from when my mom was sick. The initial shock of it was the worst. Seeing frailty in someone whose strength you took for granted was its own kind of trauma.

Lucy's eyes met mine, softening with a look of understanding that told me she'd guessed what I was thinking about.

"Matt's going to be fine." I knew she knew that, but I thought maybe it would help to hear someone say it out loud.

"I know." Her head bobbed in a jerky nod. "I know he is. It's just..." She looked up at me, her expression a mixture of worry and chagrin. "It's his bass drum foot."

I hadn't thought about that, how this injury might affect his ability to play. It was particularly unlucky coming on the heels of today's success, which they were all hoping would open new doors for them. It'd be pretty hard to walk through those newly opened doors with their drummer out of commission.

She folded her arms and hugged herself. "It's probably silly to be thinking about that right now."

"It's not silly at all. I'll bet that's what Matt's thinking about too."

"I'm not so sure about that." She was looking into the tent again at Matt, who was ashen and flinching as Ryan palpated his ankle. "But I'm sure it'll occur to him soon."

I glanced behind us, where Arwen and Corey had retreated to a nearby bench and were sitting with their heads together, deep in conversation. Hard to know if Corey had considered what this might mean for the band's immediate future. Maybe when he sobered up a little. I considered texting Wyatt, but decided there was no point yet. It wasn't as if he could do anything right now. Might as well let him enjoy the rest of his night.

Eventually, Ryan came out to give us his assessment of Matt's ankle. Corey came over to hear the news with Arwen trailing behind him, but it was Lucy who Ryan addressed himself to. He towered over her like a gentle giant, his head bent and his shoulders hunched in an attempt to make himself look smaller and less intimidating.

"The good news is there's no discernable deformity indicating a dislocation or fracture."

Beside me, I heard Lucy breathe out in relief.

"It looks like a grade two sprain," Ryan continued. "Possibly a partial tear of the anterior talofibular ligament. But I think he should get an X-ray to completely rule out a fracture."

"Okay." She had the same intent look she got in our weekly team meetings when she was absorbing Byron's directives and mentally rearranging her to-do list.

"I'm treating the swelling with cold packs right now. I want to keep Matt's ankle iced and elevated for another ten minutes, then I'll wrap it in a compression bandage and immobilize it with a temporary splint. After that he'll need someone to drive him to the ER for that X-ray."

"We took the shuttle," Lucy said fretfully. "I don't have a car here."

"I've got my car," I offered. "I'll drive him."

Ryan gave me a long look. "Have you been drinking?"

I met his gaze levelly, knowing not to take his questioning personally. "I've had three beers over the last six hours. You can give me a breathalyzer if you want."

He shook his head, giving me a crooked grin. "If you say you're good, I trust you."

A woman shouldered past us supporting a man who was flushed and staggering, and one of the other EMTs got up to assist them.

Ryan ran a hand through his red hair as he watched his colleague assist the man to a chair. "We're lucky the cloud cover's helped keep things pretty quiet here today. We had a lot of dehydration and heat-related conditions yesterday. But as the night wears on, we'll get a lot more alcohol poisoning and bad drug reactions." The man started vomiting into a plastic bag the EMT had grabbed, and Ryan turned back to us with an apologetic look. "I'll get you on your way as soon as I can."

EVERYONE WAS quiet on the ride to the hospital. Arwen sat in the front next to me, with Lucy and Corey squeezed into the back seat of my Prius with Matt. In the ER waiting room, we took up a whole row of molded plastic chairs across from a man who appeared to be asleep and a woman trying to comfort a fussing baby.

Corey had texted Tyler over an hour ago to let him know what had happened, and he finally heard back from him while we were sitting in the ER. Turned out he'd gone off with the girl at the next table to watch the band playing on the main stage. Corey had texted Wyatt as well, but he still hadn't replied. Given how much drinking he'd done, I guessed he was probably asleep by now and wouldn't see Corey's text until morning.

Eventually the woman with the baby was called into the back, and a man with a bloody towel wrapped around his hand took her place. Arwen and Corey had a hushed conversation before sheepishly announcing they were going to share a Lyft home.

"Unless there's something we can do to help," Corey said. "But it seems like you've got all the help you need."

"Sure, whatever," Matt grunted, barely looking up. His discomfort seemed to have increased as he'd sobered up over the last hour.

"We're fine," Lucy told them. "Thank you though."

Not too long after they left, Matt was finally called back.

"You two can come with him," the nurse said as she helped him into a wheelchair.

I gave Lucy a questioning look, unsure if she wanted me to go back with them or stay here and wait.

She gave me a shy nod. "Come with us," she said, her voice rough with exhaustion. "Please."

We were put in a small exam room separated from the corridor by a long curtain. Lucy and I each took one of the two small armchairs while Matt stretched out on the gurney. The nurse ran him through a series of questions and took his vitals again before leaving us alone with a promise the doctor would be in soon.

"I'm sorry we messed up your evening," Lucy said to me while we waited.

"You didn't."

She gestured around us at the ER exam room. "Don't tell me this is where you hoped you'd end up tonight."

I laughed quietly. "Okay, maybe a trip to the ER isn't one of my top ten ways to spend a Saturday night, but I don't mind being able to help."

Her smile faded a little. "But Arwen went home."

"So?"

"So we ruined your date—or whatever."

"Not a date," I said firmly. "I only ran into her by chance. We both came separately to see you."

Lucy's expression perked up enough to make the dull gray exam room seem brighter, and I wondered what would happen if I told her I still had feelings for her? Would she be glad to hear it?

Matt let out a sinus-rattling snore from the gurney, reminding me we weren't alone. How inconvenient.

Deciding this wasn't the best time or place for a romantic confession, I changed the subject. "Should you call your mom to let her know what's happened?"

Lucy glanced over at Matt, whose snoring had dimmed to a

dull roar, and I watched her expression transform into something fierce and embittered. "No, definitely not." The repressed anger in her voice took me by surprise. It seemed to take her by surprise too, because she blinked, her expression quickly shifting to regret. "I mean there's no point in bothering her yet," she amended. "I don't want to worry her unnecessarily when there's nothing she can do to help."

For the first time, it occurred to me that Lucy had hardly ever spoken about her mother. I knew she and Matt both lived at home, but beyond that one innocuous fact I knew next to nothing about her home life. Only now did I consider there might be a reason for that.

"Do you want to talk about it?" I offered quietly.

She looked down at her lap, carefully rearranging and smoothing her skirt, and shook her head. "It's nothing."

"It doesn't seem like nothing."

She didn't speak for a while. As I watched her brush invisible specks of lint off her dress, I wished I was sitting next to her so I could hold her hand, instead of all the way across the room.

"Our mom isn't..." She hesitated, and I held my breath, waiting for her to finish the sentence. "She's not well."

"I didn't know that. I'm sorry."

Lucy frowned and shook her head. "It's not—she's not sick or anything. She's just not strong. Not emotionally strong, I mean." Her gaze darted to Matt, checking that he was still asleep before she continued. "After our father left, she had a really hard time. She'd leaned on him for so much, she was completely lost without him. She sort of shut down for a while, and I had to take care of her and Matt and Becca."

"How old were you?"

"Twelve."

My heart squeezed painfully. "That's the same age I was when my mother died."

Lucy's eyes were soft with sympathy when they lifted to mine. "What happened to you, losing your mother, was so much worse. It doesn't compare."

"Your family broke," I said quietly. "One day you were a kid with two parents to look after you and nothing but kid-cares to worry you, and the next you were a twelve-year-old trying to pick up the pieces after your family fell apart." My voice was rough, both with my own painful memories, and at the thought of what Lucy must have gone through.

"I guess," she mumbled.

"When you were taking care of your mother and brother and sister, who took care of you?"

"I did." She gave a small, heartbreaking shrug. "I took care of all of us."

I swallowed thickly, overwhelmed with sadness for Lucy's lost childhood as I imagined her trying to act as caretaker to two siblings and a parent when she should have been going to slumber parties and looking forward to the next Harry Potter book. At least I'd had a father who was present enough to see to my physical well-being, and a series of housekeepers who'd kept us in regular meals and clean clothes. I'd had Ryan, who'd tried his best to be there for us, and Manny when he was home from college, and Wyatt when he was around. I'd had a lot more advantages than responsibilities—unlike Lucy.

"That must have been hard for you."

"We managed," she said, downplaying her formative childhood trauma with a familiar note of determined buoyancy.

I understood now where she'd learned her *just keep smiling* approach to adversity. Because if twelve-year-old Lucy had let herself stop managing long enough to admit she was struggling, her whole family would have fallen apart.

"Anyway, our mom got better, eventually." More false lightness and another small shrug accompanied this statement. She was still trying to act like none of this was a big deal, but she'd let her mask slip enough for me to see the truth. "But she's still fragile and easily distressed. So it's better not to involve her in something like this until it's handled. It doesn't do any good for her to know."

Which told me Lucy was still playing parent and shouldering more than her share of responsibility in the family. She'd probably been doing it this whole time, through high school, college, and all of her twenties. That was why she still lived at home. Because she was needed there. And she'd never said a single word about it the whole time we'd been dating.

That hurt a little. It served as a stark reminder that we hadn't had the relationship I'd thought we did. She'd never opened herself up to me, and I hadn't even noticed. What kind of a boyfriend missed something like that?

"Matt's lucky to have you," I said. "Your mother is too."

"Sure." It gusted out of her on a shaky breath, almost more of a sound than a word, and it cracked my heart into pieces.

I was on the verge of getting up and—I didn't know for sure, kneeling in front of her maybe or pulling her to her feet and into my arms, *something* to offer comfort to her—when the curtain was yanked back and Josie's boyfriend, Carter, stepped into the room.

"Matt Dillard?" he said, staring at his chart before he took in the three of us. His professional detachment shifted to surprise at the sight of me. "Tanner? What are you doing here?"

I tipped my chin in greeting. "I drove Matt and his sister Lucy here after Matt busted his ankle at the folk festival. Matt's the drummer in Wyatt's band, and Lucy and I work together."

Carter looked from me to Lucy. "You work for Josie?"

"That's right," she said, smiling in confusion.

He stepped forward to shake her hand. "I'm Dr. Bayliss. Nice to meet you, Lucy."

"Carter is Josie's boyfriend," I explained.

"Ah." Lucy nodded. "Got it."

"I'm going to assume that's Matt on the gurney with the bum ankle," Carter said, swiping through his chart again.

"That's right." Lucy reached over and gave her brother a gentle shake. "Matt, wake up. The doctor's here."

Matt opened one sleepy eye and raised his hand in a half-hearted greeting. "Yo."

Carter reintroduced himself and shook his hand. "I hear you're a drummer, Matt."

"I am, yeah."

"Who's your favorite drummer?" Carter asked. "Mine's Animal from Dr. Teeth and the Electric Mayhem."

"The muppet?" Matt winced as Carter started to remove the splint on his ankle.

"That's right. I just love his energy. But I suppose you think you can name someone better. Don't tell me, let me guess. Stewart Copeland? Or am I dating myself too much? It's probably Dave Grohl, right?"

Carter kept up a steady stream of banter with Matt, distracting him while he unwrapped the compression bandage and examined his ankle. I was impressed by his friendly and easygoing bedside manner. I'd never seen him in doctor mode before, having only ever encountered him at family functions where he'd mostly seemed to be biding his time until Josie decided they could leave.

"You did a real number on that ankle, all right," Carter declared when he'd finished his examination. "I don't think it's fractured, but I'm going to order an X-ray to make sure. In the meantime, I'll have the nurse bring you some painkillers. You can thank me later."

"And after that I'll be able to go home?" Matt asked.

Carter nodded. "Assuming the X-ray doesn't turn up

anything gnarly, we'll send you home with a boot and a referral to an orthopedic surgeon for follow-up."

"A surgeon?" Lucy said anxiously. "He's going to need surgery?"

"Not necessarily. Oftentimes sprains like this heal on their own just fine, but you'll want to have the ortho take a look at it and decide the best course of treatment."

Carter went on to explain all the different possible treatment options, which ranged from a few weeks in an orthopedic boot to physical therapy to surgery, and he further explained that the ortho might want to send Matt for an MRI and wait to see how his ankle was healing before he made the call about surgery. As he talked, I watched Lucy sink lower in her chair, her fingers plucking tensely at her skirt.

"Any other questions for me?" Carter asked. "Anything else I can do you for you before I go rustle up someone to wheel you to radiology?" When Matt and Lucy shook their heads, he gave them both a warm smile. "All right. I'll put a rush on it, so hopefully you won't have too long to wait."

Carter was as good as his word, because it was only a few minutes later that a nurse came in with a dose of painkillers for Matt, and ten minutes after that an orderly showed up with a wheelchair to take Matt to radiology.

As soon as we were alone, Lucy got up and started fussing with the room. First she straightened the sheet on the gurney and fluffed the pillow, arranging and rearranging everything several times until she was satisfied. Then she moved on to organizing the boxes of medical gloves in ascending order—small, medium, large, extra-large. After that, she seemed to run out of things to do and sank back into her chair begrudgingly. But she was all nervous energy, twisting her hands in her lap, glancing up every time footsteps went by in the hall, and shifting in her seat like she couldn't get comfortable.

After a few minutes she got up again, pacing restlessly around the room, which didn't allow more than a few steps back and forth. I was getting dizzy just watching her.

"Do you want to go take a walk?" I suggested, thinking a change of scenery might do her good. "I can wait here if you want to get some air or something."

"No, I'm fine," she insisted, the first words she'd spoken in ten minutes.

I watched her, noticing how her hands trembled as they smoothed her skirt, and how she avoided making eye contact with me. Something had upset her, and I wanted to know what it was.

I stood up and put myself in her path on her next circuit around the room. "Lucy."

She stilled in front of me without looking up. "Yes?"

"Tell me what's wrong."

"Nothing."

"You don't have to pretend everything's fine around me. You can tell me what's on your mind. Whatever it is."

Huffing out an unsteady breath, she pushed her hair behind her ear. "I'm worried about Matt. That's all."

"Okay." I doubted that was all, but I waited to see if she'd volunteer anything more.

"It's just..." Her jaw clenched as she shook her head. "He's going to need to stay off his foot for god knows how long, which means he'll need help around the house. And if he needs surgery, he'll need even more help and need to stay off his foot even longer." She was getting more tense by the second as she anticipated the challenges that lay ahead and the logistics of Matt's care. "And if he does need surgery, I don't know how we're going to pay for it. The deductible with his insurance is so much, and I'm sure MRIs aren't cheap, and the physical therapy, that's even more money, and he'll need someone to drive him to every appointment and—"

"Hey." I laid my hands on her shoulders, which sagged at my touch. "It's going to be okay."

"How? Do you know how? Because I don't." I couldn't see her face, but the tremor in her voice told me she was close to tears.

My hands squeezed her shoulders, trying to knead some of the tension away. "We'll figure it out. One way or another."

"*I'll* figure it out, you mean. Because I'm the one who always has to figure everything out on my own, and I'm just so tired of it. I'm so tired all the time, and I don't know what to do." Her voice broke on the last sentence, and without forethought I pulled her to my chest. She collapsed against me, and I stroked a soothing hand down her back.

"You don't have to do it alone," I told her as she clutched at me. "I'll help you figure it all out. I'm sure Wyatt would be willing to pitch in, and Corey and Tyler. And I'll bet Linh and Arwen would be glad to help too, if you asked them."

"I guess," she mumbled against my chest.

"We'll divide up the responsibilities between all of us so Matt has everything he needs. You don't have to do it all by yourself."

A sniffle. "Really?"

"Really." I bent my head and brushed my lips against her hair. "As for the money, we can start a GoFundMe. The band's got enough fans now that I'll bet you'd have no trouble raising what you need to cover Matt's medical care. Shiny Heathens could even play a benefit concert or something."

"That's...a really good idea, actually."

"Since you're so sad right now, I'll pretend I'm not insulted by the note of surprise in your voice."

She huffed out a breath that sounded amused, and when she

tipped her face up to me she was smiling through her tears. "You know that's not what I meant. You have good ideas all the time."

Ignoring the catch of my heart, I tried to keep my expression stern. "I'm glad you think so. Does that mean you'll let me help you?"

Her smile dimmed into uncertainty. "You don't have to do that. None of this is your responsibility."

"I don't need you to tell me that. I know perfectly well what my responsibilities are, and I'm capable of deciding how I choose to spend my own time. Okay?"

She let out an exaggerated sigh and dropped her forehead against my chest. "Fine. I guess."

"You don't have to figure everything out tonight. Maybe a lot of it won't be necessary. We don't know that Matt will need surgery or physical therapy yet. But if he does, there are people you can lean on for help." Cautiously, I took her face in my hands and tilted it up so I could look into her eyes. "Like me."

"Tanner..." she whispered, her fingers digging into my waist.

I held myself very, very still. So still my heart might have stopped beating and the blood ceased to move through my veins. I was painfully, acutely conscious of every place our bodies touched, the softness of her curves, and the heat of her skin.

"Why are you being so nice to me?" Her face was flushed and damp with tears, yet still the most beautiful thing I'd ever seen.

I stroked my thumb over her cheek, so tenderly there'd be no way for her to mistake my meaning. "You already know why."

Because I love you.

The way her eyes widened, I knew she understood.

I braced myself, waiting for her to pull away.

But she didn't.

She stayed right there in my arms, and her eyes stayed locked onto mine, wide-open and unblinking.

I felt like a swimmer who'd drifted so far out to sea I'd lost sight of land. My head was spinning, and when I reached for something to say, all I could find were borrowed words. "My affections and wishes are unchanged, but one word from you will silence me on this subject forever."

I nearly fainted dead away in Tanner's arms.

The man had just quoted Mr. Darcy at me.

Talk about swoonsville. But it wasn't the mere fact that Tanner had pulled a situationally appropriate Jane Austen quote out of his back pocket that had my heart beating a hundred miles an hour. It was what those words meant.

He still wanted me. He still *loved* me.

That second chance I'd been hoping for? It was right here, looking into my face expectantly. Which reminded me that I should probably get over my shock and say something before Tanner decided he'd made a mistake and changed his mind.

But what could you say to a line like that? Nothing my own head could conjure seemed adequate to the moment.

"Tanner, I—"

Can't remember Lizzie's response, dang it.

Why hadn't I read *Pride and Prejudice* more recently? Then I could have quoted the perfect answer back to him.

Before I could think of a way to finish the sentence I'd left hanging in the air, I heard Matt's voice in the hall outside, joking with the orderly. Tanner dropped his hands from my face and stepped back, putting a safe, respectful distance between us just before the curtain opened on us.

Dammit. I didn't want him to be respectful. I wanted him to kiss me until I saw stars. But now that my brother was back in the room, the window of opportunity for kissing had most definitely closed.

The painkiller the doctor prescribed for Matt had put him in a talkative mood—although not an observant one. As I went to get a tissue and blow my nose, he didn't notice that I'd been crying or that Tanner had a face-shaped damp spot on the front of his T-shirt. Instead, my brother lounged comfortably on the gurney and kept up a near-constant stream of chatter as he searched on his phone for reviews of today's Shiny Heathens show.

Meanwhile, Tanner had retreated into silence, and I couldn't say I blamed him. I'd left him cruelly hanging without an answer. I could sense his uneasiness, but didn't know how to finish our interrupted conversation with Matt sprawled on the gurney between us, tapping out rhythms on his leg.

I debated going ahead and saying what I needed to say to Tanner anyway, my brother be damned. Who cared what Matt thought, anyway? The awkwardness might be worth it to put Tanner out of his misery.

Then I realized, watching Matt stare at his phone, that I had other ways to communicate with Tanner at my disposal.

Retrieving my own phone from my purse, I opened a new text message to Tanner and composed a response to him.

Lucy: What I was about to say before we were interrupted is that I don't want you to be silent on that particular subject because I miss you desperately and I'd very much like to continue our conversation at the first available opportunity.

I stared at it for a long time, making sure it said what I wanted it to in the best way I could think of to say it. Truthfully, I was exhausted and emotionally drained, and my creative abilities were not at their best. Doubtless I could have been pithier and more romantic on another occasion, but that occasion was not tonight. It was as good as it was going to get, so I hoped for the best and hit send.

A few seconds later, Tanner shifted in his seat to slide his phone out of his back pocket. I watched him closely as he read the message. His head was bent to hide his expression from me, and my stomach knotted itself up in agony.

He looked up and his smile broke open, so sweet and so impossibly wide it felt like the sun had just risen on a new day even though we were sitting in a windowless room at eleven o'clock at night.

My cheeks ached from smiling back at him, and I reached up to press my palm to my face, which was warm and no doubt bright red and probably all splotchy to boot.

However awful I might look, Tanner didn't appear to mind, because he couldn't seem to take his eyes off my face. We sat there mooning goofily at each other for a while before I bent my head again to type another text.

Lucy: You have bewitched me, body and soul.

My fingers trembled a little as I remembered that the second half of that line was Darcy's stuttering "I love you." Would Tanner think the "I love you" was implied?

Was it? I honestly wasn't in any sort of state to know my own mind right now. That kind of soul searching and introspection would have to wait for another day.

Before I could second-guess myself further, I sent the text as it was.

Lifting my head, I watched as the message popped up on his phone. He stared at it for it a really, really long time—long enough that I started to panic a little—before he finally typed a response.

> **Tanner**: That's from the movie not the book.
> **Lucy**: I know that, Mr. English major. I was going to answer with Lizzie's response to Darcy, but I'm tired and I couldn't remember it.
> **Tanner**: Elizabeth's answer is paraphrased in the text rather than written as dialogue. Her exact words are left to your imagination.

I shook my head, smiling as I typed a reply.

> **Lucy**: I should know better than to get in a literary quote competition with you.
> **Tanner**: You pierce my soul.
> **Lucy**: That's from a different book!
> **Tanner**: But it's true nonetheless.

My heart nearly exploded in my chest. First Darcy, now Wentworth. Was there no limit to the man's perfection?

————

IT WAS another hour before we were able to take Matt home. His X-ray showed no evidence of a fracture, thank god, so he was fitted with a boot and instructed to stay off his foot as much as possible until he saw the orthopedic surgeon. I tried not to think about how much all this would cost—and how much it would set back my plan to move out of my mother's house. I'd probably need to use some of the savings I'd hoarded. Maybe all of it.

But like Tanner had said, maybe Matt wouldn't need surgery or physical therapy. I tried to hope for the best, even though hope didn't come naturally to me. Maybe I'd just need to pay for the ER bill and the appointment with the ortho, and maybe the crappy health insurance I'd insisted Matt get would cover a decent amount of it. But even if it didn't, I felt better knowing I'd have Tanner in my corner. He might not be able to make my problems go away, but he'd be there for moral support and to lend a hand if I needed it.

Thinking about Tanner made me giddy. I still couldn't quite believe he wanted me back. Of course, we'd yet to actually talk about it out loud, and I had no idea when we'd be able to do that. But we would. At some point. For the first time, I felt like things might really be okay between us—for an as yet undefined value of okay.

My mood was pretty great until we got Matt settled in the car and Tanner asked for directions to our house.

He'd never been there before, because I'd done everything in my power to keep him away. But there was no avoiding it now. With Matt in need of assistance, I wouldn't be able to stop Tanner from helping him inside.

It was irrational, perhaps, but I couldn't help feeling shame about the state of our house. I'd always been self-conscious about it in a way Matt wasn't. He'd had no problem inviting friends over in the past. Shiny Heathens had even used our garage for practice back in high school. These days Matt didn't tend to bring people around much, but that was more because he preferred to spend his time elsewhere and had better options now that so many of his friends had their own places.

I, on the other hand, hadn't invited a single friend over to our house since our father left. I'd never had sleepovers or movie marathons or boys come pick me up for a date. To be honest, I hadn't had many close friends or dates in high school. I'd been too busy trying to stay on top of my schoolwork, help my mother around the house, and keep an eye on my brother and sister. What friends I'd had mostly drifted away, and I didn't make any effort to stop them. It was the same through college. Living at home made it difficult to develop close friendships.

Even Linh and Alexis, my two closest friends, had never seen my house. When we got together, I always went to their place or arranged to meet them somewhere else. I'd make an excuse about not wanting to disturb my mother or needing to get away from my annoying brother, which was a version of the truth, just not the whole picture. They didn't know the full extent of my mother's eccentricities, my brother's oblivious unhelpfulness, or my own shame over all of it.

A cold pit of dread opened in my stomach as Tanner drove toward our house. I tried to tell myself it wasn't that big a deal. His brother Wyatt had been there before, after all.

Except Wyatt was nothing like Tanner. They might come from the same wealthy family, but Wyatt had spent his twenties working odd jobs, living in a dumpy apartment, and being almost as much of a slacker as Matt. Unlike Tanner, who kept his car spotless, wore ironed dress shirts to the office every day, and owned an incredibly nice house. Just thinking about Tanner's immaculate kitchen made me feel sick to my stomach.

Especially when he parked in front of my mother's house, and I looked out the window at our broken gutters, grimy trim, and overgrown front yard. If Tanner noticed any of it, he gave no sign as he patiently helped Matt out of the car and up the front walk. But once I had the door open and we'd guided Matt past the entryway, I saw Tanner's gaze travel around the living room, taking in the worn carpet, the sticky coffee table covered with dirty dishes, the water stains darkening the ceiling and part of one wall. As he looked at my house, I saw it all through his eyes, and it felt even worse than I'd thought it would.

He didn't say anything, of course, or let his expression betray any reaction. He would never. Tanner was far too polite for that. But I could imagine what he must be thinking. How could he not, with all his nice things and fastidious habits? Our house had to be distasteful to him, even if he was doing an excellent job hiding it.

Then things went from bad to worse, because I heard my mother's bedroom door open.

I'd hoped she'd be asleep, and we'd be able to get Matt to his room and Tanner on his way without waking her. No such luck.

"Matt?" My mother emerged from the back of the house wearing a pink satin robe, silk headscarf, and rose gold high-heeled mules. "You're home early. I'd thought you'd be out celebrating after your big triumph." When she saw Tanner she stopped, pressing a self-conscious hand to her makeup-free face. "Oh! I didn't know you'd brought a friend home. You'll have to excuse my frightful appearance."

"It's only Wyatt's brother Tanner," Matt said.

Our mother beamed her finest beauty queen smile at Tanner as she glided across the room toward him. "Another one of the King boys! I should have known by looking at you, you're all so handsome." Instead of shaking his hand like a normal person, she took it in both of hers and stroked her fingers over his knuckles. "It's such a pleasure to meet you, Tanner," she cooed, batting her eyelashes as he shifted uncomfortably.

This was yet another reason I'd never brought Tanner or anyone else I'd dated home to meet my mother. She insisted on flirting with every man she met, regardless of age, relationship, or appropriateness. I honestly didn't think she could help it. It was like she'd never learned to relate to men in any other way than by adopting this bizarrely coquettish behavior. I assumed it was something she'd picked up in her days as a beauty queen and singer that she'd never managed to unlearn.

But god, how I wished she had. It was even more embarrassing than the state of the house. The two things together were a humiliation from which I might never recover.

To my abject horror—and Tanner's—my mother was now caressing his forearm and complimenting the smoothness of his skin.

Please kill me.

"Tanner and I work together," I said in the futile hope she'd have the good grace to stand down in front of one of my coworkers. I felt like I was having an embolism. Was that the thing that made you smell toast? Because I was definitely smelling burnt toast.

Or burnt something.

"Mama, is something burning?" I asked, looking around in alarm.

The question distracted my mother enough that Tanner was able to extract himself from her clutches, although he nearly tripped over a pair of Matt's shoes in his haste to back away from her.

She looked around, pursing her lips in bemusement. "Oh right," she said, snapping her fingers. "I was making cheese toast earlier. I forgot."

"How long ago?" I asked as she drifted toward the kitchen.

"Oh goodness, I don't even remember." She pulled open the oven and made a face at the cloud of smoke that poured out. "Well, that's no good now. Pity."

Tanner was looking at me with a slightly alarmed expression, and I offered him an apologetic smile.

"You probably need to be going now," I said desperately,

hoping he'd take the hint. "Thank you so much for everything, but I think we can manage from here on our own."

He frowned in confusion and opened his mouth to reply, but before he could say anything my mother let out an ear-piercing screech.

"Matthew, what happened to your *foot*?"

My brother had flopped down on the couch and stretched out lengthwise with his booted foot conspicuously propped up on the armrest, causing our mother to notice it for the first time. I'd been hoping to avoid this moment until Tanner was safely away, but yet again my hopes were disappointed.

She rushed in from the kitchen and fell to her knees beside the couch, fawning over Matt while he told her about his sprained ankle and subsequent trip to the emergency room. Before he'd even finished, she'd burst into tears.

"Oh, my poor baby!" she wailed as Matt tried in vain to calm her down.

Tanner's expression had gone from alarmed to panicky, and I imagined my own looked much the same. While my mother sobbed over my brother's misfortune, I was uncomfortably reminded of my own crying jag at the hospital. The appalling thought that I might be more like her than I'd previously imagined compounded my embarrassment further.

After several minutes of tears, Matt finally convinced our mother he wasn't gravely injured or in extraordinary pain—though if he had been, her reaction would have been even more counterproductive—and she settled down enough to ask what he needed.

"I just wanna crash in my own bed," he said, pushing himself off the couch with a groan. "I'm beyond beat."

"Here baby, let me help you," our mother said, inserting herself under his arm as he tried to keep his balance on one foot. "Lean on me, and I'll get you tucked into bed."

I winced as my teetering mother in her high-heeled slippers tried to support my brother as he hopped across the room on one foot. Tanner started forward in concern, intending to assist, but I caught his arm and shook my head.

"They'll be fine." Taking him by the hand, I led him to the front door and outside onto our small slab stoop.

"Lucy," he said, gazing down at me helplessly.

I could practically see all the things he wanted to say tumbling around in his head, fighting to get out.

"We'll talk tomorrow. Okay?" My eyes pleaded with him not to make me have this conversation tonight. To please just go. Please let me recover my dignity. Then we'd talk. About everything.

He hesitated before nodding. "Are you all right?" he asked, smoothing his hands up my bare arms.

I let my eyes fall closed as I enjoyed his soothing touch. "I will be." Especially if he kept doing that.

And then he was surrounding me, his arms enveloping me as he pulled me close. I sagged against him gratefully, breathing in the familiar scent of him, sinking into his strong, comforting warmth. It felt like the best hug anyone had ever given, except maybe the hug he'd given me at the hospital, which had been pretty damn spectacular too. Any hug from Tanner was guaranteed to be a top-notch hug, especially today, after everything that had happened. But also because I'd missed him so much. More than I'd wanted to admit. But now I could say it, both to myself and to him.

"I've missed you," I said, my voice wavering a little.

I felt his breath catch, and he held me even tighter. "I've missed you too," he said hoarsely.

If I could have stayed there like that all night, I would have. But of course I couldn't. I needed to get back inside, and I needed Tanner to go home. So I thanked him again for everything he'd done, repeated my promise that we'd talk tomorrow, and reluctantly pulled out of his arms.

Then I turned and went back in the house so I wouldn't have to watch him walk away.

TANNER

"Did you hear what Matt did last night?" I said when Wyatt answered his phone.

I'd waited until almost noon to call my brother, giving him a chance to sleep in this morning. Me, on the other hand? I'd finally given up trying to sleep at eight a.m., after a long night of tossing and turning. I had too much on my mind for rest.

"Yeah, I woke up to like a hundred text messages from him and the other guys talking about it." Wyatt's voice was hoarse, either from the drinking or the singing or a combination of both. "I'm hoping he can work the bass drum with his left foot. I think we can leave out the hi-hat barks without losing too much sound."

"Have you talked to him today?" I asked, more concerned with how Lucy was coping than Matt. I could understand now why she'd been so stressed last night about the logistics of Matt's care. It didn't seem like she'd be able to count on getting much practical help for her brother at home.

"Nah, the texts stopped around one a.m. and everyone's been

silent so far today. They're probably all still asleep. Thanks for driving my fucking drummer to the ER, by the way."

"It was no problem. I'm just glad I had my car."

"I'll bet Lucy was glad to have you there last night."

"Don't." I wasn't in the mood for another lecture from Wyatt, of all people, about my romantic choices. Especially not now, when I was so close to getting Lucy back. The last thing I wanted to hear was a list of reasons why it was a bad idea.

"Sorry, are you saying Lucy *wasn't* glad to have you there?"

"Whatever opinion you've got about me and Lucy, do me a favor and keep it to yourself."

"What if all I was gonna say is that I think Lucy's great?"

"Was it?" I asked, not trusting him much farther than I could throw him, which wasn't all that far the last time I'd tried it back in seventh grade.

"I like her," he said, sounding for all the world like he meant it. "I've always liked her, you know." His tone was reproachful, like he was offended I'd think otherwise. "I thought you two nerds were perfect for each other until—well." There was a pause as he left the rest of the sentence unspoken. "Anyway, I tried to hold a grudge, but it's hard to stay mad at someone as nice as Lucy."

Tell me about it.

"This is a major one-eighty from what you were saying last night," I pointed out.

"Is it?" I could practically hear his shrug over the phone. "I was drunk. You should know better than to listen to me when I'm drunk."

"I'm not convinced you're worth listening to when you're sober either."

"Look, I don't want you to get yourself hurt again, is all. You're a real pissbaby when you get your heart broken."

"Your concern is truly touching. I may cry."

"I just want you to be happy, asshole. If you really believe Lucy can do that for you, then I'm rooting for you kids to work it out."

Despite my sarcasm, I was rather touched—not that I planned to admit as much to Wyatt. "I didn't actually call to talk about me and Lucy," I said, changing the subject before things got too mushy.

"Okay." Wyatt let out a long, noisy yawn. "Then what?"

"Matt's going to need to stay off his bad ankle for a while. How long exactly has yet to be determined."

"I figured as much."

"He's got to go see an ortho for a follow-up, and he might end up needing physical therapy or even surgery."

"Shit, really? Christ, that's seriously going to fuck with our upcoming gigs. And after yesterday, I was hoping we'd be able to start booking more shows."

"Yeah, it's really bad timing," I agreed. "The thing is, I was hoping you and the rest of the band could step up and offer to help Matt out some."

"Okay," Wyatt said slowly. "I mean, sure, we absolutely can, but where's this coming from?"

I hesitated. "You've been to Matt's house before, right?"

"Sure. We used to practice in his garage in high school."

"I met his mom last night when I drove him home."

"You never met her when you and Lucy were going out?"

"No. Lucy never invited me to her house before."

Wyatt chuckled. "I can guess why. Their mom's a real character, isn't she? Did she hit on you in front of Lucy?"

"She caressed my forearms." I shuddered at the memory. "It was weird and uncomfortable."

"Don't worry, she's harmless. She's one of those people who likes attention, but it's all for show."

"Gosh, I can't think of anyone I know who's like that."

"Hey," Wyatt replied huffily. "I'm a reformed attention whore, thank you very much. I don't go around caressing strangers anymore."

"Because your girlfriend would serve you your own balls for breakfast with hot sauce."

"True," he admitted. "But also, she's the only woman I'm interested in caressing, and she lets me do it as much as I want."

"Getting back to my actual point, I got the impression last night that their mom might not necessarily be that much help with Matt's recovery. At the hospital, Lucy was really stressed about having to wait on Matt and getting him to and from all the appointments he might need."

"I guess their mom can be a little flaky. Lucy's probably the only responsible grown-up between the three of them."

"Which is why I was thinking it'd be nice if y'all could help her out so it doesn't all fall on her shoulders. Maybe take turns stopping by to check on Matt and bring him meals and other stuff he might need. And volunteer to drive him to this ortho appointment and whatever else he ends up having to do."

"Yeah, for sure," Wyatt agreed. "I'll talk to Corey and Tyler once they're up. We'll get it sorted."

"Thank you. I appreciate it." Hopefully that would take some of the pressure off Lucy. The money was a whole other issue, but if she agreed to set up a GoFundMe, I was pretty confident I could make certain they got whatever they needed. Coming from a wealthy family had certain advantages—like a surfeit of wealthy relatives to hit up for charitable donations.

"You really love her, don't you?" Wyatt said.

I blew out a long breath before I answered. "I really do."

"Then I hope you two work it out. I mean it."

"Thanks. Me too."

After I got off the phone with Wyatt, I went back to restlessly waiting to hear from Lucy. I'd sent her a text first thing when I got up this morning. Just a simple, benign *How is everything today?* No pressure and no expectations. But I'd yet to hear back from her. I tried to convince myself it was because she was sleeping in and not because she was reluctant to talk to me after last night.

Either way, I figured I should give her space to respond in her own time. Only it was taking all my willpower not to message her again. At least half a dozen times I pulled my phone out and started to type a follow-up text before deleting it in frustration.

Three hours later, I was hunched over my laptop skimming through the book I'd started writing a few years ago. I hadn't touched the thing in months, but I was in dire need of a distraction, and desperate times, blah blah blah. Possibly the fact that Lucy had asked about it last week might also have prompted me to blow the dust off my old unfinished manuscript. There'd been so much else on my mind lately that I'd almost forgotten the damn thing existed until she brought it up.

I was surprised to discover how much I liked what was on the page. It actually wasn't half bad? *Huh.* Maybe I should make an effort to finish the damn thing after all.

I ended up scrolling all the way back to read from the beginning, and I got so caught up in it that I startled upright when my doorbell rang. I almost never had actual visitors dropping by unannounced, so when I went to answer the door I expected to find someone either selling something or running for office.

Instead it was Lucy on my doorstep, looking breathtakingly beautiful in a dark green sundress with thin straps that exposed acres of smooth, freckled skin across her shoulders and chest.

"Is everything okay?" I asked, flustered to find her at my house with no warning—and also wildly distracted by the sight of her bare shoulders. "Is Matt—"

"Matt's fine." We stared at each other for a too-long moment before she added, "Can I come in?"

"Of course." I shook my head at my own ineptitude as I belatedly stepped back to admit her. "Sorry, you caught me by surprise. I was expecting you to text."

She ducked her head in apology. "I should have texted before coming over. I'm sorry."

"No, it's fine," I said hastily as I shut the door behind her. "I'm sorry, I'm just—" *Jesus, could I be any worse at this? I wait all day to hear from her, and then I make her feel unwelcome.* "I'm glad to see you," I said.

Two bright spots of pink tinged her cheeks. "Are you?" she asked in a small, uncertain voice.

Did she really have no idea? Even now? I reached for her hand and twined our fingers together. "Of course I am."

"I was afraid you might have changed your mind after last night."

"You didn't seriously think that, did you?"

She ducked her head again. "It's possible I might have been a teensy bit worried about it after my mother massaged your arm."

"I haven't changed my mind, Lucy." I squeezed her fingers, letting her know I was still right here, holding on tight.

She looked down at our hands, her small, delicate fingers engulfed by my longer, thicker ones. "You can, you know. If you've come to your senses in the harsh light of day and had second thoughts, I wouldn't blame you a bit."

"I haven't had second thoughts."

She exhaled a shaky breath. "Okay."

I studied her, trying to figure out what was going through her head to cause all this doubt. "Have you changed *your* mind?"

Her eyes met mine, and my heart thumped painfully. "No. I

definitely have not changed my mind. I meant what I said. I'm yours if you want me."

I'm yours if you want me.

As her words sank in, the steel vise that had been clamped around my chest finally let go. For the first time in months, I felt like I could take an unconstricted breath.

"I do want you." I moved closer and touched my fingers to her cheek. "So goddamn much."

She strained toward me, tilting her face up, and I met her halfway. My hands cupped her jaw as I pressed my mouth against hers, giving her the kiss I'd wanted to give her last night at the hospital and again on her doorstep before she sent me home. The kiss I'd been holding inside me ever since I'd said the words "I love you" all those months ago and watched her walk away.

But I refused to think about that now or question what it actually meant that she was here. None of that mattered as long as I got to keep kissing her—and holding her, and touching her. That was enough for me. It was all I needed. I'd never ask her for anything more.

When I slid my tongue along the seam of her lips, they parted in eager invitation, welcoming me home. Kissing Lucy was like falling into paradise. Our mouths together tasted like poetry.

One of her hands slipped under my T-shirt, and sparks of electricity zinged down my spine as her soft fingers skated over my skin. When I made a low, desperate sound, she pressed her hips against me, her softness seeking my hardness. I pressed back, chasing the irresistible friction—needing it and needing her, on fire with how much I hungered for her, unable to hold any other thought in my head.

"Tanner," she moaned into my mouth, the taste of her desire rich and sweet. "I missed you. I missed your touch." She pushed my shirt up, and I helped her shove it over my head, letting it fall to the floor at our feet. Smoothing her hands over my shoulders, she kissed a wet trail across my chest. "I missed the feel of you. I missed it *so much.*"

Hot sparks of pleasure spread from low in my belly as her mouth and hands moved over my skin, claiming me as her own. When her tongue circled my nipple, I shuddered and slid my hands into her hair. Tipping her head up, I captured her mouth again, nipping her bottom lip before my tongue swept deep inside her.

She broke contact, pushed out of my grasp, and pulled her sundress over her head.

Dear Christ, she wasn't wearing a bra. She wasn't wearing anything except a pair of lacy white panties.

No, not panties, I realized as my gaze traveled down her luscious body. A *thong.*

Fuck me, when did she start wearing thongs?

I swallowed, holding myself very, very still as desire warred with prudence. Wanting too much too fast had gotten me in trouble before. I'd promised myself I'd take it slow this time, letting Lucy set the pace and tell me what she wanted. *No pressure, no expectations.*

She licked her lips and stepped forward, putting herself within easy reach. "Touch me. I missed the feel of your hands on me."

If this was some kind of test of my willpower, I was going to fail. How could I deny a request like that?

Stepping closer, I lifted my hand and touched my fingers to her throat lightly—so lightly it was barely a touch at all. Her teeth sank into her lower lip, and she leaned into me, searching for more pressure. Exhaling a sharp breath, I laid my other hand on her shoulder to hold her still. Gently, my fingers spread out around her throat, and I watched her chest hitch with anticipation. With a slow, measured movement, I dragged my hand down, over her collarbone to the top of her breast. She arched into my touch, eyelashes fluttering, and I dropped my mouth to the soft place where her neck met her shoulder.

Sucking at the tender skin, I let my hand drift lower, moving it worshipfully over the curve of her breast. A whimper shuddered through her body as my palm grazed her nipple, but I didn't linger there, instead sweeping my hand down over her ribs to her waist. My fingers tightened as I grasped her hip, and my thumb caressed her hip bone, brushing against the strip of lacy elastic below it.

She strained toward me, but I gripped her shoulder harder, holding her still. I knew what she wanted, but I also knew how much more she enjoyed it when I drew out the anticipation. I wouldn't be hurried.

"Tanner," she breathed into my hair as her head lolled against mine.

"Patience," I whispered, and sank my teeth into her shoulder. She gasped, and I licked the spot I'd bitten. "Sorry, you just taste so fucking good. I couldn't help myself."

"I don't want you to help yourself." Her voice was thready and hoarse. "I want you to take whatever you want from me."

Well, damn.

Lifting my head, I smoothed my palm up her torso to cup her breast, squeezing the soft flesh roughly. At her sharp intake of breath, I lifted my head to gaze at her face. Her eyes were greedy as they met mine, her lips slick and parted. My fingers dug into her breast with shameless, possessive want, and I dragged my thumb across her hardened nipple.

"Like that?" I asked as she let out a hiss of pleasure. "Is that what you want me to do?"

She arched her back, pressing into my hand. "More."

I lowered my lips to her other breast and felt her quiver at the touch of my tongue. She moaned when I sucked her nipple into my mouth, so I sucked harder, alternating between long, hard pulls and gentle, soothing licks while I rolled her other nipple between my fingers.

Her body shook, and she let out a whine. "I need…"

"What? Tell me."

Instead of using her words, she grabbed my hand and shoved it between her thighs.

God, she was so fucking soaked. I wanted nothing more than to shove that meager scrap of lace aside and plunge my fingers inside her glorious heat. But something made me hesitate. A tenuous shred of rationality persisted in my lust-addled brain, enough to still my fingers before they had their wanton way with her.

Loosening my grip on her shoulder, I slid my hand to the back of her neck and pressed a gentle kiss to her temple. "You know we don't have to rush into anything. If you need to take it slow, we can do that."

She turned her head, and her lips ghosted over mine as her hips bucked against my hand. "I don't need slow."

"Okay." I curled my fingers, teasing at the edge of her thong. "Tell me what you need. Whatever it is, you can have it."

I'll do anything to keep you was what I was actually thinking but didn't say. Because I knew it would sound too desperate— even if it was true, god help me.

Her hands scrabbled at the waistband of my shorts, fumbling with the button. "I just need you."

My mouth found hers again, and our tongues tangled together, fevered and hungry. "You can have me," I murmured, dragging my lips to her ear. "As much as you want, for as long as you want."

No pressure, no expectations. I'd take whatever I could get. Whatever she was willing to let me have.

"I want back what we had." Lucy's hand plunged inside the front of my underwear and closed around me.

For a second I saw stars. My knees threatened to buckle, it felt so damn good. The noise I made was half growl, half groan as my fingers slipped under her thong.

She gasped and shuddered against me, her hand tightening around my aching, hard cock.

We hadn't even made it three feet inside my front door, and I was dangerously close to coming in her hand. This wasn't how I'd pictured today going, but if this was how it was going to go, then by god I meant to do it right.

Withdrawing my hand from between her legs, I grasped her wrist and separated her fingers from my dick. Once she'd released me, I cupped her ass with both hands, jerked her hips against me, and lifted her off the floor.

She wrapped her legs around my waist and attacked me with her hot mouth as I carried her to my bedroom. I laid her on the mattress before lowering myself over her, the sumptuous scent of her arousal going straight to my head like a drug.

"You're so beautiful." My mouth moved down her body, chasing the flush across her skin. "More beautiful than a blazing sunset painted across a summer sky." Her fingers curled in my hair, her quickening breaths urging me to keep going as I covered her nipple with my mouth. "Your skin's sweet as nectar," I murmured, tracing my tongue along the underside of her breast, "and softer than the petals of a newly opened flower."

I knew her body, knew exactly what she liked. I'd made a purposeful study of it in the brief time we'd been together. That knowledge paid off now as I moved my hands and mouth over her, teasing, stroking, exploring, every touch making her shiver and gasp.

"You have no idea how much I missed your body," I whispered into her skin. "The bounty of your breasts, the arch of your back…" I kissed my way down the swell of her stomach, feeling the muscles tighten with anticipation. "The span of your hips," I said against her hip bone as my hands spread her quivering legs apart. "The succulent flesh between your thighs."

When my fingers brushed over the soaking wet triangle of lace, she made a lovely, needy sound and convulsed in a full-body shudder. Working quickly, my own impatience growing, I eased the thong down her legs and tossed it over my shoulder.

"Tanner," she moaned when I paused to take in the lovely sight of her spread out naked on my bed—a sight I'd never thought to see again. Her beautiful pussy all ripe and glistening, aching for my touch. So gorgeous, it made my mouth water. When I slid my hand through her exquisite folds, her eyes rolled back and her whole body shook with a moan.

God, she was so slick and swollen. *For me.*

"Sure you don't want to slow down a little?" I asked as I traced her entrance with a light fingertip. "I can stop anytime you want."

"Don't. You. Fucking. Dare," she gritted out between clenched teeth as she arched her hips, grinding against my hand.

I couldn't help my answering smile. I loved it when I made her swear, because she did it so rarely. "Be still now," I said, laying my arm across her stomach, and she whimpered in protest.

"I told you not to stop."

"And I told you to be still."

"Please," she whined as I continued to tease her with light touches. "Please touch me. I need to feel your hands on me. I've missed it so much."

Who was I to deny such a polite request?

"You know I can never say no to you, Lucy." I eased a finger inside her, and we let out twin moans of pleasure. As I pumped in and out of her, I stroked my thumb over her clit and felt her clench around me. Searing, silky perfection. "I've dreamed of this so many times—being able to touch you like this again and watching you fall apart beneath me."

Adding a second finger, I worked her harder, pushing her higher and closer to the edge as she gasped and moaned beneath me. It was hard to say what I liked better, watching my hand play with her beautiful cunt, or watching the expressions on her face as I pleasured her.

"I love the way you look at me when I touch you." My voice was rough and unsteady, my control hanging by a fragile thread. "I love the way you feel around me. The sweet little sounds you make. The way you taste." Bending my head, I laved my tongue over her clit, and she gasped out my name. "You like that?" I asked, glancing up at her again.

"You know I do."

"I want to hear you say it."

"I like it. I like it so much." Her fingertips traced over my cheekbone, her eyes so soft and tender my heart slammed itself against the walls of my rib cage like it was trying to break free. "I like *you*."

I had to lower my head so she wouldn't see how much those three little words—not even the big three little words—completely destroyed me.

Swallowing the tangle of emotions lodged in my throat, I tasted her again, dragging my tongue over her swollen bud, devoting myself to her pleasure, licking and sucking and fucking her with my fingers until she was keening my name.

Then I had the privilege of watching the ecstasy dance across her face as she fell apart beneath me exactly like I'd dreamed.

Sex with Tanner had always been incredible. We'd never had problems in the chemistry department. But this was a whole other level of sensation that had touched something deep inside me—something that was more than sexual. It felt like dying and being reborn.

That probably sounded melodramatic, but it was the closest analogy I could come up with for what was happening to me.

I'd always found Tanner's sex talk a huge turn-on. His perfect combination of poetic and filthy never failed to get me hot and bothered. But he'd taken me way beyond hot and bothered today. His words had seared themselves into my skin as his touch unraveled me, leaving me emotionally exposed in a way I'd never felt before.

The way he'd touched me...it was like he needed it as badly as I did. Like he couldn't *not*. It felt like worship. Like being adored, utterly and completely.

As I lay there trying to get my bearings again, Tanner kissed my thigh and flopped down beside me without a word.

His silence now was out of the ordinary as well. He tended to be a talker in bed, both during and after. Funny, since he was the strong, silent type everywhere else. Maybe he was feeling as shaken to the core as I was.

On impulse, I rolled over and pressed my face into his neck, grateful when his arms automatically surrounded me.

"You okay?" he asked, nuzzling my hair.

"Better than okay." Lying in the comfort of his arms, completely enveloped by him, was the best place on earth.

"We can stop for now, if you want." His voice was gentle, but I heard the tension in it and sensed how much effort his restraint was costing him. Not to mention the raging hard-on I could feel through his shorts.

Someone should do something about that for him.

I tilted my head back to look at him, smiling at the sight of his kiss-swollen lips and the thin sheen of sweat on his brow. His pupils were blown so wide, his eyes almost looked black instead of blue.

"Nice try," I said, "but I'm not done with you yet."

He let out a breath and kissed me, his tongue sweeping hungrily into my mouth as he pushed me back into the mattress. My body was still tingling like the aftermath of an electrical shock, and for a while I lost myself in the hot, insistent pressure of his mouth and the weight of his body covering mine.

But then I remembered the throbbing iron rod in his pants that I very much wanted inside me.

"Why are you still wearing these?" I asked, tugging at the waistband of his shorts, which hung loosely around his hips.

He sucked at a spot on my neck that sent goose bumps shivering over my whole body. "No one's taken them off yet."

"Shame on me for falling down on the job." I shoved his shorts and underwear down, and he helped me out by kicking them the rest of the way off.

His cock curved upward, thick and solid, the satiny skin pulled tight and ridged with veins beneath the fat, glistening head. It was the aesthetic ideal of a penis. And I wanted it inside me.

"Are you still on the pill?" he asked, his arms flexing as he held himself above me.

"Yes." *Thank god.* I didn't want anything between us if I could help it. "I haven't been with anyone else since you."

"I haven't either, but I've got condoms right here if—"

When he started to turn, I gripped his arm and pulled him back. "I want to feel you." My other hand closed around his shaft, stroking up and down. "Only you."

He lowered his body to mine, and our mouths met in a blazing, ravenous kiss. Our sweat-slicked limbs slid together, his hard length nudging at my slippery, oversensitive folds as he kissed me harder and deeper. When I couldn't take it anymore, I pushed him onto his back and climbed on top of him.

Straddling his thighs, I squeezed his cock and smiled at the way his stomach muscles clenched and his eyes rolled back in his head.

"Fuck, that feels so good," he groaned, digging his fingers into my hips.

"If you like that, you're gonna love this." I guided him into me, sinking down slowly.

He held himself still, his gaze fixed on my face, letting me take as long as I needed to stretch to his shape. "You good?" he asked, his voice rough and taut as a bowstring.

"So good," I sighed, taking him completely.

For a second I just stayed there like that, enjoying the feel of him inside me, so thick and solid up against all those sensitive nerve endings. He watched me intently, his eyes like dark, endless pools. The sight of his long limbs stretched out beneath me, his strong body tensed and straining as he waited for me to take the lead, inspired a humbling sense of gratitude. I was so lucky to have this man, this moment, and this chance at a do-over I wasn't convinced I deserved.

Smoothing my hands over his chest, I started to move.

"Fuck," he groaned, too far gone for pretty words. "Fuck, Lucy, I missed this."

"Me too." I sucked in a sharp breath as he arched his hips, matching his rhythm to mine. We moved in unison, slow and steady at first, enjoying the feel of each other. Getting used to having this connection again.

It didn't take long before I felt the tension coiling inside me again, and my movements grew more urgent, my muscles clenching around him as I chased the ache. He ran his hands down the backs of my thighs and up again, his fingers digging into my ass cheeks as he urged me to go harder, faster, his hips rising up to meet mine.

"Oh!" I gasped at the increased pressure. "God, yes, that's it."

"There you go," he murmured, his burning blue eyes gazing at me with unnerving focus. He was doing that worshiping thing again, but with his eyes this time as he fucked deep inside me. "You look so pretty right now. I could watch you losing it like this forever."

I braced my hands on his shoulders, my breath coming in short bursts and my fingernails biting into his skin. "Please, just —more."

Tanner lifted me up and slammed me down on him, so hard I cried out.

"Like that?" His voice was rough, on the verge of breaking.

"Harder," I begged, desperate to feel that merciless stretch again as he drove up into me. I wanted him to take me, own me, possess me inside and out. *"Please."*

His fingers dug into my hips. "Tell me I'm yours."

"You are," I gasped. "You're mine. I need you."

He lifted me up and drove himself into me again, our hips

slamming together so hard it rattled my teeth. Then he did it again. And again. Each time leaving me more boneless and closer to the edge.

"You're so perfect," he murmured and reached between us to thumb my clit, pressing my slippery flesh with firm strokes. "Look at you, how fucking gorgeous you are, riding my cock."

I whimpered helplessly, and he grabbed my hips and lifted me up again, his abs contracting and biceps flexing. The final time he impaled himself deep inside me, I threw my head back and cried out his name as sensation carried me away like a storm surge.

He stroked soothing hands over my quivering thighs and up my back, holding me steady as the pleasure rippled through me.

"Wow," I said, pushing my hair out of my face when I could finally talk again.

Tanner levered himself upright and wrapped his arms around me, holding me against his chest. Leaning into him, I rested my forehead against his, our breaths mingling and noses rubbing.

His hands smoothed over my hips, and he lifted my legs, one at a time, bringing them around his waist so I'd be more comfortable. "Is this okay?"

I hummed approvingly at the change of angle and clenched around him, smiling as it drew a groan from him. He rocked his hips, pumping inside me, and I hissed with pleasure, digging my fingernails into his shoulders as he moved inside me. It was intimate and intense, our bodies completely wrapped up in each other, so close it was impossible to tell where he ended and I began.

"Tanner," I breathed, moving my mouth to his ear. "You feel so good inside me."

We fit together so perfectly. Give and take. Push and pull. Not an inch of space between us.

"Lucy." He was trembling against me, clutching me to him. "I missed you, Lucy. I missed you so much."

"I know." I held him even tighter as we rocked together. "I'm here now. I'm yours, Tanner. You don't have to hold back anymore."

His hips bucked erratically beneath me, and his whole body convulsed as he finally let himself go.

He dropped his head against my shoulder and I rocked him through it, dragging my fingernails over his scalp in soothing circles. "I'm here," I whispered, over and over. "I have you. I'm right here."

———

I COULDN'T GET ENOUGH of Tanner's kiss-swollen lips. My fingers traced over them as I lay alongside him with my head on his shoulder and one of his arms curled around me.

"That tickles," he said, capturing my fingers and pinning them against his chest.

Not to be thwarted, I stretched up and brushed my mouth against his, enjoying the prickle of his skin against my tender, hypersensitive lips.

Kissing Tanner was my favorite thing.

Well, I reconsidered as I thought about some of the other things we'd just finished doing, *maybe my second-favorite thing. Or third.*

Okay, kissing was definitely one of the top ten things I liked to do with Tanner. Or have Tanner do to me.

Anyway.

I just really liked his mouth. And his hands, for that matter. And pretty much his whole body endealment. It was so nice and big and comforting. Perfect for curling myself around.

How had I ever thought it was a good idea to give this up? I must have been out of my mind.

I'd begun to consider the possibility that I might have been exactly that. The more I thought about it, the more I suspected I'd had some kind of stress reaction. I wasn't saying I had PTSD exactly, but the way I'd reacted certainly resembled a fight-or-flight response. What other explanation could there be for leaving a man this perfect?

"Where'd you go just now?" Tanner asked, bringing my hand to his lips and pressing a kiss into my palm.

"Hmmm?" I replied, distracted by the opportunity to touch his lips some more.

"You got all closed off and faraway all of a sudden. Tell me what you were thinking."

"I was thinking how much I like kissing you."

He released my hand and tapped the tip of my nose. "I don't believe you."

"It's true," I said. "I was. But then I started wondering how I could have given you up."

And now I'd gone and made him frown. This was why I didn't share what I was thinking more often. My brain voices made everyone unhappy, including me. I burrowed my face into his neck and wrapped my arms around him, hoping I could hug the frown off his face.

He pressed a kiss to my hair with a soft sigh and tugged my leg across his. "This isn't exactly how I imagined today going."

"How did you imagine it?"

His fingertips stroked a path up my thigh. "I expected we'd talk first and take things slow. Try spending some time together on a trial basis to see how it goes."

Right. So he'd been envisioning a big come to Jesus conversation followed by a probation period to make sure he was still willing to put up with me. And instead I'd stripped naked and thrown myself at him.

Frankly, I liked my way better. You couldn't argue with the results.

I burrowed closer. "For the record, I think it's going really great so far."

"I was going to ask you out on a date." His big hand smoothed over my hip and squeezed my ass cheek. "Woo you."

"Consider me amply wooed."

He laughed softly, his fingertips wandering lower, and the ache between my legs throbbed in response. "This wasn't how I'd planned on doing it."

I kissed his chest. "That's too bad."

"I mean, eventually I was hoping to do this. I just didn't think we'd get to it so quickly."

"Are you having regrets?" I asked, afraid of the answer.

Shifting me off him, he rolled onto his side so we were facing each other. "No," he said, his expression serious. "Definitely not." He touched my cheekbone like he was checking to make sure I was real. "I want back what we had too. But I don't want to make the same mistakes again."

"I don't either."

He gave me a measured look. "I think the best way to do that is for us both to be up front with each other about what we want —and what we don't want."

Shit, shit, shit. What if I didn't know exactly what I wanted? Why couldn't we just lie here in each other's arms forever without dealing with all the hard, uncomfortable stuff?

Because that's what we did before and it didn't work out so great, did it?

"That sounds reasonable," I said, trying to hide how nervous I was.

"And just to be clear, it's okay if we're not on the exact same page right now. But I think it's better if we at least know what page we're each on. Then we can try to find a compromise that works for both of us."

"No freaking out. Understood." I nodded, not feeling any less terrified.

There was a long silence.

"Did you want me to go first?" he offered finally.

"Maybe you should."

"Are you sure? Because the last time I went first, you pulled the emergency brake and jumped off the bus."

I deserved his distrust, but I still felt like shit being confronted by it. "I promise not to jump off any buses this time," I said solemnly. "Say what you want to say."

"Okay, here goes." He took a deep breath. "You know how I feel about you already. That hasn't changed." He paused to eye me warily, as if he was half expecting me to make a run for the door.

"Still here," I reassured him. "Still listening." I couldn't help noticing his reluctance to actually *say* how he felt about me. Which, again, I couldn't exactly fault him for. He was smart to be cautious, considering I didn't even know if I *wanted* to hear him say the words again.

God, I was such a mess. What was he doing wasting his time on me?

"That being said..." He paused again, licking his lips as he weighed his words. "The way you ended things before hurt. And I'd be lying if I said I wasn't afraid of it happening again."

I nodded, not daring to speak until he'd finished getting it all off his chest.

"But the last thing I ever want is for you to feel pressured to reciprocate. My feelings for you are mine to manage. So I want to be clear that I'm not expecting anything from you but honesty. I just want you to tell me what's going on with you, okay?"

Presumably I was supposed to feel reassured by that. He was trying to make this easy for me. But hearing about his low expectations made me feel like dirt.

I swallowed and gave him a nod that I hoped conveyed an appropriate amount of gravity. "Understood and accepted."

He took my hand and gave it a squeeze, appearing relieved that I'd listened without panicking and running out of the house. The bar was so low a baby could crawl over it. "Your turn."

"Right. Okay."

I could do this. I could be honest about my feelings and fears. All I had to do was drag myself over this baby-height bar.

"Lucy?" he prompted when I didn't say anything.

Why was this so hard? Tanner was the kindest, most considerate person I knew. I couldn't ask for anyone easier to talk to.

His lips pinched together. "This is the part where you tell me what you're thinking."

"I'm getting there. Give me a second."

Breathe. Just open your mouth and say the first thing that comes to mind. Trust that it'll be all right.

I rolled over so my back was to him. "It's easier to do this if I'm not looking at you."

"Okay," he said uncertainly.

I reached behind me and pulled his arm around my waist, scooching back until I was spooned up against him.

"Better?" he asked, dutifully assuming the position of big spoon and pulling me against his chest.

"Yes." I closed my eyes, concentrating on how safe I felt in his arms. "The first thing you probably need to know about me is that I've never wanted to be in a serious, committed relationship.

I don't want to get married. I don't want to have kids. I wasn't looking to fall in love."

When I paused to let that sink in, Tanner squeezed my hand to encourage me to keep going. If he'd noticed that I'd accidentally slipped into the past tense for the part about not wanting to fall in love, he didn't let on.

Since nothing terrible had happened yet, I kept going. "Watching my mother fall apart after my father left probably has a lot to do with that. I'm pretty sure getting married ruined her life, and getting divorced ruined it a second time."

It actually felt good to say that out loud. *Huh.* Apparently I could talk about this stuff without the world ending. Tanner was still listening and holding me tight. He hadn't even gotten upset or pulled away yet.

"So yes," I went on, feeling braver, "I'm sure there are some unresolved abandonment issues at work, courtesy of my father's decision to nope out of our lives and leave me to smooth over all the cracks in our family. And that's not even getting into the boatload of issues I have because of my relationship with my mother. But it's more than that. It's about what I want for myself, and how sometimes it feels like I'm never going to get it, which is why I don't feel like I can afford to add any more complications to my life."

"What do you want?" Tanner asked, speaking for the first time.

"Freedom." It sounded like such a small thing when I said it out loud. But for me it was everything. "I want to live my life without constantly feeling obligated to other people. I want to have my own space and not have to take care of anyone but myself. I want to spend my salary on the frivolous stuff I want to buy and do things that make me happy without feeling guilty about it. I want to be able to make selfish decisions and not be responsible for anyone but myself." I paused to take a breath, cringing at the word vomit I'd just unleashed all over him. "That makes me sound like an awful human being, doesn't it?

"No. Not at all. I think just about anyone would feel the same way in your situation." His thumb rubbed reassuring circles on my hip.

"That's why I wasn't looking to fall in love. The last thing I wanted was someone else making demands on my time."

He didn't say anything, and I had the worst feeling I'd just crushed him all over again. But I pressed on nonetheless. I'd come this far. Why stop now? Might as well get it all out.

"So when you said"—I swallowed and forced myself to say the words—"you loved me, it scared the shit out of me. I think I felt threatened or...trapped, I guess. Because in most of my experience, love means more demands and more obligations."

"Thank you for telling me that," he said quietly. "I'm so sorry you felt that way."

"Don't be sorry. Just listen." I tugged his arm tighter around me in case he was thinking of pulling away. "I thought I knew what I wanted for myself, but then I met you and...it knocked me off my axis. Because I'm pretty sure you're the best thing that's ever happened to me, only apparently I was too broken to realize it until I'd lost you."

Tanner didn't move. Or speak. I wasn't entirely sure he was breathing, even.

"Now you can say something. Please." I was clinging to his arm like a security blanket, willing him to stay. Hoping desperately that he would *choose* to stay despite everything I'd just said. *Please. Please don't leave me now that I finally know how much I need you.*

I felt him shift behind me, and the next thing I knew he'd rolled me over and his mouth crashed against mine. His warm weight crushed me into the mattress as he kissed me like a starving man, his lips and his tongue telling me in no uncertain terms that he wasn't going anywhere.

A wave of happiness swept through me, and I let out a sobbing exhale of relief. His nose gently brushed my cheek as he planted a trail of tiny kisses along my jaw.

"Does this mean you still want me back?" I asked, tangling my fingers in his hair.

His teeth grazed my ear. "Do you still want to come back?"

"No, I just spilled my guts and told you all this stuff I've never confided to another living soul because I'm on the fence about us."

He lifted his head, his mouth tugging into a heart-stopping smile. "That's sarcasm, right?"

"Yes!" I took his face in my hands and pulled his forehead against mine. "You make me happy, and I'm chasing that feeling, which means holding on to you with both hands."

I felt a million pounds lighter after unburdening myself. *Freer*, even. Maybe there was something to this sharing burdens thing after all. Maybe this was how you made a relationship work without feeling trapped. You found someone who accepted what you had to give without demanding more.

"For the record," he said, lifting his head to gaze at me, "I'm incredibly happy to be held on to by you." His erection nudged between my legs, offering solid physical evidence to support his statement.

"Wow, you feel *very* happy."

"You didn't think I was done with you, did you?" Hooking his hand behind one of my knees, he lifted my leg up and settled himself in the cradle of my hips. As he pushed into me, his gaze held mine with a focus that tied my stomach up in knots.

My eyes fluttered closed as he touched a place deep inside me, unleashing a swell of soul-deep affection. "God, I hope not."

20

TANNER

I couldn't remember the last time I'd looked forward to going into work. Usually, the sight of the creamery made my stomach curdle with anxiety. I kept a bottle of antacids in my desk drawer to accompany my morning coffee. And my mid-morning coffee. And as a post-lunch digestive. The last couple of years my antacid budget had threatened to outpace my water bill.

Huh. When I put it like that, it sounded unhealthy. That might be something I should reflect on sometime.

But not today, because this morning my stomach was shimmering with excitement as I pulled into the creamery parking lot. What an odd feeling.

Lucy was already at her desk when I walked in. She looked up and gave me a smile that sent my heart straight into my throat. Then she promptly blushed sunset pink and dropped her gaze to her keyboard.

"Are those kolaches?" Linh had swiveled her chair around and was tracking the bakery box in my hand like a cat about to pounce on a lizard.

I set the box on my desk and flipped it open. "I stopped at

Leshikar's on my way in this morning." Sneaking a glance at Lucy, I saw her smile grow wider, just like I'd hoped it would.

I knew how much she loved kolaches, and Leshikar's were the best in town. They offered plenty of delicious baked goods too, but the kolaches—a traditional Texas-Czech pastry they made from a recipe handed down through the family for four generations and guarded as closely as the nuclear launch codes —were their main attraction.

The other times I'd brought kolaches in for the team, Lucy had refrained from partaking, choosing instead to sulk at her desk, slanting longing looks at them when she thought I wasn't watching. This morning, however, she joined Linh and Arwen in gathering around my desk to accept my offering of free breakfast.

"Do these sausage have jalapeño?" Arwen asked, poking warily at the savory pigs in a blanket. "Last time I got one I nearly sweated all my makeup off."

"I'll eat the jalapeño," Linh offered benevolently. "Gimme."

"Are there any peach?" Lucy asked, trying to see around the others.

"Lots." Linh shot me an arch look as she pushed Lucy toward the kolaches. "It's almost like someone knew they were your favorite."

Guilty as charged. I tried to suppress a smile as I watched another blush travel all the way down Lucy's chest. She was wearing a sleeveless wrap sweater with a V-neck that was going to be hell not to stare at all day.

"Apparently I missed all the excitement Saturday night." Linh was still smirking at me, which meant Lucy must have told her something. But what, exactly? How much did she know?

"Oh my god! Poor Matt!" Arwen exclaimed. "You should have seen how much pain he was in. I could have cried."

"Lucy told me *all* about it," Linh said, exhaling a cloud of jalapeño. "Sounds like some of us had an eventful weekend."

Lucy's eyes met mine, and her blush told me we were both time traveling back to yesterday: her legs wrapped around me, my fingers digging into her hips, both of us breathless and—

"How's Matt doing?" Arwen asked. "Corey says he might need surgery?"

Lucy nodded as she licked peach kolache off her finger, and I struggled to hold on to my composure. "We won't know until he sees the ortho. He's supposed to call today for an appointment." She frowned, presumably worrying he wouldn't remember. Fifty bucks said she'd be calling him later to make sure he did it.

I looked at Arwen, something she'd just said triggering a suspicion. "Did you get home okay Saturday night?"

"Yeah, totally," she mumbled and jammed half a cream cheese kolache in her mouth. Now she was the one blushing. *Interesting.*

Lucy's eyes narrowed, her own Spidey senses tingling. "If Corey told you Matt might need surgery, you must have talked to Corey yesterday."

"Uh huh." Arwen finished chewing and swallowed. "I guess I might as well tell you. Corey and I sort of hooked up on Saturday." She snuck a glance at Lucy like she was hoping for her approval. It was adorable how much Arwen looked up to her, and I doubted Lucy even realized.

"Really?" Lucy seemed surprised by this development. She must have been too busy assuming Arwen and I were on a date to notice the heart eyes Arwen had been shooting in Corey's direction all night.

"Which one's Corey?" Linh asked, reaching for another jalapeño sausage. "I get the two white boys who aren't related to either of you mixed up."

While Arwen explained that Corey was the lead guitarist

and therefore the most important member of the band, Lucy was looking at me funny—like she'd expected me to have some kind of reaction to Arwen's news. Jealousy, I guess?

Which I definitely, definitely wasn't. I was far too busy trying not to stare at Lucy's cleavage to give a damn who Arwen wanted to hook up with.

"Anyway, I'm sorry we bailed on y'all at the hospital," Arwen said, turning back to Lucy. "I felt really bad about it."

Lucy waved off her guilt. "Don't worry about it. There wasn't anything for either of you to do." She directed a soft smile at me. "I had all the help I needed, thanks to Tanner."

The look on her face leveled me flat, and we stood there smiling at each other for long enough that Linh noisily cleared her throat.

"So...does anyone else have any romantic news they'd like to share with the class?" Her eyebrows lifted as she peered at us. "Anyone?"

Lucy gave me an uncertain look, and I shrugged to let her know I was fine with whatever she wanted to do.

"Well," she said, biting her lip. "Actually..." She glanced around at the half-empty office to make sure there was no one close enough to overhear. Fortunately, most of the art department took a lackadaisical approach to the start of the workday. "Tanner and I are seeing each other." Her eyes flicked up to me. "Again."

"Ahhh!" Arwen slapped a hand over her mouth to muffle her squeal of joy.

Linh pumped her fist. "I knew it! Alexis owes me a massage." She pulled out her phone and started typing, presumably to inform Alexis of the news.

"Please don't say anything to anyone around here though," Lucy added. "I'd prefer it if Byron didn't know."

"I'm so excited!" Arwen whisper-yelled at us. "You two are totally cute together."

I smiled down at Lucy. "I think so too."

———

WAS THAT OKAY? Lucy private messaged me on the company's internal communications app later that morning. *You don't mind that I told them, do you?*

I didn't, but I also knew the company had access to all our private messages and this wasn't the safest platform for discussing our relationship. I pulled out my phone and sent her a text in reply. *It's totally fine with me. But if you don't want management to know, better not to talk about it on the company's software.*

Oh shoot! she replied. *I didn't think about that.*

Speaking of...I'm guessing you don't want me telling Josie about us either?

Not telling Byron was one thing, but trying to keep my girlfriend a secret from my sister might be a little tougher. At some point, ideally, I'd like to bring Lucy as my date to family events.

I'm actually not sure, Lucy texted back. *We should talk about that. We can figure it out together.*

I liked the sound of that. Already it felt like we were being more honest and up front with each other than our last failed experiment at dating. See? Communication worked.

An hour later, Lucy messaged me again on the company app. *I need to come up with more features for our series on the company's 100th anniversary. Can you help me brainstorm?*

Absolutely, I replied, eager for any opportunity to talk to her. *When?*

Meet me in the conference room in five minutes.

———

"WE'RE SUPPOSED to do a feature related to the centennial every month this year," Lucy explained once we were seated across from each other in the conference room. "But I'm running out of ideas."

Apparently she actually did want to brainstorm and hadn't just been fishing for an excuse to get me alone. Too bad.

Resigning myself to doing actual work, I opened my laptop, navigated to the company's blog, and scrolled through it to see what kind of features she'd already done. It looked like pretty basic fare. There'd been a piece on the creamery's humble origins, one on the changes to the ice cream making process over the years, and another on the different facilities the creamery had occupied.

"Did you write these?" I asked, wincing at a profile of all the family members currently working for the company. It included an unflattering headshot of me looking like I had a stick up my ass and a glowing description of the job I'd been fired from. *Swell.*

"Yes." She looked embarrassed. "They're really boring, I know."

"They're fine," I said. "Company history isn't exactly the most exciting subject."

"It's really not—no offense." She tapped her pen against her lips, making me wish I could trade places with a purple gel pen.

"You look pretty today," I blurted, unable to help myself.

She blinked, turned a lovely shade of dusky rose, and smiled. "Thank you."

I stared down at my notebook, conscious of the clear glass wall behind Lucy facing out on the office, and the fact that anyone who happened to look in our direction would be able to see the expression on my face. Gazing at my coworker like a lovestruck meatball might undermine our efforts at professional discretion.

"Maybe something about the trends in ice cream flavors over the years? Or is that even more boring?" Lucy frowned as she rubbed her thumb over an ink stain on her finger, and I was confronted by a memory of that same finger dragging down my stomach and wrapping itself around me.

I shifted in my seat as all the blood in my body inconveniently rushed into my lap. Dragging my eyes back to my notebook, I started doodling in the margin to distract myself. "What about a retrospective of discontinued products?" I suggested as I sketched an angel who might or might not look a lot like Lucy. "We experimented with all sorts of weird shit back in the seventies and eighties—frozen fruit parfaits and rocket-shaped custard pops. It might make a decent throwback story."

"That's a great idea. People love all that retro stuff. I'll bet we can dig up some old product art and ads to run with it."

Whenever Lucy complimented me, I got this weird bouncy feeling in the pit of my stomach. Currently, my stomach was doing a gymnastics floor routine worthy of an Olympic hopeful.

Lucy wrote down my idea and tapped her purple pen on her notepad. "We should probably do something focusing on your father, but honestly I'm terrified to."

I looked up at her, frowning. "Why?"

"He's intimidating. I wouldn't want to write anything about him he didn't like. Not that he'd actually read it, probably."

"He'd have his assistant read it. And I imagine Josie would want to do a pass before it was published. She'd catch anything likely to bother him."

"I guess so."

"Are you asking me to write it?" I'd rather give myself a root canal with a rusty steak knife. But Lucy didn't know that. We hadn't talked about my father much—or at all, really. Just as she'd avoided the subject of her challenging relationship with her remaining parental figure, I'd avoided the subject of mine.

She must have sensed my ambivalence. "Not if you don't want to. I should probably be the one to write it anyway—you're too close to the subject. I can regurgitate some of the same old stuff we always say about him. I was just hoping to come up with a fresher spin."

"You know what we could do," I said, wanting to be helpful. "We could go to my dad's house and look through our old family photo albums. I know there's a bunch of pictures of Dad in there when he was just starting out at the creamery working for my granddad. And there are pictures of my dad and Manny's dad. Having some new photos to go with it might make it seem fresh."

"Would he mind?" Lucy bit her lip. "I don't want to intrude where I don't belong."

"I'll clear it with my stepmother. If we go during the workday, my dad won't be there." Which was a definite bonus. Lucy seemed to agree, because she looked a lot less nervous without the possibility of an encounter with my dad looming. "But just for the record," I added, "you're my girlfriend; you belong wherever I belong." Her answering smile made my stomach do another of those gymnastic flips.

"Does this mean I get to see all your baby pictures?" she asked, beginning to look downright excited about the field trip I'd proposed.

"If you must."

"Oh, I definitely must."

The look on her face left me flustered and inappropriately warm under my collar, given the subarctic temperature of the conference room. I returned my attention to my doodling so it would look like we were in here doing serious work instead of flirting like teenagers partnered on a group project for fifth-period history. "Speaking of my family," I ventured cautiously, "what do you want to do about telling Josie?"

There was a pause before she answered. "What do you think? You know her better than I do. How do you think she'll feel about it?"

"I don't think she'll care," I decided after some consideration. "But if it makes you uncomfortable, we don't have to tell her."

"I'll leave the call up to you."

I looked up at Lucy and shook my head. "Given that my family connection to the company creates an unavoidable power imbalance, I don't think it should be up to me. Your position here is potentially more precarious than mine."

"Weren't you just fired by a member of your family?" she pointed out, as gently as it was possible to bring up someone's recent professional humiliation.

"Yes, and I was immediately offered two other jobs with the company in quick succession." The fact that one of those jobs was awful and the other was a knockdown to entry-level didn't change the larger point. "Which proves that I'm more or less bulletproof." Whether that was entirely true remained to be seen, but I was definitely in a more secure situation than Lucy.

Her eyes were a luminous, dove-soft gray as they looked into mine. "I trust your judgment."

I could so easily lose myself in her eyes. It took me a second to rebalance and remember what we were talking about. Right —my sister, and whether or not she'd disapprove of me dating a coworker in her department. "Let me think about it."

As eager as I was to parade Lucy around on my arm everywhere I went, it wasn't a decision I wanted to make for selfish reasons. There was no need to rush into anything we couldn't take back.

"Do you want to have dinner with me tonight?" I asked, abruptly changing the subject. The longer we spent in this conference room, the more I wanted to have Lucy all to myself somewhere I didn't have to pretend not to have feelings.

Her expression turned regretful. "I'd really like to, but I can't. I need to go to the grocery store and then get home to make dinner. My mother's been with Matt all day, and they both probably need a break." Her eyebrows arched in playful accusation. "I was supposed to do the grocery shopping yesterday, but instead I was beguiled into spending the entire afternoon in someone's bed."

"Beguiled, were you?" I was definitely beaming. The people sitting outside the conference room were going to start complaining about the glare coming off my face. "Sounds serious."

"Oh, it is." Lucy was beaming right back at me. The two of us had raised the temperature in this small glass room from slightly above freezing to merely inhospitably cold.

"I could come to the grocery store with you," I offered. "I love grocery shopping. Pushing a cart around happens to be one of my favorite free-time activities."

She looked torn, which meant I had a fighting chance. "I couldn't ask you to do that."

"I'm the one asking you to let me tag along. I'll never pass up an opportunity to go to the grocery store—or spend more time with you."

Her smile warmed the room another few degrees. "In that case, I accept."

———

"I WOULDN'T HAVE TAKEN you for such a fan of Flaming Hot Cheetos," I remarked as Lucy dropped three monstrously large bags in the cart.

"Those are for Matt. Obviously." She marched down the

aisle toward the energy drinks, and I dutifully steered the cart in her wake.

Two cases of Monster Energy later, we were standing in front of the frozen vegetables. "I don't know why I even bother buying these," she grumbled as she grabbed broccoli, green beans, and carrots. "I'm the only one who ever eats them."

"Because you don't want to die of malnutrition?" I suggested.

"And yet somehow Matt manages to survive on a diet of puffed corn products, corn syrup, and caffeine. I swear, he's got the constitution of a cockroach. He'll probably outlive me by decades."

If he did, it would be because he'd managed to transfer all the stress in his life onto his beleaguered older sister.

"Do you always cook dinner every night?" I asked, trying to decide how much I should resent Matt.

"Usually. If I don't, no one else will. It's the only way I can know my mother is eating at least one square meal a day." Lucy plucked a pint of Ben and Jerry's out of the freezer case and shot me a guilty look as she set it in the cart. "Don't tell anyone."

I made a zipping motion over my lips. "No one shall hear of your betrayal from me."

"I just like a little variety sometimes, you know?"

I knew very well. I'd grown up eating the family brand every night for dessert. It was the only sweet we'd been allowed to have in the house. By the time I'd reached high school, the shine had worn off. These days I rarely touched the stuff.

"Your mom doesn't cook?" I asked, steering the conversation back to the reason we were at the grocery store.

Lucy shook her head. "When we were kids she made us a lot of Spaghetti-Os and Kraft mac and cheese. She'd heat something up for us, then sit and watch us eat, saying she was waiting to eat with Dad when he got home from work. But he always stayed late at the office and ate dinner before coming home."

Lucy's mouth pulled into a grimace. "That probably should have clued me in sooner that things weren't good, but as a kid I didn't realize it wasn't normal parent behavior."

"My dad used to do that too," I said. "Most nights we ate with the housekeeper."

"What about your mom?" Lucy asked as she passed me cans of Campbell's Chunky Soup to put in the cart.

"Before she got sick she had a busy social calendar. Book clubs, Jazzercize classes, sitting on the boards of multiple charities. She was always going out somewhere."

Lucy looked at me with sorrowful understanding. "That sounds lonely for you." We were having a heartfelt moment in the middle of the HEB.

I reached up and gently brushed some hair away from her eyes. "I had books to keep me company, which was enough for me. I think Wyatt was a lot lonelier. He's always needed more attention than I did."

"Did you not need the attention?" she asked, her eyes impossibly soft. "Or did you just adapt to living without it?"

Another shopper maneuvered a cart with a squeaky wheel around us, reminding me that the soup aisle wasn't the ideal place for delving into these murky corners of my psyche. This sort of conversation was better whispered in a dark bedroom late at night with Lucy's warm, naked body curled around mine.

"It amounts to the same thing in the end, doesn't it?" I shrugged and pretended to examine a jar of fancy bone broth. "You know what you should do? Plan some big-batch meals that can be made ahead and frozen. Then you'd only have to cook once a week."

"I've thought about it." Lucy fell into step beside me as we trundled down the aisle toward the beans. "It's just I'm usually so tired, the thought of doing all that cooking at once is daunting. Even though I know it's more work in the long run, somehow it seems easier to do a little at a time."

"I could help," I offered. "It's not like I have anything else to do tonight. I usually do a big cook for myself every weekend, and I've got some great one-pot recipes that are easy to prep."

She cut a frown at me. "I *really* couldn't ask you to do that. Keeping me company at the grocery store is one thing, but that's too much."

I stopped the cart and turned to face her. "I like spending time with you. I don't care what we're doing. Anyway, cooking with someone else is fun. And you already know we work well together in the kitchen."

Deep creases formed across her brow as she chewed on her lip unhappily. "I appreciate the offer, but it's not a good idea."

"Tell me why." I brushed her hair off her shoulder so I could squeeze it. Her neck muscles were taut as guy-wires. "I want to know what you're feeling that's put that look on your face."

She looked down at the floor and mumbled, "My kitchen's not nice like yours."

"I've seen your kitchen. It's bigger than mine. That matters a lot more than whether the counters are Formica or granite."

"That's not what I'm talking about. It won't be clean. My mother's been home all day, so god only knows what kind of state the house will be in."

"I don't care what your house looks like. You know that, right? Tell me you know that."

"*I* care," she shot back fiercely.

"I can see that."

"You grew up with lots of money in a big fancy house that probably looked like something out of a magazine spread. You already told me you had a housekeeper."

I drew back, surprised at the amount of resentment she'd apparently been harboring about my affluent background. "Do you think I'm the kind of person who's going to judge you or your family for what kind of house you live in?"

Her eyes lowered to the floor. "No."

"Whew. For a second there it sounded like you thought I was a pretentious dick."

She reached for my hand, her expression contrite. "I know you're not. This is more about me and my hang-ups than it's about you."

I squeezed her fingers. "It's okay. I'm glad you told me how you feel." Wrapping my other hand around the back of her neck, I bent down so our foreheads rested together. "I like spending time with you, and I don't mind seeing you at your house when that's where you need to be. It's a lot better than not getting to see you at all." I kissed her brow and leaned back so I could look at her. "But ultimately, it's your call."

"You really want to come back to my house and help me cook?"

"No, I just offered twice for no reason at all."

I watched her expression struggle through denial, guilt, bargaining, and finally acceptance before she relented with a gusty sigh. "All right. You asked for it. Don't blame me when my mom tries to stroke your arm again."

"Maybe that's my goal. Maybe this is all just an elaborate ploy to get closer to your mom."

She responded with a horrified laugh-shudder. "Be careful what you wish for."

21

TANNER

Lucy's house was...not in a great state when we got there, as predicted. I sensed her tense up as we stepped into the kitchen. Every counter was so covered with dirty dishes and trash—plus a half-eaten pizza that had been left sitting out—that there was nowhere to set the grocery bags we'd brought in.

"Just put them on the floor," she directed, dropping her bags next to the fridge. "I'll start clearing a space for us to work."

I set my bags next to hers and reached out for her hand before she could turn away. "Hey. It's okay. I'll help you clean up."

"Lucy?" her mother called out from the back of the house, and Lucy dropped my hand, stepping back. "My god, it took you long enough to get home!"

Mrs. Dillard pulled up short when she stepped into the living room and caught sight of me. Tonight she was wearing a heavy coat of makeup and a tight, low-cut dress that showed off an unsettling amount of cleavage.

"Oh! We've got company. I had no idea." She shot a dark look at Lucy as she approached us. "You might have given me the consideration of a little warning."

Lucy's mouth turned down at her mother's comment, and I watched her shrink in on herself before my eyes. "You remember Tanner, Mama."

"Of course I do! What a pleasant surprise!" Mrs. Dillard turned an ingratiating smile on me, extending her arms in welcome despite the irritation she'd exhibited only seconds ago.

"Nice to see you again, Mrs. Dillard." I braced myself for impact and was enveloped in a stiff-armed embrace and a cloud of perfume strong enough to overpower a horse.

"Oh honey, call me Brenda. We don't stand on ceremony in this house." She held on to my arms as she leaned back to beam at me.

Lucy's eyebrows lifted in an *I told you so* expression as her mother gratuitously massaged my biceps. "How's Matt doing, Mama?"

Her mother unhanded me and turned to shake her head at Lucy. "Helpless as a newborn kitten, poor thing. I'm just exhausted from fetching things for him all day."

"Did he start doing his range-of-motion exercises?"

"They caused him so much pain, I told him not to. I couldn't bear to see him struggle."

"He needs to do them if he wants to get better. It's important, even if it's uncomfortable."

Her mother's tone grew sharp and ugly. "Well maybe *you* can stand seeing your brother in pain. I'm sorry I'm not built as stern and unfeeling as you."

I opened my mouth to protest this profoundly unfair statement, but Lucy gave me a small, desperate shake of her head. I had to remind myself I was here to help. It wasn't my place to start a fight with her mother—no matter how much I wanted to step in and defend Lucy.

"Did you order pizza?" Lucy asked as she closed up the box and carried it to the fridge.

"No, Corey brought that by for Matt this evening." Brenda rounded on me with a broad smile, as if she hadn't just insulted her daughter in front of me. "Isn't that sweet of him? Matt's friends have all been so supportive. First Wyatt drops by with a fried chicken family meal yesterday, and now pizza."

"That is nice," I agreed, laboring to maintain a polite expression.

A smile curved Lucy's lips as her gaze met mine. "I wonder where they could have gotten the idea to do that."

Brenda turned back to her daughter with a cold, accusatory glare. "Meanwhile you're off doing god knows what when your family needs you most."

The smile vanished from Lucy's face. "What do you mean?"

"You were gone the whole day yesterday, even though you knew it was the only day you'd be free to help me with your brother this week. And today you took forever getting home from work. It's nearly six thirty! I've been on pins and needles waiting for you so I can have a little time for myself finally." As she spoke, Lucy seemed to shrink even more, and I grew even angrier as I watched the light leave her eyes.

"I had to go to the grocery store," Lucy said in a small, brittle voice. "I told you that."

"Yes. Well. You certainly took your time about it."

I didn't feel an ounce of guilt over the extra time Lucy and I had taken at the store. In fact, I wished I'd kept her there even longer. She'd certainly looked happier when we were shopping than she did right now. I was beginning to suspect the reason she hadn't wanted me to come over had less to do with the cleanliness of the house and more to do with the way her mother treated her.

Lucy opened her mouth, and I waited for her to defend

herself, ready to back her up if necessary. Instead she clamped her mouth shut again and turned her back to shove the vegetables inside the freezer.

As if sensing she was treading on some thin fucking ice—possibly due to the glowering outrage I was projecting as I fought to hold my tongue—Lucy's mother adopted a more conciliatory tone. "I'm sorry, honey. I should show more gratitude, I suppose. I know you work so hard. I worry about you running yourself ragged with all these errands and chores on top of that job. It seems to take so much out of you."

"I'm fine," Lucy replied, sounding the exact opposite.

"Well, you certainly know how to manage your own life. I just hope you're not taking on too much." Brenda's eyes alighted on me, as if *I* was the one responsible for Lucy's stress.

Of all the goddamn nerve...

"Did you get more Cheetos?" Matt called, hobbling into the living room on crutches. "Hey, man!" he hailed me with a grin. "Thanks again for all your help on Saturday."

"Oh, Matt! You shouldn't be on your feet. It scares me to death to see you on those things." Brenda clutched both hands to her heart as if she were in danger of going into cardiac arrest.

"I can handle a pair of crutches," Matt grumbled. "What am I supposed to do? Lie in bed all day?"

While Brenda was fussing over her son, I tried to edge closer to Lucy in solidarity, but she was shoving groceries into the fridge with such violence I nearly took an accidental elbow to the solar plexus.

Matt finally made it into the kitchen after waving off his mother's fluttering attempts to help, which had only succeeded in getting in his way. He shifted both crutches under one arm and made a wobbly, one-footed swoop to retrieve a bag of Cheetos off the floor in a move so precarious it almost had me sympathizing with Brenda's concern over him.

"Thanks, Luce." Matt waved the Cheetos at his sister before clamping them between his teeth and setting a tottering course out of the kitchen.

"You see what I have to contend with all day?" Lucy's mother gestured helplessly at Matt's retreating form as he made his slow way back to his room.

"Did you eat any of the pizza?" Lucy asked her mother.

"Just a nibble," Brenda answered, examining her manicured fingernails. "Do you have any idea how much fat there is in a single slice of pizza?"

"If you're still hungry, Tanner and I are going to make a couple of casseroles."

"Are you now?" Brenda arched a disbelieving eyebrow at me, as if Lucy had just announced my intention to scale Mount Everest. "A man who cooks? My word."

"I enjoy cooking," I said, glad for an excuse to contradict Lucy's mother.

"I'm sure you do," she said, giving me a knowing look that seemed to imply I was only pretending to enjoy it to get in her daughter's pants.

Which was only partially true.

"You can have some for dinner when it's ready," Lucy offered.

"Thank you, honey, but no. I'm meeting Tony for dinner at seven."

And suddenly the reason she'd been so impatient for Lucy to get home became clear.

"You've got a date?" Lucy asked her.

"Well, yes. You can't expect me to be chained to the house all day. I've got a life of my own, you know, besides taking care of my children." Brenda's mouth turned down as she reached out to smooth Lucy's hair. "You haven't been forgetting to condition, have you? Your hair's like straw, baby."

Mrs. Dillard's Jekyll and Hyde act was giving me whiplash.

One second she seemed warm and affectionate, and the next she was lashing out with a criticism or complaint. At least my father never disguised his contempt for me behind false tenderness and backhanded compliments. I always knew where I stood with him, so I was never tempted to let my guard down.

I was relieved when Lucy's mother disappeared into the back of the house to finish primping for her date. It was obvious Lucy was upset, but I was afraid to say anything with her mother potentially still within earshot. As I helped Lucy put the rest of the groceries away and do the dishes, neither of us spoke except about where they kept the breakfast cereal and which cabinet the cookie sheets belonged in.

We'd gotten the kitchen cleaned up and had just started prepping to assemble the one-pot meals when Lucy's mother breezed past us in a cloud of freshly applied perfume and air kisses on her way out the door.

After I heard her car back out of the garage, I went over to Lucy and took the sweet potato she was peeling out of her hands. "Are you okay?" I asked, turning her to face me.

"Of course. It's fine." She gave me a smile I'd only recently learned to recognize as false, and I wondered how many times I'd seen that smile before without realizing how much pain hid behind it.

I squeezed Lucy's shoulders, trying to massage some of the tension away. "It's not fine the way she treats you, and you don't have to pretend like it is."

Her jaw clenched and she lifted her chin. "You don't understand. I told you she's...sensitive. She gets easily distressed. But she's not always like that. You caught her on a bad night, that's all. I knew she'd be at her limit from looking after Matt all day."

I couldn't believe Lucy was defending her. Although her mother's disdain came in its own peculiar flavor, it had reminded me so much of my dad that I was feeling a little triggered in addition to being filled with outrage on Lucy's behalf. "It still doesn't give her the right to insult you. My god, Lucy, she called you unfeeling. I can't imagine anything further from the truth."

Her chin wobbled like she was trying not to cry. "I don't want to talk about this anymore."

Fuck. I'd been trying to make her feel better, but instead I'd made her more upset.

Wrapping my arms around her, I pulled her into a hug, wishing I was the kind of person who was better at giving comfort. Not having been on the receiving end of much comforting in my life meant I never knew the right thing to say in these situations.

"I'm sorry," I told her, pressing a kiss to the top of her head. "I'm not trying to make you feel worse. I think you're wonderful, and I see how much you do for people and how caring you are. I hope you know that."

"Thank you," she mumbled, pressing her face into my chest.

"What can I do?" I asked, smoothing my hands over her back.

"This is pretty perfect. Keep doing this."

Okay, maybe I wasn't so bad at this comforting stuff after all.

22

LUCY

Tanner gave great hugs. The best. It was exactly what I needed.

The scene with my mother had been awful. I hated that Tanner had seen her behave like that, and I hated even more that he'd seen me take it so meekly.

I knew he didn't understand why I'd done it. He couldn't possibly, because he hadn't had to tiptoe around my mother's moods every day of his life.

It wasn't as if I'd never stood up to her. I'd tried, but it always made things worse. It was better not to argue. Once she'd gotten it out of her system, her dander would settle quickly enough, and she'd be much easier to be around afterward.

I'd learned not to let it hurt me. It was only words, after all. She didn't mean most of what she said. If I let her provoke me into a fight, she'd sulk and hold a grudge for days. It wasn't worth it to defend myself against her barbs. It wouldn't stop her from doing it again the next time, and it wasn't as if she ever said or did anything *that bad*. The cuts she inflicted were only superficial. Like paper cuts. They might smart for a few minutes, but they didn't do any lasting damage.

But *god*—the look on Tanner's face. Protectiveness had radiated off him in angry, buffeting waves. For a second there, I'd been terrified he was about to jump in and stick up for me. Fortunately, his good manners and my pleading look had prevented him from rebuking my mother to her face.

Not that I wasn't grateful for his support, but I was mortified that he'd seen how dysfunctional my family was. I knew he must be feeling even sorrier for me now. *Poor, sad Lucy can't even stand up for herself against her own mother.*

And yet, I couldn't say I entirely regretted inviting Tanner over tonight. As unpleasant as my mother had been, it was nice to have him here to hold me and say sweet things afterward. There were definitely some benefits to this whole letting people into my life business.

Like Tanner's wonderful, mood-healing hugs, for instance.

"We should get started on the cooking," I said, reluctantly removing myself from the comfort of his arms.

"Hey." Catching me as I started to turn away, he surprised me with a tender, lingering kiss. "Okay," he said when I smiled in response. "Now we can start cooking."

As promised, Tanner's one-pot meals were simple and easy to assemble. There was a Greek turkey and rice skillet, and another one with chorizo, sweet potatoes, and black beans. We doubled both so there'd be enough food to last the whole week plus extra servings to freeze.

An hour later, the fridge and freezer were stacked with prepared meals, the kitchen was spotless, and I'd broken into my hidden stash of wine for us to enjoy while we dined on the fruits of our labors. If I didn't think about the stuff that happened before my mother left—and ignored the fact that my brother was in the front bedroom playing Xbox and periodically shouting expletives into his gaming headset—it was almost romantic.

For the first time, I found myself entertaining a fantasy of sharing a home with someone else instead of my usual fantasy of having a house all to myself. When I imagined getting to cook with Tanner, eat with Tanner, clean up after dinner with Tanner, and go to bed with Tanner every night, it didn't sound so bad. In fact, it sounded pretty ideal. Even better than a Fortress of Solitude.

"Do you want to see my room?" I offered when we'd finished cleaning up our dinner dishes.

Tanner's eyebrows raised. "If you're expecting to have your way with me, I should tell you I'm not that kind of boy."

I laughed as I took Tanner's hand and led him to my bedroom.

"This room feels just like you," he said as soon as he stepped inside, and for some reason it made my chest glow with pride.

He took his time looking around—showing particular interest in the quotes I'd printed out and hung in cheap frames to decorate the walls, and the cherished objects arranged on my desk and dresser—before finally sitting cross-legged on the floor to study the contents of my bookshelf.

"I recommended these to you," he said, tossing a pleased look over his shoulder when he found the Ursula Le Guin books I'd bought.

"I know, that's why I bought them. Well, first I checked them out from the library, but I liked them so much I bought myself copies to keep."

"YEAAAAH! Get shiddon, you little bitch!" Matt shouted from the room next door, and Tanner and I shared a grin.

"This must be a favorite," Tanner said, tugging my copy of *How to Be Happy* off the shelf. "It's more dog-eared than the others."

I liked watching him look through my things. The intentness of his gaze as he examined everything, and the careful, fond way he handled my treasured possessions, as if they were as precious to him as they were to me. It surprised me how much I liked having him here in my private sanctum. It felt right. Like he belonged here.

Eventually he finished looking through my books and joined me on the bed, wrapping his long limbs around mine on the narrow twin-size mattress. "This takes me back to college," he said as he wriggled against me, trying to get comfortable.

I waited for him to stop squirming before I draped my arm across his back. "Cuddle with a lot of girls on twin-size beds, did you?"

"A few. Not as many as I would have liked."

"I find that hard to believe."

"Believe it. I wasn't very good at talking to girls. I was too shy." He nuzzled my neck. "I wish I'd known you in college. I can't believe we went to the same schools all our lives and never met before last year."

"It's not like I didn't know who you were, but I didn't have much of a social life. We may have gone to the same schools, but we moved in different worlds."

"It wasn't meant to be until it was meant to be." He tugged at the neckline of my top and pressed his lips to the cleavage he'd exposed. "I love this sweater on you. It's been driving me wild all day long."

"I've never had a boy in my room before, you know."

Tanner lifted his head, his eyebrows arching devilishly. "Is that so?"

"After tonight, you can probably guess why."

His expression softened. "Is it always like that?"

"No, not always."

He kissed my sternum and laid his head on my chest, holding me tighter. "I'm sorry if my being here made it worse."

"It didn't." I threaded my fingers through his soft, honey-brown hair. "I'm glad you're here."

"I'm glad too." Matt erupted in another tirade of shouted curses on the other side of the wall. When the cussing died down, Tanner said, "I haven't told you much about my dad."

"No." When we first met, I'd assumed Tanner was protective of his privacy because of how prominent his family was and how much people loved to gossip about them. Then, as I'd gotten to know Tanner better, I'd realized he was just a private person. Like me, he didn't easily open up about himself.

"You might have picked up on the fact that our relationship is...difficult."

"I've noticed you tense up whenever you talk about him." I scratched my fingernails lightly over his back muscles, which were as tight as braided steel cables. "Also there was that whole thing where he demoted you and made you play Sheriff Scoopy."

"Yeah. There is that." I could hear the scowl in his voice. "I've never been able to live up to his expectations, and he's never let me forget it."

"What does he expect from you?"

"I'm not sure. All I know is he's never been satisfied with anything I try to do to please him. I guess maybe he wants me to be more like Nate. Driven? Confident? Uncompromising? Whatever he wants, it's not me."

"That's ridiculous," I said, cuddling him closer. "You're amazing exactly the way you are. If your father can't appreciate that, I consider his judgment severely flawed."

Tanner nuzzled between my breasts appreciatively. "I went to work for the company after college because it was what my dad wanted. Only I've been screamingly mediocre at every job I've tried to do there. If it weren't for nepotism, I never would have been promoted past merchandiser."

"That's not true. You're white, male, and conventionally attractive. You would have been promoted regardless of your last name."

His huff of wry laughter tickled my chest. "Sad but true. Either way, I'm well aware I don't deserve all the chances I've been given, and it makes me feel like shit. I know I'm taking a job away from someone else who deserves it more than me. And the thing is, I don't even like working for my family's company. I hate it, actually. I always have." He paused as if just now realizing how true what he'd said was. "I really, honestly hate it."

"Even now that you're working with me?"

He levered himself up on his elbows to look at me. "These last few weeks, getting to see you at work every day, is the happiest I've ever been in that building."

The warmth in his eyes told me how much he meant it. I touched my fingertips to his cheek, and he lowered his mouth to mine in a slow, searching kiss.

When he pulled back, his expression was somber again, his brow creased by furrows. "But just by being there I'm undermining you with Byron. If it were up to him, he'd promote me instead of you."

It was true. I couldn't deny it or pretend it didn't matter to me. It wasn't Tanner's fault, but it sucked nonetheless.

He laid one of his big warm hands along my jaw and touched his lips to my cheekbone. "I'm not going to let that happen, okay? I don't want you to worry about that."

I wanted to believe him. I knew he'd never do it on purpose, but... "It's not necessarily up to you, is it?"

Shifting onto his side, he pulled me toward him and cradled me against his chest. I burrowed into his protective embrace, inhaling the comforting, familiar smell of him.

"I'd quit before I accepted a promotion over you. But it won't come to that. Josie knows you deserve that promotion, and she thinks Byron's a brown-nosing snake."

"Did she say that?"

"Maybe not in those exact words, but close to it."

That made me feel a little better. Not nearly as good as a raise would feel, but I'd take what I could get. Hopefully next quarter's revenues would be up and my promotion would be back on again.

"If I had any other marketable skills, I'd quit my job right now." His deep sigh rumbled through his chest. "I've spent my whole life making myself miserable just to please someone who's never going to be happy with anything I do. And now I'm trapped."

For all his family money and advantages, our lives were oddly similar. We were both stuck, both of us slowly being crushed by our sense of duty to a parent who would never be satisfied.

All night, I'd been assuming Tanner felt sorry for me, but it wasn't that at all. He'd been sympathizing with me, because he knew what it was like. That was why he'd told me all this—to let me know he understood.

I raised my eyes to his and traced the reddish-blond stubble coming in along his jaw. "I meant what I said before. You're amazing. If you want to find another job, I'll do everything I can to help. I happen to be one hell of a résumé formatter and proofreader."

Up close like this, his smile was even sexier and more perfect. "You're the one who's amazing. I'm so grateful to have you in my life."

"Tanner," I whispered, overcome by emotion, and he touched his perfect lips to my cheek, rubbing them back and forth, as light as the tickle of a feather.

"I love the pink of your cheeks when you blush."

My breath shuddered, and my eyes fell shut as his mouth closed over mine. Firm and so, so sweet. A perfect kiss to match his perfect smile. My lips parted at the touch of his tongue, and I pressed my hips against him, desperate for more contact, wanting to *feel* him.

"Dude, what the *fuck* was with that potato aim?" Matt shouted in the next room, and we broke apart, laughing softly.

Tanner's smile faded as he tugged my shirt loose from the waistband of my pants. His fingertips grazed my bare skin, and his blue eyes met mine, asking permission.

I tipped my chin in the slightest of nods, and his hand slid under my shirt and up my rib cage to stroke the cup of my bra.

"I have a confession to make," he said as he tugged on my bra to expose my breast. "I lied. I *am* that kind of boy. Please have your way with me."

I let out a needy, frustrated groan as his fingers brushed my nipple. "I would love nothing more, but as you may have noticed, the walls in this house are extremely thin."

"I did notice that." He pushed my top up and bent his head, his mouth hovering over my breast. Pausing, he lifted his eyes to mine. "I can be very quiet." His tongue flicked out for a teasing taste, and I bit down on my lip to stifle a moan. "Can you?"

"I guess we're about to find out."

———

I WAS STILL awake when I heard my mother come home just before eleven. Tanner had only left an hour ago, after helping me break in my virgin bed. Our furtive, whispered gropings had made me feel like a teenager again—in a good way, not a hormonal, socially awkward, pimple-faced way. It was as if I was getting to make up for some of the fun I'd missed out on in my actual teenage years.

Therefore, I was in an unusually good mood when my mother tapped on the door of my room. "Come in," I answered softly, looking up from my book. I was in my pajamas under the covers, rereading my favorite Talia Hibbert romance.

The door opened, and my mother poked her head in the room. "I saw your light on."

"Did you have a nice time with Tony?" I asked cautiously, hoping the answer was yes. She was always more pleasant when a date had gone well. On the downside, she sometimes had a fuzzy view on boundaries, so inquiring about her dates could open the floodgates to TMI-ville. I could only pray I wouldn't be regaled with disturbing tales of Tony's sexual prowess or an excruciatingly detailed description of his penis shape.

"I did." She came in and perched on the edge of my bed. "He's such a gentleman. And so sweet! I think it might be getting serious between us."

"Already?" I couldn't help feeling concerned. "How well do you even know him?" What did she even mean by "getting serious" when he lived in Houston and they only saw each other when he happened to be driving through town?

"I know him well enough to know his heart. Don't you worry about me, I've been doing this a lot longer than you." She smoothed the duvet covering my legs. "You and Tanner King seem to be spending an awful lot of time together. What's going on there?"

I couldn't help the blush that warmed my cheeks at the mention of Tanner—which of course my mother immediately picked up on.

"Look at you! You're positively glowing." She reached out and pinched my arm. "Do you have a little crush on that nice, handsome King boy? Tell your mama everything."

I usually avoided telling my mother about my love life. It was a subject she was more deeply invested in than I liked, and her lack of boundaries could lead to intrusive questions I didn't care to answer. I much preferred to keep my private life private, and that especially included the details of my intimate partners' physical appearance and sexual performance.

When Tanner and I had dated the last time, I'd refrained from mentioning him to her altogether. As far as she knew, my acquaintance with him was a recent one. But if he was going to be coming around the house regularly, there'd be no hiding the truth from her this time.

"It's more than a crush," I said. "Tanner and I are dating."

"Are you really?" She looked surprised and a little dubious, as if she didn't quite believe I could attract someone like Tanner. "Since when?"

I swallowed the sting of her skepticism. "Since this weekend. Although we've known each other for a lot longer than that."

"Well, I'll be! Imagine, my mousy little Lucy going out with one of the King boys. Good for you, baby." She gave my knee a proud squeeze.

At least she seemed to approve of him, although I knew she was only thinking about his family's money and social status, and how much she'd be able to brag about it to all her friends and beauty clients. Speaking of which, now that my mother knew, there'd be no keeping our relationship a secret anymore. In a town the size of Crowder, the gossip would eventually make its way to Josie King.

"You just make sure you don't let him take advantage of you," my mother warned.

"He's not taking advantage of me. He's a good man, and I'm a grown woman capable of making my own decisions."

"Be that as it may." She waved away my bodily autonomy as an insignificant matter. "Make him buy the cow if he wants the milk. Don't let him think you come cheaply."

"I'm not a piece of livestock up for auction. He doesn't get to own me at any price." Her view of gender roles and male-female relationships persistently made me sad for her, because I knew she was only repeating the lessons that had been drilled into her as a girl and reinforced by her own experiences. Was it any wonder I'd been so wary of love after listening to all her "womanly" advice?

"You know what I mean," she said with a huff of impatience. "A boy like that, from a good family with more money than you can shake a stick at, he's used to taking whatever he wants and discarding it when he gets bored." Her mouth settled in a worried frown as she tucked my hair behind both my ears. "The only way you can hope to hold his interest is by playing hard to get. Make him work for it. That'll keep him coming back.

"He's not like that, Mama." I knew she was thinking of my father, who'd lost interest in her as soon as they got married. But Tanner was nothing like my father, and our relationship couldn't have been more different than my parents'.

She gave me a pitying look. "I'm sorry to tell you that all men are like that, baby. But the rich ones even more so."

23

TANNER

On Friday afternoon, after receiving Heather's permission, I took Lucy to my dad's house for a look through the family photo albums.

"Wow," she said, gazing wide-eyed through the car window as I parked on the circular drive in front of the house. "Look at this place! It's a mansion. You grew up in a freaking mansion."

The old familiar knot of dread had formed in my stomach on the drive over. It wasn't quite as bad when I knew my dad wouldn't be here, but I still didn't love coming to this house.

"Do I get to see your old room?" she asked as we walked up the stone path to the arched front door.

"I can show you the room, but none of my stuff is in there anymore. It's been redecorated into a guest room."

"That's sad. But I'd still like to see it." Lucy's hand touched my back as I fumbled with the key in the lock. "You all right?"

I set my jaw and nodded without looking at her. "There's a security camera pointed at us right now. Just FYI."

The key turned and I pushed the door open, gesturing for Lucy to enter ahead of me. She walked into the tiled entryway and came to a stop in the middle of the rug, looking around curiously. "Is anyone home? We're not going to surprise anybody, are we?"

"No, everyone's out." The smell of the house hit me in the pit of my stomach as I closed the door, and the latch fell into place with an ominous *clunk* that echoed like the slamming of a jail cell. "Heather took Riley back-to-school shopping in Austin, and Cody's camping in Big Bend with some friends."

"Right, sure."

I could guess from Lucy's face what she was thinking: *Must be nice*. I doubted she'd been taken back-to-school shopping by her mother much or gotten to go on camping trips with her friends.

She saw me looking at her, and her expression changed. "I'm sorry. I'll try harder not to sound bitter."

"It's okay to feel how you feel. We have things other people don't. You're allowed to resent us for it."

"I don't resent you. I don't resent your family either. I'm just envious. But it's petty of me, and I don't want to be petty."

"If it makes you feel any better, I hated growing up here." I shoved my hands in my pockets as I let my gaze drift around me, seeing the ostentatious decor through Lucy's eyes. The house had been designed on an aggressively Texan theme to suit my dad's tastes. Artsy black-and-white prints of oil derricks and longhorn steer adorned the stucco walls alongside collectible vintage concert posters featuring my dad's favorite Texas artists. The "formal" sitting room beside the entry was furnished with rough-hewn wood furniture upholstered with cowhide, and the handwoven rugs had been commissioned from Mexican artisans.

"That doesn't make me feel any better at all." She came closer and peered up at me, her face creased with worry. "Are you okay?"

"Yeah." I tried to smile and failed miserably. "Just some not-so-great memories associated with this place."

Lucy attached herself to me in a rib-bruising hug. "We didn't have to come. If it's too unpleasant for you, we can leave. Really."

"It's fine." I dropped my head, resting it on top of hers, and inhaled the sweet floral scent of her shampoo as I ran my hands over her back. "I'm okay. I come here all the time. I can handle this."

"That doesn't mean you have to." She backed out of my arms and punched me gently in the shoulder. "You should have told me it would affect you like this."

"Ow," I grumbled. "There's no call for abuse."

"Are there cameras inside the house?" she asked, spinning around as she squinted up at the ceiling.

"No, just outside."

"Good." She rested her hands on top of my shoulders and rose on her toes to kiss me.

I bent my head to accept her kiss and impulsively deepened it, sweeping my tongue into her mouth hungrily as I backed her up against the wall. I pressed my body against hers, and she responded eagerly, pushing her hips into me. When she shoved her thigh between my legs, I groaned and reached for the hem of her skirt.

She'd worn a dress to work today, one of those wrap dresses that clung to her curves in the most tantalizing fucking way possible, and if that wasn't enough, it had this enticing goddamn slit in the skirt that had been calling to me all day. I'd been dying to slip my hand in there, and now that we were alone, that was exactly what I did.

I grabbed a handful of her silky-soft thigh, and she made the loveliest noise in the back of her throat. It made me want to put my hands all over every inch of her body. Cradling her jaw as I crushed my mouth against hers, I dragged my hand up her inner thigh. I could feel her muscles trembling as my fingers inched higher, her breaths coming faster and shallower. I hadn't planned on letting things go this far—not here, of all places—but *god*, she was just so responsive and inviting.

I pulled my head back to look at her, devouring the sight of her rosy flushed skin and the way her eyes had gone hazy and half lidded. My thumb stroked her cheek, then parted her kiss-bruised lips. Her tongue flicked out to taste it, and I groaned.

"How wet are you right now?"

Her chin tilted up as her eyes flashed even darker. "Why don't you touch me and find out for yourself?"

I caught her earlobe between my teeth and pressed my hand against her pussy, cupping her over her underwear.

Jesus, she was fucking *soaked*, and the whimper she let out just about undid me.

My voice came out as a low growl as I spoke into her ear. "Would it be wrong if I fucked you up against this wall right here next to the front door?"

The sound she made could only be described as incoherent.

I licked the tender skin beneath her ear. "Or maybe you'd rather I sink to my knees and eat you out until you can't stand up anymore?"

I didn't plan to do it—I wasn't so mindless that I'd lost all sense of where we were. I just had to know if she'd be willing to let me.

Her answering moan and the way her hips jerked against my hand indicated her enthusiastic consent to my proposal. But instead of giving in to my shameless urges, I withdrew my hand, smoothed her skirt back down, and pressed a tender kiss to her cheek. "Better not," I murmured. "We'll save that for later."

She was pink-cheeked and shaking when I drew back, her eyelashes fluttering as she sagged against the wall for support. I, on the other hand, was feeling bolstered, my flagging spirits revived enough to face the ghosts of my past.

"You're a merciless tease," she grumbled in protest.

"I know. I promise to make it up to you." I took her hand and brought it to my lips. "Let's get this done so we can get out of here."

Drawing strength from the warmth of her soft fingers twined with mine, I led her down the hall to my dad's study. Of all the rooms in the house, this one felt the most oppressive. Even when it was empty, my father's presence loomed as large as the massive set of mule deer antlers mounted on the wood-paneled wall behind the desk.

I scanned the floor-to-ceiling bookcases. The house had changed a bit since I lived here, but not that much—and not in here. This room was my father's exclusive domain, a museum dedicated to his greatness. Framed photos of him posing with various celebrities—Bill Clinton, Ann Richards, Earl Campbell, and Lyle Lovett among them—shared pride of place with a large oil painting of the creamery's corporate headquarters building.

"Here." I found one of the photo albums I was looking for and handed it to Lucy. "You wanted baby pictures. Knock your-self out."

"Oh! Yes please." She carried it over to the big leather couch and sat down, opening the album in her lap. "Oh my god!" she exclaimed in delight. "Look at you with your chubby little cheeks! And wow, you and Wyatt look just like your mom."

"Yeah." I'd wondered sometimes if that was why Dad had been so distant with the two of us. If the sight of our faces had reminded him too much of the wife he'd lost. Then I remem-bered he'd been pretty distant before she died too. It was just how he was with us.

While Lucy oohed and ahhed over my baby pictures, I pulled down another couple of albums that I thought might have some photos we could use for the newsletter—one from Dad's youth, and another commemorating my granddad's retirement from the creamery. Settling onto the couch beside Lucy, I started flipping through the older one, past photo after photo of my dad looking youthful and brash.

"How about this one?" I asked Lucy, pointing to a photo of Dad as a teenager, working behind the counter of the old ice cream shop on Main Street.

"That's perfect."

I carefully pried the photo out of the album as she got out the photo scanner she'd brought from the office, and set it up on the coffee table in front of the couch. While I continued looking through the albums, Lucy scanned the photos I handed her.

Twenty minutes later, I'd finished going through both albums, and Lucy was working her way through the stack of photos I'd pulled out.

"Here, I'm done with this one." She handed me the older of the two photo albums. "You can put it back."

After I returned the album to the shelf, I went over to the lateral filing cabinet behind my dad's desk. Spinning the big leather desk chair around, I sat down and opened the bottom drawer. I knew my dad kept a file of press clippings that included some old promotional photos, and I thought there might be something good in there Lucy could use.

As I perused the file labels, I spotted an old brown file wallet with Reyes written on the spine. We hadn't found any good pictures of my dad with Manny's dad, so I pulled it out of the drawer, hoping there might be some photos inside. The elastic band holding it closed had lost most of its elasticity, and the scent of old paper tickled my nose as I folded back the flap and slid the papers out. It mostly looked to be legal documents related to Manny's adoption, but among them were some letters from his grandparents, and I thumbed through them on the off chance they might include some Reyes family photos.

I paused on something that looked like lab test results and ran my eyes over the flimsy, yellowed piece of paper. The tables of numbers and letters that filled most of the page made no sense to me, but two lines at the top jumped out and seized my attention:

Child: REYES, MANUEL JR.
Alleged Father: KING, GEORGE E.

My heartbeat thudded in my ears, the words on the page blurring as the implication sank in. Shaking my head to clear my racing thoughts, I squinted at the paper, trying to make sense of what I was seeing. At the bottom of the page, beneath the incomprehensibly detailed DNA analysis, were several short paragraphs of text. The very first line told me what I needed to know.

Probability of Paternity: 99.99%

I stared at it, stunned but also disconcerted I hadn't ever considered it before. Manny was less than a year older than Nate, which meant he'd been conceived while Dad was married to his first wife, Trish Buchanan. It wasn't as if my father's history of extramarital affairs was a secret. Why hadn't it ever occurred to me he might have slept with his best friend's wife?

Of course Dad was Manny's father. Of course he was.

That was why Dad had adopted Manny. Not out of loyalty to his best friend, but out of obligation to his own flesh and blood.

A son my father had never acknowledged was biologically his.

At least not as far as I knew. Had Dad ever told Manny? If he had, Manny had never breathed a hint to the rest of the family.

I thought back over all our conversations over the years, the way Manny talked about his father versus mine. It was impossible to believe he knew. His affection for my dad seemed genuine, but there was an element of gratitude underlying it—a sense of indebtedness to Dad for giving him a home.

We all treated Manny like part of the family, but—just like with Ryan—there'd always been an unspoken awareness that he wasn't a King by blood or by name. It had set them both subtly apart from the rest of us.

I'd often envied that difference and the layer of immunity it seemed to grant them from the weight of Dad's expectations. He'd been easier with both Manny and Ryan—and easier *on* them—more like the friendly father figure I'd always wished I could have had than the cold, critical father I'd known.

But Manny was Dad's son as much as I was. And Dad had known—at least since 1994, the year on the paternity test—but possibly long before that. He'd known when he'd adopted him, and he'd known through all the years since, when he'd treated Manny like an honorary son instead of an actual one.

Had my mom known? Her name was on the adoption papers right next to Dad's. Had she known she was adopting the child of her husband's affair with his best friend's wife? Or had Dad kept that minor detail from her the way he'd kept it from everyone else, letting the whole town think he was a saint doing it purely out of the goodness of his heart?

Chaotic, conflicting feelings warred in my head. In addition to shock, there was outrage at the secrecy and deception, but I also felt guilty for not being happier to learn Manny and I shared DNA. He was already one of my favorite brothers, and his kids were my favorite kids in the whole world. I should be celebrating the news that we were related.

Instead I could only feel anger on his behalf, as well as sadness that Manny had been saddled with Dad's thorny legacy like the rest of us.

I stared at the paternity test in my hand, wondering what I should do about it. Should I tell Manny? He'd want to know, surely? Or would that destroy his relationship with Dad, along with his memories of his parents? It didn't seem like something I should keep from him, but maybe he'd be happier remaining blissfully ignorant. I sure as hell wished I'd never seen this goddamn piece of paper.

"Tanner?"

I looked up and realized Lucy had been talking to me. "Sorry."

"What's got you so interested?"

"Just some stuff from Manny's adoption. Nothing we can use, but he might like to see it." I used my phone to snap a photo of the paternity test results before shoving all the files back in the wallet case. "Are you done with the scanning?" I asked as I returned everything to the file drawer and slammed it shut.

"Everything you gave me so far. Did you find anything else we could use over there?"

"No, nothing." I hadn't even gotten to the press clippings file, but I couldn't bear to look at any more pictures of my father's arrogant, smiling face. "We've got enough, right?"

"Yeah, we've got plenty to work with."

"Good. Let's get out of here."

I put the other photo album away while Lucy packed the scanner back in her bag. After casting an eye around my dad's study to make sure we hadn't left any evidence of our presence, I grabbed Lucy's hand and pulled her out of the room.

"You were going to show me your old bedroom," she said as I hustled her toward the front door.

"Is it okay if we don't? I want to get out of here."

"Of course."

"Thanks." I squeezed her hand gratefully before digging my keys out of my pocket to lock the house behind us.

We got in the car and fastened our seat belts. When I reached out to start the engine, she touched my arm.

"Tanner—"

"I'm fine," I said, blowing out a breath. "I just hit my limit for sifting through family memories."

She seemed to accept that, and we drove back to the office in silence. My mind was too heavy with the information I'd uncovered to make any attempt at conversation, and Lucy seemed to sense my need to cocoon myself in quiet. But I felt her eyes on me and the little worried glances she kept casting my way.

The employee parking lot at the creamery was already half empty this late on a Friday afternoon. The August sun rippled the air above the baking asphalt and cast blinding glints off windshields as I pulled into a vacant space in the first row. I got out of the car before Lucy could say anything and walked around to open her door for her. Hoisting her bag over her shoulder, she climbed out and peered up at me with a frown.

"Come on, let's get inside." I couldn't close the car door with her standing there, and my forehead was already breaking into an itchy sheen of sweat from the heat.

"In a minute," she said and wound her arms around my midsection, laying her cheek against my chest.

I folded into her, letting her hold me up—not physically, but figuratively. The pressure that had been building in my chest moved into my throat as we stood there quietly, wrapped around each other. Her skin was cool from the AC in the car, and for a second I forgot about the brutal heat and the very visible public space we were in.

"Thank you," I murmured when I'd pulled myself back together enough to give her a halfway believable smile.

"For what?"

"For knowing exactly what I needed." I brushed my thumb

across her cheek, which was turning red in the heat. "Let's get you inside before you get a sunburn."

"Don't be silly, I wear a daily sunscreen that's like SPF a million." Still, she'd moved aside so I could close the car door and started walking toward the office when I touched my hand to the small of her back. "What time are you picking me up tonight?"

Shit. I'd forgotten about tonight. We were going on our first real date since we'd started seeing each other again. I'd made reservations for us at Post Oak Lodge, the best restaurant in town. For the last three days, I'd hardly been able to think about anything else, but this stuff about Dad and Manny had pushed it right out of my head.

"Uh, seven fifteen, I guess."

"You sure you're okay? We can do something else tonight if you're not up to going out."

"Are you kidding? I've been looking forward to it all week."

A blast of arctic air greeted us when I opened the lobby door, and I let out a sigh of relief as we stepped inside—both for the blessed cool and for the excuse to avoid personal topics of conversation now that we were back inside the office.

We rode the elevator upstairs in silence and parted when Lucy stopped off at the bathroom, leaving me to retreat to my cubicle alone. Mumbling a greeting at Linh and Arwen, I sat down and spent what was left of the day absolutely failing to concentrate on my work.

I was unreasonably excited about my date with Tanner tonight, considering I'd seen him every single day this week. But tonight was different, because it was just us—getting dressed up for each other and going somewhere special to celebrate being together—without any coworkers or relatives around to get in the way.

As I was putting my makeup on in the bathroom, my mother tapped on the door. "Lucy, honey."

"What?" I asked as I dabbed mascara on my lashes.

"Are you decent? I need to ask you something." Without waiting for an answer, she tried the knob and pushed her way in. "Oh! Look at you, all dressed up."

"I've got a date, remember?" I'd told my mother days ago that I'd be going out tonight.

She held her phone in one hand and rested the other on her hip. "With Tanner King?"

I dipped the mascara wand in the tube. "Yes."

"Haven't you seen enough of him this week? You don't want him getting tired of you. Nothing kills desire like overexposure."

I ignored her as I applied another coat of mascara in the mirror.

"You should really start wearing false eyelashes," she said. "There's only so much mascara's going to be able to do for thin lashes like yours."

I shoved the mascara wand back in the tube and dropped it into my makeup bag. "Did you need something, Mama?"

She thrust her phone in front of my face. "What do you think it means when a man sends you a text like this?"

I cast my eyes at the ceiling, refusing to fall into that trap a second time. "Please tell me that's not a dick pic."

"Certainly not. I know exactly what to make of a text like *that*."

Warily, I glanced down at the screen. It was a text from Tony, but fortunately not an explicit one—although I could see why she was concerned.

"It sounds like he's been busy with work." I said noncommittally. Tanner was going to be here soon, and I didn't have time to hold my mother's hand through one of her relationship crises, which could easily drag on for hours.

She pinched her lower lip between her thumb and forefinger. "That's what he said, but what do you think that *means*? Is he cheating on me?"

"Maybe he's actually been busy with work." I dug a tube of lipstick out of my makeup case, and my mother thumped the back of my hand.

"Not that one. Choose something that won't wash you out." She plucked a different tube out and thrust it at me. "He waited three days to answer my last text and then claimed to be busy with work. I'm afraid he's losing interest in me."

"You don't know that." I had to admit, the lipstick my mother had picked did look good on me. It was a little dark for work, but perfect for a night out. "The fact that he bothered to apologize means he wants to hear from you. If he'd lost interest, he wouldn't have texted you back at all."

"I suppose." Frowning at me, she shoved her phone into her bra, took the lipstick out of my hand, and grasped my chin to turn my face toward her. "I'm going to let him cool off for a while before I respond," she said as she touched up my lipstick with deft strokes. "I'll make him wait on me to show him I'm not sitting around hanging on his every word."

"Don't make him wait too long," I said when she'd finished. "You don't want him thinking you've ghosted."

"That's exactly what I do want him to think. Then he'll sit up and take notice. When I finally text him back, he'll be properly grateful to hear from me." She capped the lipstick and dropped it into my makeup case before casting an appraising eye over my outfit. "You're very dressed up. Where's Tanner taking you?"

"Post Oak Lodge." I was wearing a simple but elegant sleeveless black dress with a deep V neckline. It was an old dress, but Tanner had never seen me in it before, and I liked how I looked in it. Hopefully he would too, because I was very much looking forward to finishing what we'd almost started at his father's house this afternoon.

"La-dee-dah." My mother leaned forward to examine her own flawless makeup in the mirror next to me. "I suppose a man like that can afford it."

Stepping around her, I walked across the hall to my room and fished my shoes out of the closet.

"Wear the red ones, dear." My mother had followed me and was leaning in the doorway of my bedroom. "How long do you think I should make Tony stew before I text him back?"

"I don't know. An hour?" I picked up the red heels and set them next to the black ones I'd been planning on wearing. "Really?"

"Trust me. With your complexion, you want that pop of color."

I shrugged and stepped into the red heels. "Don't wait up for me. I might not be home tonight."

"Oh, Lucy." My mother made a disappointed face. "Didn't you listen to anything I said?"

"I listened to every word, Mama, and then I made up my own mind."

She huffed in irritation. "I don't like that the two of you are getting so serious."

"I thought you liked Tanner?"

"I'm sure he seems lovely, but that's not the point."

Whatever her point was, I was saved from hearing it by the doorbell announcing Tanner's arrival. My stomach fluttered with excitement as I grabbed my bag and hurried to the front door.

My mother trailed after me. "I don't think an hour is long enough to teach Tony a lesson about taking me for granted. I think I should let him suffer for at least a day. Maybe two."

Ignoring her, I threw open the door.

Tanner stood on the doorstep, fiddling nervously with the tie he was wearing with his slacks and blazer. His eyes widened in appreciation as they took me in, traveling down my body and back up again. He opened his mouth—to say what, I'd never know, because my mother appeared at my elbow.

"Tanner! What a pleasure," she exclaimed as if his arrival hadn't been expected and he'd called at our house to see her. "How handsome you look. Why don't you come inside?"

"He can't, or we'll be late for our reservation," I answered before Tanner could. "Right?" I threw him a pleading look.

"I'm afraid so," he agreed, offering my mother an apologetic smile. "We really do have to get going."

"Good night, Mama." I kissed her cheek and stepped

outside, pushing Tanner ahead of me as I pulled the door closed behind us. "Don't look back," I whispered, slipping my hand through his arm. "Keep walking or she'll try to follow us out to the car."

———

I HADN'T BEEN to Post Oak Lodge since prom. I'd forgotten how much I liked the decor, which somehow managed to feel both rustic and fancy with its rough-hewn log ceilings, antler chandeliers, and white linen tablecloths.

"How's your rib eye?" I asked Tanner across the candlelit table.

"Good," he answered without much enthusiasm, although I suspected the problem wasn't the steak.

He'd been silent and brooding all evening—much more than normal, even. I was used to doing a lot of the talking when we were together, but it didn't usually bother me because he was such a good listener. Tonight, however, his mind seemed to be somewhere other than here on this date with me.

"My filet is excellent," I said, carving off another bite of the tender steak.

He winced. "I'm sorry, I should have asked you about it."

I tried not to take it personally, because I had an idea why he was so distracted. Something had changed in him when we were at his father's house. Whatever it was that had gotten in his head, it was still haunting him hours later.

"Do you want a bite?" I offered.

"No. Thanks." He set his silverware down and pushed his plate away.

"You've barely eaten half your steak."

"It's a twenty-two ounce rib eye. I gave it my best shot."

I dabbed at my mouth with my napkin. "I hope you plan to

take that home. It'd be a shame to let a cut of meat that good go to waste."

He nodded in agreement and reached for his water glass. He'd barely touched his wine either. Although that didn't surprise me, since he was driving.

Tanner had always been exceptionally conscientious about drinking and driving. I suspected it was partially to do with his oldest half-brother Chance, who'd died in a car accident after being hit by a drunk driver. Chance's twin, Brady, had been behind the wheel when they were hit. He'd left town not long after, and now he was the lead singer of a popular rock band. As far as I knew, Brady was estranged from his entire family. Tanner never talked about either Brady or Chance, and I wondered if his mood tonight had something to do with them. Perhaps something he'd seen at the house had reminded him of them.

Or maybe it had to do with his mother. It couldn't have been easy for him, looking at all those old photos. I hadn't realized how deeply affected he was by the past until I'd seen that haunted, bitter look come into his eyes at his father's house.

I pushed my own plate away and picked up my wineglass. As I sipped the last of it, I regarded Tanner across the table.

"Do you want to finish mine?" he offered, pushing his glass toward me.

"No, thank you." I set my empty glass down. "Do you want to tell me what's been bothering you all night?"

A pained look crossed his face. "I'm sorry. I haven't been very good company, have I?"

"You don't have to apologize. I just think it might help if you talked about it instead of keeping it all bottled up. Whatever it is."

He opened his mouth, then closed it again when the waitress appeared to whisk away our plates. I asked her to box up the leftovers and turned down her offer to bring the dessert menu.

"You sure you don't want dessert?" Tanner asked. "I don't mind."

I shook my head. "I just want you to talk to me."

He frowned. "I can't. But I promise you it doesn't have anything to do with you—or with us."

I reached across the table and offered my hand. He took it, sliding his fingers between mine. "Is it about your family?"

His frown deepened. "Yes."

We were still holding hands when the waitress came back a few minutes later. As Tanner paid the check, I tried not to think about how much this meal he hadn't even enjoyed must have cost him. He took my hand again on the walk to the car and didn't let go until he'd seen me into the passenger seat.

"Do you want to call it a night?" I asked when he'd gotten in beside me. "It's okay if you want to take me back to my house so you can be alone."

"I don't want that." He gave me an imploring look as he fastened his seat belt. "I know I ruined our big date, and I'm sorry."

"I don't care about the date. I care about you. What can I do?"

"Spend the night with me." The unhappiness in his expression ripped into my chest. "Please."

"Of course I will." I reached across the console and squeezed his leg. "Take me to your house."

———

WHEN WE GOT inside his house, Tanner walked straight through to the kitchen, shedding his blazer along the way, and took a bottle of whiskey out of the pantry. "Do you want some?" he offered, loosening his tie.

I shook my head, and he poured some in a glass and downed

it in one gulp. After pouring himself another, larger helping of whiskey, he corked the bottle and brought the glass into the living room. Taking my hand, he led me over to the couch and tugged me down beside him. I let him pull me up against him as he sagged back into the cushions.

Radagast followed us and draped himself across Tanner's leg. I petted the purring cat while Tanner silently sipped his drink, clutching my hip with his other hand.

It was a while before he finally spoke. "I found something at my dad's house today."

There it is. Now we were getting somewhere. I squeezed his leg, encouraging him to keep going.

There was a long pause before he did. "You know my parents adopted Manny when he was ten?"

"After his parents died in some kind of accident, right?" I was familiar with the basics, but not the details.

"A boating accident. They'd left Manny with his grandparents for the weekend and gone to Lake Travis."

A sense of foreboding swirled in the pit of my stomach. I had no idea what this was leading to, but given how hard it was for Tanner to talk about it, it must be something bad.

"Manny's dad was COO at the creamery and my dad's best friend." Another pause. "Allegedly."

While I was trying to parse that, Tanner handed me his glass and leaned over to pull his phone out of his back pocket, displacing Radagast, who abandoned the couch with an indignant meow. Tanner unlocked his phone, tapped his thumb to bring something up on the screen, and passed it to me.

It looked like a photo of some sort of document. I gave him back his drink so I could zoom in enough to read the text. It was a paternity test. When I saw the names on it, I stared at Tanner in surprise.

"Your dad is Manny's biological father?"

He shrugged with wry carelessness. "That's what it says."

"And I assume you didn't know before today."

"Nope." His eyes were fixed on his glass, his expression faraway and shuttered.

It was impossible for me to imagine what he was feeling right now. The closest I could come was trying to imagine how I'd feel if I learned Matt wasn't my real brother. But it wasn't the same. Not at all.

"Does Manny know?"

"I don't think so." Tanner lifted his glass and swallowed a mouthful of whiskey. "Not unless he's a lot better at keeping secrets than I ever imagined."

"But obviously your father knew, if you found this in his study."

"It was in the file with Manny's adoption paperwork. So yeah, he knew. I assume that's why he adopted him."

"But he kept it a secret from everyone." I was still trying to understand the implications of this, all the things it changed and all the ways Tanner must be hurting.

"Yep." His voice was rough with anger, his knuckles white as they gripped the glass in his hand.

I took the drink from him, set it and his phone on the coffee table, and wrapped myself around his torso like a koala bear.

His arms encircled me, and he let out a long, ragged breath as he rested his head against mine. "I really am sorry I messed up our date. We'll have a do-over so I can make it up to you."

"Whatever." I snuggled him harder. "How you doing in there?"

His fingers curled into my hair. "Better now. You're right, talking about it did help."

"What are you going to do? Are you going to ask your father about it? Or tell Manny?"

"I have no idea. What do you think I should do?"

"I can't answer that. I don't know enough about your family to advise you. What does your gut tell you?"

After a long pause he said, "Part of me wants to leave it alone and pretend I never saw that fucking paternity test."

"Understandable."

"But that feels cowardly and wrong. Honestly, I don't want to think about it anymore right now. I need some distance from it before I can come to any kind of rational decision."

"So you're saying what you need is a distraction?"

The fingers in my hair stroked over the back of my neck and downward. In this dress the whole top half of my back was exposed, so it was a pleasurable glide of bare skin on bare skin that I felt low in my stomach. "Maybe," he said in a voice that was much lower and softer than it had been a few moments ago.

I lifted my head to look at him, trying to decide if he meant it. His eyes were dark and clear when they met mine.

The hand on my back made it to my hip and idled there, rubbing small circles over the slippery crepe fabric. "Have I told you how much I like you in this dress?"

He had, as we were walking into the restaurant, but it had sounded perfunctory and distracted. Like he wasn't really seeing me.

He didn't sound that way now.

"Tell me again."

His other hand lifted to my face, his fingertips trailing a path along my hairline to my jaw. The gentlest of pressure had me leaning toward him, my body responding to his automatically. He met me halfway and lightly kissed my lips, the corner of my jaw, and my temple. "I love you in this dress," he whispered, and —*oh*, the first three words of that sentence zipped down my spine in a joyous tingle.

Before I had time to ponder that, his lips found mine again. This time he lingered there in a slow, sensual kiss as the hand on my hip slid down my thigh, under the hem of my dress, and back up again until his palm was cradling my ass cheek.

My hands smoothed over his chest as the kiss heated up, but in this dress, on this couch, I couldn't get as close to him as I needed to be. Humming in frustration, I wrapped a hand around his tie and used it to pull him up off the couch with me. "I think it'd be easier to distract you in the bedroom."

"Good idea." He mouthed a wet trail down my neck to the top of my shoulder as his fingers pushed the strap of my dress aside. "Excellent, in fact."

Taking a step backward, I tugged him along after me. He followed obediently but clumsily, distracted again, but this time by the need to kiss me some more.

"I love this dress," he said between kisses, his hands smoothing up my rib cage as we stumbled toward his bedroom. "I can't wait to take it off you."

I didn't let him take it off right away. First, I undressed him, slowly and with care, pausing frequently to kiss him and touch him, showing him with my hands and my mouth how cherished he was.

I let myself get lost in the hard planes of his body, the sweetness of his mouth, and the scent of his skin. Even though I was supposed to be cherishing him, I was the one who felt adored by the way he looked at me and reacted to my touch. The compliments and sounds that tumbled off his tongue, how concerned he was for my comfort, the tenderness with which he pushed my hair off my face.

I loved how easily he lost his composure beneath me, and I catalogued his every reaction and every single noise he made, etching the memories onto my heart and storing them away for future use. When he finally peeled my clothes off and sank himself inside me, we floated together breathlessly, smiling and shivering as our bodies moved in concert.

We took our time and took turns asking for things, giving and taking as we experimented with different sensations and positions, discovering new and wonderful angles and kinds of friction. It was worlds better than any fantasy my imagination had conjured, because being with Tanner was real, and it made me feel more alive than I ever had before.

After we'd exhausted ourselves, and the aftershocks had faded to peaceful, perfect bliss, he pulled the sheet up over us and we held each other, quietly sharing secrets and confessing things we'd never dared tell anyone else, growing closer and closer the more we talked. With Tanner's body warm and solid against mine and his cat curled up at our feet, the world felt safe and new and full of promise. I knew this feeling couldn't last, that reality would eventually dull some of the shine, but I clung to it and I clung to Tanner, determined to hold on to both as hard as I could.

25

TANNER

I knew what I needed to do—or at least what I needed to do next. I'd figured it out last night while talking to Lucy. When she'd said she didn't know enough about my family to give me advice, I realized who I needed to talk to—the person who'd always given me good advice. Ryan.

He was old enough to remember when Manny came to live with us, and knew Manny even better than I did. They were the same age, and they'd both been latecomers to my father's house. Ryan was seven when our mother married my father, and ten when Manny's parents died. He and Manny were both outsiders who'd been invited into the family and granted insider status, which gave Ryan a unique perspective on how Manny might react to this news.

After I dropped Lucy off at her house Saturday morning, I texted Ryan to ask if I could come over. He told me to bring breakfast if I was going to get him out of bed this early on his day off, so I stopped at Rita's Taqueria on my way.

Ryan was a Scottish Highland games athlete built like a grizzly bear—at six foot five inches of solid muscle, he consumed more protein in a day than most people did in a week

—so I ordered a half dozen fajita and egg tacos just for him and a couple of migas tacos for me.

When I parked in front of Ryan's house, a woman I didn't recognize was unloading suitcases from the trunk of a car in the driveway next door. I lifted my hand in a friendly wave, because that was what we did here in Crowder. Instead of waving back, she frowned and turned her back on me.

Alrighty, then.

Ryan's door opened as I approached the porch. His broad shoulders spanned the whole doorframe as he stood there yawning in a rumpled T-shirt and workout shorts.

"You got a new neighbor?" I asked as he stepped back so I could edge past him.

"Probably a new tenant." He leaned out the doorway to glance around before shrugging and shutting the door behind me. "Mr. Meckel's daughter turned the place into a short-term rental after he passed. Got all kinds of people coming in and out of there now."

His house smelled like fresh-brewed coffee, and I followed the scent into the kitchen. "You work last night?" I asked as I got down a mug and poured myself a cup.

He nodded and yawned again, pushing his half-full mug toward me for a refill. "What'd you bring me? Is that Rita's I smell?"

"What else?"

I handed Ryan his coffee and unpacked the tacos, stacking his in a large pile next to my much smaller one. While I was setting out the tiny containers of salsa, he unwrapped one of his tacos and wolfed it down in four bites.

"All right," he said, chasing it down with a slug of coffee. "I'm awake now. What's the emergency?"

I picked up one of my tacos and peeled back the foil. "It's not exactly an emergency."

"You don't ask to come over on a Saturday morning for no reason. Tell me what's on your mind."

"I found out something about Dad."

Ryan sighed and reached for another taco. "Okay."

"It has to do with Manny."

"What about him?" he asked as he doused his taco with green salsa.

"Dad is Manny's biological father."

Ryan froze with his taco halfway to his mouth. "Says who?"

I explained how Lucy and I had been at the house searching for pictures to use in the company newsletter, and how I'd looked inside the Reyes file hoping to find a picture of Manny Sr. "Instead I found this." I unlocked my phone, pulled up the photo of the paternity test, and slid it across the counter to Ryan.

He wiped his hands on a napkin and picked up my phone. I watched him closely as he squinted at it and zoomed in to read the test results.

"Fuck." He set the phone down and scrubbed his hands through his messy red hair.

"I take it you didn't know."

He glanced at me sharply. "Of course I didn't."

"Is there any way Manny knows about this?"

"No." He shook his head. "No way."

Seeing how certain he was made me realize I'd been hoping that somehow Manny might already know the truth. It would have been a relief to think this wouldn't change anything for him. Then I wouldn't have to decide whether or not to drop this bomb into the middle of his life. "Do we tell him?"

Ryan looked at me again. "Why wouldn't we?"

"Maybe he'd rather not know. Maybe he's happy with things the way they are. If I tell him this, it could blow up his relationship with Dad and taint the memories he's got of his parents. Maybe it's kinder to leave this secret a secret."

"It's not up to you to make that choice for him. It's the truth, and it's about his life—his family." Ryan frowned and scratched his head. "This information doesn't just affect Manny either. It changes Isabella and Jorge's family medical history as much as it changes Manny's."

I hadn't thought of that. But he was right.

Ryan took a drink of his coffee, set it down, and folded his thick arms across his chest. "Are you honestly willing to keep a secret like this from Manny? Do you think you could look him in the eye and say nothing?"

"No," I admitted, as much to myself as Ryan. "I have to tell him."

"There is one other option," Ryan said slowly, rubbing his jaw. "You could talk to your dad about it."

I'd never even seriously considered going to my dad with this. Which felt like a stark indictment of our relationship, now that I thought about it. "To what purpose?"

"To give him a chance to explain, and a chance to tell Manny the truth himself."

"You think he'd actually do either of those things if I asked him to? *My* dad?" George King was not a man who liked having his choices questioned, and I couldn't imagine he'd react well to having his secret uncovered.

Ryan shrugged. "I don't know. It's just an option I'm throwing out there. Ultimately it's up to you."

I tried to picture myself confronting my dad with the paternity test and giving him an "either you tell Manny or I will" ultimatum.

"No," I said, feeling a fresh surge of anger at my father for keeping this secret and lying to us all these years—not to mention treating Manny like some kind of favorite nephew instead of the natural-born son he actually was. "Fuck Dad. He's had almost thirty years to tell Manny the truth himself. He made his choices, now he gets to live with the consequences of them."

To be honest, I didn't trust my father to talk to Manny. I was afraid he'd find some way to weasel out of it or spin the facts in his favor. The man was a master manipulator—especially when it came to covering his own ass. I'd rather break the news to Manny myself than let our father do it. At least then I knew he'd get the truth and it would be delivered kindly.

Ryan dug his phone out of his pocket. "I'll text Manny to ask if we can come over and see him."

My stomach tied itself in knots as I watched him type out the message. "Now?"

He set his phone on the counter and unwrapped another taco. "Might as well. What's the benefit of waiting? Are you going to feel any better if you stew on it for another day or two?"

"I don't even know what I'm going to say to him. How do you tell someone something like this?"

"You'll tell him the truth," Ryan said. "Simple and straight-forward, just like you told me."

26

LUCY

"Where are you going?" my mother asked when she saw me putting on my shoes.

For a second, I thought about lying to her and making up some errand to avoid her turning this into a whole thing. But I rejected the impulse and told her the truth instead. "Tanner's."

Why should I have to lie or make up excuses? My time was my own to spend how I liked. I was going to my boyfriend's, and my mother didn't get to have a say or an opinion about it.

"Again?" Her lips pressed together in irritation, just like I'd known they would. "You just came from there."

"Six hours ago."

"You're spending so much time with him. I feel like I hardly see you."

"I've been here all day for you to see." Since Tanner had dropped me off that morning, I'd vacuumed the house, cleaned the bathroom I shared with Matt, done three loads of laundry, and cooked another casserole for the upcoming week's dinners. Meanwhile, my mother had touched up her roots, given herself a facial, and taken a nap.

"You were busy doing other things."

"Yes, I was cleaning the house, because if I don't, no one else will." As soon as the words slipped out I regretted them. There was telling the truth, and then there was deliberately provoking a defensive response from my mother.

"Don't use that tone with me, Lucy Jean. Your poor brother's an invalid, and I do what I can manage, but it gets overwhelming trying to keep up with everything. I'm sorry it's such a burden for you to pitch in around the house."

I stood up and faced her, softening my expression and my voice. "It gets overwhelming for me too, Mama. I need some time for myself just like you do."

"Of course you do, baby. Why don't you let me give you one of my homemade facials? We'll have some mother-daughter time."

"I can't tonight. Tanner's going through something right now and he needs me." I'd been waiting on pins and needles all day to hear how his conversation with Manny went, and he'd finally texted a few minutes ago to ask if I could come over.

"I'm sure he does," my mother said, rolling her eyes.

"Don't wait up for me. I don't know when I'll be home."

"Your brother and I need you too, you know."

What I wanted to say was, *Aren't I here for you all the time? Haven't I already given up enough of my life to be here for you? Can't I have this one little thing for me?*

But I didn't say any of that, because I knew it would hurt her feelings, and then she'd cry, and then I'd never be able to leave. Instead I stepped forward and kissed her cheek. "I love you. Dinner's in the fridge."

Then I left before she could say anything else.

When I got to Tanner's he stepped straight into my arms and hugged me. "Thank you for coming."

"Of course I came." I held him for a moment, right there in

the doorway of his house, letting him lean on me like he seemed to need to. When he loosened his grip on me, I led him into the living room and sat him down on the couch. "How'd it go?"

He looked down at his lap, rubbing his thumb back and forth across his palm. "It was—okay, I guess? Not fun, but not as bad as I feared."

"How did Manny take it?"

Tanner frowned, his thumb rubbing harder. "It's hard to say. He was pretty quiet. In shock, mostly."

I could see guilt written in the creases on his brow—the responsibility he felt for upsetting Manny's life. Scooting closer, I took Tanner's hand and twined my fingers with his. "You did the right thing telling him."

"He asked me not to tell anyone yet. He wants to talk to Dad before he does anything else. Which is understandable, I guess." His frown deepened, and I gave in to the urge to curl myself around him.

He folded his arms around me, and I listened as he described the stunned look on Manny's face, how pale he'd gotten, and how he'd shaken his head in disbelief and made Tanner repeat it twice. He told me how long Manny had stared at the paternity test, hunched over with Tanner's phone in his lap, and how Manny had held his hands against his forehead, hiding his face and whatever emotions he might have been feeling.

Tanner's voice got rougher and quieter the longer he talked, and I held him tighter, my ear pressed against his chest so I could hear his heart beating like a metronome underneath his words.

It felt good to be doing this for him—comforting him, helping him—in a way that was completely new and unfamiliar to me. Sure, I liked the way he made me feel—*you more than like it*, a voice whispered in my head, *you love it, and you love him—*

but I liked—*loved*—making him feel better. Being here for Tanner wasn't a burden, it was a privilege.

I listened as he told me how Manny hadn't seemed angry, just confused mostly. And I didn't say it, but I thought that had probably been harder for Tanner to handle than anger would have been. I could tell he looked up to Manny, even idolized him a little, and it must have been upsetting to see him shaken—and even more so to be the bearer of the news that had shaken him.

When Tanner had talked himself out, we sat there in silence for a long time, me wrapped around him, and him wrapped up in his thoughts. I let him stew for a while, figuring he needed the time and the quiet, understanding that he was the kind of person who usually processed things alone in his head instead of by saying them out loud. He'd done a lot of talking today—first to Ryan, then to Manny, and finally to me—and he'd probably depleted most of his *talking about his problems* battery.

As I lay there listening to his heartbeat, I thought about how I could help him. What did he need? What could possibly make him feel better after a day like today?

Then I thought of the perfect thing to cheer him up.

Pushing out of his arms, I sat up and squeezed his thigh. "Come on. We're going out."

He blinked at me, and I could tell he was opening his mouth to argue, but I didn't give him the chance.

"Get up." I got to my feet and tugged on his arm. "Get your shoes on." My futile tugging was no match for his body weight, and he didn't budge. "Trust me," I said, refusing to be discouraged. "I know exactly what you need right now."

He gave in and let me pull him off the couch. "Where are we going?" he asked as he shoved his feet into his tennis shoes.

"You'll see when we get there."

———

"YOU'RE RIGHT," Tanner said squeezing my hand after we got out of the car. "This is exactly what I needed."

I'd brought him to Misfit Books. Located in an old Victorian house a few blocks off Main Street, it was the town's sole bookstore and one of my favorite places on earth. I'd been coming here since I was a kid—as had Tanner, I'd learned when he brought me here on one of our very first dates. We'd spent hours wandering through the labyrinth of narrow aisles between the towering bookcases that were crowded into every room of the two-story house.

I squeezed his hand back. "Being surrounded by books always makes me feel better. It's like being wrapped in a soft blanket covered with words."

Tanner pushed the door open, and we were greeted by the cheerful jingle of the bell and the sweet, faintly woody scent of old books. Seamus Hill gave us a wave from behind the counter as he rang up a stack of children's books for a young woman and a very excited little girl who was bouncing on her toes in anticipation.

Seamus had opened Misfit Books in the eighties, before the internet and e-readers had changed the world and the way people bought their books. Nevertheless, it had managed to stay in business all these years, in part because a town like Crowder didn't have all that many places for people to go. Misfit Books had remained a favorite destination for bringing dates, bored children, or just yourself, if you were the kind of person who liked to while away an afternoon wandering amidst soothing rows of book spines.

Just inside the door was a table highlighting a selection of new releases. Other than that, and a few small collections of curated recommendations scattered throughout the store, most of the stock was either used or remaindered. A small grouping of mismatched couches and chairs occupied one corner of the main room by the front windows. An adjoining room on the opposite side housed the children's section, which featured low bookcases and a circle of tiny chairs for its pint-sized patrons. Other than those two relatively open areas, the entire rest of the shop was a cramped maze of shelves with books jammed into every available nook and cranny on both floors.

Basically, it was heaven. The sort of place where you could lose yourself for hours, exploring and searching for hidden treasures.

Tanner kept hold of my hand as we wandered through the store, pointing out books we'd read or heard about. The longer we were there, the more he seemed to relax, his shoulders loosening and his smiles coming more easily.

"I've never read a modern romance novel," he said when I pulled him into the romance section upstairs.

"You've never read Ilona Andrews?" I asked, knowing how much he liked fantasy. "Or Anne Bishop? Or Nalini Singh?"

"Okay, I guess I meant I've never read a contemporary romance where the main plot was just about two people falling in love without having to fight off any magic or monsters."

"You should try one. I think you'd like it. I mean, I realize it's one of the few genres of literature that's not marketed directly to men, but that doesn't mean men can't enjoy it. If women can still manage to read and enjoy"—I gestured at the rest of the store around us—"pretty much the entirety of Western literature that's dominated by white men, you ought to be able to pick up a romance without breaking out in hives."

The corner of his mouth quirked, and he tilted his head toward the bookcase. "What should I read first? Pick one for me, and I'll read it."

Smiling, I turned toward the bookcase and ran my eyes over the spines. "Let's see what we've got here." I tapped my finger against my lips, approaching my task with the seriousness it deserved. Recommending a book was a big responsibility, especially when it was someone's first experience with a new genre.

I dismissed all the titles I considered too outdated or better suited to longtime devotees of the genre. Also anything too dark or too silly—not that there was anything wrong with dark or silly, but I didn't think they would be the best match for Tanner's tastes. No alphas, billionaires, rock stars, or cowboys. I wanted something a little more grounded. The Talia Hibbert I'd just read would have been perfect—witty and layered and excellently steamy—but they didn't have any of her books on the shelf. Since Misfit stocked primarily used books, the selection was always a bit chaotic, which in my opinion added to the fun of browsing for books in person. I loved finding out-of-print titles, unknown gems, and forgotten favorites rather than the same selection of recent bestsellers you could get at any airport bookstore.

Speaking of forgotten favorites...

"This one," I said, plucking a dog-eared paperback of Jennifer Crusie's *Bet Me* off the shelf. "It's one of my all-time favorites."

Tanner turned the book over and scanned the back cover. "All right," he said, looking up at me again. "My turn now. Name a new genre you'd like to try."

"Hmm." I pursed my lips as I considered it. There were a lot of genres I didn't read much—history, science fiction, true crime —but which one did I want Tanner to recommend to me? I smiled when I thought of exactly the perfect one. "Poetry. I don't think I've read any since high school."

Tanner's eyes lit with pleasure as he seized my hand and pulled me through the store to the poetry section. He knew exactly where to find it in Misfit's labyrinth of book-filled rooms, tucked away in what looked like it might once have been an upstairs bathroom.

I watched him as he eagerly scanned the shelves, obviously looking for something specific. When he found it, he broke into a grin and slipped a pristine trade paperback off the shelf.

"Here." He placed a book called *Black Girl, Call Home* in my hands. "Jasmine Mans is a spoken-word artist, but her poems are almost as powerful on the page. If you like them, you should definitely look up some of her performances on YouTube."

I smiled up at him, impressed. "Is there any genre I could have said that would have stumped you?"

He shrugged. "I read pretty broadly."

"Mystery?"

"*Turn of Mind* by Alice LaPlante."

"Biography?"

"*The Immortal Life of Henrietta Lacks.*"

"You're amazing," I said and grabbed the front of his shirt to pull him in for a kiss.

He tilted his head and cupped my jaw, his lips lingering on mine before they drifted to my ear. "My English literature degree's got to be useful for something, right?"

Goose bumps shivered over my arms, and I decided we'd spent enough time at the bookstore. Mission accomplished on Operation Cheer Tanner Up.

"Let's go pick up something for dinner," I said as he kissed a path along my jaw. "And then I'm going to take you home."

Tanner hummed his approval against my neck. "What are you in the mood for?"

"You. But also a burrito as big as my head."

"I like the sound of that plan." Dropping a final kiss on my cheek, he took my hand again and led the way downstairs to the register.

"Find everything you needed?" Seamus asked when we set our books on the counter.

"For today, anyway." Tanner flipped open his wallet and shook his head at me when I started to reach into my purse.

"Enjoy it while you can," Seamus said. "Don't know how much longer the place'll be here."

Tanner's head jerked up. "What?"

"Why?" I asked in alarm.

"I'm retiring." Seamus peered through his reading glasses as he tapped on the register. "Selling the place. Been working retail hours for thirty-five years, and I'm ready to cash out and get off my feet. Do some traveling before I'm too old for it. Maybe even move closer to my grandkids."

I supposed I couldn't begrudge him that, but the thought of losing Misfit Books broke my heart.

"You can't get someone to take over the store?" Tanner asked, looking as stricken as I felt.

Seamus shook his head sadly as he pushed the card reader toward Tanner. "I surely would if I could, but I don't know who'd want to keep this old place going. The property taxes are getting too high and bookstores aren't exactly a booming market these days. Whoever buys it will probably turn it into another vape shop or one of those CBD stores that are popping up everywhere."

That seriously sucked. Big time. The unique small businesses that made up Crowder's downtown shopping district were slowly being eaten away by characterless, impersonal retail chains. Every year it seemed like the town lost another boutique or gallery, only to have it replaced by a mattress store or payday loan business.

Tanner sighed as he accepted our purchases from Seamus. "How soon?"

"Don't know exactly." Seamus rubbed a hand through his wispy white hair. "I've got an appointment with a realtor next week to see about putting it on the market. Who knows how long it'll take to find a buyer? Could be six months or six days."

I looked around the shop, bereft at the thought that this might be my last time here.

"Don't worry," Seamus said, reading my expression. "I won't close her down in the middle of the night. We'll have some kind of farewell send-off."

"A retirement party," I said, trying to put on a cheerful face.

"Yeah, exactly." Seamus's lined face split in a lopsided grin. "And a big going out of business sale too, probably."

Tanner thanked Seamus, and we took our books and heavy hearts out of the store.

———

A FUNEREAL SILENCE filled the car as I drove us to Groovy's Tacos. The prospect of losing the bookstore that had been a treasured part of our lives had dragged us both down in the dumps.

I glanced over at Tanner, but he had his face turned toward the window. I reached across the console to lay my hand on his thigh. "I'm sorry. This was supposed to cheer you up, but instead you just got more bad news."

His eyes met mine, and he squeezed my hand briefly before letting go. "It's not your fault. It was a good idea. A great idea, actually."

The traffic light changed, and I withdrew my hand and turned my attention to the road again. "Seamus used to let me alphabetize the books. I'd go there sometimes to study in college when it was too hard to concentrate at home, and when I took breaks I'd straighten the shelves to relieve stress and help me organize my thoughts."

"Of course you would." Tanner's voice was fondly teasing.

"The first time he caught me doing it I was so embarrassed,

but he said it was fine by him if I wanted to work for free. He'd leave shelves for me to organize the next time I came in."

"I used to go there after school," Tanner said. The quiet that followed felt weighty, like he was working himself up to say more. He cleared his throat. "Especially when my mom was sick and I didn't want to go home. Or after she died and I still didn't want to go home. I must have spent hours in there reading, but Seamus never seemed to mind."

Out of the corner of my eye, I saw Tanner rub his palm up and down his thigh. I reached over again, capturing his hand and pulling it across the console to rest on my leg.

He squeezed my thigh. "It was my escape. I could pull any book off the shelf and lose myself in it. Pretend for a while that I was someone else in some faraway place with a different life and different problems."

I smiled, understanding exactly what he meant. "That's why you majored in English literature, isn't it?"

My phone vibrated in the cup holder, and Tanner glanced down at it. "It's your mother. There's actually a whole bunch of notifications from your mother."

"Ignore it." She'd sent half a dozen texts since I'd left the house, asking all manner of trivial questions ranging from did we have any papaya to what was the name of the actor she liked in that football movie. I'd ignored every one. The frequency of her texts always seemed to increase when she knew I was out with Tanner, and it wasn't a habit I wanted to encourage. I shouldn't have to be on call twenty-four seven to answer every random question that popped into her head.

"You sure?" he asked. "It could be important if she's texting that much."

"It's not," I assured him.

It was early enough that Groovy's wasn't too crowded for a Saturday night, and I managed to find a parking space in the small lot behind the building, which had started life as a Del Taco, then bizarrely been converted to a bank for a few years before eventually becoming the home of Groovy's Tacos. The name was a bit of a misnomer, however, because it was Groovy's gargantuan burritos that had made them a local favorite.

"Do you want to eat here or get them to go?" Tanner asked as we got in line.

"Let's eat here." There were plenty of available tables, and I thought it might do our mood some good to be out and around people. "Is that okay?"

"Sure."

My phone vibrated in my hand and I glanced at the screen. My mother had texted three more times.

How much longer are you going to be out?

Can you stop on your way home and get me some of that peppermint tea that helps with my headaches?

Lucy??? When are you coming home?

"Do you need to answer her?" Tanner asked, frowning slightly.

"No." I shoved my phone in my purse and snaked my hand around his waist, leaning against him as we waited for our turn to order. "I don't want to live in a town without a bookstore," I said forlornly.

"Me neither," Tanner replied, draping his arm around my shoulders. "I wish there was a way for Seamus to retire without the store having to close."

"You never know, maybe he'll find a buyer who wants to keep it open. It could happen."

"Maybe." He didn't sound hopeful and I wasn't either, despite my attempted show of optimism.

As far as I was concerned, owning a bookstore would be a dream come true. But I recognized there were serious practical challenges involved. It was the kind of project you'd only take on as a labor of love. What were the odds of someone with the necessary resources, expertise, and passion swooping in to save the store?

"Hang on." I straightened, looking up at Tanner excitedly as an idea formed.

"What?"

"*You* should buy the bookstore."

He snorted. "Yeah, right."

"I'm dead serious."

The line moved up and Tanner laid his hand on my back to nudge me forward. "I don't have that kind of money. My father might be wealthy, but I'm not."

I'd assumed Tanner was set for life, but I'd never given the details of his financial situation much thought. From what I'd seen, he lived comfortably, though not extravagantly, but I'd assumed that was more by choice than necessity. "I thought you had a trust fund or company shares or something."

His jaw tightened as he shook his head. "My father wanted all of us to work for a living, preferably for the family business. If he just handed us each a big pile of money, we could go off and do whatever we wanted with it." He glanced down at me, arching an eyebrow. "Are you disappointed?"

I curled my hands in the front of his shirt and attempted to keep a serious expression on my face. "Very. Can't you tell I'm only dating you for your riches?"

The corner of his mouth quirked. "Sorry to tell you I'm just a white-collar desk jockey. But I've got a decent 401K, if you're looking to play the long game."

Before I could answer, the line moved up again and it was our turn at the counter. We placed our orders and carried our drinks to a small table next to the side window overlooking the empty patio. The heat had driven everyone inside tonight, but in more temperate weather the tiled patio was always packed.

"I'll bet you could easily get a loan," I said, not willing to let the idea go. "From a bank, I mean."

Tanner frowned at his beer. "Even assuming I could, it's an incredibly risky venture. You heard what Seamus said about the property taxes. You've got to assume the value of the property at this point is a lot more than the income the bookstore's been bringing in. It's a losing proposition."

"Not if you revitalize the business. Seamus hasn't changed a thing about that place in decades. You just need to come up with a sustainable business plan."

"Is that all?" Tanner deadpanned. "No problem."

I ignored his sarcasm. "You'd need to find a way to get more people in the door—or you could add additional revenue streams so you're not dependent on book sales alone."

"Additional revenue streams." The way he said it, quiet and sort of distracted, I knew I'd gotten him thinking about it. Which was all I wanted. For him to at least consider the possibility.

It would give him a way out of working for the family business he hated so much. But more than that, I knew it was something he'd be great at and would love doing. Honestly, it was perfect for him, if he could come up with a workable business strategy.

The creases in his brow deepened as his mind worked over the problem. "Like a gift shop, maybe?"

"Precisely," I said with an encouraging nod.

He scratched his jaw, which was sporting a longer than usual layer of stubble today. "I suppose you could sell T-shirts and other merch targeted at book lovers—book-themed coffee mugs, reading lights, e-reader covers." He paused, shaking his head slightly. "Although I'm not sure a gift shop alone would bring in enough to keep the store profitable."

"What about a coffee shop?" I suggested. "What goes better with books than coffee? And it'll get people in the door for sure."

His frown deepened. "Something like that would be a lot of work. You'd be talking about extensive renovations to bring it up to code, plus permits, inspections, licenses, food handling certifications, and who knows what else."

"Okay, but it's not like you couldn't figure all that stuff out. And you have to admit this town could use another coffee shop."

"It's true. We've only got the one Starbucks. There's probably enough business to sustain a second coffee shop. It might be enough to keep the bookstore afloat." He lifted his beer to his lips and tipped back the bottle, shaking his head again as he set it down. "It would require a lot more money though."

"If it's part of your business plan, all the costs would be rolled into the loan."

He arched a skeptical eyebrow as his eyes met mine. "Which means I'd need to secure an even bigger loan."

"With your name and professional references, not to mention the bulletproof business plan I'll bet you could come up with, I think you'd have a really good shot."

"I don't know." He rubbed his temple like he was getting a headache, but he didn't look unhappy. In fact, he looked a lot more spirited than he had when we came in. "It's a lot to take on."

"You wouldn't have to do it all alone. I'd help you, and Wyatt could do a lot of the renovations, couldn't he?" The more I thought about it, the more excited I got. I just needed Tanner to get excited about it too. "You might even find someone to partner with, or consider bringing in an investor as an alternative to a loan."

He sort of half-smiled. "I'll admit, it's a nice pipe dream to fantasize about."

I leaned forward in my seat, resting my forearms on the slightly sticky surface of the lacquered table. "It doesn't have to be a fantasy. You could make this happen if you wanted to. At least think about it. Do some research before you decide anything one way or the other. It might be more attainable than you think."

"Maybe."

"Wouldn't you want to own a bookstore if you could? Doesn't that sound like the perfect job for you?"

"Maybe," he said again, but this *maybe* was stronger. It sounded more like *possibly*.

"Just think about it," I said.

He didn't answer, but I could tell from the half-smile lingering on his lips that he would.

27

TANNER

E ver since Lucy put the idea of buying the bookstore into my head, I hadn't been able to get it out again. I'd even done some reading last night on the Crowder commercial real estate market, business loans, and the requirements for a retail food license. It was probably pie-in-the-sky, but I couldn't let go of it.

Anyway, I figured there was no harm in doing some research. Why not try coming up with a business plan like Lucy said? Even if it turned out to be completely unfeasible once I dug into the numbers, fantasizing about it was as good a way as any to kill time.

Now that it was Monday morning and I was back at work, the temptation to click over to the browser on my computer and look for resources about managing a bookstore was just about killing me. I was supposed to be writing a feature on voter suppression for the newsletter, but it wasn't due for a week and I was finding it hard to focus.

My gaze wandered up from my screen to Lucy, sitting at her desk across from me. She'd wrapped a lock of hair around her finger and was twisting it idly, her lips pursed in an adorable frown of concentration as she stared at her keyboard. My chest bloomed with warmth, and a memory surfaced of her hair spread out on my pillow last night like a curtain of pure sunshine, and her lips parting on a breathy sigh as I moved inside her.

The warmth in my chest took a decidedly southward path and I shifted in my chair. One of the downsides of working with your girlfriend, I'd discovered over the last week, was frequent, inconvenient work boners. Still, it was a small price to pay for the privilege of having her in my life.

I felt a deep sense of gratitude and a consciousness of how damn *lucky* I was to have a second chance with this intelligent, loving, incredible woman. Of course, that was followed by a ripple of apprehension. I couldn't help it. Whenever something good happened to me, I always had to brace myself for the bad luck that usually seemed to follow. Because you could never have good without bad, just like there was no light without darkness. Tip the scales too far in one direction, and they'd have to tip back the other way. The universe would seek to correct itself. Everything in balance. Always.

As I gazed at Lucy—chewing on the inside of her cheek now, her perfect pink lips twisted to one side—a giddy sense of contentment settled over me. I'd always believed in soul mates, but in the same abstract way I believed in the existence of advanced life on other planets. The vastness of the universe meant there was a chance such life existed somewhere, but the odds of ever encountering it were so statistically improbable as to be nonexistent. Sure, I might have a soul mate out there somewhere in the world, but I'd never believed I'd actually find her. It'd be like winning the Mega Millions jackpot in the lottery. That kind of good fortune only happened to other people. Not me. I'd already used up most of my good luck tokens being born into a healthy body and excessive material comfort. There were only so many blessings a person could expect in this life.

But I knew with unshakable certainty that Lucy was my soul mate. Against all odds, I'd found the person who completed me and made me whole. If you believed in the story Plato ascribed to Aristophanes in the *Symposium*, I'd been reunited with my lost missing half. Lucy was my cure for the original wound of human nature.

I'd been given an incredible, unimaginable gift. But I couldn't help remembering how great I'd thought things were between us before and how wrong I'd been. How completely I'd misread the situation—and her.

It was different between us now though. I really believed that. In the twenty-twenty vision of hindsight, I could look back and see where we'd gone wrong before and how things hadn't been as good as I'd assumed. We'd both been hiding so much of ourselves, we hadn't truly known each other. You couldn't build a lasting relationship on a flimsy foundation. The first high wind that came along would blow it all down around you.

If we were making mistakes this go-round, at least they were different mistakes. We were working on building that solid foundation—communicating more, being more honest and open with each other, exposing the messy, damaged parts of ourselves we'd withheld the last time.

I wasn't holding back anymore, and it felt like throwing open the windows and letting sunlight and fresh air into a dark, desolate room. Never in my life had I felt this close to another person. It was a little terrifying, but also invigorating. I felt more secure than I ever had—not just with Lucy, but with myself. Improbably, the more I revealed to her, the less vulnerable I felt. Seeing myself through her eyes made me feel stronger, more capable, more *valuable*. Knowing she believed in me made it easier to believe in myself.

What we had was more than just love. It was something more powerful that I hadn't even realized I'd been missing, because I'd never known this feeling existed. As I struggled to define it, the word *joy* lit up inside my head like a neon light and glowed there warmly.

Lucy had brought joy into my life.

Now that I had it, I was desperately afraid to lose it. The comprehension of what a rare and precious gift I'd been given came with a flicker of unease. How long would I be allowed to feel this way? What price would I have to pay to compensate for this bounty? There was always a price to pay, wasn't there?

But then Lucy looked up, and the way her eyes lit as they met mine—all that brightness and affection shining just for me —unleashed a flood of tenderness that washed away the apprehension. When I looked in her eyes I felt like I could handle anything.

Right on cue, as if my hubris had provoked the wrath of the gods, my phone's screen lit up with a text from my father.

Come to my office at 11.

I stared at it, consumed by the same sick feeling of dread that always came over me when I had to see my dad. How fucked up was that? Why did he affect me this way? For most of my life I'd been plagued with guilt over the antipathy I felt toward my father. It wasn't as if he was abusive or physically threatening. He wasn't a monster. A better son wouldn't feel this way, surely?

And yet, almost every interaction I'd ever had with him had been negative in some way. If he wasn't criticizing me, he was minimizing my accomplishments, rejecting my attempts to connect with him, discounting my feelings, or straight up ignoring me. Shallow cut after shallow cut until there was nothing left of our relationship but scar tissue. Was it any wonder I'd developed a conditioned response to brace for the next laceration?

So no, he wasn't a monster, but he wasn't the father I deserved. A better father wouldn't make me feel this way.

Unfortunately, I could guess what this summons was about. Manny had texted me yesterday to let me know he'd talked to Dad and "everything was fine." When I'd asked him what "fine" meant, he said they'd talked it out and he had made his peace with the truth. Which was good. If he really had made peace with it, I was relieved.

Presumably, Manny had told Dad that I was the one who'd found the paternity test and showed it to him. That was less good, but expected. I could only assume I was about to face my dad's displeasure over the role I'd played in revealing his secret.

Should be fun.

I was still staring at my phone when it lit up with another text notification. This one was from Lucy.

What's wrong?

I looked up and found her watching me with concern written on her features. As soon as our eyes met, some of my churning dread eased. Not all of it, but enough that I could offer her a reassuring smile before I typed out an answer to her question.

My dad wants me in his office at 11

After she'd read it, she glanced up at me with an anxious frown before typing her response: *Why?*

He didn't say, I texted back, *but I'm guessing it's about Manny.*

Oh no! Are you okay? Before I could reply, she added: *No matter what he says, you did the right thing.*

When I looked up at her again, it felt like stepping into a concentrated beam of sunlight on a cold day. Her concern, her compassion, and her absolute confidence in me shone in the bottomless depths of her eyes. It warmed me from the inside out, bolstering my faith in myself and unraveling the knots in my chest.

I'll be fine, I typed back and almost believed it.

AT PRECISELY ELEVEN O'CLOCK—BECAUSE my dad didn't look favorably on tardiness *or* early birds—I presented myself to Connie, my father's middle-aged assistant, and tried very hard not to think about her online dating profile.

"Hey there, Tanner! How you doing, honey?" The sympathetic look she gave me didn't bode well for my father's disposition. "Your daddy's ready for ya, so you can go right on in."

I paused at the door and took a steadying breath before I pushed it open. My father was sitting behind his desk, facing the big picture window looking out over the amusement park.

"Hi, Dad," I said to the back of his large leather desk chair. "You wanted to see me?"

For a long few seconds, he didn't acknowledge that he'd heard me. Then, just when I'd started to squirm, his chair swiveled around. With slow, deliberate movements he set down the tablet he'd been reading, removed his glasses, and carefully folded them before putting them aside. Only then did he allow his stony gaze to fall on me. "Sit down."

I did as instructed, taking one of the armchairs in front of his desk. Although I felt like a man about to face a firing squad, I endeavored to keep my bearing confident and casual—but without slouching, because that would earn me an admonition about how my careless posture made me look sloppy and timid.

My father regarded me in dispassionate silence. I waited for him to speak his mind as second after interminable second passed. My palms were clammy, but I knew better than to let him see me rubbing them on my thighs. He'd been chastising me for that particular habit ever since I could remember. *Never let anyone see they've made you sweat, son—it exposes your weak-*

ness. He'd never succeeded in breaking me of the habit entirely, but I'd learned not to do it around my father. If the lesson he'd meant to teach was that it wasn't safe to show weakness in front of *him*, then mission fucking well accomplished.

I broke first, as he'd undoubtedly known I would. "How've you been? I haven't talked to you since your birthday."

"No, you haven't." This time the protracted silence was punctuated by an ominous creak of leather as he leaned back in his chair. "But you talked to Manny, I hear."

So much for friendly small talk. I swallowed, but kept my mouth shut. Any preemptive attempt to defend my choices would only antagonize him further. Not that my choices required any defense. By rights, he should be the one on his back foot right now, but the devil would be handing out glasses of ice water in hell before my father ever admitted his own culpability.

"You had no business going through my private papers."

Of course that was where he'd start—with the offense that had been committed against him. Never mind the magnitude of his own misdeeds.

Still, unlike my father, I was willing to own up to my wrongdoing. "You're right, and for that I apologize. I was looking for a photo of Manny's dad for a retrospective feature we're doing in the newsletter. I didn't intend to unearth any buried family secrets."

"You should have talked to me before going to your brother with this."

The word *brother* hung heavily in the air between us. He'd always referred to Manny as our brother, but what had once seemed like a caring gesture now felt weighted with deception.

"Well?" he snapped. "Speak up."

I straightened my spine. "Telling Manny the truth was the right thing to do."

"It wasn't your place to tell him," he thundered back, red-faced with fury.

"No, it was yours," I replied coolly, keeping my own anger in check.

"And I guess you think you know all about right and wrong." His words dripped with disdain. "Better than me, anyway."

"I know lying to the people you're supposed to love is wrong."

He barked out a laugh. "I hope you're not actually that naive, son. Everybody lies to everybody sometimes." His gaze flicked downward, fixing on his desk. "It's just that some reasons for doing it are better than others."

"Are you trying to imply you had a good reason for lying to Manny his whole life? Other than covering up your infidelity, I mean."

My father's eyes were hard when they lifted to mine. "You obviously don't give a damn about my reasons. If you did, you would have come and talked to me first."

The bitterness leaked out of me before I could stop it. "Maybe I would have, if talking to you had ever once in my life made anything better."

I expected him to react with more anger, but instead he went scarily still. We stared at each other in a silence so oppressive it felt like the oxygen had been sucked out of the room.

My father broke the standoff by standing up. "I'll be getting all your brothers and sisters together this week to tell everyone the truth about Manny." He spoke in a tightly controlled voice, as if it was taking all his effort to hold his temper back. "Since you don't care to hear what I have to say, there's no reason for you to trouble yourself to be there."

Having said that, he crossed to the door and held it open, waiting for me to leave.

I accepted my dismissal silently, holding my chin up but refusing to look at him as I walked out.

Somehow, I managed to hold it together until I got to the stairwell. But as soon as the metal fire door slammed shut behind me, I sagged against the wall and pressed the heels of my hands against my eyes.

You'd think it would be more satisfying, standing up to my father. But there was nothing satisfying about the way I felt. It was just more of the same shit, the same poisonous stew I'd been swimming through my whole fucking life. I was so goddamn *tired*. Tired of being the only one of us trying, tired of never getting anywhere despite my best efforts, tired of feeling like this. Why did I keep doing it? What was the point? Who was I making an effort for? It sure as hell wasn't doing me any good, and my father couldn't care less.

As I stood there in the stairwell of this building that had felt like a cage for most of my adult life, I knew what I needed to do. I made a decision I should have made a long-ass time ago.

Squaring my shoulders, I walked the three flights down to the floor where I now worked. Every step of my descent cemented my resolve, and with that resolve came the satisfaction I hadn't gotten from the conversation with my father. The closer I got to my floor, the lighter and more at peace I felt. By the time I pushed out of the stairwell next to the elevators, I was practically elated.

I headed straight for Josie's office. Her door was open, and when I knocked she lifted her eyes from her computer screen and waved me inside. "Just who I've been meaning to talk to."

"Me?" I hesitated for the first time since I'd exited my father's office. "Why?"

"Close the door."

I did as asked and sat down, my own reason for coming here

temporarily back-burnered by my curiosity to know what Josie wanted with me.

She pushed her laptop aside and rested her chin in her hand. My palms prickled under her sharp scrutiny, but this time I gave in to the impulse to rub them on my thighs.

"Relax," she said. "I'm not going to bite. I just want to ask you a question."

"Okay," I replied uncertainly.

"Are you and Lucy Dillard dating?"

I froze like a possum caught on a porch rail in broad daylight. "What?"

Josie's lips spread in a slow smile. She might as well have said the word *busted* out loud. "The two of you went to dinner at Post Oak Lodge together. A date, I assume."

"How do you know that?"

She snorted. "You seriously have to ask? In this town? Someone saw you and told me. Obviously."

"Jesus," I muttered under my breath. I'd known it was bound to get around eventually, but it was impressive to see how fast the Crowder gossip mill worked.

"So it's true?" The intensity of her stare didn't do anything to put me at ease.

"Um…"

"Don't worry. You're not in trouble," she added.

"I don't care about me. I don't want Lucy getting in any trouble over this."

"She won't. Neither of you are in trouble. I just want to know. Are y'all together?"

"Yes," I admitted.

Josie's eyes lit up, and she clapped her hands like a kid who'd just been told she could have a pony. "Yay!"

I scratched my head, not sure what to make of my sister's enthusiasm. "That's not how I expected you to react."

"What did you think I was going to do? Fire you?"

"Well, no. I mean, I hoped not. But I thought you might have concerns."

"Eh." She flicked her wrist carelessly. "I trust you both to be professional. I'm just happy it's true. You two make the cutest couple. I can hardly stand it."

"Thanks?"

"So." She leaned forward eagerly. "Tell me everything. How did it start? How long has it been going on? Were you *trying* to keep it a secret?"

"It's complicated, a while, and not exactly," I answered, addressing each of her questions. As much as I might have enjoyed gabbing with my sister about my new girlfriend, I'd come here to say something else to her, and I needed to do it before I lost my nerve. "I actually need to talk to you about something else."

"Okay," Josie said, sitting upright. "Is it work or personal? Should I put on my boss hat or my sister hat?"

"A little of both, probably." I shifted in my seat, knowing she wasn't going to like what I had to say. "I'm resigning from the company. I'm here to give you my two weeks' notice. "

Her face fell a little, but she recovered quickly, becoming all business again. "Why?"

"It's something I should have done a long time ago."

"I thought you were happy? This isn't because of Lucy, is it? Because—"

"It's got nothing to do with Lucy," I said. "If anything, Lucy's a temptation to stay. It's got nothing to do with you either. Or this job, which I've genuinely enjoyed, and I remain grateful to you for giving it to me."

"But you're still leaving."

"I don't want to work for the family anymore."

"When you say family, I'm going to take a wild guess that you specifically mean Dad."

"I can't do it anymore." My knuckles whitened as I gripped the arms of the chair. "I don't want to spend another ten years of my life trying to please him. I have to get out of this place and stand on my own two feet."

Josie sighed, her brow creasing with sympathy. "I can certainly understand that. What will you do?"

I shook my head, relieved she'd accepted my decision so easily. "I don't know yet. I just...I want a chance to prove myself doing something I actually care about."

She arched an eyebrow. "Are you saying you don't care about content marketing?"

"No, I—"

"I'm kidding. Sheesh, lighten up. I get it. You want to forge your own path."

"That's it," I said. "Like you did."

"Mmm." Her smile tightened as her gaze traveled around her office. "My path still led me right back here, didn't it?" I opened my mouth to ask if she regretted coming back to the fold, but before I could she shook her head and said, "I'm proud of you. I hope you find your passion. And I'm here for you. If you need a reference, or advice, or anything at all, you only have to ask."

A swell of grateful emotion rose in my throat. Because we'd never had the chance to spend that much time together, I was only just beginning to appreciate that Josie was someone I could count on to have my back. "Thank you," I said. "That means a lot. And I'm sorry I'm letting you down. I know it's not great to quit so soon after accepting a new position."

Her shoulders lifted in an indifferent shrug. "You're not letting me down. Lucy's the one who's going to be most inconvenienced. I assume she knows about this already?"

I shook my head. "Not yet. It's something I decided just now on my way down from Dad's office."

Josie frowned. "Did something happen between you and Dad? He didn't force you into this, did he?"

"Not the way you're thinking." She'd find out about Manny soon enough. It wasn't my place to tell her. "I can stay as long as you need me to. I don't want to leave you in the lurch."

She accepted this without pressing me for more details. "As long as you come to the benefit for Chance's memorial foundation next month, we're good."

I groaned and gave her a pleading look. All these stuffy charity events were excruciating enough under ideal circumstances, but my dad would be there. I preferred not to put myself in his orbit if I could avoid it. "Do I have to?"

"Yes." Josie's eyes narrowed threateningly, a reminder that while she might be nicer than Dad and Nate, she was still as serious as a heart attack when it came to getting what she wanted. "I need you there. I can make an excuse for Wyatt's absence, but if both of you are MIA it's going to look bad. It's important for us to seem like one big, happy family, whether we are or not." Her expression softened, and the corner of her lips quirked. "But you can bring Lucy as your date."

"Right." I hadn't thought about that. It did make the prospect of all that painful socializing with wealthy donors under my father's reproachful glare slightly less onerous.

"So you'll be there? I can count on you?"

"Of course." Letting Josie down wasn't an option, no matter how I felt about Dad right now—or how he felt about me. "Speaking of Lucy," I said, remembering the other thing I wanted to discuss with Josie. "I need to talk to you about her."

28

LUCY

My head lifted as soon as Tanner walked back into the bullpen. I'd been keeping an eye out for him, glancing up every time the elevator dinged or someone walked through the office. Worry had stolen my ability to focus on work while Tanner was upstairs facing his father.

But now he was back and he looked...mostly okay? I could see telltale signs of strain around his eyes and mouth, but nothing as bad as I'd feared.

His gaze locked with mine, and he offered a small smile as he made his way to his desk.

"Is everything okay?" I asked, too anxious to pose the question via text.

He stopped at his desk and gripped the back of his chair. Something about the way he was standing there sent a spike of apprehension corkscrewing through me. "I, uh..." He glanced down briefly and back up again, looking directly at me when he spoke. "I just gave Josie my two weeks' notice."

My mouth fell open as Linh and Arwen's heads snapped up. "What?" we all three whisper-yelled in unison.

"I quit my job," he said, still focused on me. "I'm leaving the company."

Out of the corner of my eye I saw Linh's gaze ping-pong between me and Tanner.

"Whoa," Arwen said. "Why?"

"It's complicated," Tanner answered, his eyes on mine. "Personal reasons mostly."

Arwen and Linh both turned to look at me, and in the silence that followed I realized I still hadn't said anything.

I shoved my chair back and got to my feet. "Would you like to go out for lunch?" I asked Tanner.

"Yes." His shoulders dipped in relief. "Very much yes."

"Take your time," Linh told me as I grabbed my purse. "We'll cover for you."

"Thank you," I told her.

Tanner and I walked to the elevator in silence. I threw an anxious glance at Josie's office when it came into view, and Tanner touched a hand to the small of my back.

"It's all right," he said. "I smoothed everything over with Josie."

I didn't know what that meant, but I figured I'd find out as soon as we were alone.

———

"TANNER?"

We hadn't gone to lunch. After baking in the scorching parking lot all morning, my car had been hot enough to fry an egg on the dash. I'd had to roll all the windows down and crank the AC up to deafening full blast, which had made meaningful conversation near impossible. So I'd driven us to Tanner's house, because it was the closest place I could think of where we could talk in private without being observed or overheard.

Only he wasn't talking. He was sitting on his couch, looking shell-shocked.

I scooted closer and took his hand. "What happened? What'd your father say?"

He squeezed my hand. "It doesn't matter."

Clearly it did, but despite the million questions in my head, I waited to see if he'd say anything else.

"I, uh—" He cleared his throat and looked down at our hands. "It was my decision to quit. My father doesn't even know yet." His mouth tugged into a frown. "Well, Josie might have told him by now, but I didn't decide to do it until after I'd walked out of his office."

Radagast jumped up on the couch and flopped down on Tanner's other side with his back up against Tanner's thigh. His head lolled in an appeal for affection, and Tanner laid a hand on his furry belly.

"I was just so fucking done. He's never going to change. It's never going to get any better. I'm done trying with him. So I went to Josie's office and quit."

I sensed he wasn't ready to talk about what had happened in his father's office yet, so I let that lie for now. "What did Josie say?"

"She took it okay. I think she understands." He glanced over at me. "She knows about us, by the way."

"Oh." I swallowed, trying not to let my nervousness show. "Okay."

His hand squeezed mine again. "She already knew—someone saw us out together and told her—but she doesn't care. You don't have anything to worry about with her." He smiled faintly. "She actually seemed excited for us."

"She did?"

"I told you, she likes you."

"I suppose it doesn't pose a problem for her anymore since we won't be working together much longer."

"No." He turned toward me, dropping his head to nuzzle into my neck as his arms tightened around me. "I'm sorry. I know me leaving is going to make more work for you."

"Shut up. I'm proud of you." I shifted to tuck him more comfortably against me, holding him as close as I could.

He exhaled an unsteady breath against my throat as I combed my fingers through his hair.

"Do you want to talk about what happened in your dad's office?" I asked quietly, and he immediately tensed up. "You don't have to," I added, continuing to stroke his hair. "We don't have to talk at all if you'd prefer quiet."

"I can tell you."

And he did. Tanner told me everything he and his father had said to each other. But he didn't stop there. He told me things his father had said and done on other occasions. And how unhappy he always felt whenever he was around his father. How his father's criticisms and disappointment had eaten away at his confidence and made him feel weak and worthless, which only made him more of a disappointment to his dad.

A lifetime's worth of hurt spilled out of him, and I did my best to soothe it away. The more he talked, the tighter I held him as outrage burned in my chest. I wanted to go to battle on his behalf. If I'd been a Knight of the Round Table, I would have pledged my sword to defend his honor and wreak vengeance on the man who'd wronged him.

But I wasn't a knight, George King wouldn't be brought to heel by a sword, and I couldn't protect Tanner from his relationship with his own father. The best I could do was listen and hold him.

"Do you think I did the right thing?" he asked me finally.

I pressed a kiss to the top of his head. "There's no right or wrong in this situation. It's your life, and you're entitled to live it in a way that makes you happy. You don't have to work for your family's company if you don't want to. You don't owe your father anything. If you don't want to see him anymore, you don't have to do that either."

"I'll have to see him in a few weeks whether I want to or not." I felt him tense up again as he spoke. "There's a benefit coming up for the charitable foundation my dad created in memory of my brother Chance, and I promised Josie I'd be there. I owe her at least that much after everything she's done for me." He lifted his head and gave me his best puppy dog eyes. "You could come with me though. As my date. But you don't have to if you're worried it will be too uncomfortable—"

"Of course I'll come with you." Wild horses couldn't keep me away. Finally, this was something concrete I could do for him that happened to coincide with one of my not-so-useless super-powers. I could stand by his side wearing my sunniest *This is Fine* face and make cheerful conversation the whole night. I'd hold his hand, keep him company in his misery, and offer whatever moral support he needed to get him through this difficult social situation. "If you want me there, I'll be there."

Affection warmed his gaze from the inside out. "I want you with me always."

I wanted him with me always too. To share the happy moments, the quiet moments, and even the bad moments when they came. He'd already put down roots in my heart that were so deep, I couldn't imagine my life without him anymore. I wanted to fall asleep next to him every night, and I wanted his face to be the first thing I saw when I opened my eyes. I wanted Tanner in every corner of my life, even the ones I used to keep tightly guarded.

I'd never imagined I'd feel this way about anyone. My whole life I'd had to fight so hard for every scrap of independence, I'd resented the idea of anyone intruding on my hard-won private spaces. But Tanner didn't feel like an intrusion. He felt like a partner. He was everything I'd never known I needed.

For the first time in my life, I wanted to trust-fall into someone else's arms.

"Hey." Concern crossed his features at my silence, and he lifted his hand to cup my face. "I didn't mean to put any pressure on you. I know we're not—"

"I love you," I blurted before he could finish his sentence. I didn't want to hear him say what we weren't, not when I'd just realized he was my everything.

He blinked at me in surprise, pulled up short by the words that had just tumbled out of my mouth. I was a bit astounded myself, but it felt surprisingly wonderful to have said it.

"You don't have to say anything," I told him. "I wanted you to know where I stand, but I don't expect you to be on the same page. I know I'm still earning back your trust."

"Lucy." His face contorted in distress as he pressed his thumb against my lips to silence me. "Don't you know how much I love you? I never, ever stopped. Not even for a second."

"Oh." My face split open in a smile as happiness blew through me like a gust of ocean air.

"I love you," he repeated, peppering me with kisses. "So very, very, *very* much."

"Hold still," I murmured and grabbed hold of his face, settling my mouth against his.

My heart was overflowing with emotion, and there was only one cure for my condition: I was going to have to spend the rest of my lunch break showing him exactly how much I'd meant it when I said I loved him.

29

TANNER

On Wednesday evening, my father gathered the immediate family together at his house so he and Manny could tell them all the truth together.

The immediate family except for me, that was. And Wyatt, who still wasn't speaking to Dad. And Ryan, who'd elected not to go for some reason.

After he found out I'd been disinvited, Ryan had suggested I come over to his place that night so we could tell Wyatt about Manny's paternity ourselves. It struck me as odd that Ryan had chosen to skip the family meeting, so I asked him about it while we were waiting for our perpetually late younger brother to show up.

He shrugged as he thrust a beer into my hand. "I already know the news, don't I? I don't need to be there to hear the announcement."

I lifted an eyebrow as I sipped my beer, suspecting there had to be more to it than that. I'd never known Ryan to miss a family event unless he was working a shift, which obviously he wasn't tonight. Even if he knew what Dad was going to say, I'd have thought he'd still want to be there to support Manny.

Ryan took a drink of his own beer before adding, "I had lunch with Manny on Monday, and since he knew Wyatt wouldn't be there tonight, he asked me to break the news to him." Ryan's gaze sharpened as it settled on me. "He didn't know you wouldn't be there either."

I swallowed a mouthful of beer to chase the bitterness in the back of my throat. I'd had to call Manny yesterday and explain why I wouldn't be at Dad's tonight, but I'd tried to downplay our falling-out. Manny was dealing with enough already without me dragging him into my own issues with our father.

"You okay?" Ryan asked, giving me that concerned older brother frown he'd perfected over the years.

"Sure." It wasn't as if I *wanted* to be at Dad's house, listening to whatever story he'd concocted to justify lying about Manny's paternity. But I would have gone anyway to be there for Manny. It rankled something fierce that I'd been excluded as punishment for telling the truth. Plus, I couldn't help being curious how the rest of the family was going to react when Dad fessed up to his big lie.

The doorbell rang, and while Ryan went to answer it, I grabbed another can of beer out of the fridge. I met Wyatt in the living room and handed it to him.

"All right, I'm here," he said, popping it open. "What's the big news that you could only share in person?" His gaze turned on me. "Is this about you and Lucy getting back together? Because I'm pissed you didn't tell me sooner. I had to hear about it from Matt."

Ryan cut a surprised look at me. "What the shit?" He reached over and shoved me with one of his large hands, which felt like being playfully batted by a declawed tiger. "You and Lucy got back together? Were you even gonna tell me?"

"Things have been a little busy lately," I mumbled. "We can talk about that later."

Wyatt glanced between us curiously. "One of y'all wanna put me out of my suspense and tell me what the fuck's going on?"

Ryan waved him toward the couch. "Sit down."

A frown creased Wyatt's features as he sank down on one end of Ryan's black leather couch. I took the other end, and Ryan lowered himself into the big recliner.

"Someone say something," Wyatt urged when neither of us made a move to talk. "You're freaking me out."

"Go on." Ryan tipped his chin at me. "You tell him."

I broke the news to Wyatt just like I'd told Ryan. He listened quietly as I described exactly what I'd found and how I happened to come across it.

When I finished, he let out a low whistle. "Holy shit." He knocked back a gulp of beer, looking a little shell-shocked. "I can't believe I'm this surprised by something so goddamn predictable. Once a cheater, always a fucking cheater, right?"

After he seemed to have digested that part of it, I filled him in on the rest: how Ryan and I had told Manny the truth, how Manny had talked to Dad, and how Dad was supposedly telling the rest of the family right now.

"Manny's taking it okay?" was Wyatt's first question. "That's got to be a lot to process."

I looked at Ryan, who'd talked to Manny about it more than I had.

"He's all right," Ryan said. "He and George had a long talk about everything, and Manny seems like he's in a pretty good place."

"*That* I don't understand," Wyatt muttered, shaking his head. "If I was Manny, I'd want to fucking kill the old man for keeping something like that from me."

I couldn't say I disagreed, but I was trying to look at all of this from Manny's perspective. "He's the only parent Manny's got. Maybe he doesn't want to lose anyone else."

"He's the only parent any of us in this room have," Wyatt shot back. "Whatever the fuck that's worth."

"I guess maybe there were some extenuating circumstances that made it easier for Manny to swallow," Ryan said quietly.

I swung my head around to stare at him and was surprised by the guilty look he wore. "What are you talking about?"

Ryan leaned forward, setting his beer at his feet and propping his forearms on his knees before he spoke. "George told Manny it wasn't an affair."

Wyatt snorted. "Sure it wasn't."

Ryan shot him a quelling look before continuing. "According to George, Manny's parents had been trying to have kids for a long time, but Manny's dad was infertile. So they asked George to be their sperm donor."

"We don't buy that, do we?" Wyatt looked at each of us. "Do we? He's obviously lying to cover his ass."

Ryan lifted his palms as if to say *who the fuck knows?* "That's what he said, and Manny's accepted it."

I couldn't fucking believe it. Literally, it was one of the least credible things I'd ever heard. But also I couldn't believe he had the gall to make up something like that. "That's what he's telling everyone tonight at the house, isn't it?"

"Yup," Ryan confirmed softly. "Apparently, George made the Reyeses a promise that he'd always treat the kid as Manny Sr.'s natural son—and he kept it up even after they died and he adopted Manny Jr. He said it was because he didn't want to take anything away from Manny's relationship with his parents."

"Bullshit," Wyatt spat. "Of course he'd find a way to wriggle out of responsibility for this. A worm is the only animal that can't fall down."

I looked at Ryan, trying to read his expression. "Do you believe it?"

His gaze dropped to his hands, which pretty much answered my question. "Manny believes it. That's all that really matters."

Was it? It felt like it ought to matter if Dad was still lying to Manny. But maybe Ryan was right. Maybe it was enough that this version of the story was easier for Manny to accept.

Wyatt chugged what was left of his beer and crumpled the can in his fist. He slumped back on the couch, his gaze fixed on a spot across the room. "There's something I never told either of you. About Dad."

Ryan lifted his head to frown at Wyatt. "What?"

There was a long pause before Wyatt finally spoke. "Dad was fooling around with Heather the whole time Mom was sick." He paused again, clutching the crumpled can so tight I was afraid he was going to cut himself. "I saw them together one time when Mom was having surgery. They were kissing in the fucking hospital parking lot. Can you believe that?"

"Yes," I said, completely unsurprised.

Wyatt cut a look at me, his eyes narrowing. "Did you know?"

I shook my head. "I didn't know for sure, but I always assumed as much. He knocked up Heather five months after Mom died—you don't have to be Sherlock Holmes to make the deductive leap."

I took the empty can out of Wyatt's hand before he hurt himself, and went into the kitchen to get three more beers. Two I set on the coffee table, and the third I handed to Wyatt before I sat down again.

"I'm sorry you saw that." I couldn't imagine how awful it must have been for him to see something like that under those circumstances. No wonder Wyatt had such a big chip on his shoulder when it came to Dad. "Why didn't you say anything to anyone?"

Wyatt knocked back a mouthful of beer and scowled. "I told Brady."

Ah. Our absentee oldest half-brother. He and Wyatt had been pretty tight back when Wyatt was young and Brady was still around. When our mom got sick, Brady started coming over after school every day to give Wyatt guitar lessons. Until Chance died, and Brady changed. A few months later, he packed up and left town one night without a word to anyone. As far as I knew, no one in the family had been in contact with him since.

Wyatt scrubbed a hand over his face. "He told me not to tell anyone else. He said y'all already had enough to carry without adding that to your burdens."

Fucking Brady. Imagine telling a nine-year-old to keep a secret like that when his mom was in the hospital.

I glanced over at Ryan, but he had his head bowed again. No help from that quarter. "I wish you'd told me," I said to Wyatt. "*You* had enough to deal with without carrying something like that by yourself."

Wyatt grunted and took another drink of beer. His gaze narrowed as it landed on Ryan. "You're being awfully quiet over there, Big Red. You got anything to say about any of this?"

Ryan finished off the last of his beer in one long drag and set the empty on the table. "I already knew."

Wyatt's mouth fell open. "Since when?"

"Since always." Ryan grabbed a fresh beer off the table and slumped back in the recliner. "Way before Mom got sick. Before Heather. I saw George with someone, like Wyatt did. I was probably close to the same age, even. Only I went and told Mom about it."

"What'd she do?" I asked.

"Nothing." Ryan's expression was impossible to read. "It was clear she already knew about it. She made me promise not to say anything to anyone and told me to keep out of George's business." Ryan shrugged. "So I did."

"And you're okay with that?" Wyatt demanded.

A muscle ticked in Ryan's jaw as he met Wyatt's gaze. "It's not my place to be okay with it or not."

I stared at him in disbelief. It was one thing for Ryan to play Switzerland when it came to the rest of his step-relations. But I didn't understand how he could shrug this off. "She was your mother."

For a second, something that almost looked like anger flared in Ryan's eyes, but when he spoke his voice was measured. "Yeah she was, and I knew her longer and better than you two did." He rubbed a hand over the back of his neck. "You can't presume to understand someone else's marriage."

"What does that mean?" I asked.

Ryan shook his head and looked down at his lap. "Before Mom married George, we were living in a rented double-wide eating hot dogs wrapped in Wonder bread for dinner. So maybe she had her reasons for looking the other way when her rich husband played around on the side. Maybe she decided it was a small price to pay not to spend the rest of her life worrying if she'd be able to pay the rent *and* afford groceries."

I had to sit with that for a minute, the idea that my mom had married my dad purely for his money. Or maybe it hadn't been so much the money as the security. Knowing she'd be taken care of instead of having to fight to scrape by and that her kids would grow up in comfort and privilege—I imagined that had to be worth some pretty big sacrifices.

"It really doesn't bother you?" Wyatt asked Ryan. He was having a harder time with this than I was. He was two years younger than me, so his memories of our life before Mom got sick were that much fuzzier and more tainted by the rosy colors of early childhood.

"It did for a while," Ryan admitted. "But I've had thirty years to get used to it. As far as I could tell, she wasn't unhappy with him, so why should I be unhappy about it?"

He had a point. Mom had made her choices, and they'd allowed her to spend her last years living in luxury, and got her the best medical care money could buy when she took ill. I couldn't blame her for that any more than I could blame her for trying to make sure the three of us would be taken care of.

It didn't mean I had to forgive my Dad for the kind of father he'd been. But for all I knew, he'd been exactly the kind of husband Mom wanted him to be.

"Well, fuck." Wyatt collapsed back on the couch and propped his feet on Ryan's coffee table. "All this time I thought I was keeping some big, awful secret, and it turns out everyone already knew it."

The corner of Ryan's mouth quirked. "Sorry."

"What I want to know"—Wyatt pointed an accusing finger at Ryan—"is what else haven't you told us? What other secrets have you got rattling around in that vault of yours?"

Ryan laughed and pushed himself to his feet. "I'm ordering us pizza."

Wyatt reached over and smacked my arm. "Notice how he changed the subject? Closed-lipped motherfucker."

"Meat supreme?" Ryan asked from the kitchen as he peered at the menu on his fridge.

"Better make it two," Wyatt told him. "All this family drama's got me hungry enough to eat the south end of a northbound nanny goat."

I pulled my phone out to check the time and found a new message from Lucy. *How's it going with Wyatt? Everything okay over there?*

I typed out a reply as Wyatt and Ryan discussed pizza toppings. *It's all good. We're about to order pizza. I'll probably be here a while.*

"What do you think's happening over at Dad's right now?" Wyatt asked. "I'll bet you anything Nate's freaking the fuck out."

"Why Nate?" Ryan asked, wandering back in with his phone pressed to his ear.

Wyatt opened his mouth to answer but paused when Ryan held up a finger while he recited our pizza order to the person on the other end of the line.

"Sorry, go ahead." Ryan pocketed his phone and dropped into the recliner again. "Why do you think Nate's freaking out?"

Wyatt leaned back and stretched his arm along the top of the couch. "Because Manny's older than Nate. This surprise revelation means Nate's not the number one son and heir apparent anymore—Manny is."

I hadn't thought of it that way. I wasn't sure it was true either. We weren't the House of Windsor, governed by strict laws of primogeniture. As the majority shareholder and chairman of the board, our father was at liberty to name his own successor at his own whims. He could as easily hand control of the company to Josie as to Nate or Manny. Hell, he could even snub all of them and bring in an outsider to be CEO if he wanted. Although it was true that if Manny's parentage became common knowledge, it would put him on a more equal footing with Nate in the eyes of everyone else—including the board of directors—which might have some influence on our dad.

Or it might not. He could be mercurial as fuck when he wanted to be.

"You know all Nate cares about is inheriting the throne from the old man," Wyatt was saying. "Everyone always assumed it'd be him, but if Manny's a King by blood, that changes things."

"Does it?" I asked, and looked at Ryan, who offered another of his famous shrugs. He'd never had much to do with the family business, so maybe in this case he really didn't know.

"Doesn't it?" Wyatt countered. "Now which one of them is gonna be the head cheese after dad retires?"

"Like he'll ever retire." My phone vibrated under my leg and

I dug it out. "The man's probably made a deal with the devil to live forever."

Lucy had replied to my text with *I'm glad! Enjoy your fraternal bonding! I love you!* followed by a long string of emojis.

"What's got you smiling?" Wyatt asked, leaning over for a look at my phone.

"Nothing." I crammed it in my pocket, but I wasn't quite fast enough.

"Was that an eggplant I saw in there with all those hearts Lucy sent you? I take it things are going well?"

I couldn't help smiling wider. "They are."

"Damn, look at you!" Wyatt punched my shoulder and turned to grin at Ryan. "Will you look at this guy, glowing like a pregnant woman?"

"Well?" Ryan arched an eyebrow at me. "Are you going to tell me the Lucy saga or what?"

It didn't take long to fill them both in on the developments since the folk festival. When I'd finished giving them the broad strokes, Wyatt punched me in the shoulder again.

"Fuck yeah. Thank god she finally woke up and put you out of your misery."

"Congratulations," Ryan said. "I'm glad everything worked out."

"Yeah." I smiled down at my beer. "Me too."

"So what's it like going to work with your girlfriend every day?" Wyatt asked. "And does Josie know about you two yet? Because you know she's going to find out."

My smile faded. "She knows."

"What?" Ryan leaned forward. "Is that a problem?"

"No. Josie's fine with it. But, uh...there's something else I haven't told you." I paused to take a breath, anticipating their reactions to this next piece of news. "I quit my job on Monday—

not because of Lucy or anything—but I gave Josie my two weeks' notice."

"Seriously?" Wyatt gaped at me. "Holy shit, I never thought I'd see the day." He slung an arm around my shoulders and gave me a celebratory shake. "It's about fucking time you cut the apron strings. Hallelujah."

"You're gonna spill my beer," I muttered, elbowing him off me.

Ryan had stayed quiet, studying me. "Why?" he asked finally.

"A lot of reasons." I ran a hand through my hair, then smoothed it back down again. "Wyatt's not wrong that it's long overdue. I guess the last straw was finding out Dad had lied about Manny's paternity, then getting called up to Dad's office and chewed out for telling Manny the truth without asking for permission first."

"Of course he did," Wyatt muttered, shaking his head.

"For what it's worth, I think you made the right call," Ryan said.

I appreciated hearing that. I didn't regret my choice, but I felt better knowing Ryan was on my side—especially since he so rarely took sides. "Anyway, after Dad disinvited me to the family gathering tonight—"

"He did?" Wyatt cut in. "Wow. That's cold."

I nodded, staring down at my beer. "After I walked out of his office, I was just so goddamn tired of everything. I decided I'd had it. So I went straight to Josie's office and gave her my resignation."

"Does this mean you and Dad aren't speaking at all now?" Wyatt asked.

"I don't know what we are," I answered honestly. This was all new territory for me. I hadn't thought much beyond my decision to leave the family business and had no idea where it left us now that I wasn't dependent on his favor. "I'm not exactly feeling disposed to extend an olive branch, and it's not like he's ever going to offer an apology."

My father would sooner chew his own arm off than be the first to make a gesture of reconciliation, which left the burden of peacemaking on my shoulders. In the past I would have done it —eaten my humble pie to smooth things over so we could go back to pretending to get along. But I wasn't sure I was willing anymore. I'd had enough humble pie for a lifetime.

On the other hand, I didn't relish the thought of a permanent rift between us. We still were part of the same family, and I didn't want to miss family events and be divided from my siblings because of my father. Wyatt's self-imposed separation these last few months had shown me how much I valued having all of us together.

"That makes three of us now," Wyatt said. When I gave him a questioning look he clarified: "Three sons he's driven away. He keeps up at this rate, there might not be any of us left by the time he shuffles off to the Great Beyond."

"And then there were none," I murmured. It was like an Agatha Christie story, only instead of being murdered, we were being pushed into estrangement, one at a time.

"So what are you going to do now?" Ryan asked me. "Have you started looking for another job?"

"Not yet. I didn't have any kind of plan when I quit—it was more of a spur-of-the-moment decision."

Wyatt's eyebrows shot up. "Are you freaking out?" he asked, knowing how compulsively risk averse I was.

"Surprisingly no." The fear of living without a safety net had held me back for most of my life, but now that I'd done it, I felt strangely calm. "It's a little scary to think about not having a job, but on balance I feel a whole lot better, actually."

"Don't worry," Wyatt said, grinning. "I'm sure Ryan will let you move in here with him if you get desperate."

"Think again," Ryan shot back before offering me a supportive look. "Tanner's gonna be fine."

For once, I felt like I would. Even if the bookstore thing didn't work out, something would come along. I'd figure it out, one way or another.

"Hang on, I love this part." I dragged my mouth away from Tanner's to turn my head toward the TV.

He made a disgruntled sound in the back of his throat. "Don't mind me, I'm just trying to kiss you here."

It was Friday night, and we were spending it on his couch watching *Fellowship of the Ring*—though in actual fact, we'd mostly been making out.

"But it's the Mines of Moria." I swiveled back toward him, sighing as his tongue traced a path along my collarbone. "I thought you loved this movie."

"I love you more," he murmured between my breasts, his hot breath and new beard tickling the sensitive skin.

Tanner's official last day at King's Creamery had been two weeks ago, and he'd taken a vacation from shaving now that he wasn't going into the office anymore. While I'd always loved his clean-cut look, I was majorly enjoying this scruffier version of him.

In general, he'd been a lot happier and more relaxed since he quit his job. He'd been dividing his time equally between

working on his book and working on his business plan for the
bookstore. He'd even been to talk to Seamus Hill a few times
and convinced him to hold off a little while longer before he
listed the property for sale.

I was grateful Tanner had projects to fill his newfound free
time, because I'd been busier than usual at work and hadn't
been able to spend as much time with him as I liked. The day
after he'd given his notice, Josie had called me to her office to
discuss the future of the team. She'd reaffirmed that Jill's old
position would still be mine, along with a commensurate salary
bump, the second the promotion freeze was lifted. In the meantime, she'd assigned me one of the copywriters to take some of
the burden off. Then she'd told me she was invested in my
professional development and wanted to schedule regular
mentoring lunches for the two of us.

Ever since, I'd felt a lot more optimistic about my future at
the company, which had made me more motivated than I'd been
in a long time. Now that I knew Josie was seeing and appreci-
ating my efforts, I'd redoubled them, coming up with some
ambitious new plans for our newsletter and social messaging
that had me working longer hours. Between that, training the
new copywriter, and my mother's continual demands on my
time, I'd been seeing a lot less of Tanner than I had when he'd
worked at the desk across from me. Tonight was the first evening
we'd had alone together all week.

I shivered as his beard dragged across my cleavage, igniting
sparks up and down my spine. Plunging my fingers into his hair,
I pulled his mouth up to mine. "You love me more than *The Lord
of the Rings* movies? Wow, that's an awful lot."

"I know," he said, nipping my lower lip. "And I've barely seen
you for days, so if you wouldn't mind"—his palm smoothed up
my bare thigh—"I'd rather pay attention to you than some
movie."

A moan shuddered through me as his fingers crept up the inside of my shorts and brushed against the edge of my underwear.

"I love it when you make that sound," he murmured against my throat as he kissed his way down my body.

"Keep doing what you're doing, and I'll make all the sounds you like."

His hands clasped the button on my shorts. "I'm taking these off."

"Yes, please." I arched my hips to make it easier for him.

My purse started playing Carole King's "Where You Lead" from the other side of the room, and Tanner stilled at the familiar sound of my mother's ringtone.

"Sorry, I thought I'd turned that off." Since I'd been ignoring my mother's texts when I was with Tanner, she'd escalated to straight up calling me. I'd told her only to call if it was an emergency, but her idea of an emergency diverged sharply from mine.

"Do you want to get it?" Tanner asked.

"No. I'm sure it's nothing." I tightened my fingers in his hair, encouraging him to get back to the very important business of removing my shorts. He'd informed me that he was shaving tomorrow before the foundation benefit, and I wanted to make the most of that beard while he still had it.

Pushing my shirt up, he placed a kiss above my belly button, and I squirmed with pleasure as his beard rubbed my ticklish skin.

Just as he started to pull down my zipper, Carole King started singing again, and he sat back on his haunches with a frustrated sigh.

"I'll just go turn it off," I said, huffing out a sigh that matched his. "She's only going to keep calling."

He stopped me with a hand on my hip when I started to

push myself upright. "I'll get it. I don't want you to move from this spot."

"Yes, sir," I answered with a grin.

After he'd clambered off the couch, I lifted my arms over my head and stretched out in blissful contentment. Everything was finally going my way. My brother's orthopedic surgeon had said his ankle was healing fine on its own and wouldn't need surgery, the insurance company had actually approved his physical therapy, and Matt should be able to go back to work in another couple of weeks. Not only that, but he'd mastered the bass drum pedal left-footed, and the band had booked a gig in San Antonio next weekend that should cover almost half of his insurance deductible, which meant Matt's problems were no longer my problems. Hallelujah! Meanwhile, my own professional future was finally showing promise, I was madly in love with my sexy, bearded boyfriend, and I had him all to myself for the whole night. Nothing was going to puncture my happiness, not even my mother's clinginess.

"Lucy." Tanner turned around with my phone in his hand and a serious expression on his face. "You need to call your mom back."

I didn't like his expression one bit. "Why?" I asked with a sinking feeling, pushing myself up to a sitting position.

He handed me the phone, and I scanned the text notifications on the screen. "Shit." Panic set my heart racing as I swiped to call my mother back. "Mama, are you okay?"

"Oh, Lucy, thank god!" She sounded breathless and near tears. "I've been trying to call you."

"What do you mean there's a prowler in the backyard?"

"I heard a noise outside my bedroom window, and when I peeked through the curtains I saw a dark figure sneaking around back there. I don't know if it's a Peeping Tom, or if he's casing the house planning to break in."

"Did you call the police?"

"No, I was in such a state, I couldn't think straight. I'm so scared, baby. Your brother's out at band practice, so I'm in the house all by myself. Can you please just come home?"

I looked at Tanner, who'd already put his shoes on and was waiting by the door with his keys in his hand. "Of course, Mama. We're leaving right now. As soon as you hang up the phone, I want you to dial 911 and then go make sure all the doors are locked. Okay? Can you do that?"

"Just hurry, please, sweetheart. I'm near going out of my mind."

———

"THERE'S no sign of anyone anywhere on the property," Tanner said when I let him back into my house through the sliding patio door.

After we'd arrived and seen that my mother was safe and sound, he'd gone outside to check the yard, warning us to lock the door behind him. Despite my instructions, my mother hadn't called the police. She'd said it was because she didn't want to "make a big fuss and bother over something so trivial."

Though she'd had no such qualms about making a big fuss and bothering *me* with it.

"Are you sure?" my mother asked Tanner, clutching at his arm.

"I walked the perimeter twice. Even checked inside the shed and looked under the cars in the neighbors' driveways." He gave her hand a reassuring pat before gently removing it from his biceps. "Whoever it was is definitely gone now."

"If they ever existed in the first place," I muttered.

My mother cut me a sharp look. "You think I imagined it? Is that it?"

"No, Mama, of course not," I said in an appeasing tone. "But it's possible you saw something else in the dark that looked like a person."

She huffed in indignation. "I guess you think I'm crazy, don't you?"

"That's not what I said."

"You didn't have to. I know what you think of me. You've always had a mean little mind like your father. The two of you are just alike. There's never been a man so ungenerous and quick to think the worst of people."

I darted a nervous glance at Tanner. His whole body had gone rigid, and his eyes had narrowed to angry slits. In desperation, I gave him a small head shake and a pleading look. The last thing I needed was him stepping up to my defense, which would only make my mother feel ganged up on and set her off further. If I couldn't calm her down, I'd be dealing with the fallout for days. Keeping her soothed and in good spirits was the only way to make my life at home bearable.

"I promise I don't think anything of the sort," I told her in a placating voice. "Didn't we come rushing over here to make sure you were safe?"

"But you always ignore my texts these days!" Her voice rose higher, breaking slightly as her lip trembled. "It's like you don't even want to talk to me anymore."

"That's not true. My phone was in my purse, and I didn't see your texts, Mama. But I'm here now, aren't I?"

Her eyes were shiny with tears as she grasped both my hands in a beseeching grip. "You're not leaving again, are you? I don't think I could bear to be alone after such a fright."

"No, of course not," I promised. "What can I do to make you feel better? Do you want me to make you some tea? Or maybe a cold compress for your head?"

"Oh, that would be lovely. Some chamomile would hit the spot to soothe my frayed nerves." She pressed her hand to my cheek, giving me a watery smile. "Aren't you the sweetest girl to take care of me so well? Why don't you make some tea for all of us?" She turned to take Tanner's hand as she beamed up at him. "Including your big, strong gentleman who came to my rescue. Or would you rather have a beer, honey?"

"I'm okay," Tanner said, looking uneasy. "I don't care for anything, but thank you, ma'am."

"You know what we should do?" my mother said, still grasping both our hands. "We should all three watch a movie together. Wouldn't that be fun?"

"Sure, Mama. Whatever you want." I looked up at Tanner, my eyes widening in an appeal to his generous nature. "You can stay to watch a movie with us, right?"

"Absolutely," he answered, keeping his expression shuttered. "I'd be happy to."

My mother clapped her hands and squealed in glee. "Wonderful! Now Lucy, you go make us that tea while Tanner and I pick a movie to watch. Oh, and fix us some popcorn while you're at it. What's a movie without popcorn, right Tanner?"

FOR THE NEXT TWO HOURS, Tanner sat stiffly beside me on the couch as we watched *You've Got Mail*, one of my mother's favorite movies. I could feel the unhappiness radiating off him. I was equally unhappy, but my misery was compounded by my guilt over ruining his night.

At least I could hold his hand while my mother ate most of the popcorn and offered a running commentary on the movie. Periodically, I'd look over at him, searching for reassurance that he wasn't too upset with me, and he'd offer me a tight smile as our eyes locked in a wordless exchange of mutual frustration.

As soon as the credits rolled, my mother reached for the remote and started flipping through the channels, looking for something else to watch.

Tanner gave me a look I couldn't interpret and got to his feet. "I should be going. It's getting late."

"Oh, do you have to?" my mother said without looking away from the TV. "What a shame."

"I'll walk you out," I said, standing up to follow him.

"Good night, Tanner," my mother called as we headed for the front door. "Lucy, when you come back, bring me my vitamins from the kitchen."

As soon as we were outside, I grabbed Tanner's hand and tugged him toward the street where his car was parked. "I'm so sorry," I said when we were safely out of earshot of the house.

He stopped walking and turned toward me, tightening his grip on my hand. Deep lines scored his forehead in the orange light from the streetlamps. "You don't have to apologize."

"I feel like I do. I know you're unhappy about the way tonight turned out, and I don't blame you. But I'll find a way to make it up to you, I promise."

"Please don't." His hands skimmed up my arms and over the tops of my shoulders to clasp the nape of my neck. "I'm not unhappy with you."

"No, you're unhappy with my mother, who's my responsibility."

"No, she's not." The sharpness of his voice startled a flinch out of me. When he spoke again his voice was much softer, but still taut with displeasure. "Lucy, you're not responsible for your mother, or for any of the things she says and does, for that matter."

"No, I'm just the one that has to fix everything after she blows through like a bad batch of truck stop chili."

He dragged a hand through his hair in frustration. "No, you aren't. It's not your job to manage her life."

"Who do you think is going to do it if I don't?"

"She can do it herself. If she's capable of making her own decisions, then she's capable of taking responsibility for them. She can live with the consequences of her choices."

"No, *I'm* the one that has to live with them." My eyes and throat stung as I blinked back tears. "Your father's never needed you for anything the way my mother needs me, so you can't understand what it's like. But imagine if you found out he needed you to donate a kidney. No matter how difficult your relationship with him was, you'd give him your kidney, wouldn't you? You wouldn't just stand back and refuse to help him."

Tanner's mouth had tightened into a hard, flat line. "Your mother doesn't need a kidney transplant. She's manipulating you."

"You think I don't know that?" I said too loudly, causing him to flinch this time. I squeezed my eyes shut, immediately regretting my defensiveness. "I'm sorry. I didn't mean to raise my voice. It's not you I'm upset with."

Tanner gathered me against his chest, and I let out an unsteady breath as I leaned into him. "I hate the way she talks to you," he said. "You can't expect me to just stand by and watch her take swipes at you like that."

"She didn't mean it. She lashes out sometimes when she's upset, but she never means it."

"It's not just when she's upset. She does it all the time. She's constantly belittling you, Lucy. And the way she orders you around all the time makes my blood boil. You don't deserve to be treated that way."

I didn't need him to tell me that. It was the mantra I'd been repeating in my head most of my life. "What am I supposed to do about it?" I mumbled.

"You need to set some boundaries with her. Stop letting her walk all over you."

I let out a dark laugh and pushed out of his arms. "You think I haven't tried? Over and over again? It never works. It just upsets her and makes things worse for me."

"Placating her isn't making it any better either. Don't you see what she's doing? She's never going to let you have a life because she likes having you at her beck and call too much. She'll do whatever she can to sabotage your happiness in order to keep you tied to her."

Crossing my arms over my chest, I dropped my eyes to the ground. "You don't understand."

"You keep saying that, but I do. I can see exactly what she's doing to you because I've been stuck in the same kind of toxic relationship with my father—letting him push me around and trying to please him even though nothing I do will ever be enough. We've both put up with it too long. You have to stand up for yourself if you ever want to break free of your mother's hold on you."

"Stop it!" I pressed the heels of my hands against my eyes. "I don't need you berating me too."

"I'm not trying to berate you," he said miserably. "I just hate seeing you treated like this."

I lowered my hands and set my jaw, meeting his gaze levelly. "Our situations aren't the same. It's not as easy for me as simply quitting a job and finding a new one. If I walk out on my mother, she won't be able to pay her bills. Without my financial support, she'll lose her home. But since I can't afford to support myself and her both on my salary right now, I'm stuck living here until I get the raise I've been waiting for."

"Lucy—" He started to reach for me, but I stepped back because I had more to say. He swallowed, a look of anguish crossing his face before he shoved his hands in his pockets.

"This is my life," I continued, struggling to keep my voice firm despite the strong impulse to throw myself into Tanner's arms and apologize. "I'm the one who has to live it, not you. I know my mother better than you do, and I'm going to do what I have to do to make my life here more bearable. If that means placating her sometimes, then so be it. I appreciate your concern, but I don't need your input on my relationship with my mother."

How was that for drawing boundaries? Maybe now he'd believe I knew how to do it when I needed to.

Tanner rolled his lips between his teeth. I could tell he wanted to say more, but I didn't think I could stand it if he did. I already felt pulled in too many directions. This was exactly why I'd avoided relationships for so long. There was only so much of me to go around. I wasn't going to be able to keep both Tanner and my mother happy all the time. Sometimes I'd have to disappoint him like I had tonight.

I desperately needed him to accept that. If he couldn't...

If he couldn't, I had no idea where that left us.

He took a bracing breath before speaking, his gaze still on the ground. "I'm sorry." His voice was low and restrained. "It's not my place to butt in or give you advice. I overstepped, and I apologize."

I could tell I'd hurt his feelings, and it made me feel about two inches tall. But I wasn't going to take back what I'd said. I'd meant every word of it. "I don't need you to apologize. I need to know you understand. Do you?"

His blue eyes were stormy when they lifted to mine, but otherwise his gaze was shuttered—just like it had been inside with my mother—and I hated it because it meant he was hiding his feelings from me.

"Tanner?" My voice cracked as my eyes blurred with tears. Without waiting for him to answer, I stepped forward and hugged his waist. "I love you." The words gusted out of me as I pressed my face against his chest.

He took his hands out of his pockets and wound his arms around me. "I love you too." I let out a hiccup of relief and he held me tighter. "I do understand. I promise, I do. It just hurts me to see you unhappy and not be able to do anything about it."

"I'm not unhappy," I said. "Not as long as I have you."

He kissed the top of my head. "You have me. I'm not going anywhere."

"You're about to go home," I pointed out petulantly.

He grunted in amused acknowledgement. "You know what I mean." His hands gently tilted my head up. This time his eyes were gentle and loving when they met mine. "I'm always here for you, even when I'm not actually here *with* you." Another sob hiccupped out of me, and he bent down to rest his forehead against mine. "Hey. Shhh. I love you. It's okay."

I closed my eyes, too overwhelmed with relief to speak.

His fingers pushed into the hair at my temples as his lips touched mine, a warm press so tender it made my heart clench. I pressed back, needing more of him, and his tongue swept into my mouth in a slow, hot slide I felt all the way down to my toes.

Just when it was starting to get good, he pulled back. I let out a disappointed whimper, and he kissed my forehead. "We can't do this now. I need to go." Frustration roughened his voice, making it sound even sexier, which only increased my need for him.

"I hate this. I wanted to spend the night with you."

"I know." He blew out a long breath like he was trying to get control of himself. "But we'll have other nights."

"Tomorrow?" I asked hopefully.

His mouth curved downward. "Tomorrow's the foundation benefit."

"I know." I reached up to smooth his unhappy expression away, running my fingers through his lovely beard. "But after we finish drinking wine with Crowder's upper crust, then I can spend the whole night with you."

"If you're still coming, yeah." His voice had a flat quality to it. *Distant*, like he'd mentally pulled away.

"Of course I'm still coming."

"You don't have to." Instead of looking at me, he had his gaze fixed to the side, his eyes unfocused as he stared at a point beyond my shoulder. "If you want to get out of it—"

"I don't want to get out of it." I took his face in my hands, forcing him to give me his eyes. The guardedness in them made me think he was used to being disappointed by people. "I said I'd be there and I will."

That had been part of the reason I'd given in to my mom so easily tonight. She had a date planned with Tony tomorrow night, which should keep her occupied for the entire evening. If I'd gone back to Tanner's tonight against her wishes, it might have triggered a full-blown sulk. Once she got into that kind of black mood, it could spill over for days, making her even more demanding and unreasonable. The last thing I wanted was for her to decide she wasn't feeling up to seeing Tony tomorrow and cancel her plans, leaving her free to interfere with mine.

I had to pick my battles carefully with my mother. By giving her what she wanted tonight, I'd won myself enough goodwill that I'd be able to keep my promise to Tanner tomorrow, when it mattered most.

A muscle ticked in his jaw as he nodded. I could feel the apprehension radiating through every muscle in his body at the prospect of facing his father tomorrow night, and it made my heart hurt for him.

I stretched up to kiss his scratchy cheek before pulling him into a hug. "I love you, and I want to be there for you. I know tomorrow's going to be hard, but I'll be right there at your side to hold your hand through all of it. Okay? I promise."

He blew out a long breath, seeming to relax a little. "Okay."

31

LUCY

What exactly did one wear to a memorial foundation wine tasting? Tanner had told me it wasn't formal, but he'd be dressed in a suit and tie. He'd also texted me a selfie of his freshly shaven face, and I'd had to take a moment to mourn the loss of his dearly departed beard, sad I'd missed my window to bid it a proper goodbye. I'd recovered quickly, however, remembering I'd have him to myself tonight after the benefit. Beard or no beard, that was something to look forward to.

At present, I was still wearing my bathrobe as I flipped through my meager collection of dressy non-work clothes. Ruling out the dress I'd worn to Post Oak Lodge with Tanner left me with only three choices. Two were dresses I'd bought to wear to weddings over the last several years, and one was an impulse buy I'd purchased for a long-ago date that hadn't lived up to expectations.

I eliminated that one as potentially cursed by bad karma, and eliminated one of the others, a soft pink dress I'd worn to an afternoon wedding, as not dressy enough for an evening event. That left me with a midnight blue off-the-shoulder lace dress.

No bra it is. Tanner should enjoy that.

I hung the blue dress on the louvers of my closet door and turned my attention to the issue of shoes. While I was deciding between black closed-toe pumps and strappy champagne heels, my phone chimed at me from the bed, singing the cheerful trill of notes that meant I had a new text from Tanner.

Leaving now. Be there in ten minutes.

Smiling, I typed out my response: *I'll be ready!*

"Oh, *Lucy!*" The sound of my mother's anguished voice struck fear into my heart.

I looked up to find her standing in the doorway of my room with tears streaming down her face. She came toward me and crumpled into my arms, sobbing uncontrollably.

"Mama, what's wrong?" I asked, trying to comfort her as she clung to me. "Tell me what's happened."

"It's Tony," she hiccupped between hitching breaths. "He's— he's *married.*" She trailed off into an agonized wail.

"Oh, Mama. I'm so sorry." I hugged her, rocking her and stroking her hair as she cried. Once she'd calmed down a bit, I led her over to the bed and sat her down, fetching a box of tissues before sitting on the edge of the mattress next to her.

"I can't believe I didn't know," she mumbled as she blew her nose. "I had such a good feeling about him too."

Sadly, this wasn't the first time my mother had been taken in by a perfidious man. She seemed to be a magnet for them, and her good feelings were notoriously unreliable. At least Tony hadn't taken off with one of her credit cards like the last man she'd dated, who'd charged eight hundred dollars of fishing equipment before she'd even realized that the card—and the boyfriend—had absconded.

"How did you find out?" I asked.

"He called and told me. He said his wife found his phone. I

guess he had a second one he used for texting me that he'd kept secret from her. She read all our messages and confronted him."

"What a piece of garbage—Tony, that is. Not his wife." I felt even worse for his wife than I did for my mother. Imagine building your whole life around someone and having them betray you like that. Of course, that was exactly what my father had done to my mother—cheated on her most of the time they were married before eventually abandoning her and the family they'd made together. My poor mother really seemed to have a type.

"She's threatening to leave him and take their kids."

"He has *kids*?"

My mother nodded, sniffling. "Two girls in middle school."

What a tool. I hoped his wife did leave him and he never saw those girls again. Team Tony's Wife all the way.

"Did he ever mention he had kids?" I asked, handing my mother a fresh tissue.

"Nooooo." With a plaintive moan, she flopped back onto the bed and curled up on her side. "I thought I knew him, but I didn't know anything about him at all." Her voice broke as she dissolved into a fresh flurry of tears.

"It's not your fault he's a liar. At least you hadn't been seeing him very long. You'd only been on a few dates."

She shook her head as she crawled up the bed to bury her face in my pillows. "I thought I loved him! God, I'm such a fool! How could I be so gullible?"

I wished I knew. Every time she got taken in by another scumbag or some new pyramid scheme or a wellness guru selling junk that only cured you of your money, she'd ask herself the same question. And yet the next time something shiny came along, making promises that seemed too good to be true, she'd dismiss all my concerns and throw caution to the wind like she hadn't learned a thing.

"Oh, my head. All this crying's bringing on one of my headaches." She reached out a hand blindly, her face still pressed into my pillows. "Will you be a dear and make me one of those cold compresses? The ones with lavender oil to soothe my anxiety?"

"Okay, but"—I checked the time on my phone—"then I have to finish getting dressed so I can go."

"Go?" She turned her head to blink red-rimmed eyes at me. "You can't be thinking of going out? Not now."

"I promised Tanner I'd go to this benefit with him. It's going to be a difficult night for him, and he needs me there for support."

"But *I* need you!" A sob choked out of her, and she hugged one of my throw cushions to her chest. "Why does this always happen to me? What's wrong with me? Am I so hard to love?"

"Nothing's wrong with you."

She curled herself into an even tighter ball, rocking back and forth as she wept. "Then why does everyone leave me? Even you."

I looked over at the blue lace dress hanging on my closet door and the champagne heels I'd decided to wear with it. My whole body felt like it was full of lead. I was being pulled back down again, the cold, dark waters closing over me and blocking out the sun.

"Please don't leave me alone tonight. I couldn't bear it. I need my baby girl with me. Promise me you'll stay."

"I'm not leaving you, Mama." How could I, when she was so distraught? Only someone with a heart of stone could turn their back on her when she was in this kind of pain. And my heart wasn't made of stone, although sometimes I wished it was. Then maybe I'd be able to do what I wanted for once.

The doorbell rang, and my mother let out a heartrending

whimper. "Please, Lucy." She clutched at my hand. "Please don't go."

I extricated my hand and patted her on the arm as I got to my feet. "I'll be right back. I need to go answer the door, and then I'll make you that compress, okay?"

Pulling my bathrobe tighter around me, I made my way to the front entry and opened the door.

Tanner looked incredible in his suit, like something from a dream. His smile froze on his beautiful clean-cut face as he took in the sight of me. "You're not dressed."

"No." I tugged nervously at the collar of my robe.

I saw the exact moment he realized what I was about to say, because hurt flared in his expression before he slammed it shut, schooling his features to blankness. "Maybe I should have been more specific when I said the event wasn't black-tie." His attempt at dry humor fell as flat as a ruined soufflé.

"I'm so sorry," I said, feeling miserable.

"It's fine."

"I know it's not."

"What do you want me to say?" A flicker of anger sharpened his words, and he shut his eyes for a second. When he opened them again, all that empty blankness was back.

"My mother just found out her boyfriend was married." My tone was pleading, willing him to understand and forgive me for disappointing him. "She's legitimately a wreck right now. I can't leave her."

He clenched his jaw and dropped his gaze to the ground. "Right."

"I *can't*. If you could see her—"

"I believe you." His cold brusqueness sliced right through me.

I rubbed my aching chest. "I know I promised I'd be there for you tonight and I'm letting you down, but she's curled up in a fetal position on my bed right now, sobbing her eyes out." I was on the verge of tears myself. What was I supposed to do? My mother was fragile. She needed me. Yes, Tanner needed me too, but he was stronger than she was. He'd be okay on his own.

He stood motionless without looking at me or saying anything, the two feet of distance between us feeling more like two thousand miles.

"I'm so sorry," I tried saying again.

His expression grew pinched. "Please don't apologize."

"What can I do? How can I make this better?"

"You can't," he said and it felt like a slap. His lips pressed into an unhappy line. "What I mean is you don't have to do anything. I understand."

"Do you?"

There was a long pause before he answered. When he spoke his voice sounded detached and robotic, and his eyes remained fixed on the ground. "Like you said last night, you know your mother better than I do. It doesn't matter if I think she's taking advantage of you. It's not my business or my place to interfere. You have to do what you think is right, because you're the one who has to live with your choices."

I swallowed thickly, feeling every one of the words he'd just thrown back at me like daggers. "Will you look at me, please?"

He lifted his eyes to mine. They were devoid of all emotion except one: *resignation*. Like he'd known this was coming all along.

Guilt washed over me as I remembered the hesitancy I'd seen in his expression last night. How reluctant he'd been to believe I'd come through for him. He'd anticipated disappointment, and now here I was, fulfilling his low expectations.

He gave a small, heartbreaking shrug in an attempt at nonchalance. "You have to stay. I get it."

"I'm sorry."

Another flare of anger broke through his expression. "Stop apologizing."

"You *are* mad at me. You keep saying you understand, but you don't. Not really. I know I've disappointed you and you're upset with me, but I don't know what you expect me to do. Turn my back on my mother when she's crying?"

His face betrayed no emotion as his eyes stared into mine. There was nothing but that blank, dull flatness he'd constructed to hide his hurt feelings. "No," he said quietly. "I would never ask you to do that."

"Tanner." My voice broke as tears rose in my throat.

I started forward, and he took a step back, putting himself out of my reach.

My heart cracked in half at his rejection.

"I have to go," he said, lowering his eyes to the ground again. "I promised Josie."

The words hung in the air between us, pregnant with unvoiced reproach. Tanner was someone who kept his promises, and I wasn't. I couldn't have felt lower if he'd scraped me off the bottom of his shoe.

Without another word, he turned his back on me and got in his car.

32

LUCY

After I watched Tanner drive away without so much as a look back at me, I reached into the pocket of my bathrobe for my phone. My lungs burned like I was suffocating, and my eyes were blurred with tears as I navigated to my contacts and called Wyatt.

"Hey, Lucy," he answered, sounding surprised. We'd exchanged texts in the past about band practices and performances, but I wasn't sure I'd ever called him before. "What's up?"

"I need to ask you for a huge favor."

"What's wrong?" He must have been able to tell from the sound of my voice that I was crying.

I wiped my eyes on the sleeve of my robe, not caring that I was smearing my carefully applied makeup. "I need you to go to your family's charity fundraiser thing tonight at the winery."

There was a long pause. "Why?"

"Because Tanner's going and—" My chest hitched and I blew out a breath, trying to get control of myself again. "He didn't want to go because your dad's going to be there, but he promised Josie he would. So I promised Tanner I'd go with him for moral support, only now I can't go. Something came up, and we had a fight, and now he's upset and he's going to be there on his own. And I know you don't want to be there either, but I'm asking you to go for Tanner's sake. Can you please do that? Will you please go and make sure he's okay? He needs someone tonight, and it can't be me." I'd been speaking so fast I was breathless by the time I finished voicing my request.

"Are *you* okay?" Wyatt asked. "Where are you? Do you need me to come and get you?"

"No, I'm at home."

"Do you need me to come and get you from there?"

"No, I'm fine." His gentlemanly concern warmed a teeny bit of the ache in my heart. "Can you go to the benefit for me?"

"Won't Ryan be there?"

"He's working a shift."

"Yeah, okay," Wyatt said. "I can do it. I'll leave as soon as I throw on some clothes." Rustling sounds came over the line, as if he was already moving around and getting ready to go.

I let out a long, shaky breath. "Thank you. I really appreciate it."

"It's no problem," he said, even though I knew exactly how big an ask it was. Wyatt hadn't seen or spoken to his father in months, and now I was potentially forcing them into a confrontation. Yet another thing for me to feel terrible about. "You said you and Tanner had a fight?" he asked me.

I swallowed around the lump in my throat. "Yes."

"How bad a fight are we talking about? You didn't break up, did you?"

The question brought on a sob, and I pressed my hand against my mouth to stifle it. As much as Tanner had tried to hide it, I'd seen how hurt he was. And it wasn't like I could offer him any assurances that things would be different or get better anytime soon. He hadn't said anything about breaking up, but once he'd had time to think things over...

What if he decides he wants to be done with me?

"I'm just trying to gauge how much consoling he's gonna need," Wyatt added at my silence.

"I have to go," I choked out. "Just...look after him, okay?"

"I will, but—"

"Thanks, Wyatt." I hung up before he could say anything else.

Now that I knew Tanner would have someone coming to support him, I needed to put my own feelings aside so I could be there for my mother. Wiping my tears away, I took a few bracing breaths before I went inside the house.

My mother was sitting up on the bed when I went back into my room. "How'd your young man take the disappointing news?" she asked, dabbing at the corners of her eyes with a tissue.

I couldn't bring myself to answer her question. I was still too upset to talk about it without risking a complete breakdown, and I certainly didn't want to talk about it with her.

She made a moue of sympathy at the look on my face. "Oh, baby girl. Don't you worry about him. He'll be just fine. It does a man good to be reminded he's not the center of your universe."

"I forgot to make your compress," I said, wishing she'd stop talking about Tanner like she knew anything about him. She hadn't seen the wounded look in his eyes. She didn't understand how generous and selfless he was, or that he was the last person in the world I ever wanted to hurt.

"Forget about that silly compress. My headache's feeling better already just knowing I have my sweet girl here with me." She reached for my hand and pulled me down to sit on the edge of the bed beside her. "You know what we should do tonight? We should get in our pajamas, put on beauty masks, and watch another movie together. Won't that be nice? Just us girls. Who needs men, right?"

"All right. Whatever you want." I tried to smile even as my heart twisted, thinking about Tanner and how badly I'd let him down. How much more miserable tonight would be for him because of me. Instead of making it better for him, I'd made it infinitely worse.

"There you go." My mother pinched my cheek. "There's that smile I love. You go wash all that smeary makeup off your face, and I'll pick out a nice detox mask for you."

I looked at her—really *looked* at her, for the first time since she'd come into my room crying. "You're not wearing makeup. Why aren't you wearing makeup?"

She blinked her bare, natural lashes at me. "What do you mean?"

"You told me you had a date with Tony tonight. He was supposed to be meeting you for dinner at seven thirty."

"He called and canceled. I told you that."

"When did he call to cancel?"

"I don't know." She flicked her hand carelessly. "Why are you asking me so many questions?"

"Because you aren't wearing makeup. If he didn't call to cancel until you came into my room crying, why hadn't you put on your makeup for your date?" It took my mother a full forty-five minutes to apply her makeup, and she always—*always*—started on it early to make sure she had plenty of time before she had to leave.

Her shoulders lifted in a shrug as she studied her nails. "He may have called a little earlier than that."

I stood up and walked away from her, trying to calm my pounding heart as an ugly suspicion rose inside me. "How much earlier?" When she didn't answer, I turned around and repeated the question. "How much earlier did he call?"

She threw her hands up in exasperation. "It was earlier this afternoon, okay? Honestly, what does it matter?"

I gaped at her, utterly dumbfounded. "So you found out he was married *hours ago*? And then you—what—sat around calmly and waited until I was about to leave before you decided to have a breakdown over it?"

The way my mother's lips pursed told me everything I needed to know.

"That's exactly what you did, isn't it? You deliberately waited to make a scene until you knew it would ruin my night out with Tanner."

She got to her feet, her expression growing hard as she rested her hands on her hips. "Don't you raise your voice to me, Lucy Jean!"

"I'll pitch my voice however I please." Her betrayal sat in the back of my throat like acid, making every word burn as it came out. "Are you even *upset* about Tony? Or was it all an act to earn sympathy?"

My mother blinked wide, incredulous eyes at me, her lower lip trembling. "Of course I was upset. What an awful thing to suggest! What have I ever done to make you speak to me this way?"

"Are you *kidding* me?" I felt like I was losing my mind. How could she not understand what she'd done wrong? "You intentionally sabotaged my date with Tanner—and possibly my whole relationship with him. Why would you do something like that? Because you wanted me to stay home and put on face masks with you?"

She bent her head and covered her face with her hands. "How dare you speak to me like this, and after everything I've sacrificed for you. What a cruel, unkind child you are."

"Stop it! Just stop! You obviously don't care a damn about my feelings, so why on earth do I spend so much time caring about yours?"

My mother let out a high-pitched wail like I'd shot her and ran from the room in tears.

"You're unbelievable!" I shouted down the hall after her.

The only response was the sound of her bedroom door slamming shut, followed by loud crying.

All this time, I'd been bending over backward to make her life easier, and she'd been playing me to get what she wanted. Tanner was right. She was never willingly going to let me have my own life. Every time I tried to grab onto some small piece of happiness for myself, she'd find a way to ruin it. She'd keep taking and taking, just like she always had, without giving anything back unless it suited her.

And I'd gone along and let her get away with it at the expense of everything that was important to me.

My legs gave out beneath me, and I sank to the floor in front of my dresser. Pulling my knees to my chest, I bent my head and wept into my folded arms.

"Lucy, what the fuck?"

I lifted my head to find Matt in the doorway of my room looking like he'd just gotten out of bed.

He frowned at me, hobbled a few steps closer on his orthopedic boot, and ran a hand through his messy hair. "What happened? Are you okay?"

A sob tore its way out of my throat, and I bent my head again, too upset to offer my brother an explanation.

He lowered himself awkwardly to the floor beside me, and his arm settled around my shoulders. "Hey. It's okay. Don't cry. Whatever it is, it'll be okay."

He sat there with me, patting my back and mumbling consoling words while I cried myself out, disgorging the emotions I'd been bottling up for years, grieving for all the things I'd missed out on or denied myself and the years of my life I'd never get back.

All of it for someone who didn't care about me.

The realization brought a profound sense of sadness. She was my *mother*. How could she treat me so carelessly? She was supposed to love me. Maybe she did, in her own twisted way, but not in the way I deserved. Not in the way I'd tried to love her.

When I'd cried out the worst of it and my breathing had calmed again, I lifted my teary face and looked at my brother. "I can't take it anymore."

"What?" he asked, leaning forward to snag the box of tissues off the bed.

I took one and blew my nose. "Mom."

"Well, yeah," he said matter-of-factly. "What'd she do now?"

I told him everything. Not just the fact that she'd manufactured a breakdown to manipulate me into canceling my plans, but also all the little ways she'd been trying to come between me and Tanner for weeks, leading up to the fight we'd had tonight. But I didn't stop there. I also told my brother how I felt stuck living at home, trapped by the commitment I'd made to help our mother financially, and how I felt like I was drowning, and every time I caught sight of the shore, she pulled me back under the water. I told him how tired I was of doing everything around the house all the time on top of working a full-time job and paying the majority of the household expenses. How I felt taken for granted and taken advantage of, not just by our mother, but by him.

When I'd finished unloading all my pent-up grievances, my brother looked at me like I'd told him the earth revolved around the moon. "Shit," he said quietly. "I had no idea you felt that way. I thought you were happy with the way things were."

I stared at him in disbelief. "Seriously?"

His shoulders lifted in an innocent shrug. "Happy enough, anyway."

"You thought I was *happy* doing all the cooking, cleaning, and shopping for all of us without any help?"

He rubbed the back of his neck, looking ashamed. "I thought you did all that stuff because you liked doing it yourself."

"You thought I liked doing dishes and scrubbing toilets?" What kind of loser nerd did my brother think I was? Sure, I appreciated order and cleanliness, but had he honestly thought I was so dull and pathetic that cleaning the house was something I did for my own enjoyment? I was so irritated I socked him in the shoulder. "I like living in a clean house, you asshole. That doesn't mean I like doing all the work myself."

He winced in embarrassment. "I thought you didn't mind. You always seemed fine with it."

"I wasn't fine! None of it is fine. I feel like I'm losing my mind all the time."

"Okay, but Luce, you never, ever complain or ask for help."

"Are you kidding? I ask you to do stuff all the time!"

He rolled his eyes. "Sure, stuff like, 'Hey, Matt, can you do the dishes?' Never once have you said, 'Hey, Matt, I feel like I'm going out of my fucking mind, and I really, really need some help here before I completely lose my shit.'"

"Would that have worked?" I asked.

"I'm listening now, aren't I?"

A slightly hysterical laugh bubbled out of me, and I bent my head to my knees again, overwhelmed by the ridiculousness of it all. Was that seriously all it would have taken? All this time, I'd assumed my brother had seen my frustration and failed to care. Had he really been that oblivious—or had I been that good at pretending?

"Look, I'm sorry," he said, shifting beside me. "I know I haven't been as helpful as I should have been. If I'm being honest, I've always known I should be doing more around the house—but I swear I didn't realize things were that bad for you. You're right that I took you for granted. I suppose I got used to you taking care of everything the way you always did for us when we were kids. I never thought about what that must have been like for you."

I turned my head to look at him and let out a long, shaky breath. "It sucked. Like, a lot."

"I get that now. I'm really sorry." He stared down at his lap, frowning. "The thing is, I've sort of gotten into this habit of switching off when I'm at home, you know?"

"Yeah, I've noticed." I didn't bother to keep the bitterness out of my voice. All this honesty and expressing my dissatisfaction was coming more easily to me the more I did it.

Matt scrubbed at the side of his face, keeping his eyes downcast. "That's the only way I can deal with Mom. I tune everything out so it can't get to me."

As soon as he said it, something clicked into place. Suddenly I saw my brother in a whole different light—all the hours he spent locked in his room with his headphones on, losing himself in video games and self-medicating with weed. It was his coping mechanism. I'd assumed he didn't care about anything, but he was only trying to survive his own unhappiness.

"Does it work?" I asked him.

"Eh. Kinda," he said with a shrug. His eyes returned to mine guiltily. "But I guess it leaves all the burden on you, doesn't it?"

"Yeah, it does."

His brow furrowed as he looked at me. "You know you don't actually have to do all that shit for Mom, right?"

I let out a bitter laugh. "Oh, okay. Well in that case I'll just stop. So what if the house falls down around our ears? While I'm at it, I'll quit paying the bills too and let the debt collectors come take everything away and put you and Mom out on the street."

"I can support myself if I have to."

I arched a dubious eyebrow at him. "Can you?"

"Yes," he muttered. "Probably I should have started doing that a long time ago."

"Probably." I didn't try to keep the sarcasm out of my voice. I might understand my brother better now, but that didn't mean I was prepared to let him off the hook.

"Okay, but you never *asked* me to," he said with a defensive jut of his chin. "I thought you had it all under control. If I'd known you were struggling, I would have worked harder so I could pitch in." He poked an accusing finger into my arm. "This is what you get for pretending everything is fine all the time."

I supposed he had a point. It wasn't exactly fair to fault someone for not reading your mind. I'd nagged him about working more hours and cleaning up after himself, but I'd never told him *why* I needed him to do it. I'd never let him see how much pressure I felt or sat him down and asked him to help me pay down Mom's debt.

Just like he'd never told me why he spent so much time checked out and trying to ignore everything that was going on around him at home. My brother hadn't been okay either, and I hadn't noticed his struggles any more than he'd noticed mine.

"You and Mom are exact opposites," he said. "Mom acts like she can't do anything when she's not half as helpless as she seems. And you're always doing too much for other people and pretending you can handle it when you can't." His expression grew serious again as his gaze met mine. "Mom's a lot stronger than she lets on, you know. She can do stuff for herself when she wants to. She just knows if she doesn't, you'll come along and do it for her. Where do you think I learned it from?"

I leaned my head back against the dresser as I contemplated what he'd said. If tonight had shown me anything, it was how much my mother was capable of. Deep down, I'd probably suspected the truth long before now, even if I hadn't wanted to accept it. Because if I accepted it, I'd have to *do* something about it—and I didn't know if I was strong enough to do that.

When I didn't respond, Matt nudged my arm with his elbow. "She's playing a game of chicken with you, Lucy, and you're letting her win."

I sighed and rubbed my forehead. "I know I am, but I can't just let the car crash."

"That's what she's banking on. But the car's not going to crash, I promise. You need to start putting your foot down with her. Trust me—once she realizes you're not going to do everything for her, she'll start doing it herself."

"Will she? I'm still paying off her debts from the last time I left her to make her own decisions unsupervised."

"Because she's always known she could lean on you to clean up any mess she made. Look, I'm not saying you have to cut her off cold turkey. Start by drawing lines with small, manageable stuff and build from there. But you have to hold firm and not cave."

"She's going to fight it. She's going to make it *so hard*." It gave me a stomachache thinking about it. The tantrums, the sulking, the petty rebellions. The hurtful words. It would all get so much worse and make her that much harder to deal with.

"I know," Matt said. "But I'll help you. You don't have to do it all by yourself. When you're ready to talk to Mom, we'll do it together and I'll back you up."

"Do you mean that?"

He answered with an earnest nod. "It's past time I started pulling my weight around here. I'm gonna try harder to help you out more—for real this time—but you have to promise to *tell me* when you need my help." His mouth pulled into a scowl as he waved his hand at the boot on his foot. "I'm a little limited while I'm dragging this fucking thing around, but I'm mobile enough to do some shit, at least. And I'll help deal with Mom for you. Once I'm able to drive again and can go back to work, I'll take more hours so I can pay my share of the household expenses." He grinned. "Who knows? I may even try to get a better job that pays a decent salary."

"Let's not get too carried away," I said, meeting his smile with one of my own.

He jostled my arm again. "But there's something you have to do first before we do any of that."

"What?" I asked warily, anticipating something unpleasant.

"Wash your face, put on that fancy dress"—Matt pointed a finger at my closet door—"and go to your boyfriend's highfa-lutin shindig tonight."

33

TANNER

"You made it," Josie said, leaning in to kiss my cheek. Her gaze darted around before fixing on me with a frown. "Where's Lucy?"

I struggled to keep the tension out of my voice. "She couldn't make it."

I nearly hadn't made it myself. I'd spent a good ten minutes sitting in my car out in the parking lot, psyching myself up to turn off the engine and come inside. The last place I wanted to be right now was here in this room trying to make pleasant small talk with my father's wealthy society friends and business associates.

Josie's frown deepened as she gave me a probing look. "What's wrong?"

"Nothing. She had a family thing come up." I cleared my throat, looking around for one of the waiters I'd seen circulating with trays of wine. "What do you have to do to get a drink at this thing?"

The main tasting room at the winery was packed with people. It wasn't the largest space, and it was too hot outside for anyone to take advantage of the picturesque courtyard beyond the two sets of French doors. Inside was rather uncomfortably warm as well. Having so many bodies crammed into the main room seemed to be taxing the building's climate control system.

Josie raised her hand, and a waiter appeared out of thin air at my elbow. He recited his little spiel about the different wines on offer, and I selected one at random, having not listened to a single fucking word he'd said.

"Thank you," Josie said, and the waiter disappeared, back into whatever parallel pocket dimension he'd teleported out of in the first place. It honestly wouldn't surprise me to learn Josie had an army of magical imps at her beck and call.

"Better?" she asked after I'd gulped down a mouthful of whatever white wine I'd chosen. It tasted like ashes in my mouth, so probably a chardonnay.

"It's good," I lied and took another drink, figuring the more I had, the better it would taste. Hopefully.

"I was asking about you, not the wine. The chardonnay tastes like sucking on a wet campfire."

"I was thirsty, I guess. It's hot out there."

The searching look Josie gave me said she wasn't buying my act. "Is Lucy all right? It's nothing serious, is it? Her family thing that came up?"

"Lucy's fine. Everything's fine." The words came out sounding choked, and I looked down at my wineglass. "Boy, you're right. This wine really sucks."

"You want to talk about it?" Josie asked, still not referring to the wine.

"I don't. But thank you for asking."

What was I going to do? Tell Lucy's VP that we'd had a fight over the fact that she'd let her mother manipulate her into breaking a promise to me, and I felt like I couldn't rely on her? That it hurt to know I'd never be her priority, and she'd always put her mother's needs over mine? Except that wasn't even the part I was most upset about—it was the creeping fear that Lucy was going to keep pulling away from me, using her family as an excuse, and there wasn't a goddamn thing I could do to prevent it.

Yeah, none of that was the sort of stuff I could casually blab to Lucy's boss.

Josie patted my arm. "No more bringing up Lucy. Understood."

I glanced around and was relieved not to see my father anywhere. Josie's mother was here, however, working the room as usual. She held a seat on the foundation's board, along with Josie, Nate, and my father, but Trish was the guiding hand behind most of their operations, including this annual benefit.

"Where's Carter?" I asked, and Josie's smile went rigid.

"What do you say we put him in the 'don't ask, don't tell' bucket as well?"

"Fair enough." I clinked my glass against hers and swallowed another mouthful of the terrible wine. "Are all the wines this bad or did I just choose poorly?"

"You picked the worst one. Drink up and we'll get you a glass of the blanc du bois, which is quite respectable for a Texas winery."

"Are you a wine snob?" It struck me as odd that I didn't know something so basic about my own sister.

"I've been known to dabble for sport," she replied with an arch smile, lifting her glass to her lips.

"Is Nate gay?" I blurted out, my mind still circling around things it seemed like I should know about my own siblings.

Josie nearly choked on her wine at my non sequitur. "Why on earth would you ask that?"

"I was just thinking about how little we all know each other, and I've never known Nate to have a girlfriend, so it got me wondering."

"He's not gay."

"Are you sure?"

"Of course I'm sure."

"So he's had girlfriends that you know of?"

"Yes." Her expression grew thoughtful as doubt crept in. "Back in high school, anyway."

I raised an eyebrow. "Not since?"

"I wasn't around much after high school, in case you didn't notice."

"He's never mentioned anyone to you?"

"We don't talk about that sort of thing. It's not Nate's style." She grew thoughtful again as she sipped her blanc du bois. "But he definitely liked girls when he was a teenager, because I walked in on him and Ashlee Teagarden once when he was enthusiastically rounding third base."

"Huh," I said. "All right."

Josie hooked her arm around mine and shepherded me through the crowd of mingling guests. "I'll tell you what." She gave me an evil smile as she tapped on a suit-coated shoulder in front of us. "You can ask him yourself."

I clamped my mouth shut, fixing her with a baleful glare as I realized the suit coat she'd led me to belonged to Nate.

He turned around, his expression narrowing with suspicion as he regarded us. "Ask me what?"

Josie smiled at me expectantly, her eyes twinkling with mischief. When I refused to speak, she looked at Nate and her smile grew even wider. "Tanner wants to know if you're gay."

"Why?" He gave me a puzzled look. "What makes you think that?"

"I didn't think anything one way or the other," I clarified. "It just occurred to me I didn't know, and I didn't want to make assumptions."

"I'm not gay," he said, frowning at me.

"It's totally cool if you are," Josie told him. "I could build a great Pride Month campaign around you next year. Are you sure you're not bi? Or ace, maybe? I can work with anything on the sexuality spectrum."

Nate rolled his eyes. "Your selfless show of support is overwhelming. Or it would be, if I wasn't so inconveniently straight."

"Too bad." She smirked at him. "For a second there I thought you might be more interesting than I'd estimated."

His answering glower looked almost amused. "Sorry to disappoint you by being attracted to women."

I marveled at how easily he accepted Josie's ribbing. Never in my life had I dared to tease Nate, and I doubted I'd get the same tolerance if I tried. Then again, he and Josie had always had a different sort of relationship with each other since they'd grown up together in the same house.

Josie's smirk grew wider. "Ashlee Teagarden wasn't an aberration, then?"

At which point I had the pleasure of seeing Nate blush, which was a first in my recollection.

He shook his head, laughing under his breath—something else I didn't see him do much. "You're never going to let me live that down, are you?"

"Never," Josie said, laughing along with him.

"When's the last time you had a girlfriend?" I asked Nate, taking advantage of his affable mood.

He snorted. "When do you think I'd have time for a girlfriend?"

Josie's eyes widened. "Don't tell me it was Ashlee Teagarden!"

"No." Nate directed a sour look at her. "It wasn't Ashlee Teagarden—but it wasn't that many years after her either."

"Ouch," Josie said.

Nate squared his shoulders, bristling. "I do fine, thanks. Just because I have neither the time nor the desire to commit to a relationship doesn't mean I'm spending all my nights alone."

His declaration unfortunately reminded me of Lucy, which reminded me of our fight, which brought on a fresh bout of melancholy. I tried to chase it away with another mouthful of the appalling chardonnay, but that only made me feel worse.

Gazing around the room in the hopes of spotting one of Josie's magic teleporting waiters, my eyes came to rest on the enormous banner hanging from the ceiling. It was emblazoned with the logo for the Chance William King Memorial Foundation, along with a photo of Chance himself, smiling and forever youthful while the rest of us aged beyond him.

"He would have turned forty this year," Nate said, noticing where my attention had caught. "Can you believe that?"

"Brady *is* forty," Josie murmured. "As of last month."

"Sure." The corners of Nate's mouth flattened. "Wherever he is."

Josie gave him an odd look. "He lives in New York. It's not some big secret. He's got a whole website with his tour schedule on it."

"You really haven't heard anything from him in all this time?" I figured if anyone had, it would be one of them—or their mother.

"Not a word," Nate said. "Brady might as well be dead too."

"I guess I always thought he would have reached out to one of you at some point—or maybe you'd reached out to him. It seems weird that we all pretend he never existed when he's out there living his life in plain sight."

Nate scowled. "He made it pretty clear he didn't want any of us in his precious life. I'm just honoring his wishes."

"I guess he's probably hard to get in touch with," I mused. "It's not like you can just look up a rock star's phone number or message him on Facebook."

"His management team is easy enough to contact," Josie said. "If you wanted to get a message to him, you could probably do it that way." At Nate's look of surprise, she shrugged. "I used to think about it—especially when I was living in New York. It was weird knowing we were in the same city. I always used to look for him on the street and wonder if I'd bump into him at my coffee place one day."

Nate turned a sharp gaze on her. "You never did it?"

"Bump into him at my coffee place? No."

"Reach out to him through his manager."

"No, I never did that either."

Nate grunted, his gaze fixing on something across the room. "There's Dad, finally. I need to go talk to him."

Stiffening, I turned my back to the direction Nate had headed, not wanting to see my father's face. Especially tonight, after what had happened with Lucy, I wasn't in any kind of head space to deal with him.

Josie gestured and a waiter miraculously appeared—I swear to Christ out of thin air. My sister took my almost-empty glass and exchanged it for a full one before thanking the server and sending him back to his magical other-dimensional space. "Drink this," she said, putting the fresh glass of wine in my hand. "It makes a better liquid courage than that burned sawdust they're calling chardonnay."

"Thanks," I muttered, raising my glass. She was right, the blanc du bois was much better.

"Well blow me down and call me Dusty!" Josie smacked me on the elbow and pointed across the room. "Do my eyes deceive me, or has Wyatt Earle King deigned to grace us with his presence tonight?"

I turned in surprise. Sure enough, Wyatt was making his way toward us—in a shirt and tie, no less—with Andie in tow.

"What the hell are you doing here?" Josie asked, giving Wyatt a hug.

"Oh, you know." He shrugged. "I thought you might miss me."

Josie gave him a hard pinch on the cheek like our Grandma Cookie used to do. "I did, actually."

While Josie greeted Andie, I gave Wyatt a searching look. "Seriously, what are you doing here?"

"I'll explain later." He craned his neck to peer around. "Do they have any beer at this thing or is it just wine?"

"We're at a *vineyard*." Andie rolled her eyes at him as she released Josie from a hug. "Or did you not notice the acres of grapevines we drove past on the way here?"

And yet, within a few minutes Josie had somehow managed to track down a beer for Wyatt, in addition to a glass of the blanc du bois for Andie.

"You're not here to do anything stupid like confront Dad, are you?" Josie asked Wyatt as he tipped back his beer.

"God, no," he said, dragging the back of his hand across his mouth. "Not if I can help it."

"Good." Josie directed a menacing look at him. "I would appreciate it if you could be on your best behavior so I don't have to spend my whole day tomorrow dealing with a PR disaster."

Wyatt arched an eyebrow. "What are you afraid I'm going to do? Punch him or something?"

"I'd like to think you wouldn't physically assault a senior citizen," she replied coolly. "I'm more concerned about the two of you getting into a verbal altercation in a room full of wealthy donors and reporters."

"Then maybe you should be giving him the warning, because I assure you I have no interest in talking to the man. If he chooses to start something with me, that's on him." Wyatt gave Josie a sour look. "I see you're still Team Dad, even after everything that's come out."

"The only team I'm on is my own," Josie shot back. "It's my job to maintain the company's positive public image, irrespective of my own personal feelings."

"What are your personal feelings about the Manny revelation?" I asked her. "It's your mother he cheated on, after all."

Josie darted a glance toward Trish, who was holding court on the far side of the room, before turning back to us and lowering her voice. "It's hardly news that Dad cheated on my mother—she made it a matter of public record when she filed for divorce. But in the specific case of Manny, there was no affair."

"Come on," Wyatt said with a derisive snort. "You don't actually believe that lie."

Josie cut a sideways look at him. "It's not a lie, as it happens. I was skeptical too, so I asked my mother about it, and she confirmed his story."

"Your mother backed him up?" I said in surprise. Dad and Trish put on a nice show of cordiality for the sake of public appearances, but in private their relationship was a hell of a lot less amicable than they pretended.

Josie nodded. "She told me that Uncle Manny and Aunt Rosa came to them and asked Dad to be their donor. Mom was dead set against it, and she and Dad had a huge fight about it. But he was determined to do it, with or without her blessing."

"Well there you go," I said, shaking my head. "I guess he was telling the truth."

"About *that*," Wyatt grumbled. "Even a broken clock tells the truth once a day."

"Twice a day," Andie murmured, giving him a fond smile.

"Let's not go giving the old man too much credit." Wyatt draped an arm around her and pulled her closer so he could kiss her temple.

Their unwavering devotion to one another hit me hard in the pit of my stomach, and I lowered my eyes to the floor. I'd expected to have that with Lucy tonight, but instead I'd had to come here alone. That in itself wasn't a tragedy. I missed her so much my bones ached with it, but I could survive one unpleasant social occasion on my own. What scared me was what I saw when I tried to imagine our future. I knew Lucy's mother would keep trying to come between us, and I had a sinking feeling she was going to get her way.

I didn't want Lucy to be caught between us like a handkerchief on a tug-of-war rope, but her mother had no such scruples. She'd keep forcing the issue, testing Lucy's loyalty and monopolizing her attention. She was a textbook narcissist, just like my father. Though their personalities and the tactics they deployed were dissimilar on the surface, they were both prideful, thin-skinned, and self-centered, requiring constant appeasement but unwilling to compromise themselves.

I'd have no choice but to stand aside and watch while Lucy's mother rolled right over her. What other option did I have? Make Lucy's life even more difficult by placing additional demands on her? I couldn't do that to her. I wouldn't. And Lucy had made it clear she didn't welcome my advice on the subject. If I tried to come between her and her mother, it would only drive more of a wedge between us.

"I suppose I'd better go check in with my mom," Josie said with a sigh. "Keep an eye on these two, will you, Andie?"

"That's what I'm here for," Andie replied cheerfully.

I regarded my brother and his girlfriend with renewed curiosity. "Why *are* you two here?"

Wyatt's expression grew somber. "Lucy called me. She said you'd had a fight and begged me to come and check on you."

"She did?" My throat had gone dry, and the words came out sounding like they'd been dragged over sandpaper.

"She was really upset." Wyatt's tone held a note of reproach. "You want to tell me what happened?"

I swallowed and shook my head. "It's complicated."

Andie moved to my side, shooting Wyatt a warning look as she hugged my arm. "He doesn't have to talk about it if he doesn't want to."

"Look," Wyatt said, rubbing his forehead, "I know you feel an obligation to come to shit like this for the family—"

"I'm only here because I promised Josie." I generously refrained from mentioning that it was Wyatt's presumed absence that had necessitated my presence in the first place. There were photographers in the hall outside the tasting room, and I'd had to smile and pose in front of a step-and-repeat banner on my way in. There'd be pictures online and in the next edition of the local paper—maybe even the *Austin American-Statesman*—and both the foundation and the creamery's PR department would issue press releases about the event, name-checking all the family members and high-profile guests in attendance.

"Fine. You officially showed your face, and people have seen you. You performed your duty like the stand-up guy you are. Now you can get out of here and go patch things up with Lucy."

My jaw clenched. There was nothing I'd rather do, but showing up at Lucy's house tonight would only make things worse for her. "I can't."

"Jesus, don't be proud. Go talk to her. Grovel if you have to."

"I'm not being proud. Trust me, it wouldn't help. She doesn't want me there."

"She wouldn't have called me if she didn't want you."

"I have an idea," Andie interjected. "Why don't you ask Lucy what she wants?" She spun me around and pointed across the room.

Lucy stood just inside the door.

I almost didn't believe my eyes at first. Her face had been

burning a hole in my heart all night, and for a second I assumed my mind was playing tricks on me.

But if Andie could see her, that meant she was real. Lucy was here. Wearing a stunning blue lace dress that showed off her bare shoulders as she scanned the crowd, looking for someone.

Me. She's looking for me.

Wyatt's hand smacked me between the shoulder blades, shoving me toward her. "Go get your woman."

As I took a stumbling step forward, Lucy's gaze turned in my direction. Our eyes locked, and she offered me an anxious, tentative smile.

The whole room and everyone else in it faded away as my feet carried me toward her. Once I got up close, I saw how pale her skin looked beneath her makeup and that her eyes were red and puffy from crying.

"Are you all right?" I asked as I guided her over to a quieter spot removed from the main crowd of wine drinkers.

She drew in a breath and nodded. "I'm fine."

My heart hammered in my ears as I gazed down at her. "What are you doing here?"

"I realized that here was where I wanted to be. I'm not too late, am I?"

Her words crashed into me, igniting a blaze of hope in my chest, and I let my smile break free.

Relief washed across her expression, and her chin wobbled as she opened her mouth to speak. "Tanner, I—"

I grabbed her face and kissed her. Our mouths clashed together in a desperate, heartfelt union, and my tongue plunged into her heavenly mouth, simultaneously claiming her and giving myself up to her completely.

The burning need to touch her nearly overwhelmed all reason, but before I forgot myself entirely I managed to pull back, breaking off the kiss just short of making a public spectacle of ourselves. She let out a soft whimper of protest, and I rested my forehead against hers, unwilling to let her stray too far away from me again.

"I love you," I said, sliding my hands down the side of her neck.

"I love you too." She gripped my wrists like she was afraid I'd try to get away—as if I'd ever do any such thing. "I'm sorry I didn't come sooner. I should have chosen you before."

"No, I'm sorry I made you feel like you had to choose." My thumbs settled in the hollows above her collarbone, stroking the soft skin. "I know what a difficult situation you're in, and I don't want to make it harder for you. I just want to make you happy. I want to make things better for you, not worse.

She shook her head. "I want *you* to be happy. I hate that you were disappointed."

My lips drifted to her temple, and I breathed in the sweet scent of her perfume. She smelled like orange blossoms and vanilla. Like pure sunshine. Like joy. "I can live with a little disappointment."

"I don't want you to. I never want you to be disappointed in me." Her fingers tightened around my wrists.

I pulled my head back to look into her eyes so she'd know how much I meant what I was about to say. "I wasn't disappointed in *you*. I could never be disappointed in you. I always wish I could have you with me, but I never want to become another burden in your life."

"You're not. You were right when you said I need to set boundaries with my mother. I've always known I should, but it was too hard to do it alone. But I'm not alone anymore. I have people I can ask for help now."

"You can always ask me for help."

Her eyes squeezed shut as she nodded. "I know that." Opening her eyes again, she pressed her hand against my cheek.

"You can always ask me for help too. And I won't let you down the next time. From now on, I'm prioritizing the people in my life who prioritize me."

I covered her hand with mine. "What happened with your mother?"

A pained look darkened her expression. "I don't want to talk about that right now. I promise I'll tell you, but I'm not ready to think about it yet."

"Okay." I frowned in concern as I brought her hand to my lips. "Whatever you need."

She set her jaw, tilting her chin up with a look of determination. "What matters is that things are going to be different from now on. I had a long talk with Matt tonight, and we're going to work on making some changes at home together. I'm going to be better about asking for help, and he's going to be better about offering it."

"That's great. I'm so glad."

"I know it's not going to be easy, but it'll be worth it to finally be able to live my own life instead of being a supporting player in someone else's."

My heart felt like it was going to burst, I was so relieved for her. She deserved so much—she deserved every happiness in the world—and I swore to myself I'd do everything I could to make sure she got it, even if the only thing she needed me to do was love her and support her while she fought her own battles.

I pressed my lips against hers in a tender, cherishing kiss. She kissed me back with relish, winding her hands around my neck and sinking her fingers into my hair. As I felt her body relax against mine, I knew with certainty that we were going to make it. This love between us was stronger than any challenges we might face.

"Ahem," Wyatt said behind me, tapping my shoulder.

Reluctantly, Lucy and I ended our kiss. I hooked my arm

around her waist, tugging her against me as I turned to regard my interrupting brother and his girlfriend.

"You looked like you were done talking." Andie's gaze bounced between us with a barely contained smile. "Does this mean everything's okay again?"

Lucy gazed up at me with soft, loving eyes. "Everything's better than okay. It's perfect."

"Halle-fucking-lujah for that," Wyatt said, flashing a grin.

Lucy slipped out of my grasp and hugged him. "Thank you for showing up tonight."

His cocky expression softened. "Anytime. Thanks for looking out for my annoying older brother."

I arched an eyebrow at him as Lucy fitted herself against me again. "I'm the annoying one? Really?"

He tugged at his collar. "You're the reason I had to put on a tie and show up at this goddamn event."

"That would be my fault, actually," Lucy said.

Wyatt winked at her. "I choose to blame him, irregardless."

"Don't wink at my girlfriend," I growled.

"*Y'all*," Andie whisper-yelled urgently. "Nobody panic, but your dad is coming this way."

Sure enough, a glance behind me revealed my father heading toward us with a stony look on his face and Manny trailing a few steps behind him.

34

TANNER

"Fuck," Wyatt muttered under his breath.

Lucy pressed herself against me, and I felt her hand tighten on my waist, offering reassurance. The four of us—Lucy, me, Wyatt, and Andie—stood in a stiff, silent row, watching as my father and Manny approached.

As they came to a stop in front of us, Manny offered a supportive smile that I didn't know whether to take as a good sign or bad one.

My father's gaze drifted over Andie and Wyatt, then me, before settling on Lucy. I bristled, ready to go off like a fucking car bomb if he formed his lips to say anything unkind to her.

"I don't think we've met." My father smiled and extended his hand. "I'm George King."

Whenever our dad smiled, you could see where Wyatt's charisma had come from. Dad could be equally magnetic when he wanted to be, but it wasn't a side of him we got to see often. He saved his charm for people he wanted to impress, which didn't customarily include his family.

Lucy detached herself from my side to shake his hand, giving him one of her brightest smiles. I doubted anyone but me could tell how nervous she was. "I'm Lucy Dillard. Tanner's girlfriend." When she said the last word, her chin lifted with an expression of pride that caused my heart to lodge itself in my throat.

"It's a great pleasure to meet you, Lucy." My father's eyes actually *twinkled*, if you could believe it. It was a damned good act. He really seemed every bit the amiable, kindhearted good ol' boy he pretended to be for the benefit of the general public. "I hope we'll be seeing a lot more of you in the future."

When my father let go of Lucy's hand, I released the breath I'd been holding. "This is my brother Manny," I told her, avoiding my dad's eyes.

Manny stepped forward to greet her, and she offered him a warmer, more genuine smile as they shook hands.

My father sidled over to address Andie next. "Good to see you again, Andie. How're your folks doing? They enjoying the weather up there in Maine?"

"Yes, sir," Andie answered, meeting his gaze fearlessly. "My mom said the high last week was only seventy-one."

"Boy, if that doesn't sound like heaven compared to the dog's breath weather we've been having this month. You be sure to give your mom my best the next time you talk to her, all right?"

"I will," Andie said, her polite smile never wavering.

My father then turned his attention to Wyatt. There was an ominous silence as the two of them eyed each other, and I saw a muscle tick in Wyatt's jaw.

Dad was the first to break. "I saw you perform at the folk festival," he said in a more subdued but still surprisingly genial voice. "You sounded real impressive up there. Very professional." He cast a glance over at Lucy, his expression warming. "You too. That's a beautiful voice you've got."

"Thank you," she murmured.

Wyatt still hadn't said anything, and there was another awkward silence as our father regarded him again.

"You've got a lot of talent," Dad said finally. "I'm proud of you, son."

"Thanks," Wyatt mumbled, sounding confused.

Then it was my turn. I lifted my chin as my father's gaze focused on me.

"You quit your job," he said, dropping the Bubba act completely and sounding a lot more like himself—or at least the version of himself I was most familiar with.

"That's right," I answered.

"You figure out something else to do yet?"

No way in hell was I telling him about the bookstore. The last thing I needed was his negative energy getting in my head and making me second-guess myself.

"Not yet," I answered tightly and clamped my lips together, ready to hear how aimless and irresponsible I was, and how I'd let him and the whole family down.

Instead, what he said was, "I know you've never been happy at the company, so I hope you find whatever it is you're looking for." He glanced at Lucy again and gave her the exact same wink Wyatt had given her. "Looks like you've already made a pretty good start." His attention swung back to me, and his smile faded again. "I'm proud of you too, Tanner. Taking your destiny in your own hands requires a lot of courage."

I swallowed, too surprised to speak.

Dad laid one of his hands on my shoulder and the other on Wyatt's. "I'm glad you boys made it tonight. It means a lot to have you here." He gave our shoulders a squeeze before letting go and flashing a smile for Andie and Lucy. "Y'all enjoy the rest of your evening."

Then he walked off, leaving us to stare after him in stunned silence.

"What the fuck was that?" Wyatt said after Dad had disappeared back into the crowd.

"I have no goddamn idea." I narrowed my eyes at Manny. "What did you do to him? Did you drug him? Hit him in the head? Cast some sort of spell on him?"

Manny laughed and held up his hands. "Nope."

"Did you replace him with a clone? Or is this one of those alien shape-shifter situations?"

"I didn't do anything," Manny said, shaking his head. "I think he honestly just wanted to mend fences."

"Bullshit," Wyatt muttered.

Manny shrugged. "Maybe he realized he didn't want to lose any more sons."

"Shit, c'mere," Wyatt said, grabbing Manny. "I just remembered I haven't hugged you since I found out we're related."

"We were always related." Manny ruffled Wyatt's unruly hair as he let him go. "But now I know why my daughter's devilish smirk looks so familiar."

Wyatt flashed the devilish smirk in question. "It's only right and proper that she takes after her favorite uncle."

I looked over at Lucy, and she squeezed my hand, smiling up at me. "That wasn't so bad."

"No," I agreed, still a little dazed. "It wasn't." I pulled her toward me and brushed a kiss against her lips. "Do you want to get out of here?"

"Whenever you're ready."

"I'm ready. I'm *so* ready." Keeping Lucy close, I turned to address the others. "We're taking off."

It took another few minutes to make our goodbyes and do all the giving and receiving of hugs required before we were allowed to leave, but finally Lucy and I completed our exit and stepped out into the sweltering night.

Once we were alone under the stars with nothing but the empty cars in the parking lot and the surrounding rows of grapevines as witnesses, I pulled her against me and lowered my mouth to hers, sinking into her glorious sweetness.

My hands roamed over her body shamelessly as I pressed myself against her. I needed her close to me and needed her skin against mine. As much as I loved the dress she was wearing, it was preventing me from touching her all over her beautiful body. I was going to need to do something about that very soon. But to do it properly, I'd have to drive her back to my house. It was a long drive—at least twenty minutes, during which I'd need to have my hands on the steering wheel instead of on her —and before I undertook it, I wanted to taste as much of her as I could without risking indecent exposure.

"Tanner," she murmured as I suckled at the soft skin beneath her jaw.

"Lucy," I growled against her throat, thinking of how I was going to lavish her with attention until she was moaning my name, begging me to do sinful things to her.

"Tanner, I have to tell you something."

"Go ahead."

"I can't focus when your mouth is doing that."

"Good. That means I'm doing it right."

"Tanner, stop." When I stilled, she tightened her fingers in my hair and pulled my head back, capturing my attention with her eyes. "I owe you an apology."

I opened my mouth to protest, and she silenced me with a finger on my lips. "Hush. Just listen."

I gave her a solemn nod of assent. And then, because I couldn't help myself, I sucked her finger into my mouth and bit it.

"I'm being serious," she chided, failing to suppress a smile.

"Me too." I formed my face into a grave expression. "I'm being extremely serious. Please proceed."

Shaking her head slightly, she blew a breath out through her nose before she spoke. "I'm sorry for saying that I don't want your advice about my relationship with my mother. That was wrong of me." Instinctively, my lips parted to argue, but she quelled me with a look, reminding me she'd asked me to listen. "I do want your advice—about everything, including my mother. I value your input and trust that you want what's best for me. I always want to hear what you think, and I promise from now on I'll listen to what you have to say and give it due consideration." The corner of her mouth twitched into a smile. "Then I'll make up my own mind for myself."

My lips curved to mirror her smile. "I wouldn't expect anything else. And likewise, I always want your advice and opinions. I love your strong mind." I placed a solemn kiss on her forehead. "And I love your soft heart." I bent and pressed my lips to the exposed skin at the top of her breast before lifting my mouth to her ear. "But right now what I'd really like to do is love your gorgeous body, if you'll let me."

She shivered in my arms, and her lips found mine, pressing against them warmly before pulling into a smile. "Take me home, and I'm all yours."

EPILOGUE
TANNER

"You close to being done for the day?" I asked as I pushed my way through the plastic sheeting Wyatt had hung to keep the sawdust kicked up by his remodeling work from blowing through the whole bookstore.

He glanced over his shoulder, in the middle of coiling up a heavy-duty extension cord. "Just cleaning up now and putting away the last of my tools."

I'd taken possession of the bookstore two weeks ago, after securing a loan to finance the purchase of the property and the cost of upgrades and renovations. In the end, I hadn't been able to raise all the cash for the down payment on my own. I'd needed to accept help from my family, but it had come from an unexpected source. Ryan had offered to put up half the down payment in exchange for a silent partnership in the business.

Shortly after our mother had married my father, she'd taken out a life insurance policy with Ryan as the sole beneficiary. Smart woman that she was, she'd wanted to ensure her son would be taken care of without relying on the goodness of his new stepfather's heart. I'd known about the money, and known that Ryan had used it to buy the house he lived in. What I didn't know was that he'd only used half of the payout, and the rest had been sitting in an account earning interest all this time.

I'd had qualms about accepting money from Ryan, but he'd told me he wanted to do it, not just for me, but because he'd always meant to invest it, and he couldn't think of a better use for it than keeping the town's only bookstore open. What convinced me, however, was when he told me it was what Mom would have wanted him to do.

It felt right and fitting that I had my mom to thank for making my bookstore plans a reality, since she was the one I'd inherited my love of reading from and the one who'd first brought me to Misfit Books. It also felt right that Wyatt was taking point on the renovations for me. He'd had to outsource some parts of the remodel that were beyond his expertise, but I'd entrusted him to hire and oversee the contractors and crews for those jobs, and the rest of it he was doing with his own two hands.

"Lucy's on her way over," I told him. "Do you and Andie have plans tonight? You want to come to dinner with us?"

Lucy had moved out of her mother's house and into her own apartment last month. Things with her mother hadn't exactly been smooth sailing, but I was proud of the way Lucy had been slowly but surely extricating herself from her mother's dependence. I was also impressed by how much Matt had stepped up. He'd stood shoulder to shoulder with Lucy when they'd explained to their mother how things were going to change, and he'd borne the brunt of Brenda's gripes and grievances since Lucy had been absenting herself from home more and more. Once his ankle had healed and he'd been cleared to drive again, he'd also started working more hours and contributing to the household expenses.

The additional income had been enough to allow Lucy to rent a one-room garage apartment from Andie's aunt, Birdie

Fishbaugh. It wasn't all that much bigger than her old bedroom, but Lucy had been enjoying having a space all to herself for the first time in her life, and I'd been enjoying the hell out of the extra privacy and independence it afforded her.

"Can't." Wyatt stooped to gather some trash off the dust-covered floor. "We're having dinner at Birdie's tonight with Josh and Mia. But I'm sure she wouldn't mind squeezing two more around the table if y'all want to join. You know Birdie, she always makes enough food to feed a football team."

"I'll ask Lucy when she gets here." I gazed around at the half-finished coffee shop space. "It's looking good in here. I can't believe how much progress you've made already."

We were putting the coffee shop where the children's section used to be and enclosing two porches to expand the interior of the store. The new children's section would be where the back porch used to be. Meanwhile, the front room next to the coffee shop would host a curated selection of book-themed gift items and rotating displays of featured book recommendations.

"Yeah, it's starting to take shape." Wyatt dragged the back of his hand across his forehead as he surveyed the coffee bar and prep counters he'd already put in. "Did you see the invite to family dinner at Dad's next weekend?"

My eyebrows lifted. "Yes, but I can't believe you did. Don't tell me you're actually reading the family group text?"

Wyatt flipped his middle finger at me. "Are you going?"

"Probably. Are you?"

We'd maintained a cautious truce with our father since the foundation benefit. Not that I'd seen all that much of him, but on the few occasions I had, he'd stayed on his good behavior. I wasn't sure what had brought about the transformation, but as long as Dad was willing to keep the peace, so was I.

"I don't know." Wyatt scratched the back of his head as he tossed a screwdriver into his toolbox. "Andie thinks I should, so I guess I probably will." He slammed the toolbox shut and dusted his hands off on his jeans. "Let me ask you something. You're not about to propose to Lucy, are you?"

I frowned at him, wondering where the question was coming from. "No."

"You sure about that? Because you have a history of moving fast when it comes to that girl."

"Why are you asking?"

Wyatt dropped his gaze and rubbed the back of his neck. "Because I'm fixing to propose to Andie, and I don't want you stealing my thunder before I get a chance."

I stared at him in surprise. "You're proposing to Andie?"

"That's what I said." His chin tipped up defiantly, like he was expecting me to try and talk him out of it.

Breaking into a grin, I stepped forward and pulled him into a hug. "I'm so happy for you."

"She hasn't said yes yet," he grumbled, shoving me off him.

"When are you asking her?" I couldn't stop smiling. Wyatt and Andie were getting married. My restless, commitment-allergic little brother was settling down with the woman he loved. It was about time one of us besides Manny got hitched. But if you'd told me a year ago Wyatt would be the first to fall, I'd have thought you were crazier than a soup sandwich.

"I'm not sure yet. I need to figure out how to do it. I want it to be special for her, you know? I was hoping you could help me strategize, since you're so good at all that mushy stuff."

"I don't know how good I am at it, but I'll help however I can."

"Thanks. I'm kind of nervous about it, I guess."

"Andie loves you. And you're already living together. You don't have any reason to be nervous."

"Maybe." He ran a hand through his hair. "Don't tell anyone yet, okay? Not even Lucy."

"No, of course not," I promised. "Just let me know when you want to strategize." I wondered how long it would be before they gave me more nieces and nephews. Hopefully not too long. I couldn't wait to see Wyatt as a dad.

A car pulled into the parking lot outside and the engine cut off.

"That'll be Lucy." Wyatt pointed a warning finger at me. "Remember, not a word."

I made a zipping motion across my lips as I backed out of the room.

Lucy was letting herself in the front door as I emerged from the curtain of plastic sheeting. She wore a big, happy smile on her face, and she launched herself into my arms, wrapping her legs around my waist and planting a kiss on my mouth.

I caught her easily, accepting her kiss and the soft weight of her body against mine. "Hi there."

"How was your day?" she asked as she dotted enthusiastic kisses all over my face.

"It was good, but it's a lot better now. How was yours?"

She wriggled out of my grasp and dropped to her feet in front of me. "It was great. My day was great."

"Did anything happen?" I asked, wondering what had her sounding so cheerful.

"Nope." She shook her head, smiling up at me as she ran her hands over my chest. "Nothing interesting at all."

"You're in a good mood."

"Why shouldn't I be in a good mood when everything's going so great? I've got my new apartment, you've got your bookstore, and we've both got each other." Her hands traveled up to my face, and her fingers sank into my beard. She really seemed to like me with a beard—so much that I was considering throwing away my razor for good.

"That is all very true," I agreed as my gaze dropped hungrily to her lips.

Before I could bend my mouth to hers, she let go of me and stepped back, out of easy kissing range. "I realized today there's only one thing missing that could make all of this more perfect."

"What's that?" I asked, impatient to kiss her again.

"We should get married."

My mouth fell open as my heart slammed itself against the wall of my chest. "What?"

"Are you serious?" Wyatt shouted, throwing back the curtain of drop cloths.

"Oh, hi." Lucy gave him a sheepish smile. "I didn't know you were here."

"Apparently," he said, giving me a *what the fuck?* look.

"You can go now," I told him. "Please leave."

Shaking his head, he tramped past us into the back of the shop. I turned to watch him depart, using the interruption to force a few deep breaths into my lungs. When I heard the back door slam behind him, I swiveled to face Lucy again.

She was down on one knee on the filthy, dust-covered floor.

"Don't do that," I said, growing increasingly panicky. "You'll ruin your nice pants."

Lucy ignored me and stayed right where she was. "Tanner Townes King, will you marry me?"

My whole body felt leaden as I moved toward her. "Please get up." I grasped her elbows and gently pulled her off the floor.

She got to her feet and looked at me expectantly. When I didn't immediately say anything else, she started to frown.

Then she started to look scared.

"Oh god," she said, backing away from me. "Oh shit. Oh *no*."

"Lucy—"

"I'm such an idiot! I just assumed you'd say yes. I thought

you'd want to get married, but you don't, do you?" Her voice broke on the last few words as her eyes flooded with tears.

"Stop. Come here." I closed the distance between us and folded her into my arms.

"I can't believe it. You're saying no, aren't you?"

"Shhh," I murmured, stroking her hair. "I'm not saying no."

"Are you saying yes?" Her voice sounded small, and I hated that I was the one who'd made it sound that way. But this was too important to do wrong.

"I think we need to talk about it before I say anything at all."

"That doesn't sound like a yes." She tried to pull out of my arms, but I held her tighter, refusing to let her go.

"I love you," I said, cradling her trembling body against my chest. "Don't you dare start doubting that's true."

She sniffled into my shirt. "But? There's obviously a but. What is it?"

I let go of her so I could see her face but kept my hands on her shoulders to prevent her from moving too far away from me. "Is getting married really what you want?"

"Why would I ask you to marry me if it wasn't what I wanted?" She had her head bowed, hiding her eyes from me.

"Because you think it's what *I* want."

"Isn't it?"

I took her face in my hands and made her give me her eyes. "I thought you didn't want to get married. That's what you told me."

"That was before. A lot's changed since then."

"Has it?"

She pulled out of my grasp and walked a few steps away, pressing her fists against her eyes. "If you don't want to marry me, just say so."

"That's not it at all. Of course I want to marry you."

She swiveled back to face me, blinking her wide, beautiful

eyes in surprise. "You do?"

"It would be my honor and privilege to be your husband. But I don't want you to think you have to do this for me. How many times have you told me how much you wanted your independence? You've finally made your dream come true and now you want to give it up? When you've barely even had time to appreciate it?"

Her mouth opened and closed again. I could see her thinking about what I'd said.

"I'm not going to take your dream away from you," I told her. "Yes, I would love to have you as my wife, but I don't need to marry you to be happy. I'm happy just having you in my life. But if we rush into a decision like this for the wrong reasons, you might regret it and end up resenting me. And I could never, ever forgive myself if that happened."

She blinked as her eyes filled with more tears. I took a hesitant step toward her, and she propelled herself into my arms, squeezing me hard around the rib cage.

"You don't get it at all," she mumbled into my shirt.

"What? Explain it to me."

She pulled back to look at me, smoothing her hands up my chest and grasping my shoulders. "You're my dream come true. *You are.* Not my apartment. All that freedom and independence I craved? I needed it so I could choose what I wanted for myself. Remember when I told you I wanted to make selfish decisions that made me happy? This is the selfish thing I want because it will make me happy. I want to marry you and share a home with you and spend every day of my life with you."

I frowned, afraid to let myself believe it. "Are you sure?"

She gave me a shake. "Yes! Will you stop trying to be noble and just accept my proposal already?"

"Yes."

Her eyes widened. "Was that a real yes?"

"Yes," I said solemnly. "I will marry you."

She burst into the most beautiful smile I'd ever seen. All Lucy's smiles were beautiful, but this one topped them all, because this one was a concentrated beam of pure joy, and it was coming from my future wife.

I swept her into a kiss, bending her back a little as I pressed my mouth to hers. When we finally broke apart, I brushed my nose against hers and took a breath. "However—"

"Nooo!" She groaned and dropped her head against my chest. "No buts. I hate buts."

I tried and failed to suppress a smile. "I know for a fact you adore my butt."

She tweaked my chest, narrowly missing my nipple. "I'm referring to a different kind of but right now."

"It wasn't a but, it was a however."

"I don't like those either."

"Will you hush and listen?" I slid my fingers into her hair and massaged the base of her neck. "I think we should have a long engagement."

She lifted her eyes to mine with a frown. "*How* long?"

"You just signed a one-year lease on an apartment, so we should definitely wait at least that long. Maybe even longer. There's no reason we have to rush, is there? I'm not going anywhere. Are you?"

"No."

"So let's not hurry. Let's enjoy being engaged for a while. How many times are we going to be engaged in our lives?"

Her eyes narrowed. "It better just be the one."

"Exactly." I kissed the tip of her nose. "Let's make the most of it." My heart was filled with so much happiness it felt like it was going to fly out of my chest.

"All right. That sounds reasonable, I guess. But just so you know, I'm probably not going to be okay waiting any longer than a year. Enjoying our engagement is fine, but I mean to make you my husband."

"And I mean to make you my wife." I touched my lips to hers in a soft, lingering kiss, letting all my love overflow.

No doubt we'd make plenty of missteps and hit our share of bumps in the road, but I wasn't worried about that anymore.

We were a team, and together we were strong enough to take on the whole world. It wouldn't always be easy, but nothing worth having ever was. What mattered was that we'd always be there to pick each other up. We'd be together. The surety I felt in Lucy banished all my fears and made me excited for the journey that lay ahead.

We were at the beginning of something magical and wondrous.

The rest of our lives.

I was about to suggest we get the hell out there and start celebrating when my phone started ringing. It was the ringtone I'd assigned to my family, which was odd since they almost always texted instead of calling. Giving Lucy an apologetic look, I fished my phone out of my pocket and saw Ryan's name on the screen.

"Hey," I said, answering it. "Can I call you back? I'm in the middle of something right now."

"Is this Tanner?" asked a woman's voice I didn't recognize.

"Yes." I frowned. "Who's this?"

"My name is Maggie. I'm Ryan's next-door neighbor. I'm calling because you're listed in his phone as his emergency contact, and he's had an accident..."

---

*Read Ryan's story in **PINT OF CONTENTION**, the next book in the King Family series...*

ABOUT THE AUTHOR

SUSANNAH NIX is a RITA® Award-winning and *USA Today* bestselling author of rom-coms and contemporary romances who lives in Texas with her husband. On the rare occasions she's not writing, she can be found reading, knitting, lifting weights, drinking wine, or obsessively watching *Ted Lasso* on repeat to stave off existential angst.

———

CPSIA information can be obtained
at www.ICGtesting.com
Printed in the USA
BVHW080336100122
625855BV00004BA/172